# DRIVER

## IGGY BLACK

ANGRY PUNK PRESS

# 1

Pops used to say there's nothing worse than a thief.

I never told him I shoplifted a pair of headphones from the corner store when I was fifteen.

He used to look at me, a reddish tan covering every part of his face but where a hard hat sat. Son, real men work hard. Everything in this house, everything I got, you got, your mom, your big sister, is because of my sweat and blood. I earned it with these hands. Then he'd take off his yellow vest, kick off his steel-toed boots, and he'd be one with the couch. Twelve hours a day, five days a week, sometimes more than that for a nine-hundred-square-foot house in Buffalo, New York, whose white planks needed repainting and whose walls were thin enough to hear the rat in the other room.

Pops, I don't want that.

You don't know what you want. You're a kid.

The first time I ever heard of The D3vil's Krew, I was thirteen years old on a field trip from one of those dinosaur museums the school administrators send the kids to because they can't think of nothing else. Y' know, they got to get rid of the kids, but they can't cancel school, laws or something like that.

There was a kid Pops didn't like me hanging out with, who listened to a lot of Marilyn Manson and Insane Clown Posse and bragged about having knives in his backpack. Yeah, they're pretty badass, kid said. Pretty dangerous.

I'd forgotten the name D3vil's Krew until I heard it again on the news after Pops had gotten up from his afterwork nap and realized it was dinner time. A stolen ATM, he grumbled, damn. There's nothing worse than a thief, Nolan.

The tablecloth was the American flag. Jesus and his disciples watched us during his Last Supper above our kitchen table.

I was fourteen. I didn't like Brussels sprouts but I ate them because Ma liked it when I did. I asked for a motorcycle. I knew we didn't have money for a motorcycle. Pops said when you get old enough and work real hard, you can get a motorcycle. Then he poured back a Bud Light he didn't know I didn't like because he didn't know I'd drunk any.

I asked Pops why he put me and my sister in sports and afterschool activities even though he had to work extra hours to afford it.

He said something about integrity.

I said I don't want to do those things.

He said something about integrity.

I said, I think I want to be a writer when I grow up.

He said, be realistic.

The first thing I ever drove was a motorcycle. Sixteen years old. I told Pops if he got me driving lessons, I would work to buy myself a bike. He agreed to it. I never told him I bought myself a motorcycle from gambling and selling my Adderall to kids at school. He never asked what I did at my job.

Sometimes Pops would look at me like, why can't you be more like your sister, but he never said it.

That bike cost me two years and two thousand dollars. A hundred lucky lady rolls and fifteen bottles of "lost" Adderall. A long walk to the house of a guy who said he could sell it to me for cheap. She was a beautiful bike, black and sleek. Sports bike. Looked brand new even though she was a few years old. Nobody ever told me that that bike would be the only thing between me and a homeless shelter when I got old enough and smart enough to realize Pops was right when he said you got to bust your ass to make ends meet. Money doesn't fall from the sky, son. It ain't a human right either. It's something you got to sweat and grind for, and then when you do, you can at least keep your lights on. If you work extra hard, you can have as many motorcycles as you want. Harder than that, you'll own a motorcycle shop. One day it'll all pay off.

It never paid off for him.

Pops believed an overworked body was a trophy. I believed an overworked body was the law of a broken land. But you had to do what you had to do.

We both could agree on that.

When I was seventeen, Pops bought me a truck because he said a car was for a woman to pick up kids and drop them off at school and soccer games; a truck was for a hard-working man. One day, son, you're gonna take that truck, and you're gonna make money with it. You're gonna pick up a beautiful woman in it, and she's gonna have your beautiful babies, and you're gonna use the money you made with it to buy that beautiful woman and those beautiful babies a beautiful house, three-stories high, six bedrooms, five and a half bathrooms, a hundred presents under the tree every Christmas. If I hadn't broken my leg at work, he said, I'd have moved up in the business and done the same for you guys, but it's still on the way.

Pops never got promoted.

I didn't make use of my truck except to drive it to parties and back, sneak out, and pick up girls. An old brown and tan 1990s GMC truck Pops found at a used car dealership. It didn't make me any money, but it got me to a couple of concerts, it got me laid in the back of a movie theater. It got me to my own apartment when me and Pops couldn't agree to disagree anymore.

I once grew my hair past my shoulders. He told me to cut it.

I once asked if I could pierce my eyebrow. He told me not under his roof.

I once got caught with a joint in my mouth. That was the final straw.

I told him I needed room to breathe.

He said, then get some room to breathe.

I'm eighteen years old; I don't need this shit.

Watch your language in my house!

I can make my own money. I'll get my own job. I'll live out my dreams as a writer.

I suggest you do then.

Ma tried to stop me, my sister tried to deescalate the situation, but I grabbed my things, and I grabbed my keys and me and that ol' truck hit the road. Sort of. I lived in that truck for a short period because I had no money.

My first real job was as a pizza delivery driver. It paid seven dollars and twenty-five cents. Anything else I was supposed to make in tips. Sometimes I did and sometimes I didn't. I found an apartment across the state in the Bronx where the brick crumbled and the air smelled like musty socks, and I lived between a hoarder and a porn addict. Ma would call, sometimes, and make sure I was still alive, and I'd tell her, yeah. I'll let you know when I'm dead.

Rent went up every year. Seven twenty-five wasn't going to cut it. I got a job as a package delivery driver when I turned twenty. Fourteen dollars and thirty cents. Better. But the water was still cold, dinner every night was still a question, and I couldn't move out.

I worked second shift. Out there until midnight. Twelve to fifteen hours, Monday through Friday, sometimes Saturday. Sorry, Pops. Maybe you had a point.

One morning, I got off from a late shift. Peak season. The ground was covered in snow. I yawned, blinked my eyes a bunch of times, turned up the radio, but I dozed off. Next thing I knew, my truck almost turned a Mercedes Benz into an accordion. No one was hurt. The other driver got out with minor scratches, I had a few bruises, but my truck was totaled. It was that feeling you get when you're staring down at a problem but there's nothing you can do about it. You keep looking for an answer, but there isn't one. Then you panic. You're wishing this whole thing was a nightmare. You're thinking it is. It's got to be. But it's not.

I had no truck, and because I fell asleep at the wheel, I was ruled at fault, so I had to pay for the other guy's damages. Put me in debt. Would take a lifetime to pay that thing off.

Car insurance is a joke.

So, my bike got me to work and back. It was all I had. I tried to find a closer job in the city, but I guess all nearby employers were wiping their asses with my resumes.

Rent.

Utilities.

Gas.

Payments for the wreck damage.

You're spending more money than you're making.

One day you learn food stamps are your friend.

By twenty-five, I was making more money than I was at twenty, but I was still at the same job. Still a driver. Eleven a.m. to eleven p.m. Some days earlier. Fifteen dollars an hour.

Sometimes they told me I was the best damn driver they had.

# 2

The third time I heard of The D3vil's Krew, I had the news on before heading off to work.

My apartment was the size of a suburban kid's bedroom. One couch that's also your bed, that's also your dresser, that's also where you store all of your shit. A studio apartment, peeling linoleum, and a leaky faucet. I didn't grow up in a beautiful house, but it looked better than where I lived now.

Maybe it wasn't the third time I'd heard of The D3vil's Krew. Maybe I'd heard of them some other time and didn't realize I was hearing about them. Maybe I wasn't hearing about them then, but I always assumed it was them.

*"In other news, a convenience store was robbed last night. The suspects were seen in Halloween masks—"*

I turned off the TV. If Pops were there, he'd have said, what a bunch of low lives. Get a job. And I'd have agreed.

I threw on my uniform, my hat, my badge. I grabbed my keys off the counter. Got my lunch container out of the fridge.

Yesterday, I wrote a short story about a guy who didn't know he was an ant until a horde of other ants ate off his wings and forced him to become a slave for the queen. But all he had to do was mate with her to keep the colony going. He was forced to have sex with a powerful woman. That ant had it better than me.

I was going to write it Saturday, but they told me I had to work Saturday. I hated when that happened.

I zipped my lunch in my backpack and headed to work.

Sometimes, when riding down the street and seeing the graffiti on the buildings, the cigarette butts and beer bottles on the concrete, crushed takeout cups, broken glass, used needles, stray cats and shaggy dogs, cardboard boxes and wooden pallets, when I smelled the mildew and cigarette smoke, felt the bumps of the broken concrete beneath my tires, I could at least say, this place has character. This place is human. As we are. If there were no social regulations or rules in place. It's us at our darkest, our lowest, our most fragile, our most honest. When we're not pretending. Sometimes I loved it as much as I hated it.

I worked out of town. Had to drive to commute. I got there three minutes before clock-in, everyone standing around the punch-in clocks waiting for that minute to turn so we could get going. If I gazed too hard at everyone's faces, the crowd we stood in, the drained and soulless expressions, I'd realize we looked like a bunch of zombies. I'd realize I was one of them, and then I'd laugh.

Everyone clocked in one by one. Friday, I was late delivering packages due to traffic. Saturday, my tire caught a nail. That didn't stop them from yelling at me.

Same route. I liked that. But I didn't like the road there. Too hectic.

When you first start a job, it's this brand-new thing. Kind of exciting, really. You're optimistic. Might even like it. You learn the ropes, you get good at it, but then months go by, years, and it's the same thing over and over again. You don't even think about it anymore. My ankles hurt from the number of times I jumped in and out of a van. I still liked it better than pizza delivery.

I delivered one hundred and ninety-three packages that day. A neighborhood that seemed rich to me, but maybe not to a 1950s sitcom mom. Green grass, a neighborhood pool, a sprinkler system in every lawn, a passcode to get through the gate, four bedrooms, three bathrooms, pure breed dogs, the whole white picket fence. I never lived like that. Used to want to, never stopped wanting to, especially as a kid because I knew some kids in school who grew up on the nicer side of town. Kids with doctors and lawyers for parents. Kids that lived in McMansions and complained about how they didn't get a new cellphone for

Christmas, but their lives were better than mine and much better than what I ended up with after I flew the coop.

A twelve-hour shift. One hundred and ninety-three packages. I got a tip from a middle-aged woman who I think wanted to have an affair with me when her husband wasn't around, and I got yelled at by an old man in a polo shirt because I parked too close to his driveway. So, what else was new?

I was supposed to get my monthly evaluation that night. Last month, I got excellent feedback. The month before that, satisfactory. I never fell below neutral.

All month, I hadn't missed a package. Except for three days of too much traffic and a flat tire, I'd delivered everything on time. I had more excellent feedback than anything else. I'd trained new hires for this position.

I planned to ask for a management position. Three dollars more. Less physical strain. Five years. I'd earned it.

The manager asked me to step into the office, take a seat in front of the desk.

"Nolan, you've worked very hard these past five years and have been a great contributor to our company."

"Thank you, sir."

"We really appreciate you working extra hours and coming in on Holidays."

"Thank you, sir."

"But unfortunately, the company is facing financial difficulties."

I didn't say anything.

"This has nothing to do with you or your work efforts. You truly have been a great asset to our company."

"So...what? Are you cutting my paycheck?"

"No..." he sighed. "We're going to have to let you go."

My face paled. "Are you...are you firing me?"

"No. You're not fired. You're getting laid off."

"But I've been here five years. You said I was one of your best drivers."

"You are, and this is a difficult decision to make, but we have drivers that have been here eight, nine, ten years...some of them forty, and we have to cut our losses."

"Cut your losses? I'm not some bad habit." It felt like someone dropped a brick on my chest. I couldn't breathe. Damn near cried just waiting for myself to wake up from what should've been a nightmare. "I...I've got rent to pay..."

He nodded.

"I've got utility bills..."

He nodded.

"Gasoline..."

He nodded slowly, with a look on his face that resembled pity, but he was going to go home in his SUV, to his three-bedroom house, take care of his mortgage, his bills, buy his wife something nice, watch Netflix, and get his paycheck on Friday. Just part of the job. We got to cut our losses. Just part of the job.

"I'm really sorry."

I jumped out of my seat and threw my chair back so hard it smashed against the wall. I slammed my hands on his desk and stared him dead in the eyes. "Sorry? You're sorry? This is my livelihood. I live in a shithole, surviving off food stamps, and all you have to say is you're sorry? Go fuck yourself!" I grabbed his laptop and smashed it on the ground. I climbed on top of the table, grabbed him by his shirt collar—

I didn't do any of that. But it made me feel better to imagine it.

What I actually did was shake my head, press my lips together, and pretend like tears weren't stinging the back of my eyes. "Don't worry about it. I understand. You gotta do what you gotta do for the business. This world don't run on feelings." I forced a smile and handed him my badge, got up, shook his hand. "Thanks for the years of employment."

I turned and headed for the door.

"Hey, Nolan."

I stopped, looked back.

"Good luck." Maybe he really meant it.

I wrote a story about a guy who thought he was a peasant until he realized he was the dirt the cows shit on. He thought he was a peasant because, when he looked up, he saw peasants feeding the cows, farming the land, but then he realized *they* were watering *him*, he wasn't watering anyone else, and finally he stopped looking up. He looked down at his own place in the world, and realized the only thing there was dirt. And shit.

Rent was due.

I used to say I would make that writing thing take off. Publish a novel. A short story collection. Somebody was going to read it one day and say, this is the best goddamn thing I ever read. Make a movie out of this. Give this guy a Pulitzer. Pops showed me all the books from all the other people who said the same thing. They only sold ten copies.

The night I lost my job, I looked up information about unemployment online. I didn't understand it all because I wasn't that good at being an adult yet. I spent most of my time trying to find another job. I didn't call Pops and tell him what had happened because I didn't want to hear what he had to say. I didn't call my sister because she would've called Pops.

Rent was due.

I put in a bunch of applications the same night and drowned myself in Jack Daniels. Seemed like everything wanted you to have some sort of experience.

Requirements:

Five years of experience in an office setting. Ten years of experience operating a forklift. Fifteen years of experience in graphic design. Two hundred years of experience in assembly. Five hundred years in everything. Every-goddamn-thing. Who the hell has that kind of experience? Eight hundred, seven thousand, and fifty years working with Photoshop. Proficiency in Adobe. Know Microsoft like the back of your hand. So close to Excel it pours you a glass of wine before it fucks you up the ass.

What sort of experience did I have? I could drive a van.

I looked at the clock. Any normal night I'd have still been at work. I'd have been hating it. I'd have been wondering about the number of packages I had left, the amount of time before midnight, how much sleep I could get—I should've been happy I didn't have a job. I lost my job. That's a good thing. I ought to chill.

I was too poor. Chilling was for folks with retirement funds or inherited riches.

I lost track of time putting in applications.

Jesus Christ! Rent was due.

What if I got a knock on my door? Hey. Hey, you, kid. Yeah, you, with the wavy hair your dad would've made you cut if you were still living with him. You in the same sweaty work shirt you've been wearing since you got laid off because you didn't get any sleep last night, lying around in your socks and underwear, looking like a dark-haired Jesus if he became a drunk and gave into meds. Yeah, you. Remember that contest you entered a couple of weeks ago? Yeah, you know the one, when you were desperate enough to take a poll on one of those sketchy websites because some shill on the internet said you could earn money from it. Remember? And in this one, they offered you a $10,000,000 prize. Well, it turns out that it wasn't just a scam to get your information so they could sell it to spammers. Turns out it was legit.

And then they'd give me one of those giant envelopes. Here. Now get out of this shithole and make something out of your life.

Then I'd use the money to market my books. My books would become bestsellers. Somebody would make a movie, and I'd be a rags-to-riches story. No more of this shit. No more looking over my shoulder every time I'm out in the parking lot late at night. I'm getting me a Lambo. I'm getting a penthouse in Manhattan. I'm king of the world! I'm turning that ten mil into twenty, that twenty mil to thirty, that thirty mil to forty.

The fire alarm in my kitchen went off. Damn. I forgot I warmed a quick meal in the oven. I ran in and turned off the oven, put out the smoke. It wasn't the first night I would be eating black ashes. Wasn't the last either.

Rent was due.

I spent the rest of the week staring at my emails. The only emails I got back were spammers and rejection letters. I put in a number of applications to truck businesses that offered to pay you while they train you to get your CDL. I could make six figures with a job like that. If nothing else, I applied for more delivery driver positions. Thing is, every single one of those jobs do background checks on you. They ask if you've been in any wrecks in the past five years, and well, we all know what happened to my truck. Damn.

Within a couple of weeks, I'd gotten a total of three interviews, all of which ended in the ol' thank you for your interest in our company, but we have decided to proceed with other candidates. Started to feel like there was no hope out there in that big-ass universe that apparently thought me a joke.

I believe it was a Monday or maybe a Tuesday I finally got a phone call. Early afternoon. I'm sprawled out on the couch with my arm hanging over the side like a dead guy. The TV was mumbling. The fan was turning. The blinds drew a shadow on the cheap carpet like Etch A Sketch lines. I was surviving on leftover microwave noodles.

*"Two men were arrested for drug trafficking that led to a shootout today at..."*

Can't do the time don't do the crime. What about people who bust their asses at a nine to five? Nine to nine? Nine to twelve? Nine to whenever they say you can go? Contribute, dammit. Get a job like everyone else. That was coming from me. I used to gamble in the back of the school, sneak items in my pocket when no one was looking, smuggle them out of corner stores. Fifteen and stupid. Twenty-five and learned the value of breaking your ass for a paycheck. If you really want something, work for it.

I sounded like my father.

I was half asleep, half dead. The phone buzz startled me something good. I almost didn't answer. With job searching comes job sites. With job sites comes your information getting to spammers. With spammers comes some broke kid as desperate for work as me reading whatever half-assed page their employer gave them to try and sell me insurance. I couldn't deal with that at the moment. I grabbed the phone off the armrest.

"Hello, may I speak to Nolan Castro?"

"Uh, yeah," I rubbed my eyes. "Speaking."

"Hi, this is Chelsea Carter, a recruiting agent at Drop and Ship Solutions. We received your resume online. It looks like you have five years of experience as a delivery driver. That correct?"

I sat up, almost laughed. "Uh...yes, ma'am. I worked for a previous shipping company."

"Great. What got you interested in applying for our company?"

Drop and Ship Solutions. It had been about a month since I'd lost my last job, and I'd made ends meet with unemployment checks. I'd put in at least a hundred applications since then. Which one was Drop and Ship Solutions? How was I supposed to remember Drop and Ship Solutions? There's a lot of Drop and Ship. Say something generic. "You guys have been around for a long time, and I want to work for a reputable company."

"That sounds awesome. May I ask why you're looking for a new job at this time?"

"I was laid off my last one. Company had financial difficulties."

"I understand. We read through your application, and your resume looks really good..."

It does?

"Would you be interested in coming in next week for an interview?"

Fuck yeah! "Yes. I'm available anytime."

"Wednesday at three sound good?"

"Perfect. Thank you."

# 3

I couldn't remember the last time I hung out with a group of friends.

I buttoned my shirt in the mirror, put on my suit coat, pulled out my collar. Looked like a guy a fifteen-year-old version of myself wouldn't recognize.

When was the last time I had any friends? High school? Had to be.

I slid my feet into black dress shoes that'd been buried in my closet for five years, put my foot up on the edge of the couch and tied my laces.

I think the last time I really did anything with a group of people was when we ditched the prom. Yeah. I remember that. Because prom was lame, and at house parties, we could get away with drinking alcohol. I was dumb then.

Now I was a salesman, a lawyer, a substitute teacher, a timeshare agent, looking in the mirror, making sure the dress coat teenage me said I would never wear didn't have any crinkles in it, checking to make sure the creases Pops used to make me iron into my slacks were sharp, pulling my hair into a bun. I wasn't ready to cut it yet.

Living cooped up in that apartment put an emptiness in my chest I don't think I addressed enough. Sometimes, I'd talk to the porn guy next door, but I didn't want to touch his hand. I couldn't visit the hoarder's place. The couple down the hall had too many kids. I worked too many hours, anyhow. Or I was looking for a job. Either way, I didn't have time.

Sometimes I could talk to my sister. Might go out with her and her husband once every three months or so, to dinner, something like that. She had that life, y' know? Ma and Pops were proud of her because she did the thing they said, went to college, found a husband who makes six figures, and got the hell out of that shit hole. She was the housewife my parents set her up to be. The ideal child they wanted. And they could brag about her at family get-togethers I stopped going to and talk about how she's opened a shop with the crafts she makes, how well her husband's doing in his career, and then they'd look at me and not say anything, but I knew what it meant.

Drop and Ship Solutions was ten minutes from my old job. What are the odds? The weather report didn't say it would rain. Good. But I hoped the air hitting me on my bike wouldn't funk up my suit. I put on extra body spray just in case.

"Do you have reliable transportation?"

The HR office at my old job didn't look as good. The windows at Drop and Ship were like those big modern windows you see in rich people's homes, and I was on the second floor. I could see the whole parking lot, my little black bike sitting alone amongst a sea of cars and trucks. The walls were some kind of white wood. I hoped I didn't have a smell.

I nodded. "Yes."

"Great. Why do you want to work for this company?"

I smiled, but it was forced and probably shaky and unconfident. I rehearsed but forgot everything. "Well..." Never say well. "I know you guys have been around for more than twenty years." Give an exact number. "Twenty-five years, more specifically." Or was it twenty-six? "You ship worldwide and are one of the leading services for both businesses and...everyday people."

She smiled. "I see you've done your homework."

"Of course."

"What are your strengths?"

"I'm..." Jesus, I suck at everything. "I'm determined. I'm a hard worker. I enjoy learning new skills and am very teachable." Too generic. "I get things done on time *every* time. I'm extremely detail-oriented, and I'm a great team worker as well as independent." Say something they want to hear. "I've got a lot of years of experience in this position, and I know it like the back of my hand."

"That's good." She nodded. "What would you say your weaknesses are?"

Damn. Trick question. I hesitated and stopped myself from scratching the back of my head once I realized I was doing it. "I'm...Early in my work history, I found it difficult to accept criticism, but as I've grown older and gained more experience, I've learned to take criticism and apply it to my work, making me a stronger worker...overall."

She nodded.

"I can also be a perfectionist." Too much.

"How do you work under pressure?"

"Pressure motivates me."

"How would your old boss describe you?"

"I always get things done on time."

"In your previous job, were you tardy more than three times within a year?" Yes. "No."

"In your previous job, how many times did you call in within your last year?" Five times. "Never."

"Why do you want to work for this company?"

"Because it's a positive work environment and its values align with my own, which has been a huge priority throughout my career search."

"Last one."

I let out a discreet breath.

She typed on her computer. "Where do you see yourself in five years?"

Damn. I didn't write that one in my notes. I rubbed my lips together. I couldn't even envision myself in five years. Who the hell knows where they're going to be in five years? Five years prior, I was twenty years old. I'd just gotten my last job. There's no way I could've known five years later, I'd have just lost it, sitting nervous in front of an HR rep with brain fog. "Uh..." too much hesitation. "Uh..." Just say something. "Five years from now I see myself...growing and developing in a career. Developing my skills, my talents, and being a part of something that is larger than I am. Yes." I nodded. "In five years, I'll be settled in my career."

I stopped at a Waffle House before going back to my apartment because I couldn't look myself in the face. Holy shit, did I blow it. What kind of answer was "its values align with my own"? What values? Elaborate. Too late.

I didn't get home until the sun looked like a radioactive tangerine. I'd brought back half a burger with me that I threw in the fridge and knew I'd never touch again. I dropped on the couch, scrolled through my phone as if some miracle would pop up there—hey, you just won a million dollars for no reason! Come collect your prize.

If you lie on the couch too long and think too hard, you start to realize nothing matters. And then all the effort you put in is just for the universe to discard like an expired batch of fruit. You can think that shit is wine all you want, but sooner or later, the realization's going to hit. Then what do you do? You end up on the couch. You chew some Nicorette.

I didn't take off nothing but my shoes and dress coat and left them on the floor where I dropped them. Grabbed myself a beer before me and my pillows were spooning. Turned on the TV.

*"A break-in happened at West Fort Boulevard today during—"* I couldn't take any more news. I turned the channel. *"...just had their first bundle of joy today. A bouncing baby boy..."* a celebrity baby that'll never have to work a day in their life. I turned to Hulu. I missed Netflix because it had the shows I was watching, and I didn't have to sit through any commercials. But streaming without commercials was for working people. Or celebrity babies.

I fell asleep with a beer in my hand and the TV on.


I got a phone call that I first thought was a dream.

"Yes." I laughed with a groggy voice. I had to rub my eyes and smack my face because the call woke me up. I'd slept until two p.m. Hadn't had any breakfast, hadn't brushed my teeth. My shirt was soaked in beer. "Yes. Next Monday, right? Nine a.m.? ...Absolutely. Thank you. Thank you so much!"

My first day on the job, I showed up thirty minutes early just in case. They had me in one of those boardrooms with the other new hires, where they go over the job on PowerPoint and have you sign a bunch of papers. I didn't start training until the next day. The new route was a lot different than my old one. They had me delivering to businesses instead of neighborhoods. I worked fewer hours, but I was making a higher wage, about three dollars more, and if I put in overtime, maybe I could move up. Get a better apartment, some actual furniture. A car. They gave raises every year, so once I got some seniority, who knew what I could get?

Things were looking up.

I was coming back from work late one night. I decided I'd put in some overtime. Probably wasn't the best time to pick something up from the convenience store. There was no one else out there, and all I wanted was a snack.

I'd worked the job for about a month now. Sounded like they liked me. My first evaluation was excellent. I started to hear my father's voice in my head about how hard work pays off, and I didn't scoff at it. I actually nodded. But when I parked my bike and got off, I sighed.

You can't live in an area like mine and not feel like something ain't right. Here I was, getting off work after twelve hours, and all I could afford were streets with gas stations where the paint was peeling off the walls and there were only two pumps because the other two had been out of order for over a year. The *Open* sign was flickering, and the crumbling brick was covered in dirt, grime, and graffiti. The windows were barred because they had too many break-ins too many times. It had character, but it was less than what forty hours or more a week should get a guy. Kind of makes you look up at the universe and ask, what's the point of any of it? You're scared to die, I guess. Maybe that's the point.

I looked over my shoulder like I always did in this shady neighborhood. If I were smart, I'd have bought myself a Taser or pepper spray. Pops said that was for women. Men go toe-to-toe or learn to shoot a gun. When I went toe-to-toe with other boys back in school, I got grounded.

There was a group of guys standing around an ATM. One of them pulled his cigarette out of his mouth and looked me dead in my eyes. I turned away from him immediately. Out there in those streets, you're in the wild. You don't make eye contact with another male because that's a challenge. Stay off their territory and take care of your own damn business. Maybe I should've learned how to shoot a gun.

I went in, grabbed a pack of chips and a stick of beef jerky. The cashier added up my items, and I kept looking over my shoulder. You get that feeling inside, y' know? Like something ain't right. You can't tell if that's anxiety because you know what side of town you live on or if the feeling's legit. It's not like I hadn't been punched in the face out there before. Or mugged.

"Eight dollars and fifty cents." The cashier caught me off guard.

I took out my wallet and paid in cash. "Thank you, sir."

I walked outside. That same group of guys were still there. I kept my eyes forward, but I could feel them watching me. I could hear them laughing, talking amongst themselves, their footsteps.

I headed to my bike. Their footsteps were getting closer.

I started walking faster. They started walking faster. I started running. They started running. By the time I got to my bike, they were right behind me.

"Look," I put up my hands, "I don't want any trouble."

One of them downed a bottle of liquor. "Hear that? He don't want any trouble."

They laughed. Had to be about five or six of them, smoking, drinking, smelling like cigarettes and musk.

"We don't want any trouble either," the same guy said.

I didn't like this guy's face. I didn't like the look on it. I didn't like his crooked nose or the scar over his eyes. I didn't like the way he looked at me with a smirk, walking around my bike, stroking his chin, with his friends standing around laughing and flicking cigarettes.

I put my hand on my bike handle, but before I could swing my leg over, he grabbed the other handle.

"That's a nice bike you got there," he said.

I made eye contact with him, and everything froze like reality crashed and the earth stopped turning.

One of those guys grabbed me from behind and threw me on the ground. I got up, but another one punched me in the face. I swung at one of them but missed. Swung again and hit one. Got punched in the stomach. Too many of them. I shoved them off me best I could but ended up on my ass. One of them kicked me in the chest, and I fell back against the concrete. My limbs were sore. My lip was bleeding. The metallic taste of blood ran down the back of my nose and burned my sinuses. The world was tilting and spinning, and everything around me doubled like I'd gotten fucked up on fifteen shots of whiskey. The growl of my bike engine made the ground rumble against my back. I could hear those guys laughing, the clomping of their footsteps. All I could make out through squinted eyes and blurred vision was that guy riding off on my bike, the other guys jumping into a car. Then they were gone.

# 4

What makes a guy take another guy's bike?

Does he just not know what it means to that other person? Or does he just not care? I guess there's no clear answer to that. It's the kind of thing that's too hard to put thought into right after it happens. Right after it happens, you just want to fuck somebody up and make them pay for what they did. Reliving that incident over and over and over again from the time you're kicking yourself for leaving your shit out there by itself to the time you're tasting your own blood as it rolls down the back of your throat, lying back to the ground, ass to the ground, hearing the gears of your own dollars and maintenance fees ride off. The thing that's getting you to work and back is gone, and there's not a damn thing you can do about it. And then you got to ask yourself, is it my fault for being stupid, or that guy's fault for having no empathy? I don't know, but I blamed myself more than anything. The what ifs, rolling around in my head like an overplayed song. Or maybe I was the one without any empathy. Maybe that guy needed a bike. Too much to think about. Too much going on in my head. What was I going to do about it? Cry?

That car accident I was still paying for fucked up my credit. No new ride. Not anytime soon.

I took an Uber to work the next day. That was $100.

I spent $500 by the end of the week, an additional hundred for Saturday shifts. That came to $2000 a month. That was more than rent on transportation alone.

Sometimes shifts started early. Sometimes they started late. I'd have to reschedule my ride.

"You're late."

"I'm sorry. My driver canceled."

"Second time this week."

"I'm sorry. Could you override it? Just one last time."

I started taking the bus to work. That was less expensive than a rideshare. The bus stop was a thirty-minute walk from where I worked.

"I'm calling to let you know I'll be late today."

"What happened?"

"One of my bus routes cancelled."

I could see the management looking at me and talking amongst each other before I hit my routes. This happened more than once. I put in extra hours, helping out other areas of the facility, not just for the extra money but to prove I was willing to work. Nighttime bus rides meant only a few people, most folks on their phone. As long as you didn't bother them, they didn't bother you. Late-night bus rides meant you and maybe one other guy. Maybe he's eyeing you. Maybe he's wondering what you got in your pockets. I've seen guns tucked under shirts and knives clipped to belts. I didn't make eye contact with anyone.

Bus rides meant early rising to meet at the stop. Getting off late meant going to bed late. I was getting four hours of sleep. First two months on the job. I'd mixed up a few packages. I dozed off at the wheel. Careful. That's how I lost my truck.

"Nolan, can I see you in my office, please?"

"Yes, ma'am."

"Are you getting enough sleep?"

"I'm trying. I live in the city. Still working on getting a ride. But I've got a lot saved up, so it shouldn't be too long."

My end-of-the-month evaluation was unsatisfactory. Last month it was neutral.

Good speed. Decent accuracy, but where we're most concerned is you not showing up on time. She sent me a copy of my evaluation, which they never do, and I stared at it the entire bus ride home. I stared at it from the bus stop to my apartment. I stared at it after I passed out on the couch. I don't even think I knew what I was looking at anymore.

My head ached. My throat was sore. I was shivering. It'd been that way for a while, but I ignored it. I think I'd gotten a fever. I'd have seen a doctor, but my health insurance hadn't kicked in yet. I was sprawled back on the couch. I didn't eat anything because my stomach wouldn't accept food. And it was late. I needed to work in the morning. I needed to get some rest. Maybe I'd feel better once the sun rose. I couldn't call in.

I balled up my evaluation sheet and threw it on the floor. I rolled over and passed out.

I was my Pops.

When I woke up the next morning, my sinuses were clogged, my throat was swollen, my head was pounding. I fixed myself a bowl of oatmeal, but that was puke in the toilet in less than five minutes. But I'd been tardy too many times. I couldn't call in. I threw on a jacket, even though it wasn't cold and hurried to the bus stop.

I clocked in on time. Had the cold sweats. I went to the bathroom, grabbed a napkin, and wiped my face in the mirror. I was pale, and there were dark rings under my eyes. I looked at my watch. Those packages weren't going to deliver themselves.

I walked to my van, hunched over with my hand over my stomach.

"How are you doing today, Nolan?"

I didn't even know the manager was standing there. "I'm good."

She furrowed her brow. "Are you sure? You look like you're running a fever."

"No. I'm just tired. Long night."

She crossed her arms. "I think you should go home."

"It's okay. I got it."

"No." She shook her head. "We can't have anyone sick. The other workers could catch it, and it'll affect your job performance. Besides that, you'll be touching packages. We can't have that. Just..." she sighed "...take the day off. I'll find someone to cover you." She started walking off. "And Nolan," she stopped, "if you're not feeling good, just call in. I'd rather have you not be here than come to work sick."

If I'd put in a year, I could've used a sick day, but I think I would've ruined it by calling in late too many times to have accumulated that shit anyway. Wasn't like I could argue with her. Maybe she'd understand. First two months on the job, and look at me. I looked like the incompetent teenager naïve about a job until they're told about that eight-hour shift.

I went home and fell back on that same couch I might as well have started an intimate relationship with. I coughed. Wrapped myself up in a blanket. It was the stress. I knew it. I'd been knowing it. I'd just been ignoring it. Sometimes you're just lying there, y' know? And when you tune out the rest of the world and let your own mind have a conversation with you, it tells you stuff you don't want to hear.

I think it was right there, curled up in my blanket like a silkworm too in love with the warmth of the cocoon to have the balls to make itself vulnerable to reality, when it dawned on me for the first time. Life's only about survival. Food. Water. Shelter. Money. Either you have a job or you die looking for one. You're on top with all the gold or on the bottom beneath a heel. Either way, you got to make that cash. That cash is the blood and the breath and fuel of your body. It's the god of this world. You either make that cash or you die trying.

Maybe that's why somebody stole my bike.

When I was a teen, they asked me what I wanted to do for a career. I told them I wanted to be a writer, and they told me most folks didn't make a lot of money doing that, so I told them I wanted a cool job.

Tenth grade, advisor's office. I'm an attitude-ridden, punk fifteen-year-old, and she's like, what kind of a cool job?

I don't know, I tell her, just a cool job. Something I can brag about, I guess. Something fun.

She asked me what I was good at.

I told her I could write. Maybe. Sometimes. I like to think I can.

They gave me an aptitude test. It said I was creative, but it said I was a lot of things. Every job popped up on that list, graphic design, doctor, lawyer, teacher. Either I was good at everything or nothing at all.

They told me I should consider college, and I did. Pops wanted me to go. Wanted me to apply for some scholarships, but I didn't make scholarship grades. I'm glad I didn't go to college. That would've been tuition bills.

Guess it was inevitable I'd be driving package delivery for a living.

I didn't feel perfect two days after the manager let me take the day off, but I felt good enough to go to work. I clocked in on time. I put my lunch in the fridge. I did my route. I didn't mix up any packages. I got everything out on time. I came back to the facility by the end of shift. The manager asked me to see her in her office. I'd seen this before.

"How are you doing today, Nolan?"

"I'm good. Thank you."

Long pause.

She clasped her fingers on the desk. "You've been with us for almost two months, and while you've been doing a good job on your routes, it looks like you're having trouble coming in on time. Or at all."

I forced a smile. "I'm sorry, but I only missed the last two days. I was sick. Remember? You gave me those days off."

"Right. But, the way our system works around here, it accumulates all the time you put in. So every day you miss, every tardy, every time you leave before the end of your shift, it takes a point."

"I thought you overrode it."

"I can only override so many times."

"I'm saving up for a car right now. It's just really difficult with rent and bills...I mean, I'm on food stamps—Christ!" I dragged my hand down my face. "I'm sorry. I-I'm sorry...I don't mean to..."

"No. Don't worry about it. I understand. It's difficult, but you said that you had reliable transportation when we hired you—"

"I did—and I do. I just—someone stole my bike, so at the moment, I'm having to catch a ride either by bus or..."

She shook her head.

"Just give me one more month. I can have this thing solved..."

She shook her head.

"Please."

Long pause.

"I'm sorry," she said. "I understand it's difficult, and I wish you the best of luck, but I have to make the best decision for the business. We are very grateful for your contributions to this company, but we have to cut our losses."

I swallowed. "Please. Just give me one more month."

She shook her head.

"I can prove to you that I can be here on time. I'll work extra Saturdays—"

"Please turn in your badge."

I sighed, dropped my elbows on my lap, rubbed my temples. Nothing I could do about it. I took off my badge and set it on her desk.

I got up. "What am I supposed to do?"

"I understand, it's difficult."

I started for the door but stopped, turned around. "Please stop saying that. You don't understand. At all. It ain't just difficult. What does difficult mean to you? Difficult is solving a math problem. It's—it's trying to figure out what the manual's telling you when there's something wrong with your computer." I slapped my hand to my chest. "My only real form of transportation got stolen. I've lost two jobs in less than a year. I'm living in a dangerous area on a dangerous side of town, busting my ass just to pay rent to stay in a place where hearing gunshots outside my window is just status quo, and the only thing anyone can ever tell me is it's difficult. I wish it were just difficult."

She stared at me with her mouth open.

I put my hands in my pockets and dropped my head once I realized what I'd said. "I'm sorry. I didn't mean to go off like that." My face flushed. "Thank you for the opportunity."

*He's David and Goliath.*

*He started off small, a fragile, narrow-chested man, bones protruding, body wilting, but one day he threw a rock at a giant. Then he grew to gargantuan size.*

*He's powerful. He can lift mountains over his head. He can smash buildings with his fingers. He battles monsters with his bare hands, and when the palms of his hands are covered with calluses, and his tendons are torn, he doesn't give up. He keeps fighting because if he doesn't, people will die. Monsters will eat everyone. The world will become chaos. When he keeps fighting, when he puts in everything, and his body is bruised and battered, he gets stronger. He grows. And he has to take on bigger opponents.*

*But one day he realizes there're too many monsters, and they're as big as he is. Or bigger. And he realizes that he can keep fighting them, and if he does, he'll keep growing and growing and growing. His back will reach the moon. His head will reach the stars. His eyes will be able to see the entire universe. The monsters will keep coming, and they'll keep growing and they'll become more and more powerful. Who will defeat them?*

*And then, when he's reached his maximum size, when he becomes unstoppable, the most powerful being in the universe, the greatest that ever lived, when he becomes God, who will defeat him?*

"Hey, Pops. I need your help."

By the start of July, an envelope was under my door. Two months, and I again had no job.

"That the only time you call? When you need my help?"

*Electricity service will be shut off on or after the following date unless the bill has been paid...*I crumpled the note and hurled it across the room. Rubbed my temples. "Sorry. I've been super busy, and I just don't got a lot of time."

He chuckled. "I'm joking."

My unemployment application was rejected because I was fired, which was considered my fault. I was back to the old drawing board, only it was worse because, since I was fired from my last job, new jobs wouldn't even look at me.

"What do you need help with?"

I rubbed my face.

"Hello?"

I stroked my brow. "I lost my job."

The job placement service got in touch with me, but the best I got out of them was a temporary position assembling phones. It kept me afloat for a month, but it only paid nine dollars an hour. At least I didn't have to drive.

"After five years?"

"No. It's a different one. I got laid off a couple months back. Got a new job, and it worked out, but somebody stole my bike. I had trouble getting to work on time. I got no job."

"So, you got fired?"

Silence.

"Yeah." I nodded. "I got fired."

"So, I guess what you're wanting now is money from me."

"Look, they're about to turn off my electricity. I only need it until—"

"Nuh-uh, son. Remember what you said when you left the house?"

"I know, and I'm sorry. I was young and stupid—"

"A man's gotta do what a man's gotta do. Know what a lot of guys your age are up to? A wife, a few kids and a nice house. You don't have the money, you gotta figure it out."

"I know, and I will, but it's just for the moment. I'll pay you back."

"Sorry, son. I can't help you."

"Please—"

He hung up.

How the hell is a guy supposed to pay for his electricity without any money? How the hell is a guy supposed to get money without a job? Is there a God up there? Does He give a flying fuck?

I called my sister.

"Hey...Nolan? Long time, no see."

"Yeah. Sorry about that. Say, I really need your help."

Pause. "Is this about money?"

"I just need it for the month. I'll pay you back—"

"You didn't gamble it all away, did you?"

"What? No. You know I haven't gambled in years."

"What'd you need it for?"

"I lost my job. Both. It's a long story."

She sighed. "I guess I could ask Steve. Hold on...Nolan? Hello?"

"Yeah."

"He doesn't think it's a good idea. I don't either. We helped you out when you were living in your truck..."

"I know."

"And how did you lose your job? Or jobs? You had two?"

"I told you. It's a long story, but I got laid off. The second one, someone stole my bike."

"I'm sorry, Nolan..."

"Katelyn, they're gonna turn off my lights—"

"I'm sorry." She hung up.

# 5

Pops used to say with desperate times come desperate measures.

I was at the store one day. I'd filled my basket with as many groceries as my food stamps could afford. I liked to walk down the electronics aisles because I knew I couldn't buy anything.

Cellphones, tablets, laptops, desktops, TVs, Bluetooth stereos, game consoles—there was a version of me out there in the multiverse who had all that stuff. A three-story mansion, five cars, a private yacht. He wasn't looking for a job or trying to figure out transportation. Wasn't embarrassed to talk to folks because he didn't want them to find out he was on food stamps. He had enough money to feed the world. That me existed. Somewhere.

But the me in this universe, standing in a superstore with a basket of SNAP-bought groceries, he was staring too hard at a phone on the display table. Newly released phone. I don't remember the model or even the brand, but it could probably sell for a couple of hundred.

Nobody else was around. I shook my head.

I ain't a thief.

I stared at it.

Wasn't like it belonged to anybody. It was just sitting in the store. A store from a business chain that probably had two billion dollars. Probably more. What difference was a couple hundred dollars going to make?

I looked over my shoulders.

They probably wouldn't even notice it was missing.

If I could just figure out how to get the sensor off. Or maybe if I ran for it, they wouldn't catch me.

I grabbed it and stuffed it in my backpack. I looked around to make sure the coast was still clear. A few other shoppers, but they weren't paying attention. I started for the exit, left my groceries on a shelf with folded pairs of jeans.

I hurried with my head down, and the workers took notice. I realized I'd have to act natural, but that was easier said than done.

I made it to the double doors where the security guard sat. Just a little old man, probably retired, looking for something to do. I hurried past him, and the detectors went off.

"Hey!"

Somebody grabbed me by the shirt. Store manager; at least it said so on his nametag.

I jerked.

"What's in your bag?"

"Nothing."

"Let me see."

"Shit." I don't think I fully realized what I did until I looked at the phone. I don't even think I weighed the pros and cons before I took it. It kind of just happened like you're thirsty, you drink, you're hungry, you eat.

I dropped it and ran out the door.


Food stamps don't pay for beer. I ordered water.

Sometimes you got to pretend. You pretend hard enough, you can trick yourself you're drunk. Convince yourself you're too intoxicated to pay attention to the time. Maybe that wasn't it. Can you be intoxicated on stress? If so, I wasn't pretending.

Or maybe I just gave up on life. Sometimes you reach that point where you feel like there's no reason, y' know? No point. You're breathing, you're feeling,

you're experiencing, but it's all in vain. You got nothing to live for, and that's
when the time just starts moving, and you don't realize it until you look at the
clock.

2:00 a.m.

"Alright, man. We're closing up."

I put my phone in my pocket. "Sorry. Didn't realize how late it was."

I was the only one in this bar. Me and the bartender. A tiny bar, no tables. Just
a bar counter, bar stools, Coors Light, and flickering neon. It's too late for this
shit. Damn. Gotta go home in the dark.

"What'd you do today?" he wiped the counter. "What's got you so down?"

I said it with a smile, but it wasn't real. "I tried to steal a phone. Didn't get
away with it. I ain't proud of myself."

"I've been there."

I walked out of the building wishing I was drunk. The mind is louder when
you're alone. Not a whole lot of people around. Not a whole lot going on.
Broken bottles and cigarette butts. Graffiti I appreciated more than my father
ever would.

I went to the bar furthest from home because I wanted a long walk to clear
my mind. Now I regretted that decision. Took the shortcut home through the
alley. Pops used to say, never take the shortcut. The long route builds character,
but I was tired, and I had a long way to walk. There weren't any prostitutes in the
alley tonight. Looked empty, but I didn't feel good in my stomach. I think I felt
the way a gazelle probably does when a lion's stalking him. I didn't see anyone's
shadow until I got halfway down the alley. When I passed a set of concrete steps
with rickety rails. Then I saw there were four of them. Beneath the fire escape.
All merged together on crumbling brick held together by concrete and scum.

I thought, for a second, I should turn around and go back, but they weren't
looking at me. I'd just gotten robbed. What were the chances of it happening
twice in such a short period of time? That was naïve.

I walked past them, and they weren't like the guys that stole my bike. One of
them had a gun. I didn't look back at them, but I heard their footsteps slapping
against puddles and kicking concrete rocks. If I started running, they'd start

running too. Then I figured if I acted cool, they'd leave me alone. That ain't a defense mechanism I ever heard before.

"Give me your wallet."

I threw my hands up. "I don't have it."

"You think I'm fucking with you?"

I looked behind me and saw straight down the barrel of a desert eagle. I gulped. "I'm not lying. I don't have my wallet. I hardly got any money at all. I'm jobless. I'm about to be—"

"Shut the fuck up." He jerked his head at the other three. "Check his pockets."

They patted me down. "He's got a cellphone."

"Anything else?"

My heart pounded. "Please."

"Shut up!"

I saw his face. He could kill me anyway. I glanced behind me. I could die there or die trying to escape. I hightailed it.

The gun went off.

The bullet hit me in my thigh. I clutched my wound and dropped on the concrete. They kicked me in my stomach, my chest. Blood squeezed through my fingers. I tried to scream, but my breath got trapped in my lungs.

"Help!" I couldn't catch my breath. "Somebody help me!"

I thought I was dead. I closed my eyes, but nobody was hitting me. When I peeked, somebody punched one of those guys in the face. He struck another's nose with his elbow, and when the guy with the gun tried to shoot him, he dodged the bullet, grabbed his arm, and twisted the gun out of his hand.

Don't judge a book by its cover, they say. I won't pretend like a judgment is never true, but that wasn't this guy. He wasn't a big guy at all. He was small. Skinny.

He picked the gun up off the ground and pointed it at my attackers. "Get the fuck out of here!" and all those guys ran out of the alley like a bunch of scattering roaches.

He was the only man I ever met who had the characteristics of a mouse and a tiger all at once.

He knelt beside me. "Let me see it." He had a rasp in his voice, dry, lower than a voice I was used to on a guy his age.

I moved my hand.

"Looks like it's just a flesh wound."

He was nobody's stereotype. His jeans were probably a size twenty-nine. He had on a black tank top, hair to his shoulders. I almost thought he was a chick at first glance. Had brown hair with one braid hanging down in the front and one in the back. He was tatted up. Tattoos on his arms, tattoos on his face, on his neck, on his fingers, studs on either side of his nose and beneath his lip, a ring above his eyebrow.

"I don't have a job." I quickly shook my head. "I don't even know if I qualify for Medicaid. What if I don't? I can't go to the hospital. How am I supposed to pay for that? What if..."

"Hey...hey. Look at me, alright? Look at me. Quit worrying. It only grazed you, alright? I'm gonna take care of you." He got up. "Can you walk?"

It was a struggle, but I got on my feet.

"It looks ugly, but it's not that bad. I've dealt with worse. I live right around here. I can take you back to my place, fix you up. That good?"

I nodded.

I made a joke about how this wasn't the first time I'd been attacked within the last couple of months. He didn't laugh.

His apartment wasn't any bigger or prettier than my own. I had trouble getting up the stoop, but he let me balance on his shoulder.

He took me up a flight of creaky stairs and put his key in a door he had to shove two times before it opened.

"Go lie on the couch," he said.

He had a photo of a toddler taped to the wall. A biracial kid with brown wavy hair and green eyes. Cute kid. He had photos of himself with other people. He had illustrations on notebook paper. Fingerpaints and crayon art of scribbled houses and smiling suns that could only look real in the imagination of a child.

You could see every room in the unit, no matter where you stood. His floors were tattered and his windows were smeared. The room smelled like mildew and cigarette smoke, and you could hear every bus, car, train, and voice outside through the walls, but the pictures kind of made you forget about all that. Kind of made you remember that there's more out there than getting shot in the leg. Maybe life's about something.

I dropped back on the couch, still had my hand gripping my wound, thinking I'm going to die, but at least I wasn't going to die alone. Even if the guy was a stranger.

He got a bottle of rubbing alcohol from the kitchen cabinet, bandages and cotton swabs from the bathroom, medical tape and scissors from the closet, and he set it all down one by one on a fold-up table he dragged out to the living room.

He wrapped the belt around my thigh and pulled it tight. "This is gonna hurt." He opened the bottle and poured alcohol on my leg.

I bit down and sucked air through my teeth.

He took a lighter and knife from his pocket and heated the blade. "You might wanna close your eyes." He pressed it against my wound, and I screamed like a bitch. Felt like lightning shot through my nervous system. Sweat soaked my whole body. My chest heaved so hard I thought I'd crack my ribs, yet it still felt like I couldn't get enough air.

I finally did what he told me, but I could feel hot steel pressed against my open skin.

"Where are you from?"

I clenched my teeth, held my breath, let it out harsh. "Buffalo."

"Yeah? How long you been here?"

I bit back the pain. "'Bout five years."

"What brought you this way?"

"I left my parents' house. Needed to find a job." I breathed. "I lost it, though. I actually lost two of 'em recently. Trying to find a new one."

"Sorry to hear that."

I didn't open my eyes until I heard the knife click. I stared at the pictures on the wall. Maybe I'd forget about the pain.

He poured alcohol on my wound, and I felt like my whole body had been skinned. I started reading things. Anything. Everything. Book covers. Posters. Cereal boxes. *Is it better to out-monster the monster or to be quietly devoured? -Friedrich Nietzsche. 1984-George Orwell.*

I noticed the letters on the side of his neck. "Who's Caelin?"

He dipped the cotton swab in the alcohol and rubbed it on the scrape on my arm. "My son."

"That him over there?"

He glanced at the photo on the wall. "Yeah. You can tell?"

"It's the eyes."

He unraveled the bandage roll. "Do you have any kids?"

I shook my head. "Nuh-uh."

He wrapped the bandage around my arm, grabbed a cotton swab and dipped it in the alcohol. I sucked air through my teeth when he rubbed it on my cheek. He snipped a square of bandage and taped it to my wound.

"You've done this before. Haven't you?"

"A couple of times." He dipped another swab in alcohol. "What's your name?"

"Nolan."

"Friends call me Pip."

"Pip?"

"Yeah, Pipshank. Like Pipsqueak. On account of my size. But I don't squeak."

I laughed.

"You like that? Other times, they call me The Mad Twink."

I laughed harder. He cracked a smile for the first time since I'd been there.

I cleared my throat. "Say. Why'd you help me tonight?"

"You looked like you needed it."

"Thank you. You probably saved my life."

He shrugged. "I wasn't gonna let you get killed." He swabbed my forehead. "What were you doing out there in the alley?"

"Needed a drink. Somebody stole my bike, I lost my job. Thought I'd take the shortcut home. Dumb. I know."

"You don't got a gun?"

"Nuh-uh."

"You should. The streets are dangerous. Especially at night."

"What were *you* doing out there?"

He hesitated. "Business." He patched up my forehead, then reached in his pocket. "This yours? It's got your picture on it."

"Hey. My phone. Thanks."

"It was lying in the alley."

"One of those guys must've dropped it when they tried to steal it."

He pulled the gun from under his shirt and set it in front of me. "I don't need it."

"I hardly know how to shoot it."

"There's a shooting range not far from here."

"I'm trying to save money."

He reached into his back pocket, took out his wallet, and handed me two twenties. "Don't worry 'bout paying me back."

"Thanks."

He grabbed his lighter, got up. When he turned around, I got a look at the tribal tattoo on his back. I could only see half of it, the rest was covered by his shirt, but it looked like devil horns. At the time, I wondered if that was just how I was interpreting it. He had what looked like "666" scarred on each shoulder blade.

He grabbed a pack of cigarettes from the counter. "Do you smoke?"

"I'm trying to quit."

"Mind if I..."

"It's cool."

He leaned against the counter, stuck a cigarette in his mouth, lit it.

"You said you were out there doing business. What does that mean? You got a job out there or something?"

"You can look at it like that." He blew out a cloud of smoke. "If you want."

"You any better than those guys that attacked me in the alley?"

"Probably not."

I paused. "I'm sorry."

"Don't apologize for nothing. The world doesn't apologize, so we shouldn't have to apologize either."

"I apologize a lot. I got a lot of shit going through my head ever since I lost my job. Lost two jobs in less than a year if you can believe that. Now I'm fucking around with resumes and applications, hoping some money's gonna rain down on me like God dropped His wallet, but every day it's spam calls or getting mugged—they're gonna shut my lights off sooner or later. All I wanna do is scream at the top of my goddamn lungs. Only thing I can do is write it all out."

"I get that."

"I told off my last manager." I chuckled. "After she gave me the boot."

"Did you apologize?"

I chuckled again. "Yeah."

He smiled, shook his head.

He rolled his lips together, took a long drag, gazed at all the pictures on his wall as if he forgot he was in the room with me, having a conversation with himself. "The world's tough. The system's a bitch. The best thing we can do is protect ourselves and survive. Place like this, you ought not to be out there alone. Fat cats got bodyguards and foot soldiers. We got each other."

"Yeah. I've been thinking about that. My whole family sort of ditched me, but I guess I can't blame 'em. I've made mistakes—"

"We all make mistakes."

I sat up and grabbed my phone. "Hey, man, I'm about to get out of here, but let me get your number. Maybe we can go for a beer or something one day."

"Sure."

We exchanged numbers, and I lifted myself off the couch best I could with all my wounds.

"Say." He pointed at the gun. "Don't forget that."

I grabbed it, almost tucked it into the front of my pants like they do in movies, but I was afraid I'd shoot off my dick.

"Come on." He jerked his head towards the door. "I'll drive you home."

Pip drove an orange 1970s Dodge Challenger. He listened to classic rock and the blues. When the music slowed or the light turned red, he'd sit back and wouldn't speak. Nobody could know what was happening in his head, but it was like he stepped outside of his body, took a walk, and when he'd come back, he was reluctant to tell you where he went, either because there was a truth there he wish he didn't know, or he didn't want to take you with him.

"How old are you?"

He pulled up in front of my apartment. "Twenty-one. Why?"

"You just look young. That's all."

I opened the door.

"Are you gonna be alright?"

I nodded. "Yeah."

"Something goes wrong, don't be scared to give me a call. Remember to clean those wounds every day. I can't help you if they get infected."

"Got it." I stepped out of the car. "I meant to ask you earlier, what's the tattoo on your back?"

"You ever heard of The D3vil's Krew."

I furrowed my brows. "Sounds familiar."

"Look 'em up."

"Nice car, by the way. Is it yours?"

"No."

"Whose is it?"

"I don't know."

# 6

I told Pip I'd meet up with him for a beer down at the bar one Saturday night.

I didn't have any money for beer, but he took care of it and threw in a basket of fried pickles. We sat at a side booth where the window flyers looked like real-life pop-up ads, and the TV above the bar hung just low enough to flash moving colors across names, cartoons, and dicks carved into the table.

*"An Arizona factory worker was rushed to the hospital after collapsing while operating a forklift in scorching temperatures reaching 109 degrees..."*

"That oughta be a crime." I guzzled a cold beer.

The ceiling fan turned, and the neon signs looked like somebody scribbled on the walls with star jizz. Bud Light, Coors Light, Budweiser, a flashing silhouette of a chick's bikini where one side of it didn't light up.

When I looked outside, I saw crumbling brick and rusted staircases, cheap cars, broken glass, alleys with piles of trash, a shirtless old guy sitting on a stoop with a backpack and a liquor bottle, but if I looked hard enough, I'd see the lights of tall buildings—corporate offices and penthouses, Mercedes and Porsches and Bentleys, billboards and marquees, suits and ties, Billionaires' Row. And if I stood on top of the building, I guess I'd see everything, like a field that the rain only hits one side of. If I took an airplane and jumped out of it, which side would I land on?

I took a swig. "I never had fried pickles."

"You should try one. They're good."

I did, and it tasted like what pickles would taste like if they were fried.

"How's your kid?"

"He's good." Pip nodded. "He's starting preschool in a few months. I swear, just yesterday, he was this little bean wrapped up in a blue blanket. He's gotten so big." He smiled, but it was short-lived. "I wish I could see him more."

"Are you and his mom not together anymore?"

"We don't hate each other. Nothing like that, but sometimes you have to do what's best for other people. Especially when they're people you care about." He got quiet. "I still see him. Take him out over the weekends. I wanna be in his life as much as I can."

I didn't know what to say to that.

"How've you been since the incident?" he asked. "Feeling any better?"

"Yeah. I've got a pretty bad scar, though."

"Scars will tell ya whether or not you lived in this world."

"Yeah." I nodded. "I guess so."

"What about money?"

"I was able to work something out with my utilities company, so they're not gonna turn off my electricity. At least not just yet. I need a job, but I ain't got any offers yet. What the fuck's a man gotta do to make some money 'round here?"

He didn't respond.

"I asked Pops if he'd help me out. Pfft. I already knew the answer to that, though. I asked my sister and—we get along. It's just. I dunno. Maybe you get it. You got an older sister?"

"Yeah." He took a drink. "Well...sort of. She's actually my mom...biological-ly."

"What?"

"Me and my birth mother were raised as siblings."

"Why?"

"We grew up poor. Uneducated. Regular-ass, run-of-the-mill white trash—you get the picture. Too many people in a two-bedroom apartment. My grandma was my mom, my great-grandma was my grandma, my uncles were my older brothers, my aunt was my little sister, and my mom was my older sister. She got pregnant with me when she was ten, so my mom, *her* mom, had to raise me with her other kids. She already had three, all with different dads. The first two, she got out of prostitution." He shook his head. "The shit we do for money."

"Ten?" I started to mouth *wow* but stopped when I realized it. "Are you serious? Did they ever catch the guy that...?"

He shook his head. "*She* took advantage of *him*. There was a kid that lived down the hall, just turned thirteen. They used to hang out, and apparently, one day, she just..." he shrugged. "She showed him something."

"But she was only ten years old."

"Yeah. Tell me about it. But it's not all cut and dried. Turned out, her grandma knew a couple of guys. Said her mom got her started at nine years old, too." He shook his head. "The shit we do for money."

"I...damn." Stories like that will make your breathing stop and your skin go numb. Ride through your nervous system and gets trapped in your brain. "Sorry to hear that."

He shrugged. "No use apologizing for it. What's done is done." He slid a pickle in his mouth and chewed on it a long time, took a drink. "I had two older brothers and a stepdad, and I used to wonder which one of them was supposed to be my father. My stepdad was probably the closest thing to it, but he went to jail when I was about five. I didn't even know my sister was actually my mom until I was, like, eight years old. You don't ask a whole lot of questions about shit like that when you're that age. It's just sort of shocking, I guess. Maybe because you don't figure you're the only one. It's not until you get older that you realize how fucked up it all is."

I could look at the person sitting across from me, and I could ask what every single one of his tattoos meant. Black ink across his fingers. Black ink down his arms. Around his neck and on his face. I could ask him why his voice was so low and raspy, how many cigarettes he smoked a day. Then I could ask myself how I was feeling looking at somebody like that. Was it awkward? Was it wrong? Maybe it was pity or judgment. I don't know. But there's something about when you meet a person, look at that person's tattoos, the lines on their face, the scars on their skin, the direction of their eyes. Take a big mirror and wonder what somebody else is looking at on you. It's shit like that that might make you feel ungrateful. Or disadvantaged if I was staring at a cashmere suit instead of the dangling black threads of ripped-off t-shirt sleeves.

"Did you ever have a dream?" I asked.

"Dream?"

"I dunno." I took a swig. "I used to think I'd be a writer."

"Guess I never really thought about it. No." He shook his head. "I never had one."

I nodded.

"I guess if I did," he tapped his fingers on the table, turned his gaze towards the window where the city put lights in his eyes, "it might've been waking up in a house and a family that's happy. That sounds cheesy." He put the beer bottle to his lips but didn't take a drink. "That's a good question."

"I looked up The D3vil's Krew. Since 2007? That true?"

"What?"

"That's what the site said. It said it wasn't confirmed, but people think it's been around since 2007. Said it was started here. In New York."

He nodded. "Yeah."

"But there wasn't a whole lot. Like, there ain't lots of information about it." I lowered my voice. "About you. There ain't a whole lot about you."

He wiped his mouth. "You don't gotta whisper."

"That how you make your money?"

"Yeah."

"But how? Why? You don't rub me as...I dunno...that kinda guy."

"What kind of guy were you expecting?"

I shrugged.

He took a bite of fried pickle and a gulp of beer.

"What made you join something like that?"

"Can't tell ya." He shook his head. "It kind of just...happened. Looking for money. Knowing my girl was pregnant and trying to figure out how I would provide for her and my son as a seventeen-year-old kid. Guess there were a lot of factors." He picked up a pickle and held it between his fingers long enough to probably forget it was there. "I'm a fourteen or fifteen-year-old kid. I go out to the diner around the corner a lot because at home, there's always some shit going on, and I just feel like I need to breathe. I get into a whole lot of fights in school, and I'm skinny and shy. I just need to breathe. Every time I go, there's this guy named Richie. He's older than me. He's an adult, but he doesn't judge me like the other adults do. He's more confident than I am, and he's looking at me like the son he never had. He's always coming in with these other guys, and if one of those assholes from school comes in and says something to me, those guys defend me, and Richie's telling me that I need to get some confidence in myself and learn to protect myself. And, I dunno, I just started hanging out with those guys. Sometimes missing school. And they taught me how to fight, how to stick up for myself."

He tossed the pickle in his mouth. "He said, the world don't give a flying fuck about you or your son. All it cares about is your money. You know what they say, if you can't beat 'em, play their unfair game by your own rules." He took a swig, slammed the beer down on the table. "The world's not going to wait around for you to get your shit together. When it wants to play dirty, you gotta play dirtier."

"But how? It's wrong."

He relaxed his shoulders and sighed. "Do you believe in God?"

"I'm not sure."

"Know why I don't believe in God? Because if there were a God, I don't think that He would make living things have to eat to survive. Because in order for a living thing to eat, that means another living thing has to die." He put another pickle in his mouth, slowly chewed. "And those at the bottom of the food chain have to do whatever it takes to survive. By all means necessary."

"Have you ever killed anyone?"

He didn't say anything.

I didn't either.

He combed his hair to the back of his head. "The only thing in my life I'm proud of is Caelin. Everything else can burn in Hell."

Pip had on a three-piece suit and a striped tie. What a crazy fucking dream.

"Tired of being poor? Tired of having no money? Feel like they're gonna turn off your lights and throw you out on the streets with nothing but an unkempt beard and a bottle of Jack Daniels?" His voice didn't sound like Pip's. It was high-pitched and flamboyant. He had a briefcase and a smile that looked like someone pumped fifteen years' worth of Botox into his cheeks. Everything was fuzzy, like a cheap commercial. It even had those buzzy lines going up and down like an old TV, but mist was surrounding our waists like we were at a ghost's birthday bash.

What a crazy fucking dream.

"Do we have a job for you!" He pointed at me.

"Me?"

"Yes, you."

"What?"

"You don't have any experience. You've lost two jobs. You made terrible grades in school, and you're a desperate son of a bitch." A PowerPoint popped up out of nowhere, and he pulled a pointer stick from behind his back. "Our aptitude test shows that you would make a perfect...drumroll, please..." Confetti exploded from the sky and spilled down over my head. "Outlaw!"

"You're crazy."

"See why so many average people like yourself are becoming outlaws today! It pays your rent, it doesn't require any education, and it's perfect for unskilled fuckups like yourself."

I shook my head. "I'm not that desperate."

"What do you got to lose?" He stopped smiling and actually looked at me seriously, for once, with a face that was more recognizable as Pip and not like I was a part of some cheap local ad. "What do you got to lose?"

I woke up.

What a crazy fucking dream.

I didn't have enough money to pay next month's rent. I didn't get any callbacks or job offers. The homeless man who occasionally slept out on my stoop was picked up by the cops last night. Any day, they were going to shut off my electricity.

The next time I met up with Pip, we went out to the same bar, only this time, afterward, he told me he was going to take me someplace remote, a place where he liked to go to think because where there were too many buildings and too many cars, too many people and media and voices, you forget what the sound of your own mind is like. Then you don't know who you are. A clay model shaped by the hands of everything else but you.

It was nightfall. He drove me out to a park. There was no one out there. Said he went out there by himself, most of the time, but he thought it would be good for me.

Across the bridge, the city looked like a mural on the earth's wall. He turned away from it, and I followed him down a trail made of stone and dry soil.

"Where do you guys usually hang out?"

"Who? You mean D3vil's Krew? Why?"

I shrugged. "Curious. I guess."

"You don't wanna join nothing like that."

"What happened to not waiting on the world? Playing dirty?"

"You ever played dirty before?"

"There's a first time for everything."

He shook his head.

"Why do you do it? Why don't you get out?"

"It ain't that simple."

"Why not—"

"Cause it ain't." He stopped walking, sighed, stared out at the wiggling lamp lights and distorted tree branches that looked like melted crayons on the pond's black ripples. "You ever step in water you thought was shallow, but you don't realize how deep it is until you're drowning?"

He faced me.

I stared at his expression until I realized it wasn't changing.

I put my hands on my hips, hung my head. "I don't got anything. My family won't help. My electricity's about to get shut off. I didn't even have money for rent this month. I've been getting fees, and soon enough...I won't even have a home." I rubbed the back of my neck, lifted my head, and stared him in the eye. "I got nothing to live for."

I followed him to an open area between low-hanging tree branches and hairlike vines.

He squatted on the ground and raked his fingers through the grass. He gazed out at twinkling stream waters, put a cigarette in his mouth, lit it. Before it smelled like cigarette smoke, the earth smelled like a planet I forgot existed. Soil and grass. Ripe tree leaves. The ambient ensemble of waterfalls and rustling leaves. Restless breezes and velvet winds.

"If you want," he said, "I can take you out to the spot. Let you meet 'em, but I'm letting you know, you might not like it."

"Thanks."

He crossed his legs out in front of him, put his arms behind his head, and dropped back against the grass. I think he forgot I was there for a minute. He gazed up at the sky, eyes darting back and forth so that the lights ran across the whites to his pupils like shooting stars.

"You ever just stare up at the night sky?" he said. "You oughta do it some time. You do it hard enough, you start to feel like you can see the whole universe. Sometimes I look up there and wonder if somewhere out there, there's a better version of me." He took the cigarette out of his mouth. "Guess it's better not to know. If you know everything, there's nothing left to hope for."

I sat beside him, stretched my legs out in front of myself, and craned my neck. There weren't enough stars in New York, but there was a crescent moon and a deep purple sky that encapsulated the entire city, the pond, the stream, and the trees, and went on as far as the imagination could create it, and out there, there were stars and more moons, and planets, comets. You soon realize you're not the only thing that matters. You realize how small you are, and then you realize you're a part of something much bigger than you.

"Sometimes," he said, "when I stare at it hard enough, I forget this world even exists."

# 7

Pip said it used to be a church. Back in, like, the seventies.

An anarchy sign looked like fresh blood, but it was dry, chipped, and runny, even though the paint hadn't dripped in years. It had dried against the building's rough texture and seeped between cracks in the wall, whose dust and decay probably hid what used to be red brick. The windows were all boarded up except on the second and third floors, which had glistening spiderweb cracks and scratches that made my skin itch. A rusty chain-link fence encircled the building like a rampart bought at the discount store, and weeds and roots crawled through the cracks of the pavement, reaching across the ground and climbing the fence like they were breaking from the grave.

The building had been tagged and spraypainted so many times there were tags on top of tags, and the left side had so much done to it, it looked like the poor man's Sistine Chapel. Middle fingers and marijuana plants, dollar signs, tongues, skulls, *Fuck the police!*, guns, anarchy symbols, *If Not Peace then War!*, zombies, vampires, Satan in sunglasses, inverted crosses, 666, a black-winged angel. But it looked good. Really good. Eyes with every fiber and eyelash detailed down to the glisten across the iris. Hands with every tendon and bone pronounced like you could reach up there and shake them. Fingernails where even the dirt stains were dotted in.

I got out of Pip's car and stepped out on a sidewalk that looked like it would crumble and break into a sinkhole as soon as my foot touched it. The pavement was smeared with street chalk.

Pip opened the gate. I followed him to a rusted metal door with a code lock.

He flipped through his keys, found a small bronze one, stuck it in the lock, and punched in the code. The lock clicked. He twisted the knob, shoved open the door.

Sat right there on the wall. Looked like the anarchy sign. More dried paint and spray blotches. Below it, the same symbol Pip had on his back ran down the brick. Cracks ran across the concrete floor. Tangled wires drooped and hung from the ceiling like tangled vines from some crazy cyberpunk jungle. It smelled like mildew, cigarettes, and booze. I heard people laughing around the corner, rock music, clanking beer bottles, clacking billiards balls, the generator humming outside. You might think you were standing outside some old dive bar if you didn't know better.

"Hey," a low voice came from around the corner. "Pip's here."

"Say, Pip, what'd you bring us?" Another guy laughed.

"You guys seen Richie?" Pip walked me around the corner, where the concrete was as dusty and cracked as it was at the entrance. There was a rustic ceiling lamp with a single light bulb hanging on the ceiling by a chain and hook. The wood burner had rust stains, with a long pipe that ran up the top and a glass door you could look through and see the ashes and charcoaled wood. There was a green couch in front of it with holes in the fabric, and a black and white plaid chair that looked handmade. A brand-new TV on the wall played something nobody paid attention to.

They had a barrel for a trashcan next to the bar. A record player cabinet that looked vintage until you realized it played Bluetooth. A round wooden table by the wall with six chairs. A galley kitchen with an old firewood oven, a microwave, and a refrigerator nobody's seen since the nineties.

Movie posters and neon beer signs on the brick. A memorial plaque with names and photos of mostly young people, young men, hung on the wall just behind the bar counter.

A lanky dude in a crop top bent over the pool table, aiming at the cue ball until he glanced up at Pip. "He's in his room."

I didn't know it yet, but that guy's name was Mike. Most of the time that I would know Mike, he had on the same beanie he wore that day or a backwards hat, hair hanging dirty blond over his shoulders and down to his waist, eyes droopy like he was perpetually high off his ass. His tattoos weren't like everyone else's. They were colorful. Abstract. He had more than anyone in the group, and when I would later ask him where he got them, he said he did most of them himself.

He shot pool with a guy named Axe. Biggest dude I ever knew. Had a shaved head with *D3K* tattooed on the side. Shoulders broad as a semi-truck and a chest just as hard, and then you had to wonder, in a competition between him and the truck, who could throw the hardest punch. His neck was as wide as his head, and his jaw was a cinder block. His shirt fit him tight, though his pants were baggy, and then I wondered if the dude skipped leg day.

There were four of them in this room, five if you included Pip, shooting pool, sitting on the bar stools. When I first saw Jackie, I didn't know she was a woman. She was the only woman. A broad-shouldered chick, a muscular chick, had a frame like an MMA fighter. She had on baggie cargo jeans and a black tank top. She kept her hair black and short, sort of a pixie cut on the top, but shaved on the sides like a pixie mohawk. She had a beer in her hand, a cigarette between her lips, cursive above her eyebrow, a piercing in her lip. Sat on the barstool like she'd seen enough shit in a day.

First time I saw Arin, he had his laptop on the bar counter, but he was looking at me, studying me while downing a beer. He kept his hair in dreadlocks, long and red, shaggy, his beard trimmed into a goatee. He wore a tie-dyed t-shirt of a band or brand or movie that I'd never heard of, joggers, and socks with sandals. The kind of guy, when you saw him with a book, it was Shakespeare or James Joyce, and then you had to ask yourself, where do we draw the line between the high and the low when yesterday's Darwin and Newton are wearing ripped jeans, tattoos, piercing their ears, and polishing their nails chrome blue today?

He pulled his beer from his mouth. "Who's that guy?"

"He's a friend of mine," Pip said. "You seen Richie?"

"I told you," Mike hit the cue ball, "he's in his room."

"What's he doing? He asleep?"

Mike snorted a laugh. "Hell if I know. I ain't knocking on that door."

Pip sighed, jerked his head. "Come on."

He took me across the room and banged on one of the doors. "Hey, Richie?" He banged again. "You in there?"

It took a minute, but the knob turned, the door opened, and I was smothered by a pillow of tobacco and nicotine.

He leaned against the doorway and took the cigarette out of his mouth. "What'd you want?" He had a black bandana wrapped around his head, hair down to his shoulders that was kind of blond, kind of red. Had a young Axl Rose vibe to him, but his eyes were so pale they were almost white, so it looked like I was staring into bare pupils. When that didn't draw your attention, the scars on his face did, one big one on the side that all but comically looked like a cross, or the 666 tattooed above his eyebrow, the inverted cross tattooed under his eye, the gap between his two front teeth.

He had tattoos on his arms, his neck, his chest, his fingers, tribal tatts, inverted pentacles, an anarchy sign on his shoulder that didn't make him stand out from the rest of his crew, but he had words on his forearms and chest that did. Maybe poetry. Maybe lyrics.

"Who the fuck's this?" he asked.

"Guy I met a couple weeks ago. Helped him out after some punks tried to mug him in the alley."

"What'd I tell ya about bringing people here without telling any fuckin' body? He got an ID? You know anything about this motherfucker?"

"He ain't a cop, Richie."

"You don't know what the fuck he is. Looks like a Guido hipster to me."

"He ain't a cop, Richie. You think a cop's gonna be out in an alley without a gun or a Taser waiting for some white trash scallywag to come and save him? No backup or ambulance? You gotta be out of your mind. Look, he's got a manbun. What kind of cop wears a manbun."

"So you got some sort of beatnik, hippie, street Jesus. Where the fuck's he from? What the fuck does he want?"

"Money," I said.

He got in my face. "Alright. Whatcha got?"

"Me."

He raised one eyebrow, smiled sarcastically. "What? You running some sort of male prostitute ring, now, Pip? I ain't into that. Find somebody else." He slammed the door.

I banged on it. "That's not what I meant."

He opened the door back up. "Who are you working with? Where are you from? I got money, but I don't got time, so you wanna make a deal with me, spit it, or we're done."

"I'm not looking to make a deal."

"Then what the fuck are you looking for?"

"I wanna join your team."

He paused, stared at me a long time, then busted out laughing. "Team." He slapped me on the shoulder. "You hear that? Anyone who calls it that doesn't know a gun from a dildo."

They all laughed. Even Pip cracked a smile.

Richie's complexion changed, and he glowered at me, showing the whites of his eyes like a mad dog. "Get the fuck outta my church before I beat your ass into human pulp!"

He almost slammed the door again, but I stopped it with my hand. I balled my fist. "I'm serious."

He glanced at his guys, back at me, sneered. "This stupid son of a bitch ain't playin'."

"I'm not. I got no job, and I got no money. I'm a downtrodden, desperate motherfucker, and I've got nothing to lose."

"That it?"

"That's it."

He took his cigarette out of his mouth, threw it on the ground, stomped it out. "Get out of my fuckin' way. Mike, get me a fuckin' drink. Get me another fuckin' cigarette while you're at it. Holy fuckin' shit. You." He pointed at me. "Come here. Sit."

I followed him across the room and sat in the plaid chair.

"No. Never mind. Stand."

I got up, and he took my seat.

Mike brought him a beer and a pack of cigarettes. He popped it open, put a cigarette in his mouth. Mike tossed him the lighter.

Richie stared at me for a long, uncomfortable minute while the ripples of his cigarette smoke drifted across his eyes. "You ever been in a jail cell?"

I swallowed.

"I didn't think so. You like warm meals? A comfortable bed? It ain't nothing like that. It smells like shit, and you feel like a fuckin' animal. And there's no mercy from those people on the outside. Oh no," he chuckled, "once you're in this business, you ain't the shit beneath their boots. You ever been shot before?"

"I've been hit by a bullet."

"I mean really been shot. I mean felt that shit rip straight into your flesh, and you don't know if that son of a bitch is going to send you to hell tonight or leave you running from death yet another day. And you can't call an ambulance about it 'cause if you call an ambulance, they're gonna ask you too many questions and send you on your way to the fuckin' cage, so you gotta get that shit out yourself or get somebody else to do it, and you don't know how many arteries that shit's been blocking off just to give you enough time to turn your life over to Jesus. You ever watched somebody get shot? You ever shot somebody? You ever stood over a body and watched it go from a living breathin' person to an inanimate piece of meat right before your eyes?"

I swallowed.

"I didn't fuckin' think so." He took a drag. "You say you got nothing to live for. Tell ya something, I got nothing to live for. He's got nothing to live for. He's got nothing to live for. She's got nothing to live for. He's got nothing to live for, and that asshole who just brought me my drink's got nothing to live for, either. We sacrificed that for this bitch right here. It didn't come because the government knocked on our door and said, 'Hey, would you like some free shit?' We sacrificed, baby. Paid the tithe, and there ain't a fuckin' refund." They nodded. "What's got you wantin' in? You stupid?"

"Maybe. I'm desperate."

He tapped the ash off his cigarette, got out of his seat, and slapped me across my face.

I bit down and balled my fists.

"That it?"

"I don't got no family to turn to. I lost my job and can't find a new one. They're gonna kick me out of my apartment soon, and I don't wanna be a bum out on the streets getting my asshole plugged by guys like your posse."

"Oh-ho-ho, you hear that? Guys like my posse. So what? You think you're gonna run down here, get some of my money, and all of your problems are gonna be gone? Do I look like the poverty fairy to you?"

"I need some security."

"Call the fucking cops."

"This system don't care about a poor man."

"Ha! You ain't seen a proper ass-raping from this system yet."

"You don't know what I've seen."

He slapped me across my face.

I kept my fists balled, my chest out. I don't know why I was intimidated by him. He wasn't taller than me. Matter of fact, he was the shortest person in the room aside from Pip. He wasn't bigger than me either—cut, but not bigger.

He took the cigarette out of his mouth, grabbed his beer off the table, and chugged.

"I grew up poor. You think I haven't seen shit?" I tightened my fists. "I've robbed before. I've made my money the hard way, and I've seen what desperate people do under desperate fuckin' measures."

He wiped his mouth. "You ever kill somebody?" He put his beer on the table, stepped up to me until I could feel his breath in my face. He stared cold into my eyes. "Could you?"

I rubbed my lips together.

"Huh? You think you got the balls to take another life? First time I ever killed somebody, I was fourteen years old. I couldn't sleep a wink that night or any night for that matter. That shit tormented me like it was violating me down in its basement. Every day, that scene played over and over again in my head. But, you know what? I did it again. And I did it another time after that. And every time I did it, the more detached I became. I've seen so much blood on my hands, I wonder what color they used to be. And now, I haven't had a nightmare in years. I don't fuckin' dream at all. I don't even remember the way it felt the first time I took a life. What the hell is fear anymore? Now, everything in my chest is as numb as the left side of my fuckin' face."

I stared into his bare pupils, at the scar running down his cheek.

"Know what I think? I think you're weak shit."

"I ain't weak."

"Yeah?" He slapped me across my face. "That feels like a pussy to me."

I tightened my fists.

"You ain't ready."

"I'm ready."

"You ain't fuckin' ready."

"I'm ready.

He slapped me again. "You ain't fuckin' ready. That's why you let another man slap you in the face and don't do shit about it."

"I've heard gunshots. I've seen ambulances carrying away dead bodies. Neighbors' units getting broken into, people wailing, all their shit gone. You think I ain't had nightmares? It's been shit like that every day for the past five years, and I ain't ready to walk out into that world broke and alone."

He slapped me across my face.

I slapped him back.

He punched me in the face, and I fell back against the floor.

I sat up, pinched my nose.

He squatted beside me. "If you got nothing to live for then what the hell are you still doing alive?"

"I ain't ready to die yet."

He grabbed me by my hair and lifted my head. The ash dropped off his cigarette and the smoke curled around my face. "Sounds about right." He stood. "Get the hell out of my church."

## 8

My electricity went out.

No lights. No TV. I tried calling my electricity service, but the battery on my phone was down to three percent. I sighed, grabbed my charger, and headed to the café down the street.

I wrote a story that morning about a guy who had superpowers until he realized he didn't. It was all just a fantasy he believed because he never questioned it, but I didn't finish it because my electricity went out.

Richie wasn't wrong. I was stupid. But you have those moments where you want something for one reason, and then when you can't get it, you want it for another.

I'd gotten a note under my door that told me I had yet another fee for my late rent payment. One more of those, and my next warning would be eviction. Then what?

I'd watched an old guy with a backpack, thermos cup, and a grimy, holey shirt pound the pavement with a *Need Money, God Bless* sign. I'd seen a bunch of guys like that. Jack Daniel's and holey sneakers. I could get a tent and put it up in an alley somewhere, camp out at the subway station, live out the remainder of my couple of years getting drunk until the alcohol destroyed my liver. What a way to go. Maybe I'd stumble across a dropped lottery ticket, find out it's a winner.

From tent to mansion. Maybe they'd make a reality TV show about me, give me a movie deal.

Dreaming ain't solving problems.

I still had that gun. I wasn't planning on killing anybody. It wasn't like I was a stranger to crime. Or something like crime. Shoplifting headphones as a teen was a crime, right? I wasn't a stranger to it. Just rusty, but I could do it again. And I wasn't planning on staying long. Do a couple of dirty deeds just until you can get yourself an actual job and be done with that life before you ever have to spill any blood. A seasonal position. Is there such a thing as a part-time criminal?

If not for the money, at least to prove myself. I couldn't put it on a resume, but I could at least say, hey, I did that one thing, and if I did that one thing, then I could do anything. Or maybe I could put it on a resume. Experience: three months of marketing by making business transactions with drug lords.

I could hit the gym and build some muscle. Learn some fighting moves so I could make a good impression. First impressions are lasting. I once went into a job interview with two different shoes on. I didn't notice it until I left the house. Too anxious, too much to do, too little time. I might've gotten the job if one shoe wasn't black and the other brown. First impressions are lasting.

My electricity service said there was nothing they could do. Go figure. I learned to live halfway off-grid for a time, battery-powered lamps and lots of trips to the café. Foods and drinks in an ice cooler. Lots of trips to buy ice.

I thought I'd call and ask Pops for help again, but I already knew what he would say. If he knew I was trying to make money the criminal way, he'd lock me up himself.

You got to do what you got to do to make ends meet, son.

And I'd say, I agree with that.

Huh?

I agree with that.

There's no excuse for breaking the law.

And I'd say, tell that to the guys who stole my bike.

Playing by the rules doesn't work, Pops. The rules don't care. The rules got no empathy or human understanding, so why should I play by the rules when the rules failed me one too many times? I don't plan on staying with Richie and those guys long.

Seasonal criminal.

I binged videos on fight moves and self-defense. I used to be able to fight a little bit when I was in high school. I'd won a couple, but that was all chaotic nonsense. Other animals seem to have a natural instinct for how to fight. We human folk have to learn everything. There's a technique to everything. When did there become a technique for kicking somebody and punching somebody out? Couldn't have always been, but I guess when one guy knows a technique, and you're out there throwing your fists everywhere like a damn monkey, the technique guy has the advantage. Brawns *and* brains, I guess. Something like that.

I made jogging a regular thing and practiced those punching moves I learned on my pillows. With no electricity, there wasn't much to do but exercise. I didn't grow a six-pack in twelve days, but I at least felt some confidence.

I watched some motivational videos. Don't fake it 'til you make it. Be it! If you stand confident, you feel confident. Believe in yourself, and anything is possible.

By the start of August, I hadn't had a lot of time to prepare, but I also hadn't made any money. I sat up in bed going back and forth with myself whether or not I wanted to take a bus ride out there and prove myself to Richie. I didn't make a good first impression, but I could try again.

Money or have my ass thrown out on the street. No shelter, no food, or not much. No security. Depression. I was going to die anyway. If I was going to die anyway, I was going to die fighting.

There'd never been such a time in my life when I really felt like nobody cared. Who was in my corner?

I had a bit more confidence. Even some survival cred if you want to throw in adapting to my lack of electricity.

Did I really want this? Is this what I really wanted? Or is this what I really needed? And then I had to ask myself something because I knew a part of me wanted this for more than just the money. Last year, crime was bad; tonight, I was trying to join in. Is that what happens when your pockets go empty? Or was it just me?

I put in a lot of work to ready myself. I was going out to that church again the next day. That was for damn sure.

I knocked on the door.

Mike cracked it open but not all the way. He peeked at me through the crack, and maybe he did or maybe he didn't know I could see his gun pointing at me from below. "What do you want?"

"I wanna talk to Richie. He here?"

"What about?"

"I was here about a week ago. I was wanting to join D3vil's Krew."

Mike squinted, then maybe he remembered my face.

I raised my hands. "I don't got any weapons. You wanna pat me down, go ahead."

"Give me a minute." He closed the door.

I waited.

The door opened. "He's not seeing any visitors today."

"Tell him I'm not going anywhere until I talk to him."

He looked at me seriously, but then he cracked a smile of yellow teeth, crooked incisors. "You're a stubborn motherfucker, aren't you?"

I shrugged.

He looked over his shoulder. "Ay, Richie. He said he ain't going anywhere."

"Goddamn." Richie came to the door and peeked at me. "Just let his ass in."

Mike opened the door all the way. He held up his hand before I could come in. "Stop. Raise your hands." He patted me down. "You're good."

They were all there—big man, Axe, sitting at the bar; little man, Pip, leaning against the pool table; Mike walking in looking like he's stoned off his ass; red dreadhead, Arin, sprawled out on the couch, and Jackie, the only chick, behind the bar counter.

"Hey, hey, hey," Arin said, "look who's back."

Pip crossed his arms and turned away from me.

Richie was in my face before I could breathe. "The fuck you doin' back?"

"I'm not done yet."

"I am."

"I'm not. I want in. Now, either you're gonna let me in, or you're gonna kill me. Which is it?"

Richie wasn't much for breaking eye contact with anybody, and I couldn't let him see me shake or know that my heart raced as I said what I said.

This could go either way.

"Why do you want this so bad?" he asked.

"I told you. I'm desperate." If I shook, he'd know how the cold look in his unnaturally pale eyes made me uneasy or that I wondered how he got those scars on his face. "You never gave me a chance."

He stepped back. "Hit me." He patted his cheek. "Right here. Hit me right here on the face."

They're all watching me. Axe's pouring back a beer, Mike's smoking a joint, Arin's got a smile on his face like he's excited, and I see Pip drop his head and rub his temples.

I'd been practicing punches. Been hitting the gym. Learned some fight moves, even if it was the armchair way. Built a little bit of confidence.

Richie patted his cheek, and truth be told, there wasn't a thing in this world I wanted to do more for the past week than deck him. I tightened my fist, pulled my arm back, swung for his mouth.

He caught my hand mid-air.

I tried it with my other fist.

He caught that too. "That the best you got?" He let my fist go.

I swung at him again, but this time, when he caught it, he threw it back at me and hit me in the face with my own fist.

I fell on my ass.

"Quit hitting yourself," he said. "Get the fuck up. Let's go again."

They laughed, but I got up. I swung for his stomach this time, but he grabbed my arm, swung me around and got me in a chokehold. He laughed. "You throw like a bitch."

He shoved me to the ground. "Come on, faggot. Get the fuck up."

The humiliation made me feel smaller than a cigarette butt after you worked overtime. I grit my teeth, charged at him.

He grabbed me and threw me on the floor. "What a pussy."

I got up. "I ain't done yet."

He turned his back to me. The audacity. But I couldn't blame him. My shoulders slumped in defeat.

I turned around and left.

I went out to the front yard. The more I thought about it, the more it spread like a dye drop in a cup of water. Kind of starts off small, but once that shit settles in, it takes over your whole body. I wanted to curl up somewhere. Die.

I opened the fence door but stopped when I heard footsteps coming my way. "Hey."

I turned around.

"Hey, kid." Jackie stopped by the fence. "Let me tell you somethin' 'bout Richie. You can't break on him. Truth is, he likes you. If not, he would've had us haul your ass out of here before you got a word in."

I scratched the back of my head. "I don't know."

She dragged her hand down her face. "He's calling you a bitch and a pussy. I *got* a fucking pussy. You think he instantly looked at me and said, 'That's the one I want'?" She swatted me on the shoulder. "It's resilience, kid. Come back here tomorrow and let him know you still ain't done."

When I showed up the next day, I didn't knock on the door. I banged on it. I imagined a bullet through my skull, or a knife in my gut, or getting beat to a bloody pulp right there on the floor. I told that dude he was either going to let me join or kill me, and the way it was going, it didn't look like it was going to be the former, but Mike opened the door, and he didn't have his gun this time. He let me right in.

Everybody was there again, and Arin said, "Goddamn. This is getting good. I should've grabbed some popcorn."

"Where's Richie?" I asked.

"I'm right here, you hardheaded son of a bitch." He marched into the room. "And I'm gettin' real tired of your ugly mug."

"You wanna throw a few punches, I'm ready, but I told you. I want in."

He crossed his arms, stared at me for a long time, like he was trying to figure me out.

He took a pack of cigarettes from his pocket, popped one in his mouth, lit it. He snapped the lighter closed, put it in his pocket, pointed his cigarette at me. "You're the stupidest motherfucker I ever met." But he didn't say it with disdain this time. His tone softened, if Richie's tone could be soft.

He took the cigarette out of his mouth. "What do you know about us?"

I furrowed my brow. "Not a lot. I mean, there's not a lot about you out there. Guess that's a good thing."

"Why do you think you'd be a good fit?"

A job interview? I blinked. I didn't study. "Uh…" Shit. Don't stutter. "I'm strong." Too vague. "I ain't afraid of nothing." More specific. "I've done this before. I've been desperate. I've done what I've had to do to survive, and I protect the people who fight alongside me. When I was in high school—"

"I don't give a fuck about your pubescent years." He crossed his arms. "You got any weaknesses?"

Damn. Recycle. "Criticism. I don't take criticism well." That doesn't work for this gig.

"Like what? What'd you mean?"

"I'm a perfectionist. I want everything to be just right, and when I screw up—"

"You sensitive?"

"No."

"Where do you see yourself in five years?"

Was this serious? How the hell do you answer that question? Why do they always ask that question? Who the hell knows where they're going to be in five whole years? "Making money." I nodded. "That's where I'm gonna be. I'm not going to be a useless, homeless fuck out on the street. I'm gonna make my money and do whatever it takes to keep it."

"Really?" He slowly walked up to me. "'Cause I see you dead."

"I won't be."

He took the cigarette out of his mouth and blew a cloud of smoke in my face. "Why not?"

"Because I'm resilient."

I looked at everyone's faces. Dumbfounded expressions appeared to be contagious. Jackie had a sort of smile on her face. The room was so quiet, you could hear a fly fart.

"That so?" Richie stepped back, pulled the cigarette out of his mouth, and dropped it in the ashtray on the bar counter, but he didn't turn his back to me. "We'll see about that tomorrow."

# 9

I still wasn't officially in. I could change my mind.

Had I exhausted all my options? Or was I jumping in too soon?

It would only be for a short time.

I could turn around, go back, and pretend like none of it ever happened. I hadn't committed any real crimes yet. They didn't want me anyway. I didn't have to take it.

It was only for a short time.

They drove me out to a gas station. Midnight. Empty parking lot. One guy at the cash register. Get in there, grab a pack of beer, get out of there without the cashier catching you. Run. We'll be right here. You can't do that, you can't be in D3vil's Krew.

I've shoplifted before. I've never shoplifted beer. I've never driven up to a convenience store in the middle of the night, grabbed a whole six-pack, ran out the door, and jumped in my car before I got caught.

What if the cashier had a gun?

I've never wandered right in, right in front of the cashier, walked around like I was shopping, took off with a whole six-pack, ran as fast as I could, jumped into a vehicle, and hoped nobody saw my face and nobody was on my ass.

The cashier was going to call the cops.

When I shoplifted before, I was a teen. I slipped small items into my pockets, wore earphones out of the store I put in my ears while pretending to try on clothes in the fitting room, wore t-shirts under my t-shirts.

Was it worth it?

They didn't give me a gun. They drove me in a white van. Mike drove. I had on a black hoody. Pulled the hood over my head even though it was August.

Get in there, get out. Hurry the fuck up. You freak out, you waste time, you're getting left behind.

I took a deep breath. Opened the van door. Empty parking lot. Moths buzzing around flickering white lights. Marlboro. Play Lotto Here.

The door dinged when I opened it. A mirror in the entrance distorted the top of my hood. I looked down. I had my hands in my pockets. The cashier had his earphones in, stared at his phone. A young dude. Maybe a teenager.

Maybe I could grab the beer and get out before he noticed me. Walk right out with it like nothing happened. I casually walked to the fridge. I didn't even know what beer to get. Budweiser, Coors Light, Bud Light. Did it matter? I opened the door and grabbed a six-pack of Coors.

The cashier wasn't looking. He laughed at his phone.

I turned around and hurried to the door. But not too fast. He'd get suspicious.

"Everything good, sir?"

Damn.

I turned around. Slowly. "Yeah." I nodded. "Everything's good."

I kept my head down, away from the camera. The van headlights beamed. The clock was ticking. They'd know if I went up and paid for this shit. I'm sure they were watching me through the window.

I scratched the back of my head. "Actually. Do you guys have...uh...Budweiser? Maybe in the back? I didn't see any in the cooler."

"We actually don't sell alcohol past twelve. Sorry 'bout that, sir."

I nodded, walked back towards the cooler. I watched him out of the corner of my eye.

He looked back at his phone, tapped the screen.

I took three steps back.

He chuckled, but he didn't look up at me.

I hightailed it.

"Hey!"

But I didn't drop the beer like I did the phone I tried to steal from that other store, and I didn't give him enough time to grab me. I don't know if he had a gun or if he was even chasing me.

They threw open the door soon as I ran out, took off before they closed it, and sped out of the parking lot.

But that one was easy.

"The real test," Richie said. "You gotta get up close in person."

I didn't know what that meant until they put me out on a sidewalk the next day after asking me if I ever picked a pocket.

I told them no.

"Then you're going to figure it out today."

How do I even know he's got a wallet?

"Get his phone."

They picked out a guy who was bigger than me, taller than me, a white t-shirt, gray jeans.

"Guy like that don't fuck with anybody." Richie took the cigarette out of his mouth. "So be careful." Then he shoved me out the door.

They waited in the van.

My target was on his phone, leaning up against a building, foot on the brick wall like he didn't care lowlifes like me were out scoping the streets for folks like him minding their own business.

I could do this like they do in the movies. Peasant kid, always running through some marketplace or alley somewhere, says hi or bumps into a person, and the next thing they know, their wallet's missing. You don't realize how unrealistic TV and books are until real life happens. Then your heart's racing, your palms are sweating, and you can't think because you're in some sort of fight or flight mode. You can't do either. You got to pass your initiation, or you can say goodbye to a roof over your head and hello to cold beans and ass beatings on the streets.

Don't think about it. Because the more you think about it, the more you'll panic, but if you don't think about it at all, you can't strategize. Pretend it's a video game. Also fiction. But if it were a video game, what would you do?

Probably talk to the dude. Small talk. What's up? Weather's nice today. Do anything fun this weekend? Eye the wallet. Grab the wallet. Get the hell out of there.

"What's up?"

He glanced from his phone. "Hi. How ya doin'?"

"Pretty good." I leaned against the wall beside him. "Nice weather. Huh?"

He shrugged. "Yeah. Pretty good."

I could see the lump in his pocket shaped like a square. I scoped the area for cops. Pedestrians. A white van ready to leave me behind. No cops.

He wasn't paying attention.

I moved my hand to his pocket but pulled it back.

"You waiting on somebody?" he asked.

I paused, nodded. "Meeting up with some friends. We're going out...new restaurant just opened."

"That one right up the street?"

"Uh...yeah."

"Cool. Cool." He hadn't looked at me at all throughout this conversation.

I moved my hand towards his pocket, slipped it in.

He wasn't looking at all.

I grabbed his wallet with the tips of my fingers, pulled it up.

"The fuck you up to?" He grabbed me by my shirt.

"Nothin'."

"It don't look like nothin'."

No way in hell I was getting that wallet. I slapped his phone out of his hand.

He swung at me, and I dodged his punch.

I reached for his phone. He shoved me. I swung around and punched him in the face. He stumbled. I grabbed his phone. He chased after me.

I ran to the van, pulled the door handle, but it was locked. I pulled it again, banged on the door. "Open the door!"

He grabbed me by my shoulders and threw me on the concrete. I rolled over. I still had his phone in my hand; I couldn't lose it. I got on my feet and punched him in the face. He swung for mine. I blocked his punch with my arm and took off.

"Shit," I said under my breath. "What the hell are they doing?"

I turned around, swung at him, but he dodged my punch.

He grabbed my shoulder, kneed me in the stomach. I stumbled back and fell on my ass, clenched my gut, but I didn't let go of the phone.

He raised his foot to stomp me. I got off the ground. Finally, the van doors opened. I spit a wad of blood and hurried over there with a limp. He grabbed my arm from behind.

Jackie and Axe jumped out. Jackie shoved him off me. Axe punched him in the face. He stumbled back, but he didn't fall.

Jackie grabbed the phone from my hand and threw it to him. "Take it. We don't need it."

They climbed in after me and shut the door. Mike sped down the street.

I collapsed on the chair and wiped the blood off my lip. Looked up to Richie's black pupils dilated in the dim ceiling light.

"I guess he held his own pretty decently," he said. "What'd you guys think?"

A mix. Yes. No. Shrugs.

Pip had his arms crossed and was staring at me with a face I wished I could read.

"He got the phone," Jackie said. "That was the objective."

"Nah, the objective was a wallet, and that guy had a wallet." He leaned forward, tapped his index fingers together, and stared at me like I was an unfinished project.

I swallowed.

"One more task. Meet up at twelve midnight."

You hadn't played any real games, Richie'd told me. Easy mode with no boss levels.

At midnight, they gave me a gun. "Do what you've got to do with that," Richie said, "but don't make rash decisions."

Every house on that street probably cost over a million dollars.

"So what do I gotta get? A passport, social security card...?"

They told me to come in a black hoody, black t-shirt, black pants and shoes. Gave me a ski mask to put over my face. Oak trees and three-car garages. Green grass and sprinkler systems.

"You could, but I want a Bible."

We pulled up at a stop sign where the sprinkler waters splat against the window and left streaks that looked like rotting blood.

"A Bible?"

"Yeah. Don't matter which one."

"What if they ain't Christian?"

He looked back at me with a face that didn't tell me shit.

I put my mask on. "Which house?"

"The one at the end of the street," Richie said.

"Who lives there?"

"Guess we'll find out."

I opened the door.

"There's a playground a block down on the right. We'll wait for you there."

I got out, stopped, turned back to Richie. "What if a security alarm goes off?"

"Then you'd better run like hell."

He shut the door, and the van rode off.

Chances were, they did have a security system. House that big. Who knew who was living there? Might've had a gun. I had a gun too. I barely knew how to use that thing.

I didn't step into the yard until I checked for a security camera. Wasn't like I had a plan if I'd found one. Maybe I'd shoot it, but I didn't see one. Didn't see one of those fancy doorbells people kept getting either. Must've been something else. House like that, it wasn't like they couldn't afford it.

They had a cross on the door, a Jesus statue in the corner of the front porch, so I guessed there'd be no problem finding a Bible.

In movies, they always went through the windows. I'd have to break that glass, and that would be too loud. I crept to the front door. Looked under the welcome mat. No key.

I stared at Jesus's judging eyes.

I lifted the statue. I didn't even believe in Hell. But if I never felt the flames singe my ass before, that'll do it. I grabbed the key off the stone and put the statue back exactly the way I found it.

I took a deep breath, squeezed my eyes shut, and unlocked the door. All I needed to do was creep in there, find a bookshelf, find the first Bible I saw, and get out of there before somebody showed up. Wasn't like I had to drag out a TV. What the hell did he want with a Bible anyway?

I didn't shut the door. When you're doing shit you got no business doing, there's no such thing as tiptoeing. Your feet are heavier than a death metal riff if it swallowed thrash metal and louder than both combined. Everything makes a noise. The floors, the staircase, the walls. You don't even have to touch it. It's creaking and cracking. The wind's hitting the windows. The clock's ticking. The A/C's humming. You're breathing too loud. It's too dark, but you don't want to turn on the lights. They'll be calling the cops, popping a bullet in your ass. They're peeking down the stairs right now. They're watching you. They're watching you from their rooms. They're whispering to each other to get quiet, and somebody's coming downstairs with the shotgun.

It wasn't like I could tell them I come in peace. Put my hands up in the air. Don't mind me. I just want your Bible. I'm here on an initiation so I can join a band of criminals. Just let me grab your personal item, and I'll be on my way.

I pulled my phone out of my pocket and hit the flashlight app. Big house. Two sets of stairs. A whole lot of rooms. I made a left.

The kitchen. Polished wood floors and marble counters. A Persian rug beneath the breakfast table and satin curtains over the bay window. Damn. If I'd been raised in a house like that, I'd have been driving Lamborghinis instead of delivery trucks.

I went through the drawers. Forks and spoons. Cookbooks and recipes. But why would anyone keep a Bible in the kitchen? I turned around and tip-toed out of there. I went back to the foyer, took the hallway between the two staircases. A piano. A living room with a chess table and a bookcase but no Bible. I did a double-take. Encyclopedias, DVDs, vinyl records, novels. No Bible. I scratched the back of my head. Who'd have thought it'd be this difficult? With that cross on the wall and the angel statuettes on the fireplace, you'd think there'd be at least one Bible.

I crept out of there. Past the piano, down the hall. A bathroom. A laundry room. A bedroom. The door was closed. I pressed my ear against it. No snoring. I took a step back, gripped my gun.

I didn't go in.

I went back to the foyer. Upstairs were probably just more bedrooms. Maybe a game room. I wouldn't have the balls to go in there, either. Maybe it was time I gave up.

I hadn't searched the parlor yet, though. I sighed. Last spot.

I shined the light in first. They had a nice pool table in there. Red fabric, carvings in the wood—damn thing probably cost more than my whole soul. There were red leather seats in the middle of the floor, bookshelves against the wall, a coffee table in front of the fireplace, a Bible. Right there in the middle of the table. A big one. White leather. Golden letters. Golden edges. I hurried to it but stopped. I gasped. My heart skipped. My breath caught in my lungs.

I wasn't alone in there.

An old woman. Tight gray curls, drooping cheeks, wrinkles around her eyes and mouth. Maybe ninety years old, sitting in the lounge chair against the wall. Quiet. I don't know if I'd woken her up. If she'd been there all night. Maybe she'd already called the cops on me, but her eyes were open.

She didn't say anything, but she watched me.

I walked slowly toward the Bible, my fingers wrapped around the grip of my gun.

But it didn't matter.

I wasn't about to shoot an old lady.

But I kept my eyes on her as much as she kept hers on mine. She didn't try to make a run for it. Maybe she realized that wasn't a good idea. But it was the strangest thing I ever saw because this old lady didn't look afraid at all, sitting in the dark. By herself.

I picked up the Bible, tucked it beneath my arm.

"Are you going to read it?"

I paused. How do I answer that?

I walked backward, turned around, and headed for the door.

Nobody was out on the street. Maybe it would've been smart to run, but I didn't. I walked down to the playground, like they said, and they were out there, parked on the side of the road. I opened the door.

"Did you get it?"

I handed Richie the Bible and dropped down in the seat like I'd just run a marathon.

He looked at it, front and back, leafed through the pages. "This is an old Bible," he mumbled. "Could probably sell it for a good price."

He handed it back to me. I didn't know what to do with it, so I put it on the floor.

"Alright," he said. That was it. "Take us back to the church."

When we got back, they left me downstairs by myself. I couldn't hear anything upstairs. Only the ceiling light was on. I sat in that plaid, tattered chair like I was a jacked-up accessory that came with it. They could be discussing anything up there. How to kill me, where to dump me. If they should keep my ass for ransom, not that that would get them much.

Finally, they all came downstairs, except Richie. Mike jerked his head to the side. I followed them to the other side of the building. He opened what I first thought was a closet door until he turned on the lights to the basement steps and a hall that smelled like piss.

They let me go down first. I stopped where the light didn't reach. They stepped down the stairs like shadows rejected from the light, surrendering to the dark.

Mike hit the light, and a bulb flickered on above my head. "Richie will be here in a second." Everything lay in shadow except where the light left a spot, so as far as I knew, the basement could've gone on forever, and it looked like it because the only walls I could see were the ones beside the steps.

They had a throne in the middle of the floor. Maybe not made of real gold. Might've been a fancy dining chair, but it had golden embroidering, velvet red padding, a medieval style. The feet were shaped like lion claws. The top rail was shaped like a crown. Everything but that throne was covered in dust. Its reds and golds burned against the colorless backdrop like a flame.

Richie came down. He handed me a plastic bag with my license and social security card. If Pops were there, he'd have told me how stupid I was for giving my identity to people like them.

It ain't the only stupid thing I've done in recent days, Pops.

Everyone got out of the way for Richie.

"How'd you like driving?" He turned to me and crossed his arms.

"It was a job."

"You got laid off after five years and fired from the next one about two months later. Jesus! How'd that happen?"

"I worked out of town. Had to drive to commute. Somebody stole my bike."

"Rough life, huh?"

I shrugged.

"Tell ya a little 'bout us, who we are, what we are. We been around since 2007. This here is house crew. Call 'em house crew because we run with each other. At times there were more of us. At times, there were fewer. Over the last sixteen years, D3vil's Krew's branched out. Now we got guys on the East Coast, the West Coast, the North and the South. We got guys in London and Tokyo. We're all over the fucking world. We can be anybody. We can be everybody. We got guys in schools. We got guys in law enforcement. We got guys that enlist in the army just to get the training because when D3vil's Krew shows up, we don't show up like a bunch of pussies.

"And all that started right here in New York City, the very place you're standing. This crew you're looking at was the one that started it all. The OG. You're looking at a literal fucking king.

"You saw the names on the wall. Bobby Samuels, beaten to death by five guys in an alley. Snake Jake, shot by the cops. Sin's in the cage. Larry moved out to Texas and don't know when his execution date is. And they never found Q-man's body. Look around this room. How many people do you see?"

I parted my lips.

"Six, right? What if I told you there was a time when there were ten of us? Fifteen? That number shrinks and grows depending upon how bad God wants to punish us that day. When you become a D3vil's Krew, you leave everything important to you at the door.

"I could've been shit at the bottom of a pair of Valentino's, but I said fuck that. I started an empire. We pay the cost so we're not someone else's shit. We're one body. It's ride or die. I sacrifice so he survives, he sacrifices so she survives, she sacrifices so he survives. We live, breathe, eat, and sleep for the Krew. Traitors die. Snitches die. You got any objection to that life, walk."

"I got no objections."

"Good. Once you're in this thing, you've made a promise." He stared me in the eyes.

I hesitated but nodded.

He introduced me to everyone in the group—big man Axe, stoner Mike, red dreadhead Arin, Jackie, the only chick. "And Pip," he said. "You already met him. Now that you're acquainted," he dropped back on his throne, "they're gonna kick your ass."

Pip was the first to punch me in my face, and before I could gather what had just happened, I was on the floor. They kicked me in my sides. They kicked me in my shoulders. Axe lifted me off the ground by my shirt and punched me to Jackie, who punched me to Mike, who punched me to Arin, and they punched me back and forth to each other until the floors and walls were spinning around me. All five of them.

My eye swelled shut. Blood ran down the back of my throat.

All I could see was a blurry light and a tilting double of Richie sitting on his throne, one leg over its arm.

I couldn't breathe. I thought I would die.

Richie raised his hand. "That's enough."

I fell on my hands and knees, gasped in as much air as I could. Blood clogged my throat with an iron taste. I spit a wad, raised my head.

Richie got off his throne.

The floor tilted as he walked to me. He grabbed my hair, lifted my head until I was staring into the gap between his two front teeth, doubled against a blurred smile.

He punched me in the face but kept hold of my hair so I couldn't fall over. He punched me again. He kneed me in the jaw. He kneed me in the nose. He kneed me in the eye, and the pain became so much my body went numb.

He let go and stepped back.

I stayed on my hands and knees, wheezing. I stuck my tongue through a space in my gums and spat another wad of blood.

He knelt down, grabbed my hair, and lifted my head so close to his face I could see the faded greens crossing with the white-blue fibers in his eyes. "Pick up your tooth." He patted my cheek. "Keep it as a trophy."

## 10

Pops used to say tattoos were for sailors and men in the military. Unless you plan on fighting for our country, I suggest you keep your skin clean. Back in my day, tattoos meant something. Now they're just trendy trash young boys like you throw on your body because you think it makes you special, and then you call it art.

I told him when I moved out, I was going to get the coolest tattoo. Not because it made me special, but because it's art. Body art, Pops.

He said I'd better not bring that shit around his house.

I never had enough money to get a tattoo.

After initiation, I didn't go outside for about a week until my face looked better. Except to get ice. If anyone asked me what happened, I told them I got into an accident on my bike.

They didn't know my bike had been stolen.

I'd gotten an eviction warning under my door. Next time it would be an official notice.

I've had that nightmare before. Where I'm out on the street, got no food, got no shelter. I never die in my dreams, but some things are worse than death.

I'd had that dream more than once.

The basement at the church looked smaller when more than one light was on, but that didn't make it small. You could almost see everything, though. The shooting range in the back, the punching bag inside a chain-link fence where the floor was covered in mats and the walls had mirrors, and then there was that metal door in the back corner with a caution sign.

Beneath the staircase, they had steel bars that looked like a tiny jail cell standing in the corner. I didn't even want to think about what they did with that.

The walls were tagged in the basement just as much as upstairs. Pipes ran on the side of the brick. Wires drooped from the ceiling.

When I pictured getting my first tattoo, I imagined I'd finally saved at least a thousand dollars to get something really good. Maybe a pen since I like to write, a skull to add some badassery.

I never planned to get one on my back.

I was face down on a tattoo chair. Mike had a foldable table next to me that he used to hold the ink. The pain was moderate, but after the shit I'd faced the past few days, maybe everything was.

"How long you been doin' this?" I asked.

"Tatts?" Mike sprayed my back. "Shit." He chuckled. "Before I was legally old enough."

"Are you licensed?"

He laughed again. "Hell no."

"I was looking at the ones on your arm. You did some of that, huh?"

"Yep. Sure did. It took ages to build this up. Got a whole canvas like I always wanted." He wiped my back. "Since I was a kid. I used to want to do it professionally. Goddamn. That seems like a forever ago."

"Did you paint that mural on the side of the building?"

He chuckled. Didn't say nothing, just chuckled.

"I used to draw a whole lot," he said. "And paint. Nobody ever told me I was worth a shit at it—"

"You are. You definitely are."

He paused for a sec, and I assumed he took that time to smile. "Thanks, bro."

"What got you into it?"

"The imagination, man. Just...the imagination. 'Bout the only thing there is that can be whatever you want it to be. Where you can make your own reality, and nobody can steal that away from you. I wasn't the happiest kid. My mom had a boyfriend I don't wanna talk about. But yeah," he lifted the needle, "you can probably figure out why. Some moms put their kids before anyone else. Some moms don't have the money or enough love to do it. But on really bad days, when you're too small to hop on the bus and get away. Hell, too young to even get what's going on..."

I glanced up at him.

He tapped the side of his head. "Imagination. Who the hell can take that away from you?"

I shivered as the needle nibbled my spine.

"Get yourself a pencil, a few paints. Who the hell can take that away from you? Bonus points if you can heighten that shit up with some psychedelics. Maaaaaaan!" He laughed, then he got quiet. "Sometimes I look at this world, and everything is bleak. Catch my drift? There's no meaning. But when everything goes black..." his voice softened, "...takes a few colors."

I nodded.

"I lost my faith in everything a long time ago, but I keep thinking that maybe I'll find it again in art."

"Was that your dream? To become an artist?"

"I don't know." He put his machine on the table, showed all his teeth when he smiled and slowly shook his head. "Maybe it still is."

He sprayed a rag with rubbing alcohol, but it felt more like corrosive acid when he rubbed it on my back. He grabbed a different rag off the table and dropped it in front of my face. "Bite down on it. This is gonna hurt like shit."

He grabbed a razor blade off the table. I closed my eyes and did what he said.

The blood tickled my shoulder blade and ran down my side. He did the other side. A tiny amount of blood collected beneath my chest.

He poured alcohol on a rag and pressed it against my skin. "Did you want another one?"

"Another?" I asked.

"Yeah. I can get ya anything. Arm? Leg?"

"For free?"

"Yeah. I like doing it."

"Maybe not now." I blinked a bunch of times. Never thought I'd get two tatts for free. Even if the first was hardly my decision. "Maybe later."

"Alright. Let me know when. I'll hook you up." He put his utensils back in the case. "There's a mirror over there if you wanna check it out."

"Actually," I said. "You got a bathroom?"

"Yeah. Up the stairs next to the table when you first come in."

I went upstairs to the bathroom. Turned on the light. The only thing that separated the shower from the rest of the bathroom was a curtain. They had a shower nozzle they installed to the wall, a large tin bucket underneath it. No drain. Just a bucket. I never asked Mike, Arin, Jackie, or Richie what the squatting life was like, but it made sense why Axe and Pip weren't doing it.

The toilet had a note above it.

*This toilet incinerates piss and shit.*
*DOES NOT FLUSH!*
*Please cover bowl with sheet before use.*
*You don't, you're cleaning it!*

I looked in the mirror. My face was almost completely healed. I turned around.

The blood of "666" ran down my back in red streaks and crusted residue. "666" on each shoulder blade. That tattoo Pip had on his back.

Now I had one on mine.

Looking at it, I didn't feel how I thought I would or how I think I wanted. I'd never really been a part of anything in my life, other than my family, and that didn't last. Never belonged to anything. Never thought about it.

It was for the money.

I probably had only a week or two before the landlord had enough of my shit and put me out. Then what would I do? Squat out here with Richie? I wasn't that crazy yet.

But did I even have time to get the money? And then all the late fees. The power wasn't going to turn itself back on.

I sat on the toilet, but I didn't use it. I didn't even know how to apply that sheet thing or whatever the note was talking about. If you looked at it hard enough, this bathroom almost looked like a regular bathroom. Wonder what it was before it became a bathroom, if it was anything at all. Probably another bathroom. Don't know if the shit around here was bought or stolen, but a sink, a shower curtain, a mirror, a toilet, even a vent. A vent, but there wasn't any air coming out. The grooves in the wall were weird. I tilted my head, squinted my eyes. I peered through the vent's cracks.

I got up and went through the cabinet. Found a screwdriver.

I listened.

Didn't hear anyone outside the door.

I unscrewed the vent. It dropped down, and I wasn't wrong. A safe. It had a code on it and a fingerprint identifier, but it looked unlocked. Maybe they didn't close it all the way or there had been an error. If I were smart, I'd have left it alone, but I was curious. And I wasn't smart.

I opened it.

A Godsend? Maybe more than that. The Devil's send.

Rolls of bills piled in there. Thick rolls. Fat rolls. Obese rolls. Fives. Tens. Twenties. Fifties. Even some Benjamins winking at me.

I put the door back the way it was, closed the vent, picked up the screwdriver. I almost stuck it in the screw, but my hand shook.

Don't be that damn stupid, Nolan. If it wasn't my voice, it was Pop's voice, or anybody's voice who had some sense. But this was probably already dirty money. Could dirty money get dirtier?

I opened the vent.

Maybe one roll. Just one. The smallest. Just enough to pay my rent and get my lights back on. Nothing more. I could replace it as soon as I got enough money.

I grabbed a roll of hundreds, stuck it in my pocket, closed the safe. I messed up.

It beeped, and the latches locked.

I pulled on the door, but it wouldn't budge, which meant there was no way I was getting back inside to replace the money. All I could do was hope no one would notice.

I quickly screwed the vent shut.

# 11

"Did you wanna watch a movie?" Pip's TV would've been a nice size if it were a computer monitor. It sat on top of plastic filing cabinets that doubled as a clothing dresser. "What'd you wanna watch?"

I shrugged. "What's streaming?"

He pulled up one of those jailbreaking sites I never took the time to try and figure out. "What happened with your lights?"

I paused. I'd deposited the money I stole from the safe soon as I got out of there that night. Did it with a sweaty hand. Made the bill just in time, even paid off those late rent fees, but I didn't sleep.

"I got it taken care of."

"You know," he scrolled through the movie titles, but I don't think he was paying attention to what he was doing, "if you need any money, just ask. I can help you out."

"Uh..." I scratched the back of my head. "Thanks."

I had a tattoo on my chest that probably would've cost me a thousand dollars if I'd gone to see a professional artist. Skeleton fingers holding a feathered pen. Raven silhouettes, an eye for the moon. It had all the quality of a professional tattoo. In many ways it was better than what most professionals can do. But I got it for free.

"That little girl you were telling me about. The pregnant ten-year-old."

He grabbed two beers out of the fridge. "My sister?"

"Yeah. Where's she at now?"

He handed me a bottle. "She got out of rehab about two years ago, but she's doing good now."

"I can't quit thinking about it."

"Yeah? What's that about?"

"I dunno. I don't hear stories like that a whole lot, y' know." I popped open the beer, took a swig. "When I do, it sticks with me. I try to figure it out, y' know. I'm a writer. Or something like that. I don't know why. But I am. Listening to Mike talk a while back, you weren't there, but he said something that stood out to me. He said he's always trying to restore his faith through art. Maybe I'm trying to do that. Problem is, I don't even think I know what faith is. Is it God? Is it hope? It seems to be one of these words like, uh..." I snapped my fingers. "Love, y' know? Or Beauty. Uh...truth...it's, it's, y' know..."

"Abstract?"

"Yeah. Yeah. Abstract. Do I sound like an idiot?"

He shook his head.

"And then I hear stories like your sister's. Your...*mother's*. What the hell do I do with that? Do I cry about it?" I lifted the bottle to my mouth but didn't take a drink. "Do I *write* about it?"

The pizza was here. Pip got up and answered the door.

"What's her name?"

"Tammy. I can give you her contact information if you wanna talk to her. She's real down to earth."

"Yeah-yeah. Do that."

"I'll text it to you." He set the pizza on the counter, unfolded the plastic table, pulled it out in front of the couch. He opened the box. "I asked for extra stuffing. See how they rip you off?" He put the pizza on the table and sat next to me.

"How much do you make?"

He grabbed a slice, and maybe it's because I'd been saving money too hard to get any food outside of what food stamps covered, but the cheese pulled and stretched and broke off the edge of the bread as he lifted it to his mouth, and the pepperonis slid down the melting cheese. The smell rose into my nose and made my mouth water like Heaven made it rain.

"That's hard to answer," he said. "It varies."

"On average. How much would you say you make in a year?"

He took a bite of pizza and chewed on it for a long time.

"How much you got right now?"

"Couple of thousand."

I grabbed a slice. "Did you ever think about it? Having a regular life?"

"I think that was off the table soon as I was born."

"Maybe not—"

"This ain't the life." He chewed, swallowed. "It's just the only life I know."

"I'm sorry, it's just...you're young."

"I know." His phone vibrated. He got up. "I'm the baby of the family. Not my blood family. The other one." He grabbed the phone off the counter and hit the button. He stared at the screen. If I'd never seen Pip's eyes light up, I was seeing it then.

"Hi, Daddy."

"Hey, little man. What you been up to?"

"Nothin'."

"Nothin'? Nothin' at all?" He laughed, but his face had more than one emotion, like his eyes and the corners of his lips were having a conversation about two different things. He combed his hair out of his face.

"Mommy let me have a cookie."

"Did she? Was it good?"

"Yeah, but she said, only 'cause I clean my room."

Pip sat on the couch, and I could see the little boy in the video. A mess of brown wavy hair all over his head, green eyes that stood out against his brown skin. The little boy in the picture above Pip's head, only here he was moving and breathing, smiling, big round eyes and pink cheeks.

"Can I come play at your 'partament, Daddy?"

"My apartment? Not tonight. Tell ya what, I'll come get you this weekend. How's that sound? We can go out to the park."

"Are you gonna go work tonight?"

Pip got quiet. If I hadn't been looking at him closely, I would've missed the whites of his eyes turning red, the tear in the corner of his eye before he blinked and pretended it wasn't there. He cleared his throat. "No, Cay. Daddy doesn't have to work tonight."

"I drewed a picture. Did you wanna see?"

Pip nodded. "Yeah. Let me see it."

Caelin disappeared from the screen, and when he came back, he had a crayon scribbling of a sun with a face, a tree with an owl, and a guy with black scribbles all on his arms standing next to a kid with curly brown hair. Both had ice cream. Both had green eyes.

"That's amazing, Cay." Pip rubbed his mouth.

"Mommy said she put it in a fwame."

"She should. It's really good."

"Want me to draw one for you, Daddy?"

The kid was cut off by a door opening in the background. "Caelin, what'd I tell you about playing on the phone by yourself?"

"But, Mommy, it's Daddy."

"Elijah?" she said, but Pip didn't speak.

She sighed. "Tell Daddy good night. You gotta go to bed."

"Night-night, Daddy."

Pip waved his fingers. "Night-night." The screen went blank, but he never stopped staring at it.

When I was seventeen, I was trained as a pizza deliverer. It was my first job.

Grab a pizza and go. Don't keep the customer waiting. If the customer waits too long, they get a free drink. That's on you, kid.

What happens if I can't find a place to park?

Find the closest parking spot.

Cars lined down both sides of the street. Parallel parking. Honking. Almost got run over by a bus.

They didn't train me. They ran through the rules and threw me out there.

Everything I knew about fighting, I learned from having been a short-tempered teenager. But the chaotic punches thrown at other short-tempered teenage boys were different than the ones that were going to get thrown at you when it's the real deal.

Those boys out there don't show mercy, Jackie said. They won't stop until you're dead.

I'd wrapped my feet in white bandages. Took my stance on a workout mat enclosed by a chain-link fence in the corner of the basement. The pen, as they called it.

When I looked up, I saw my face in the mirror, my form, knees bent, fists clenched, fingers wrapped in the same kind of white bandages as the ones around my feet.

The veins in Jackie's arms were as prominent as the lines in her muscles. She poked me beneath my chest, and it knocked the breath out of me. "Hurts, doesn't it?"

I rubbed my stomach.

"That's your solar plexus. Good weak spot. There's also the nose, the throat, right up under the nose, and if all else fails," she struck the punching bag with her knee, and it bobbed back and forth, "go for the balls." She stepped aside. "Show me what ya got."

I punched the bag twice with both fists.

She nodded. "Alright," walked around me, "nice form. Let me see." She took my hand. "Protect your fingers." She moved my thumb.

"Hey. Thanks for helping me out when you did."

"Sure thing." She stepped back and got in a fighting stance. "Don't ever let somebody tell you you're not good enough. You want something, take it." She waved her fingers. "Alright. Take a swing at me."

She blocked my punch. "Good," she said. "But surprise me. Don't hesitate. Distract me with an uppercut, then go for the kill."

"How long have you been in D3vil's Krew?"

"A long, long time."

"How long is that?"

"Maybe thirteen years. Give or take." She stepped back, grabbed her water bottle off the floor, took a drink. "I got kicked out on the street when I was, like, sixteen. Used to hang out with this girl named Lacy. God! I loved that chick. We got into a lot of shit together back in those days."

"What happened to her?"

"Nothing happened to her, really. I mean... I don't know. I'm always thinking about her. Wonder if she still thinks about me." Her eyes drifted. She glanced at my face. "Oh," she chuckled. "Sorry." She shook her head. "I grew up in a strict household. Wasn't like we had a whole lot of money or nothing like that, but I had a dad who liked everything in its place." She raised one eyebrow. "You're laughing."

"Strict and broke. I get that."

"Check that out. See? Small world, huh?"

I nodded.

"Didn't make no sense. The man was a damn drunk. Every cent that could've been spent on making sure the lights stayed on went to whiskey and beer, but he had the nerve to pretend he was living the 1950s sitcom life, like that little girlfriend he used to bring around was going to turn into a housewife and do anything more than cheat on his ass. Damn hypocrite. But I guess if you keep pretending, you'll start believing. Maybe I need a little bit of that."

"I take it he didn't like your friend."

"Lacy? Hell, no." She laughed but got quiet afterward. "Sometimes I think my dad just wanted me to be better than he was. Sometimes. But other times...I don't know what's going on in somebody else's head."

"I get that. I've had that with my own pops."

"I knew I had no business hanging out with that girl. She taught me how to shoplift. Took me out one night, we got a bunch of piercings and tattoos in some back alley that probably should've given us tetanus." She made soft punches on the bag. "That girl had a whole lot of problems at home. A whole lot. And she didn't talk about that shit to nobody but me. I used to think her life was some special kind of fucked up. Used to feel sorry for her until, one day, I looked at my own life, and I said, maybe there's a whole lot more there that I've been ignoring." She struck the bag with her knee. It bobbed back and forth, vibrated until it stopped.

"I got kicked out," she said. "And when I did, she was out there waiting for me because her mom kicked her out two days before. We got on the subway, rode off to Destination: God knows where, and we did what we do. Squatting and hustling. Drugs out the ass."

She swung her hands back and forth, got in a fighting stance, and took a swing at the bag. "We both got arrested for breaking into a dollar store one night. A dollar store. I mean, for God's sake. If you're gonna go to jail, do it stealing a Louis Vuitton." She shook her head. "Did three years. We ended up in different penitentiaries, and I ain't seen her since. Don't know if she's in jail. Don't know if she's dead." She kicked the bag. "I just hope wherever she is, she's in a better place than we were then."

I grabbed a towel and wiped the sweat off my face.

She put her hands on her hips, threw her head back. "After I got out, I started running with a gang of girls. We took care of each other, but it didn't last long. I found out about Richie through a guy who knew a guy who knew one of my girls—" she waved her hand. "Long story short, he's telling me about how he and Mike didn't have nothing to turn to when they were teenagers, ran away—I'm telling you. It's a small world we live in. So, I started hanging with them and the next thing I know, I got a tattoo on my back that looks like a cross between Satan and fancy G-strings."

"Have you ever worked a job?"

"What the hell's that supposed to mean?"

"Nothing. Just asking."

"Nah." She popped her neck. "Truth is, this is the only thing I've ever had any skill at. Kind of fucked up, but hey, you get what you get. I didn't even know where I was headed until one day I looked up, and here I was. Guess some folks find their place in a career, some folks find it in a family, and other folks like me..." she shrugged "...we got our own place in the world." She picked her towel up off the floor, patted her face with it, and threw it around her shoulders. "Come on. I'm gonna show you a few kicks, then we gotta get moving."

"Have you ever had a dream?"

She raised one eyebrow.

"I used to think I'd be a writer."

She looked at me a long time with a face I couldn't read. "You know how to shoot a gun?"

"Barely."

She stared at me like I was an alien. "Guess it's gonna be a long night, huh?"

I liked working with Jackie the most. Jackie was my favorite.

You don't realize there are so many bits and pieces to this thing. You're thinking, okay, I'm just going to get out here and sell some drugs. Steal a couple of things. Learn how to shoot a gun. Punch a few guys in the face.

There was actually homework. It was fill in the blanks, all about how you don't say, I'm planning on stealing a Volkswagen tonight. Instead, I'm planning on taking a Volkswagen for a test drive tonight.

You don't steal the money from the register, you count the paper in the box.

I'm visiting the neighbors to check out their TV.

I'm picking up medicine for a friend.

I got three bags of sugar in the backseat.

I finally saw what was on the second floor of the church. That's where they gave me my written lessons, at a folding conference table in the middle of the floor. Might've looked somewhat professional if there hadn't been metal folding chairs. Had a dry-erase board in front of it. It made me feel like I was back in school, but where schools had motivational posters, globes, and textbooks, this place had a gun safe and a turned-over ATM wrapped in chains by the wall.

There wasn't a teacher's desk. There was a green metal desk with filing cabinets and three computer monitors I only ever saw Arin sitting at.

He showed me how to access the dark web one day. When I was a teen, I read stories about that place. Creepypasta. Internet campfire tales. That's where the snuff films are uploaded. Violent murders. That's where secret societies discuss their plans to summon the Devil. It's all on the dark web. Demonic activity.

Uploaded photos of the body parts of serial killers' victims. Decapitated heads of war prisoners.

It's all on the dark web.

The only thing he showed me was how to buy and sell illegal shit. Drugs. Hacked Amazon gift cards. No demons.

You'd think they'd just give you a gun and throw you into action. Nope. Lessons were thorough. They weren't shitting. I learned anatomy through the Krew. All the bits and pieces of a gun, how it worked, how to put one together. I probably learned more with them than I ever did in school.

And every day, I was in the pen in front of three tall mirrors, watching my stance, watching my body grow and develop defining rips in its muscles. Street fighting ain't just a bullshit thing people go out there and throw their arms and do. There's an art to it.

There's an art to shooting a gun. There's an art to stealth.

When I started to see a change in my physical form, and I knew the differences between an AR-15 and an AK-47, Richie came into the pen with me and a punching bag that put calluses across the edges of my knuckles. He pulled his hair up into a ponytail and took off his shirt.

He had black feathers tattooed from the top of his chest to the lower part of his abdomen, finely detailed and spiraling into six wings that were covered in eyes as pale as his own, staring at me, staring at everything. He had verses on his chest, verses on his stomach, verses on his arm, on his side.

*I polished my gun tonight.*
*The angels said a prayer, and the crows took flight.*
*I hope that God can hear me cry*
*And knows that snakes don't always lie...*

*...You say I'm a monster. I'll be your monster.*
*I'll devour you whole and shit out your bones.*
*I'll absorb your power, destruction, everything you own...*

*And he causeth all, both small and great,*
*rich and poor, free and bond,*
*to receive a mark in their right hand, or in their foreheads.*
*Revelation 13:16*

He had scars. Scars all over his abdomen, all over his chest. Long scars. Short scars. Scars that were as illustrated as everything else on his muscular canvas.

He dragged the punching bag out of the way.

I took a deep breath and closed my eyes. When Richie entered a room, it was hard to feel natural. It was a wound exposed. You're injured, and a predator's standing nearby. All your weaknesses are brought to the forefront. You're naked. You're weaponless.

But then you remember, you got to put that shit away. And that's part of why you feel that way to begin with.

"Let's go," he said. I already knew what that meant.

I got in my stance. I clenched my fists. I took a swing.

He blocked my first punch and dodged my second, but I got him in the cheek with my third. He kneed me in the stomach, punched me in the jaw.

I swung twice at his head, and he dodged both.

"You're swinging before you're thinking," he said. "Think quick."

I tried to surprise him with an uppercut. It didn't work. He dodged, came around me, got me in a chokehold from behind.

"Let's go again," he said.

I blew out a breath, got in my stance.

He swung at me. Got me in the cheek. "This is street fighting. No one's going to give you time to prepare."

Now I was getting mad. I aimed at his stomach. He jumped out of the way, came back around with a kick to the shin.

I stumbled.

"Come on. Let's go."

I tightened my fists. "How'd you learn to fight?"

"Experience."

He swung at my face. I dodged it. I aimed for his jaw. He blocked it. I aimed for his nose. He blocked it. I went for an uppercut, and when he raised his arm to block it, I struck him in the mouth with my left fist. Hard.

He licked the blood off his lip. Stepped back. Nodded. "Alright."

Street fighting, the contemporary dance to martial arts ballet. The slam poetry of martial arts. The jazz and rock n' roll of fighting.

I grabbed my towel off the floor and wiped the sweat off my face. When I dropped my towel, I felt a sharp knock on the back of my head. I already knew what that was. I raised both hands.

"Turn around."

I had no idea if that thing was loaded.

"This is the streets," he said, "We don't play fair."

I ducked out of the line of fire and grabbed his arm.

He kicked me in the shin, knocked me on the floor, pointed the gun at my face. "Pow. Pow. You're dead."

I sat up.

"You move, he shoots, so do what he says. If he wants to kill you, you're already dead, but what's more likely..." he tossed me the gun.

I got off the floor.

"Point it at my head."

I hesitated but did what he said.

"What are you gonna do?"

I hesitated.

He shoved the gun away from his face, grabbed my arm, and pushed the barrel into my stomach. "That's the kind of shit you need to be prepared for."

# 12

It's crazy.

You're a part of something. It's bigger than you. It's been around for years, and only a few days ago, you were on your own.

I wrote a short story one day about a grain of rice that wondered why nobody would cook him—until he realized he wasn't the only grain. When he found a batch of rice, he was no longer just a grain. And now he could be cooked.

Say you're walking around town, and you've got a tattoo and carvings on your back that mean something, and anyone else could have that same tattoo. Could be the waiter, could be the custodian, could be a schoolteacher. Anyone could be D3vil's Krew. It happened sometimes that I'd see the mark on someone's shoulder blades, and when they saw mine, it was like we were old friends. Might buy me a beer. People who'd I'd never met in my entire life, but there was a brotherhood.

I'd find myself back and forth at the church, and not always because of obligation. Friday, I went out to lunch with Pip and Jackie. Saturday, Arin came with the three of us to the bar.

Sometimes, we'd just sit around watching whatever stupid thing was on TV. Sometimes, we'd go out to make a bonfire behind the church. Throw a bunch of shit in a trashcan, set it on fire—guess that made it a trash fire, but it had all the character of a bonfire. And we'd sit back, play a drinking game, shoot the shit. Pip would stare up at the sky. I'd close my eyes and pretend I was at a camp where the log cabin sat on the shore of a lake and the moon dropped a spotlight over my head.

Sometimes Axe would stop by the church with a homemade cream cake or crème brulee. Then I'd have to imagine this big muscled tattooed son of a bitch in a pink apron and oven mitts, and I'd laugh. But it was hard to get Axe to talk about anything. I'd sit down with him at the bar counter. He might have a cigarette. I might have a beer, and I'd try some small talk on him. How'd your day go? What you been up to?

The most you'd get out of him was a shrug. Or an, *I've been good.* Might even ask how you've been.

He might give you a short smile or a chuckle if he sees you're chuckling. But his eyes never met anybody else's. His focus stayed on the floor, like he was always gone, always off in some other place, some other time, and whatever facial expression he may have forced would fall right back down into a pensive gaze.

Hey, Axe, I might say. How long you been in D3vil's Krew?

He'd stub his cigarette out, take a quick glance at my face. How's about a few cupcakes? And he'd say it with a smile.

Nobody questioned Axe about that. But he made damn good cupcakes.

Nights were long. Not in a bad way. In the way that they were long back when I was in high school, and I would sneak out knowing Pops was going to have my ass the next day. In the way that they were short.

When I worked regular shifts, nights were getting home late. Kicking off your shoes, taking a shower. Getting ready to repeat it all soon as you got up the next morning. Nights were routine. Maybe you could squeeze in a movie or that series you started way back when and haven't been able to catch up to. Weekend nights were supposed to be for writing. Weekend nights were for sleeping. So were the days.

D3vil's Krew nights didn't come with routine. There were no shifts or cycles. No expectations. D3vil's Krew nights could be anything. Maybe you don't meet up with them, maybe you stay at home. Maybe they want to show you something. Teach you a new thing. I learned how to weld with The D3vil's

Krew. Some might argue my first gig was filing the serial numbers off guns. Tedious shit.

Sometimes shit was fun. Sometimes shit was weird. One time, Richie smeared purple lipstick across his mouth, smothered his eyes in black makeup, poured liquor all over himself, and invited us out to the bar for a drink. Come midnight, he punched some guy in the face and started a whole brawl just for the hell of it. That guy he punched fell back onto another guy who punched that guy who punched another guy, and that guy punched another guy. Then *that* guy punched another guy, and the whole bar was punching and kicking and rolling on the floor, beer spilled everywhere, bottles shattered, glass all over the floor, women with their tits hanging out of their shirts, blood, and cut skin, broken tables, turned over chairs. Richie sat back and watched it all from the top of the bar counter with a cigarette and a shit-eating grin.

Sometimes when you're sitting around at the church, you're looking around at the tattered chairs, the concrete floor, you're sitting in the ol' bar stool, you're watching Netflix start the next episode but nobody's looking at it, you're watching Pip scroll through his phone, you're watching Arin on a laptop, Axe coming out the kitchen with a red velvet cake he just baked in some old firewood oven, and Richie's laughing and going on about his mother, god-damn that bitch was crazy! That bitch hated my guts! he's saying, and Mike's nodding and laughing along with Richie about how much Richie's mother hated him. The sun's setting, the clock's ticking, you're wondering how many years they've squatted in that building. You're wondering how old the couch is, you're wondering how they keep up maintenance, where'd they get their appliances? Who knew who first? How old's the church? How'd they connect all these wires? How the hell do you bake a cake in a firewood oven? How'd they install that thing to begin with? The stove too? Why does Richie's mom hate him so much? Why's the TV on if no one's watching it? Is it always on like this? Sometimes, when you're sitting there, you're tapping out, you're having an almost out-of-body experience, you're asking yourself, where do I fit into all of this?

I'm the guy who stole money from the safe.

One night I was sitting at the bar counter. Pip didn't show that day. Axe left before me. Arin and Jackie were either in the basement or in the room. I'm sitting back with a beer. I stopped keeping up with the time because I didn't work a job anymore.

We met with each other earlier that day upstairs around the conference table, and they talked about some things that I didn't understand because I hadn't been around that long, but I had to come because I was a D3vil's Krew now. Pip didn't come because he promised his son he'd see him that day. Told Richie it's the kid's first day of school. Preschool. He ain't missing it for the world. Richie told him, fine. Whatever. Learn the art of a fuckin' condom.

If I ever told Richie no, he'd rip my face off with his teeth.

But I was sitting back with a corner of beer left, late at night, when everything settled, and the church was quiet. Richie and Mike were sitting on the couch. I don't even know if they knew I was still back there.

It wasn't nothing big. But they were talking. Just talking. Stuff like, remember when? Remember the time? Say, what about that time when...

Might start talking about D3vil's Krew. Might start talking about music. Might start talking about life. Might get angry about something that happened a long time ago that I didn't know shit about.

They might laugh. They might pause. They might start talking slow. Light a cigarette and watch the smoke curl.

Nothing big. Just something I paid attention to.


When I put in job applications, I put in for everything, including on-call jobs. But a part of me hoped they'd never get back to me.

"Hello?"

"I swear to fucking God, Nolan, if you keep ignoring these fucking phone calls, I'm gonna cram a rifle up your ass!"

"I'm sorry...I'm sorry...I haven't been ignoring you; I just didn't know you called. What is it?"

"I need you here. Tonight."

My first gig. I don't know who, why, what; Richie said they just needed me to drive. They'll take care of the rest.

So, I took a bus out to the church. 12 a.m. Monday. Everybody was there.

They kept the van parked in an old garage attached to the building with a rusty manual door covered in spray paint. I'd never driven their van before, but it looked like the ones I drove for delivery. Same steering wheel. Same mechanisms.

Richie got in the passenger seat. Everybody else got in the back except Mike, whose job it was to open the gate.

I started the van. "How much am I getting paid for this?"

"Drive." Richie slammed the door shut.

I backed out. Rain drizzled on the windshield, and I turned on the wipers. Mike opened the gate. I drove out onto the road and waited for him to get in the van.

Richie'd told me the street, but I didn't know where I was going.

"Take a left," he said. "Make a right when you get to the next light."

I did what he said.

"Bout time we got ourselves a driver," he said under his breath, staring through a film of rain on his window. I don't think he knew I heard him.

These slums weren't empty. Prostitutes. Druggies. People like what I'd just become.

There was a guy walking along the sidewalk with his hands in his pocket, his hood over his head.

Richie leaned to the side. "That him?"

"Looks like him," somebody said from the back, but I didn't get a look at who it was. Sounded like Mike.

"Get closer."

I drove the van up just behind the guy in the hoody. He glanced back, then he took off.

"Go after him."

I didn't know this guy or what he did, but I stepped on the gas.

"Don't let him get away. He's headed for the alley."

I swung the car right. Almost hit a woman, so I slowed down.

"The fuck are you doing? Step on it! He's gettin' away."

I slammed the gas, chased the guy into the alley. The van gained on him, and soon as it was close enough for the headlights to paint him white, I let go of the gas, jerked left so I wouldn't hit him.

"Jesus Christ!" Richie reached over and grabbed the wheel. The van jerked right, tossed the guy over its hood, and he rolled over and fell flat on his face.

Guns clicked. The doors opened. They all got out. I sat back and repeated under my breath, *it's just part of the job.*

The guy got up and started running, but they jumped him, punched him, kicked him. Richie put a gun to his head.

They opened the back of the van and threw the guy inside. "Cut the headlights," Richie said.

I did what he told me. I could see them through the rearview mirror, lit only by the dim and blinking red and yellows of alley lanterns gleaming through the windows. When my morbid curiosity got the better of me, I kept looking, but most the time, I stared forward, watched the windshield wipers stroke hazy ripples across the glass, listened to them squeak.

"Where's my fuckin' money?" Richie said it calmly at first.

There was a rustle but not a response.

"I said, where's my fuckin' money?"

"I don't know," the guy cried.

I was Jamie Foxx in *Collateral*. I was Ryan Gosling in *Drive*.

"We've been through this before, man, too many times before, and I'm gonna start cuttin' off fingers if I don't get an answer."

"I told you. I don't know—" He screamed an earsplitting shriek. I don't know why, and I don't know what happened, but I heard a crack. "I swear to God," he heaved, "I don't fucking know. He's still got it. He told me he'd get back to me."

Crack! His scream was so shrill it raised the hairs on my skin.

"When?" Richie said.

The guy heaved. "I-I don't..." He screamed so hard it rolled back into his throat and came out like a gag. I squeezed my eyes shut. "I swear to God I don't know."

Richie lowered his voice. "This time, I'm gonna drop you off, but you're gonna relay a message to him. In three fucking days, I want the money in my pocket. And let him know I'm being real, real generous. You got until 11:59 p.m., and if you're one second short, so help me God, the morgue's getting an extra paycheck. Nolan, take us west."

I froze. My heart pounded in my throat. My eyes and hands were paralyzed until I felt Richie's cigarette-funked breath warm the side of my face. "Get us outta this fucking alley! Is that too fucking hard for you?"

I blinked my eyes, wiped the spit off my cheek, and stepped on the gas.

It was just part of the job. Whatever went on with this guy had nothing to do with me. I headed west.

Richie directed me to a rowhouse about three miles away. "Right up there," he said. "Two sixteen. Drop him off."

I pulled over to the side of the road, slowed the van.

"Did I tell you to stop? Keep rollin'!"

I rolled. They slid the door open, tossed the guy on the sidewalk, and he tumbled onto his back. The streetlights exposed bruised skin and swollen cheeks through the rearview mirror. A man who could barely move, slowly lifting himself off the ground.

I swallowed. Just a job.

The rain drizzle turned into a shower that thumped against the metal and splattered the windshield.

"What was that about?" I kept my eyes on the road.

The itching burn of a freshly lit cigarette tickled my sinuses.

"Long story." Richie snapped his lighter closed. "It ain't important. Just drive."

I blew out a breath. Just a job.

About a week later, Richie said he needed to meet with me. He sat upstairs at the conference table. I took a seat in front of him.

He got up and unlocked the gun safe. AK-47s, AR-15s, Glocks, Desert Eagles. A door covered in assault rifles, shelves full of shotguns, pockets full of handguns and bullets. He pulled out a leather briefcase with golden combo locks. "You hold up your end of the deal, you get paid for what you do. That's how we work 'round here."

He sat back down and opened it. The inside was divided into sections like a cash register drawer. Fives in one section, tens in another, twenties, fifties, and hundreds.

He took out a band of twenties. "There ain't a cop or judge or contract that's gonna make sure we get what's owed to us." He set the money on the table. "If they don't pay, you don't get paid." He closed the briefcase. "So sometimes we gotta do what we gotta do."

I grabbed the money, flipped through it, and smelled the satisfying scent of what was probably a mix of cocaine and dirty fingers.

"You're dismissed."

# 13

He cooked it in the basement instead of the kitchen.

In a sauce pot on a portable burner on top of a folding table. Buckets and bowls, a pile of empty gas cans. Bottles, lighters. Baking soda, plastic funnels. A balance scale. Spoons. Vials and eyedroppers. A bunch of stuff I didn't know what it was. Bags of cocaine. How'd the burner fit on the table? Brick walls in a room about the size of a closet. Maybe it was a closet before the building became a base.

Shelves on the walls full of vials and empty boxes, full boxes. Spray containers, plastic tubs, metal scraps. Screwdrivers and a welding gun. On the wall, posters of the periodic table, that photo of Einstein where he's got his tongue sticking out, *Never Trust an Atom, They Make Everything Up!*

Said crack wasn't the only thing he cooked down there.

Arin had on a lab coat but a tie-dye shirt underneath. Said he didn't need the coat. Just made him feel like something special. He stirred a pot of shit I might've thought was grits if I was naïve enough. "You wanna smoke some?" He laughed.

"I'm good."

He slapped me on the shoulder. "I'm funnin' with ya. Unless you got money." He was one of those guys who got real close when he talked to you. Made sure there was constant eye contact so you couldn't avoid looking at his face no matter how hard you tried. "How much do you think this stuff can sell for?"

I shrugged.

"Take a guess."

"Twenty dollars?"

"A little more."

"Thirty."

He shook his head.

"Fifty."

"Keep going up."

I opened my mouth but stuttered.

"One hundred ten dollars. A gram."

"A hundred ten? You serious?"

His laugh came out as a hiss. The substance hardened into some dry, clay-looking shit.

"How'd you end up here?" I asked.

"Same as you. The Almighty."

"But was it your first choice?"

"I don't think it's anybody's first choice. I went to Princeton. Got a degree in chemistry."

My breath caught in my throat. "You're joking, right?"

He shook his head. "Nope."

"You could've been a scient—"

"A scientist. I know. I thought I'd become a chemist after I graduated." He glanced at the table and nudged me with his elbow. "I guess in a way I did." He laughed.

"So what happened?"

"Nothing happened." He blew air through his lips. "Just didn't go the way I had planned. I ended up in coding."

"Did you like that?"

"Hell, no. It paid good, but it was shit. Worst job I ever had. IT tech. You ever deal with a smooth brain that doesn't know how to reboot a computer? Man!" He slid me a pack of plastic baggies. "Here." Dropped a spoon in front of me. "Bag this shit."

I opened the pack and pulled out a baggie, looked at it front and back as if that would teach me anything about drugs, how much a gram was, or how any of this shit worked.

When I got a spoonful, I froze before I dumped it in. Someone's going to buy this. They're going to smoke it. They're going to get addicted. They're going to come back for more. They're going to OD. And I'm going to look back on it, and I'm going to say I asked Richie earlier that day if there was anything I could do to make extra money, and he told me if I helped Arin out with the drugs, I'd get a larger cut.

My hands were the ones that touched the baggie.

"Then I did software engineering," Arin said, "which was better than IT, but not that much. Paid more."

"What was wrong with that?"

He blew another breath, twisted his lips from side to side, shook his head, shrugged. "I dunno. Wasn't my calling, I guess."

"What brought you out here?"

He wagged his finger at me. "You already asked me that."

"But you were already making money."

He cocked his head from side to side. "Yeah…"

"How'd you end up doing this?"

"Like I said. Money. I could quit my coding job, go full Walden and live off the land, or I could quit my coding job and try something dangerous."

"You ever have a dream?"

"I used to want to be, like," he shook his head with a sheepish grin, "a spy when I was a kid. Remember how…? Wait. How old are you?"

"Twenty-five."

"Oh…pfft. You might be too young, but when I was a kid, they had all this spy shit coming out. Movies and TV…holy shit. It was, like, a trend." He turned his eyes towards me like he expected me to say something.

"When you're a kid," he said, "you have dreams. When you're an adult, you have life goals. My life goals didn't work out, but I still had to make money, and truth is, I don't hate this.

"I make more money than everybody else here because of my role in the Krew. I could have my own place. Probably a pretty decent one, if I wanted to. Problem is...I don't want to. There's something freeing about showering in buckets and cooking my meals in a woodfire oven. Like nobody's putting a rope around my throat and jerking it back every time I fall out of line. I like it here. I know I shouldn't. I know I'm gonna die young."

It was hard to read his face. Maybe passion. Maybe thirst or regret, but whatever it was, it contradicted the nonchalant tone of his voice.

"And the best part about it...I don't deal. That's what those guys do. My job is right here. Got my own office." He gestured to the posters on the brick. "One day you realize life is the same ungrateful routine over and over and over again, and then what? You die. Suddenly, I quit my job, I dug around on the dark web, and I got in touch with Richie. Let him and the guys put a gun to my head just so I could tell them I can build a bomb, I can crack a safe, I can make bullets. Just let me put my skills to use."

He jerked his head towards the table. "Finish bagging that stuff so we can get it out of here."

"It doesn't make you feel like the bad guy?"

He opened and closed his mouth, rubbed the side of his neck. His brows drew together, and he turned his eyes to me. "Freedom has a price."


"Stupid."

The end of Pip's cigarette burned tendrils of smoke that climbed my nostrils and tightened around my senses the more I denied it.

"Sometimes," I said. "I can be real stupid."

The TV was on the Netflix home screen. The couch was more comfortable than what an old, tattered couch should be, and that still shocked me even after having sat on it enough times. The atmosphere sounded and felt and smelled like a rundown dive bar, beer bottles clinking and cue balls clacking, cigarette smoke and buzzing neon signs. But it was always like that at the church, when you got Axe and Mike shooting pool and Jackie and Arin at the bar. Richie might be in there with everybody else; he might be in his room; he might be someplace nobody fucking knows. But that's what the church looked like. That was a typical photo.

"We're all stupid at some point." Pip stubbed his cigarette out in the ashtray on an end table that wasn't an end table but a crate. "That's life."

"It's kind of funny now." I chuckled. "But maybe the dumbest thing I ever did was leave my bike by itself in a convenience store parking lot. At night. No lock."

"Talkin' 'bout when you got it stolen?"

"Yeah." I nodded. "I let those guys kick my ass. One of 'em hopped on it, the rest of 'em got in their car, and it was gone. Just like that. Damn. If I knew then what I know now."

"Did you get a look at 'em?" Richie came up behind the couch, and I guess I forgot he was in the room, or maybe I didn't ever know he was there. Maybe he came in and sat down at the bar when I wasn't looking, but if the cigarette Pip just burned out wasn't enticing me to pop one in my mouth and light it up, then the ribbons curling above my head from Richie's fresh would do the job.

I hesitated to respond. That's just how I communicated with Richie, spending most of my time trying to read him and figure out whether he hated my guts or was alright with me. "Sort of," I said. "The guy who got on my bike, I can somewhat remember his face."

"What'd he look like?"

"He had a crooked nose, a scar over his eye."

"What was he wearing?"

"A black hoody."

"Any brand?"

"I feel like it might've been some knock-off brand of uh...Nike."

"Did you get a look at the car? Anything like that?"

"It was kind of an old car. Maybe a 2000s model. A black Mustang."

"What store did this happen at?"

"Shell. The one across the street from Lou's Tires."

"Nerd, can you do anything with that?"

Arin took his beer from his mouth. "Might take me a minute, but I'll see what I can do."

I got a call from Mike the next day to meet them at the church. Said, we're gonna get your bike back.

I didn't know if Arin had magic powers. Or if he knew the name and face of every goddamn body in the city, but he said it might take him a minute. It took him less.

He'd texted me a picture of my bike thief the night after I told him about the incident. *This the guy?* I told him yeah. They had me come over the night after that, and Arin showed me the dude's name and social media, where he normally hangs out and with who. I don't know how a vague facial description and a generic car could lead somebody to that information, but it happened. So, we left that night.

I never asked them why they did it. It was almost like there was an unwritten reason that they thought I already knew. That's what they do, I guess. I had that tattoo on my back. The carvings on my shoulder blades. That's what they do.

I drove. We rode around the area Arin told me my thief hung out in a lot. I never tracked down a guy before. I rode slow. Eyed everyone on the sidewalk. Kept his picture in mind. I didn't think I'd find him. Seemed kind of crazy. The kind of shit that only happens in movies. I felt like I was in a movie. Maybe I was a bounty hunter going after the guys on the Wanted signs. Maybe a thriller. Maybe I was a cop keeping an eye on a suspect. That's ironic.

At night, everybody kind of looks the same. You got streetlights that give you a shot of people's faces, but you're driving on the street, and there's shadows, and you're having to squint to get a good look at everybody. I might not have noticed him if I hadn't seen my bike first. Still polished. Paint still good. And it looked like those same guys. All of them.

"That him?" Richie asked.

"Yeah." I pulled over and got out of the van. I was walking faster than I was thinking. Seeing my bike again was like having my baby ripped out of my damn arms and running into the kidnapper unplanned. I just wanted to hug her.

The guy turned away from laughing with his friend and drew his brows together when he saw me. "Don't I know you? Shit."

My guys jumped out of the van, and when they did, they didn't do it meekly or with hesitation. They were a pack of lions going after a meal. They didn't even run. They walked. But they walked with powerful steps, shoulders back and chest out, no eyes towards the ground, no meandering. Confident strides. Authority. I felt all-powerful. It filled my lungs, charged through my bone marrow, and released into my veins. My body was energized. My muscles were tight. And the looks on these guys' faces weren't anywhere near close to the sneers they displayed when they stole my bike.

My guys jumped their guys, and the brawl was on. Punching. Kicking. Aggression. Testosterone. Blood. Spit. Sweat. There were seven of us and four of them, and my guys knew what they were doing. This was going to be easy.

When they had bruises on both sides of their faces, blood streaming from their noses, swollen lips and blackened eyes, they ran. Surrendered the keys, threw their arms up in the air, and hightailed it.

I had a bleeding lip and a nosebleed, but I also had my bike. Besides, it was kind of fun.

I tossed Mike the van keys, and nobody said anything else. Almost like nothing had happened.

They got in the van and drove off, and I got on my bike like I thought I'd never get to do again and drove back to my apartment for the first time since I had a job.

I never knew the bumping beneath my tires could feel so good.


I'd been invited.

Every Krew member in the metroplex showed up. Friends and comrades. Women in patent leather, fishnet stockings, high heels, and straps. Men in patent leather, fishnet stockings, high heels, and straps. Loud music, alcohol, drugs. LED lights. Twirling light batons. There were three hundred people. There were four hundred people. There were five hundred people down in the basement that shouldn't have been able to hold that many people. Glow-in-the-dark paints, LED shoes and clothing items, and if you went down there, you were going to run into someone who would ask if you wanted to gamble. One hundred dollars on the big guy! Because there were cage fights in the pen, and you might even get somebody who asked you if you wanted to participate. I almost participated, but Axe went in, and I said fuck that. But Axe's winning streak ended when he got K.O.'d by a guy five times smaller than him. A whole lot of booing from the audience. A whole lot of wasted money. I'd have laughed if I hadn't bet on Axe.

I met a guy there who said his only job in D3vil's Krew was to handle house crew's phone plan and bank accounts. That was it. He didn't fight. He didn't deal. He didn't rob. He stayed at home. His only job was to keep the phone plan and bank accounts under his name. Said they paid him a good sum of money to do it. They make the money, he said, but my name's on the bank account.

I asked him how he got a role like that, and he said he didn't know. Maybe if he wasn't drunk, he would've been able to remember. A D3vil's Krew member but with a regular life. Easiest job in the world.

He offered me his services. Said it would help keep my name and activities confidential. "Y' know," he poured down the rest of his beer, "in case something happens."

I thought about it, but I didn't have the money to spend. I just wanted his job.

I met another guy who called himself Cracker Joe. That may not have sounded the same to him as it did to me. I talked with him in the back of the church where you could get out of the crowd and sit out by the trash fire, with folks sitting on mismatched folding chairs, standing around with a bottle or cup of booze.

This kid, with his thick-framed glasses and his hair combed back like a yuppie from the 1980s, looked more like a guy who collected Marvel figures than anybody associated with The D3vil's Krew. But he was a member. Showed me his tatt and everything, but he wasn't from New York. Lived out in Jersey. Said he used to hang out with Arin back in the day.

"Why Cracker Joe? Where'd you get a name like that?"

"I can crack a safe."

"That all you do?"

"No, but I'm good at it. Not everybody's got the skill." He threw back a cup of liquor that I think got him tipsier than he was willing to admit. "How'd you end up here?"

"Long story. It begins with me losing my job."

"Yeah? How'd that happen? What kind of job you do?"

"I was a driver at Drop and Ship. Somebody stole my bike. I worked way out of town. Had to drive to commute, so when my bike was stolen, I was pretty much fucked. Tried to make it work. Couldn't."

"Wait a minute, you were a *driver* for a business, and you lost your job because you had to *drive* to work." He laughed in a way that let me know I wasn't wrong about how much he was buzzing.

"We just got the thing back, but now I make sure I keep it inside. You come out here a lot?"

"Nah." He shrugged. "I usually stay in New Jersey, but Arin gave me a call, told me about the party. Plus, there's a business transaction I might wanna make."

"What's that?"

"Guns."

I didn't know enough about illegal gun exchanges to pretend like I did, so I kept my mouth closed.

"I hear you guys have got a decent inventory. I wanna check them out. Maybe we can negotiate a good price." He looked at me like I could help him out with that.

I took a swig of beer and looked out at the fire before he could get any ideas.

That was the last thing I remember before I got too much booze in my body or a strip of LSD that made the later part of that night a mix of contorted objects, chaotic rainbows, and my face melting. Maybe it was the drugs, but I felt like I became one with something that night. A Kaiju of sorts, a gigantic being that could be destructive when it wanted to be destructive but graceful when it exposed its vulnerability. I couldn't write a creature of this caliber.

As I danced in the basement and watched bodies move, feet stomp, fists pump, heard the rambunctious music and calls of the crowd, felt the intensity of the cage fights where blood was spilled for laughter and camaraderie, I was a part of something. I was one of many cells that made up an entire body.

I'd been to parties before. I'd been to a bunch when I was a teen. I'd danced and drank and fucked and got shit-faced and fucked-up on every pill and leaf and cookie and drink a kid my age shouldn't have been having. I'd heard loud music and seen the twirling lights. The girls doing stuff girls ain't supposed to do and boys doing stuff boys ain't supposed to do. I'd been in a crowd, a congregation, back when I was in high school, though it'd been a long time since then. I'd done it. But I ain't never felt like I belonged somewhere, and that moved through me more than the music and the drugs.

# 14

In October, we took a trip.

They called them "tours." A thing they did where they rode from state to state and committed heists at different stores. Had to build some profits, Richie put it. Told me I'd be driving.

When I was a kid, I used to go on road trips with my ma, pop, and sister. Used to visit family halfway across the country. Two days in the car. Lots of bickering between me and sis. Dad rock. McDonald's for dinner. Cramped legs.

I hadn't had a vacation like that since I was fourteen. I've got to say, even with the arguments with my sister or my pop's shitty music collection, I liked looking out at the trees. Liked the way the soil smelled when it wafted through the cracks of the window. I liked the way the vibration of the station wagon felt against my back when I closed my eyes and how that feeling just after I woke up from a good nap heightened my senses. Car games and road signs. Stops at cheap, cramped motels because who the hell could afford to stay at a Holiday Inn? Punching my sister in the arm every time I saw a Volkswagen Beetle. Ma would turn around and snap at me, if you keep that up we're turning the car around.

I never believed her.

Pissing on the side of the road when the next rest stop was an hour away. My sister held her piss for hours before ever doing something so, as she put it, "barbarous." It made me laugh.

Sometimes you don't realize something is gone until you look out your window, and one thing brings it all back, and then you say, damn. I never realized how much I missed this.

This wasn't a road trip. My head knew it. My senses didn't. I didn't know what to look forward to on this trip. We talked about it at meetings around the conference table before we broke out into a smoky room and a game of poker. Strategies and preparations my attention span wouldn't let me get the full picture of. We were about to do some illegal shit was all I could conclude. But I knew what I signed up for when I got into this gig. Pops used to say, you got to work for the money. Richie said you got to chase the money. Far as I'm concerned, that meant the same thing. So, I got to get the money. Put everything else aside and just do it.

I was scared. I was excited. I was curious. I was unprepared. My nerves were sometimes on edge riding that long next to Richie because I couldn't always tell what was going on in his head or what he was feeling. He didn't talk much that trip, and when I thought about it, I guess he usually wasn't too much of a talker, even riding for hours in the car where the rest of the crew could be laughing or bickering just like me and my sister used to.

He didn't listen to anything but rap, punk rock, and metal, especially thrash, and when he got into music, he really got into it. The car was short on gasoline when "Wanna Be a Baller" came on, and he bobbed his head and sang along, feet up on top of the dash. He knew every lyric. I started to let him know we were running out of gas, but I didn't want to interrupt him. Not because I thought he'd get mad, but because I was enjoying it. When that song went off, another one came on—*Rage Against the Machine*. I realized if I didn't say something now, we might be pushing the car, and that was going to be my ass. But it didn't interrupt his jam. He reached into his pocket, pulled out a couple of twenties, and continued banging his head like I never said anything.

The kind of stuff that inspires writing.

The van had that soil smell I was used to from road trips as a kid. The vibration from the motion beneath my legs.

The night before, I stayed the night at the church so we could leave early. It was the first time I ever showered in a bucket. I slept upstairs in the room where Arin and Jackie slept in bunkbeds. Had my own mattress on the floor that they said used to belong to another member who was no longer with them. I don't know if he died or ended up somewhere else.

They had a brick staircase in that room that answered my question about that mysterious third floor I was always looking at when I stood outside the building. They never told me I couldn't go up there, but they never took me up there either. I waited until they were asleep before I gave into curiosity and crawled off the mattress. I couldn't sleep anyways.

I hit a light switch at the end of the staircase, and like most of the joint, a single bulb lit up. But it wasn't what I expected. I thought I might find a pike of stashed drugs, another gun safe, maybe even a skeleton or two. It wasn't nothing like that.

It was a library.

Books, stacked up on shelves as high as the ceiling, some of them in piles, some of them leaning, some of them stacked neatly, some of them old, some of them new. Dust particles drifting in the dim light, coating the book covers, and cobwebs drooping from the shelves and corners of the room like the dried hair of a mummy. Binders and piles of papers, old newspapers. They had a chess table in the middle of the floor. Framed newspaper clips, old photographs—one of them was of the church. An old black-and-white image, probably before it was abandoned and became the base for The D3vil's Krew.

I started thinking that all of this had been there before D3vil's Krew showed up. Used to belong to the church, and they never did anything with it, but there was a handwritten manifesto on two separate pages of notebook paper side by side in one large frame.

*If you're tired of seeing homeless folks camp out on the streets, you're D3vil's Krew. If you're done with the tyranny of Wall*

*Street, you're D3vil's Krew. If you're done being a lap dog, rolling over and playing dead, subservient to a master that keeps a chain around your neck, you're D3vil's Krew. The D3vil's Krew's not an organization; it's an ideology. It lives and breathes in the bones and the blood of millions of people whether they're willing to dig in there and recognize that or not...*

*Don't bend over and take it.*

*Richard Bryant*

I won't pretend like I remember the whole thing or even read it all, but *Don't bend over and take it* made me pause.

I tried not to think about it too hard.

I grabbed a leather binder off the shelf that just said *History Book* in black ink. Opened it. There were photographs inside, mugshots, notebook paper covered in sloppy writing and scribbled-out words. A magazine article dropped out and drifted to my feet. I picked it up.

*What caused Grace Redemption Church to go bankrupt?*

I remembered when that happened.

Before I put the article back in, I read a sheet of notebook paper hooked inside the binder. It was kind of hard to make out; some of the ink was smeared, and a lot was scribbled or crossed out.

*In 2014, Jeffery Howard, a church pastor for Grace Redemption Church, made a drug deal with Richie Bryant and The D3vil's Krew.*

I skimmed.

*With the money made from the drugs, Jeffrey Howard was able to get his business even further off the ground, opening five more Christian stores in the country, turning him into a millionaire and televangelist within one year.*

I skimmed.

*Jeffrey Howard met with The D3vil's Krew at a rooftop lounge in Manhattan to discuss payment terms Bryant argued were already negotiated. Howard, however, argued D3vil's Krew were not "mafia tier," as he put it, and refused to pay the agreed amount.*

I skimmed.

*Shortly after their meetup in Manhattan, The D3vil's Krew burnt down the church and fifteen of the twenty stores Howard had opened in select locations across the country.*

My lack of sleep hit me when we got on the road. Mike drove while I was out, and as soon as I woke up, I was back on the wheel again, so I knew next time not to let Richie know I was awake.

In Virginia, Richie had me pull up to a mobile home with weathered wood and discarded tires on the lawn. Splintered porch steps and a rickety rocking chair you could hardly see in the buzzing porchlights that made the house look like it was glowing in the dark.

We got out, and the moon was smiling and frowning at me at the same time. Rocks and dry leaves crunched beneath my boots, and the frigid breeze blew the pungent scent of oil-soaked mud into my nostrils. The sky was navy blue behind the cluster of black trunks and branches that looked like old bones the more they lost their leaves.

The steps creaked and wobbled as we climbed them. All of us. Me, Richie, Pip, Jackie, Arin, Mike, and Axe huddled around the doorway. I must've been the only one who didn't know where we were.

Richie banged on the door. "Hey. It's us." He banged again, leaned against it with his fist and forearm. "Open the fuckin' door. It's cold out here."

A shirtless dude in pajama pants opened it. I don't remember his name, but his pants had Snoopy piloting his doghouse like a fighter jet. Kind of thing you had to look at twice to confirm before you realized Snoopy was also smoking a cigarette.

"Hey, Richie," he said. "Glad you guys could make it. Who's this? Got yourself a new goon?"

"Yeah." Richie pointed his thumb at me. "He's from Buffalo."

"Come on in." He turned around, and there was that tattoo again. The one on their backs, the one on mine. All the way out there in Virginia.

"When's your first stop?" he asked.

"Tomorrow night," Richie said. "We gotta do it. Our profits are dropping. We never recovered from that deal with that crackpot pastor back in '14. Push comes to shove, we might have to take from the safe."

My heart jumped. The safe? The one I stole from?

"Money's hard. You gotta do what you gotta do to get it."

The house smelt like cigarettes and freshly cooked soup. Rust gave the vents skin disease. The carpet had holes. Felt like the floor was made of cardboard. It creaked when anyone stepped on it, and I thought it would cave in if I stepped too hard. The kitchen faucet leaked. The TV was on *Breaking Bad*.

He shut the door behind us, and they started talking about things I didn't know anything about because I was the new guy. I didn't even know what we were doing there. Nobody told me anything. Just drive.

He fed us a bowl of soup, which was the first thing I'd eaten since our first stop on the road, and if I weren't so hungry, I might've been able to admit it tasted like vinegar and onions. I was hoping Axe would pop out one of his recipes and replace the taste. Now that I think about it, if I'd have said something, he probably would've.

If you've ever sat around with a group of people, and everyone knows each other and everyone had experiences with each other, they're all laughing with each other and telling stories, then you know the feeling. You laugh when everyone else laughs because everyone else is doing it. And then, when they start talking seriously about something you don't know nothing about, you make the face that everyone else is making, like you know what's going on. You're there because everyone else is there, and you're kind of waiting for the convo to move on.

And it did, but when it did, Snoopy Pants took us to the back room and unlocked a large gun safe. Made me think about when Cracker Joe talked about house crew's inventory. Lots of guns, assault rifles, handguns, shotguns, non-guns, bowie knives, grenades—Snoopy Pants had more weapons than house crew, probably twice as many.

He tossed three on the bed. "Got these imported from Russia about a week ago."

"I like 'em," Richie said. "How much you willing to negotiate?"

Seemed like everybody bought something for themselves. I never been in any illegal gun buy situation, so I didn't know what to do. Felt like the naïve dork kid who didn't know the other kids were going to do drugs at the party.

"You looking to buy anything?" Snoopy Pants gestured to me.

Everybody else bought something, and it was kind of like when you say you're not drinking tonight, only to take a few shots because everybody else is having a good time getting wasted. But I didn't buy a gun. I bought a bowie knife. Halfway because I didn't want to be left out and halfway because it looked cool. Then when I bought it, he explained shit to me about that knife and what it could do, the different parts, clips and spines and serrations, words I'd never heard before, like my ass had been trained in the army and I ever used one of these things before. I held my chin up like I knew what he was talking about and tucked it away under my shirt because I'd seen them do that in movies. I spent forty buck on that thing.

They didn't say it, but I figured we were staying the night there. Guess that's probably why we stopped there in the first place. When time came for us to go to bed, Snoopy Pants said he had three rooms in the house. Two had a bed; one had a cot folded up in the closet. Obviously, one of those beds was his.

"Richie's taking the other bed," he said. "The rest of you guys will have to figure it out."

"Mike can have the cot," Richie said, and he, Snoopy Pants, and Mike left the living room.

"Dibs on the couch," I said.

Pip pulled a roll-out mattress from under the couch. "Guess I'll sleep here." If I'd have known about that, I'd have called dibs on it instead.

"I'll take the lounge chair," Jackie said, and Arin and Axe got some sheets out of the closet and took the floor.

So I'm stretched out on the couch in the dark, eyes wide open, staring at the shadows of tree branches and crooked blinds the porchlights sketched on the wall, and I'm thinking about where I am. Ever have one of those moments where you realize you're a thing in the world experiencing and witnessing it from a single perspective? And then you ask yourself how you got there. Feeling your own body, your own bones inside your skin, and the exact place where you are?

I don't know if anyone else was asleep. I doubt it. I know Arin was on his phone. I got up and climbed over the edge of the couch so I wouldn't step on

Pip. I'd hardly seen the "shank" side of his name, but it was there for a reason, and I didn't want to find out the hard way.

I went to the bathroom, took a piss, and then I had that moment again, looking in the mirror in the house of some stranger. This time last year, I'd just gotten off from work after a long shift. I probably worked overtime. I delivered hundreds of packages that day. My manager gave me an evaluation. Said I did a good job, but I need to pick up the speed.

Tonight, I was staring at my face in a stranger's bathroom in another state after watching a gang illegally buy guns. They had the same tattoos on their backs as me. Shit like that almost gives you an out-of-body experience. If I stared at myself too hard, I'd be wearing a delivery driver uniform. I turned around. I had a tribal tattoo on my back that looked like the devil. The number 666 carved on there twice.

I also paid my rent that month.

I left the bathroom and heard my phone vibrating on the couch. Grabbed it. "What are you doing calling this late? It's, like, twelve in the morning."

"I know," she said. "Sorry. Something's been on my mind for a while."

I went outside to the porch. Hoped I wasn't too loud. This was the last place I wanted to be mistaken for an intruder, all those guns lying around.

I leaned against the porch rail. "What's this about?"

"Me and Steve have been talking it over, and...you're my brother, his brother-in-law, and we shouldn't have turned you away like that."

"Oh...you mean about the money?"

"Yeah. We should be there for you. After all, we're family. So, if you need it, we can help you out. At least until you get on your feet good. How about we get together and discuss it?"

I stared out at the trees. Lost my train of thought.

"Hello? Are you there?"

"I'm not home right now."

"Oh, where are you?"

"On a trip. With some friends. It's...they're taking care of the costs."

"Oh. Maybe we can get together when you get back."

I turned and looked at the house. "Know what? I don't need it."

"No? Are you sure?"

"Yeah."

"Cause...I mean...I know it's hard to make a living wage these days, and me and Steve are fortunate to be where we're at—"

"I don't need it. It's like Pops always said, right? A man's gotta do what a man's gotta do. Thanks. But I got it taken care of..."

I thought we'd been disconnected.

"Hello?"

"Nolan, I don't want you to feel like you can't come to us for help."

I hung up the phone. The breeze blew through my t-shirt. My muscles stiffened. I went back inside.

The whites of Pip's eyes gleamed in porchlights that shadowed the rest of his face. Had his arms crossed under his head as he gazed towards the ceiling. "What was that about?"

I climbed over the edge of the couch and got under my blanket. "Family shit."

"Yeah?"

"Uh-huh. My sister called me. Wanted to know if I still needed help paying for my apartment."

"What'd you say?"

"I got money."

"I went to pick up Caelin the day before we took off."

"How's he doing?"

The porchlight glinted across his teeth when he smiled. "He's doing good. Sounds like he likes school. A hell of a lot different than me, that's for sure." He chuckled.

I yawned, curled up beneath a thin blanket that wasn't long enough to cover my feet, and snuggled my face into a flat pillow.

"He asked me something crazy the other day."

"What was that?"

"A spider died in his room, and I guess it upset him. And then he asked me if it went to Heaven."

"Kids say the darndest things." I chuckled.

He nodded, "Yeah, they do. But how do you answer that?" He stopped smiling and turned his head to me. "How do you tell a child that spiders don't go to Heaven?"

# 15

They put an earpiece in my ear and a gun in my hand.

"Nerd's our surveillance." Richie pulled his ski mask over his face, his hood over his head. "He's scoping out where the cops are in this area, so he tells you to go, you go. He tells you to wait, you wait. You do what he says, when he says it. Got that?"

I looked in the rearview mirror. Arin had a laptop. Everybody was dressed in black. Combat boots, hoodies, ski masks, semi-automatics.

Three a.m.

The white light flickered and moaned on the side of the building like it was dealing with a headache. The red letters on the Open sign lit up one by one. Cigarettes and beer ads. Vacant gas pumps. The glare through the windows turned the building into a neon spot against a black backdrop and left a glowing residue on the concrete that reached as far as the crack running beside the van's tires.

"Stay out of the light," Richie said. "I'll let you know when."

I cut the headlights and drove to the side of the building.

Richie grabbed a black duffel bag from under the seat. They got out.

What do you do when your nerves are banging on your bones like there's a fire in your gut? Your fingers are rattling. Your chest is heaving. And then, you look back to another day, and you don't know how you got there.

What do you do to rest your nerves when they're screaming something scary in your head and it echoes across your skull from wall to wall until it leaves your brain pulsating?

First real stop on the trip. My palms are sweating. My stomach's churning. I've got my eyes shut, waiting to hear a gunshot.

I don't know who's in that convenience store. I don't know how many people. I don't know what's going on in there.

A part of me doesn't even believe this is real. I'm just sitting at a gas station. Met some folks about a month back. Just joking around and told me they were criminals. Those aren't real guns. They're Nerf guns. They're gonna come back out. Maybe they bought some beer, a pack of gum. This isn't real. None of this is actually happening.

I met some criminals. They carved 666 into my back. We're running a heist. And I don't know what the hell's going on in there.

Just part of the job.

Arin's in the back. He's not saying anything. I'm waiting for him to tell me the cops are on our asses. Get the hell out of here! Slam the brakes! They're shooting!

He's not saying anything.

I examined every road on my way down there. I read every street name. Memorized every stop sign, building, mailbox. If something goes wrong, where do we go? Cut the parking lot, break right. There's an alley up ahead. Or we make a right, a last-minute left at the fork. I planned it out. Had it all in my head. This is what I'll do if something goes wrong.

When I got to thinking about that, I got to relaxing. Let my mind drift. Forced it to. This is a video game. This is the scene in your next novel. What if a car pulled up in the parking lot? A mysterious car. A car without a license plate. What if a guy gets out? He's not a regular guy. He's a big guy. A big, *big* guy. Eight feet—nuh-uh. Make him nine. He's nine feet. He's got boils all over his skin. He's got no shirt on. No shoes. Torn jeans. He's got a mask on his face. It looks like a pig. A boar. He goes into the convenience store. The cashier gets a gun from under the counter, shoots him, but he doesn't fall down. It only angers him. He digs the bullet out of his skin and throws it back at the cashier. It hits the cashier in the chest, the cashier falls back—

"Start the van!"

I jumped, looked in the rearview mirror.

Richie and the rest of them sprinted around the corner. "Start the fucking van!"

"Let's go," Arin said.

I started the van, put it in reverse, slammed the gas. They dodged the bumper. I slammed the brakes. They threw open the doors. Richie tossed the bag in the front seat. They all jumped in.

"What the fuck! What the fuck!" Richie yanked the mask off his head. "I told you to pull up!"

I gulped. "Sorry."

"Drive!"

I slammed the gas. The tires screeched, and the van bumped and jolted everyone and everything inside. I made a sharp right and sped onto the road.

"Slow down," Richie said, but my foot was lead. "I said slow down."

I swallowed and tightened my grip around the steering wheel.

"Hey!" He whipped his head towards the window and back at me. "The cops aren't on our asses right now, but they will be if you don't slow the fuck down."

I took a heavy breath and eased my foot off the gas.

"Go the speed limit. Make a right up here. Don't give 'em any reason to think you're suspicious."

Not looking suspicious was a lot to ask for when we just robbed a convenience store, but I did what he said.

Flashing red and blue lights raced down the other street.

"They're probably looking for us," Richie looked out the back window, "but there's a lot of white vans in the world. I don't even know if anyone got a look at this one. Make a left. We're crossing state lines."

My nerves eased some when I pulled onto the highway, but my chest was still tight.

Richie unzipped the bag. "Sweet baby Jesus, I think I'm in love! Ka-ching, ka-ching, boys. First stop, and this money's already tasting better than pussy."

"Let me hold it," Mike said.

Richie tossed it to him.

"Goddamn."

Heard Jackie say we're off to a good start. She tossed the bag back to Richie. I tried to keep my eyes on the road. "Was anybody in there?"

"The cashier," Mike said. "A few customers. Nobody, really."

"How many?"

"Just drive the van," Richie said.

"Bout four people total," Mike said. "We got in and out pretty smoothly."

I let out a breath I didn't realize I was holding.

We stayed at a motel we found on an empty back road where the only thing nearby were pine trees you had to bend your neck to see the top of. One room. Richie took a bed. Mike took a bed. The rest of us were on the floor. We got there at five in the morning when the sun was still down. At twelve p.m., we hit the road again.

Nobody'd knew what we'd done. We were driving with the rest of the cars like we were one of them.

"I'm hungry," Richie said. "Pull over at the next place you see."

I pulled over at a dingy truck stop in North Carolina. When I was a kid and used to go on road trips with my family, truck stops meant bathroom breaks and greasy burgers. Cool souvenirs and candy.

When we walked into the truck stop diner, the greasy smell hit me. I was nine years old again. What a thing it does to the mind when you have to remind it you're not on vacation.

We had guns in the van. A bag of dirty money.

"Can I take your order?"

It didn't feel right because I knew something she didn't know.

"Yeah," I avoided eye contact. "Just a...a burger."

Patrons of a diner, employees, and truck drivers. I'm the guy who drove a van last night for a gang of criminals robbing a convenience store.

It's not like the diner would look different. Like the walls were supposed to melt in, the windows were supposed to shatter, the color of the room would turn green and orange. Everyone would look at me with giant, bulging eyes and say you committed a crime! You committed a crime! I didn't have a sign that said it. My body wasn't a different shape from any regular guy my size. Criminals didn't have a special kind of voice or a special kind of face, so why did I expect everybody to know what I did? Like the world and reality were supposed to flip and warp. There are eight billion people in this world doing eight billion different things, eight billion concerns, and yet, for some reason, mine felt like the biggest.

I sat at the table with the rest of The D3vil's Krew. They didn't look the way I felt. Did *my* nerves show?

Two cops walked in. They didn't even glance our way. They fixed themselves a coffee.

There are guns in our van.

A guy in a trucker hat stopped and asked us if we were from New York or New Jersey. Richie told him New York.

I waved hello.

There was a bag of stolen money in our van.

Richie made conversation with that guy. I couldn't understand how he could be so friendly with people. So casual.

This was it. Just part of the job.

The Krew was laughing. And then, before I realized it, I was laughing too. I was laughing. I laughed. Because Mike told a joke.

And it was funny.

We broke into a pawnshop late at night before we left North Carolina. Some little shop in the ghetto, with bars up and down the windows, and I said to myself, if the cops show up, we're going to have to jet. Up the road, left turn, hide in that alley between the two abandoned buildings you'd miss if you weren't looking.

Richie broke the glass with the end of his gun, slid his hand through the bars, and unlocked the door. The alarm went off, and I sat there sweating, but

I breathed. Kept myself calm. They've done this before, I said to myself. They know what they're doing.

We got a flat tire in Kentucky, and someone pulled over to help us replace it. He asked us where we were headed. Richie told him it was a weekend trip. Finally got some vacation time, but before we know it, it's back to the office.

I don't think most people consider how many folks they walk by on an average day have committed burglary or arson, run a heist. Committed murder. But every time I walked by somebody after I got involved with The D3vil's Krew, that's all I could think about.

By our fourth run, I didn't feel the dread burning my veins like I did before. I was still anxious, but the anxiety I felt before with the sweat from my palms soaking the wheel, waiting for a gunshot or police sirens, took on a different form. Went from being the feeling you get when you're cowering before a monster to the feeling you get when you're standing before it with your fists balled.

Then I felt like I had it, and on our fifth run, when we drove away with a load of money that wasn't ours, I laughed. Instead of fear running through my veins, now there was excitement. It became a game.

Pull up to the building. Look for cameras. Stay out of the light. Listen. Wait for the signal.

I had this.

In Kentucky, we robbed two corner stores and a pawn shop. In Illinois, we broke into a drugstore. The clock's always ticking. The cops are always around whether you see them or not.

Sometimes, we stayed the night in a motel. Sometimes, we stayed at the places of Krew members who lived nearby. Night after night of springs in my back or hard floors. I couldn't sleep anyway.

If you turned on the TV or the radio, you might hear a story about a corner store or a drugstore, convenience store that was robbed. The suspects drove a white van. And what should've made me hide or quit energized me. Felt like I was about to run a marathon. I was about to jump out of an airplane, go paragliding. Yet at the same time, I couldn't stand in the shower water without my heart racing, my breath getting short, and the nagging in the back of my head arguing with the voice that prepped me for our next run.

It's going to come to an end. It's all going to come to an end. You're going to fuck up. You're going to get caught.

You're going to get in there and you're going to get out. You got the best damn crew there is. They're veterans. Sixteen years. They've been at it sixteen years.

It's wrong. It's immoral. It's going to get you in trouble. It's going to get you prison time.

It's going to get you paid.

In Ohio, I did what I always did. Midnight. We're at a drugstore. We ain't the only folks there. There're three cars in the parking lot. I pull the van into a tight alley where the walls look like they're closing in on you if you stare at them too long.

It looked like a small town. Not even a mile back, there were trees. The buildings looked like some of them had been around for a hundred years, and a lot were boarded up, falling apart. It had a divided road that separated our building from the building across the street, and I had to go all the way down to turn around just to pull up in front of the drugstore. But this was the building they chose, for reasons—I guess that was for The D3vil's Krew to know when they decided on that shit.

My heart was racing, my pulse was spazzing, but it felt more like I'd drank three energy drinks than the fear I felt before.

Tonight was different.

"Pull up," Richie called me on the headset. "We're heading out."

I put the van in drive.

"Wait," Arin said. "Stay where you are. There's a cop on the road, but he's on the other side of the street. Just give it a minute."

I looked at Arin through the rearview mirror. "Did someone call them?"

"I don't think so."

I put the van in park.

"Alright," Arin said. "He's gone."

Richie paged me on the speaker. "Put it in drive, Nolan—"

"Wait. Looks like he's coming back around."

"What the hell, Nerd?"

"Lay low," Arin said. "He's heading this way, but he's in the other lane. He doesn't have his blinker on. I don't think he's gonna stop here—Really? That's not even legal."

"What's going on?"

"He just turned in from the wrong lane."

"Jesus fucking Christ. Start the van, Nolan."

"No. Don't. You come out of there right now, he'll see you."

"Goddamn. Start the van."

"You wanna turn this into a shootout?"

"If we got no choice."

I squeezed my eyes shut. "What do you want me to do? You want me to pull up?"

"Yes," Richie said.

"Stay put," Arin said.

My chest tightened. "You told me to do what Arin said."

"Now I'm telling you to pull up."

"If you guys come out now," Arin said, "we're done. Shit."

The cop rolled past the alley I was hiding in. I inched up just enough to see him. He parked by the side of the building.

"Maybe we can go through the emergency exit," Richie said.

"On the other side of the building?" Arin shook his head. "He's parked too close. He'd probably see you."

Two cops got out.

"Damn. They're going in."

"We gotta go—"

"Stay put. Richie, get behind a counter—or—damn—find a place to hide."

"What then, jackass? You don't think one of these assholes aren't gonna alert the cop?"

I took a deep breath, exhaled. Don't panic. Exhaled. Gather your thoughts. There's a two-way street. Trees less than a mile from here. You saw a slight right that was easy to miss. The emergency exit's on the opposite side from where you're parked.

Get rid of the cop car.

"Say, Richie," I said, "go out through the emergency exit."

One cop opened the door for the other.

I pulled my pistol from my jacket and floored it.

"What are you doing?" Arin clenched the seat.

I slammed the brake in front of the cop car, rolled down the window, and popped a bullet in the tire.

Before I could get my foot back on the gas, gunshots went off inside the building. One. Two. Three. Pop! Pop! Pop! That one second felt like time stopped and everything froze but the gasping of my breath and the pounding in my chest. I skidded into the alley, slammed the brake, jerking the van and me and Arin and every stolen sack of money forward. I looked through the rearview mirror. I didn't see nothing but scattering dust and a flickering light. My heart sank, but there was my crew, all five of them, hooded up, masks and guns and a bag full of money, hightailing it out of the building with two cops on their asses.

Pop! Pop! One bullet broke through a drainpipe. Another just missed the windshield. My crew jumped in the van, and I sped off before they closed the door.

The cops were probably calling in backup, but they didn't have a car they could drive. I had a head start. I slammed the gas. Head forward, turn left. Wrong way. I swerved and just missed a head-on collision with a truck.

Police sirens. Blue and red lights.

Turn right.

The trees are up ahead. Slight right. They haven't found us yet. You got this.

I sped through the trees and slammed the brakes. Cut the lights. I couldn't promise we weren't visible, but the only thing we could see outside those windows was the shadowed bodies of tree trunks and a darkness that swallowed everything.

I didn't say anything. Nor did Richie. Arin didn't. Pip didn't. Jackie, Mike, Axe—nobody said jack shit.

But everybody was looking out the window, waiting to see those blue and red lights go by. If they did. Or if they were going to stop and pop us until our brains replaced the seats.

Sweat ran across my eyebrow. My limbs tingled.

Blue and red lights. Like they knew where we were, like they were on us. The lights raced past us, and they were gone. The sirens faded to a distant whistle.

We kept staring out that window long after they disappeared. Everybody did.

Richie broke the silence. "Holy...fucking...shit." He sounded stunned at first, maybe lost or dismayed, dumbfounded, but then he laughed. "Did you see that?" He laughed harder. "Ride or fucking die, baby. Nolan flew us outta here like a goddamn bird." He slapped me on the shoulder. "He's a fuckin' bird."

They all laughed, and I wanted to let my ego take over, but if I did, I'd probably do something stupid. "We ain't out of the woods yet." Unintentional puns aside, I waited at least an hour before I started the van up again. I didn't turn on my headlights until I hit the highway. Took a route different than the way we came when we entered the city. Had Arin tell me where the cops were headed on his scanner and hightailed it out of that fucking state before this bird lost any damn feathers. No stops. Just a long road trip up ahead.

I don't know what happened. No one ever told me.

We headed back to New York. We stopped a night in Pennsylvania. Rented a room at a motel off the highway.

Sometimes D3vil's Krew talked about shit I didn't know anything about. Either because I wasn't there when it started, or I just wasn't paying attention.

We didn't need to stop in Pennsylvania, but Richie said he had business to take care of. I said, what business?

Old business. Shit that's been going on a long time. Shit that needs to be dealt with.

He told me to drive them out to some old, broken town where there was as much graffiti and trash on the ground as there was shattered glass and crumbling brick. Bullet holes and boarded buildings. Cigarette butts and beer bottles. Pallets piled up in alleys where trash bags overflowed the garbage bins.

I don't know what it was about. I didn't get it. Some guy they had some beef with. Some guy from way back when. Some guy who ran with some other group of guys who did this thing because that thing. And betrayal. And money.

If you listen to them in the back of the van, you could pick up some stuff when they were talking amongst themselves. But it didn't make no sense.

"Stop the van." Richie had me pull up behind some abandoned parking garage in an area that had been fenced off and had only one streetlight. There was a white SUV parked beneath it. Richie and the rest of them got out. I stayed in the van and kept it running.

I'm going to make this story short.

There were some other guys and there were my guys. Those guys stayed in the SUV. My guys were on foot. The guy in the driver's seat said something to Richie. Richie said something to him. Then they started shouting.

"Bullshit!"

"Fuck you!"

"I'll kill you, motherfucker!"

Richie pulled a Glock and pointed it at the guy's head. I couldn't tell if the guys in the backseat had guns out, too, but they had to deal with the rest of the Krew's guns making eye contact with them.

"I don't want this to get messy," Richie said.

"Fine," the driver said.

They put their guns away.

Someone in the back shouted, "Fuck you!"

"Drop it!"

"Traitor!"

The door swung open, they tossed that guy out onto the ground, and sped onto the road. Disappeared. He got off the ground and hightailed it. Everybody but Richie chased after him. They jumped him. Punched him. Kicked him. He put up a good fight, punched Jackie in the face, kicked Mike in his side, but everybody else put a gun to his head. He threw his arms up.

"Fuck you!" he spat.

Then Richie walks up. "Get out of the way." They made way for him, and he tucked his gun in the back of his pants.

He punched the guy in the face. The guy stumbled back, and Richie punched him to the ground. He got up and charged at Richie. Richie whipped out his gun, shot him in the thigh.

"Fuck!" The guy fell on his knees and clenched his wound. He slowly lifted his head. "Go to hell."

Richie laughed. "I've been there, baby. I'm the motherfuckin' Devil. I'm the Devil *and* God, It's my fucking will, now, bitch, and I'm about to pronounce judgment."

Fast as I blinked, he popped him. Pop! Pop! Pop! And when I thought it was done. Pop! Pop! Two in the chest, two in the stomach, one in the face.

I stopped breathing.

Richie stood over the body with the gun hanging in his hand. "Clean this shit up 'cause I ain't going back to jail."

# 16

*I watched someone die yesterday.*

*He wore blue jeans and a hoody. He looked like everyone else. I don't know what his name was. Or if he had a family or any friends, but he lay on the ground, and he stared at me as his blood seeped into the gray cotton of his jacket.*

Sometimes he still stares at me.

The night before we left Pennsylvania, we celebrated the money-making and the end of the "tour" at a strip club.

We went to a strip club the night after we tossed a body.

Richie smoked a cigar at a table, sitting with Mike and other folks, two women clinging to his arms. Arin stuck money down a dancer's stocking. Jackie made out with a chick on her lap. Axe didn't come because, as he worded it, unlike us animals, he respected the opposite sex. Pip was nowhere to be found, and me—I sat alone.

The music bumped, and I didn't like it because I couldn't unhear gunshots everywhere I went. At some point, everybody's going to be dead. I am, everyone in that club. I had to wonder, how many of us will die at the hands of someone else?

The drinks were good, the ladies were beautiful, especially for a cheap club like that, but no amount of alcohol could remove me from the moment I heard those gunshots. No matter how the pink and purple lights flashed, hips

rocked, breasts flopped—crystal heels and fishnet stockings, alcohol and cigarette smoke—it was all red. Everything was red. I was not there. I was not in my
body. My flesh, my muscles, my mind were numb. Pale. And the flashbacks hit.

Richie picks up the bullet shells. Axe and Mike grab the body. They're going
to put it in the van. The same van I'm driving.

Richie tells me where to go. I can't move. I can't breathe.

Ay, Richie says. Nolan, you got this?

Huh?

I asked, do you got this?

I hesitate, and he looks at me for a long time. When he does that, I don't
know if he trusts me anymore. I don't know if he's thinking I'm unreliable. I
don't know if he's trying to figure me out.

I nod, tell him yeah, I'm good.

I couldn't have fun knowing what I did. I could try. I could try to forget about
it, be like everyone else, close my eyes and let the music shake my bones. Get lost
in the curves of the female form. Drink until I'm dizzy. I could pretend. But
the reality was, I was still in the van. We were still riding down the road with a
corpse in the back. I still saw someone die right in front of me. God! The road
was bumpy; the street was empty. That guy wasn't moving anymore.

We were at a strip club smoking and drinking, throwing money and watching
dancers like everyone else. How many people here have killed someone?

There were guns and a bag of dirty money in the van.

Those girls were being showered with dirty money. I bought a drink with
dirty money.

I watched someone get shot last night.

Everybody's body was just a body—the patrons, the dancers, the bartenders,
mine. Everybody's body was just a body. But money was money. A body stops
moving, but money never stops flowing. That guy was moving. He was running.
He was fighting. Then he wasn't.

Holy shit, I watched someone die last night. I was involved. I was an accom-
plice.

The van ride was quiet when we picked up the body. Nobody said a damn thing. It wasn't like that on the way there. They chattered behind me. They had conversations about mundane shit like movies and overrated bands.

"Another shot." That drink wasn't going to do shit for me.

"You okay, kid?"

"Yeah. Long day. Thanks."

"You've had a lot of drinks. Hope you don't plan on driving tonight."

"You got a cigarette?" I hadn't smoked a cigarette in almost a year. The flavor of that thing tasted like honey and regret. It wrote the angel's names in cursive. It smelled like the Devil's cooking. "Thanks."

"Hey, take it easy."

If Pops knew where I was, what I was doing, what I'd been up to, there's no telling what he'd say. I'd say, there was a rabbit hole, Pops. One day you're standing outside that thing, but the next thing you know, you tripped, searching for a way out of your situation, and you don't even realize it until you look up and you say, well shit.

I smoked that cigarette until the end burned my fingertips, and when my fingers smelled like nicotine and what was left of the cigarette crumbled into the ashtray, I left that joint.


"Do you ever wonder what song will be in your head when you die?" I didn't realize I asked that out loud.

"All the time." Richie had one foot on the dash.

The crumbling pavement had no other cars on it, a road with sparse street-lights that lit it just enough to prove it led you one way into the dark. Just beneath the blot of navy-blue clouds, the road broke off like it was the end of the earth, but every time you reached the end of the earth, just more road up ahead.

"When was the first time you killed someone?"

"When I was fourteen." Richie's voice was probably the calmest I'd ever heard it, had that gravelly fry. "It was an accident. Some bullshit I got into, me and some guys I used to hang out with. There was another group of guys we had a beef with. I didn't know nothing about that shit because I was a pubescent twat at the time. I just did what they told me. They jumped us, and we wound up throwing fists. I had my gun on me, and I told that dude I'd shoot. I didn't have the balls to actually do shit like that yet. I was talking out my ass, but he tried to get the gun from me, and it went off."

"You've been in this gig a long time, huh?"

"I've been in this gig since I was twelve."

"Why?"

"Pfft. You're asking me."

I nodded.

"I guess when you're a kid and the only thing you know about the world is that you're poor and your ma's crazy, shit just happens."

"I get that—"

"And it don't even gotta be a conscious decision. It's like, one minute you're fucking around with, like, Ninja Turtles or something—I dunno. Normal kid shit. Then the next thing you know, your ass is out selling dope on the corner, hoping you can rake in enough because your ma's struggling to keep the lights on. How does that happen?" He shrugged. "I don't fuckin' know. But it does."

"What about your pops?"

"Never met him."

"How come your ma hated you so much?"

He chuckled through his teeth. "She was a crazy bitch. Crazy, crazy bitch. Haha. Wasn't no telling what you were gonna get out of that lady. One minute, she's reading you a bedtime story, the next, she's jerking your arm out of its socket because you spilled cereal on the floor. Knocking you upside the head with household objects, and you don't even know what you did.

"She held down a job for a while. At least fourteen years, I think. Used to strip down at Club Kisses. Know why she got fired? She wasn't Best Girl anymore. Lost the title to some blonde with fake tits. Said, why choose silicone when these double D's are real? Ol' Ma! She was Best Girl for, like, ten fucking years, and when they gave it to that other girl, holy shit," he laughed, "she went Mike Tyson on her ass. In the bathroom. Slammed her face into a fucking sink. I told you that bitch was crazy." He stopped laughing, stopped smiling altogether. He cleared his throat. "I don't think she hated me. I think she had her ups and downs, short temper. Maybe some chemical imbalances going on in there or some bullshit that happened to her when she was a kid. Plus, living where we were living, she probably just needed somebody to talk to but never got it. She tried." He paused. "I think she tried."

"Why'd you start The D3vil's Krew?"

He took his leg off the dash, sat up straight. "The first time I got shot, I was seventeen years old. I died on the hospital bed. Woke up in Hell. The Devil looks me in the eye, and he says, 'Son, you ain't done yet.' Showed me my whole life before he sent me back to this good-for-nothin' world, but he was right. I wasn't done. And there's still work to do.

"After Ma got fired from her job, she had to go back into prostitution. Wound up picking up some cop who dragged her ass off to the cage. I wasn't gonna let 'em send me to live with my cunt of a grandma, so one day, I knocked on Mike's door, and I said, 'Mike, let's get outta here. Let's go. 'Cause you got nothin' to go back to. I got nothin' to go back to. Let's stop pretending we fit in. Like we don't see the world for what it is. Let's quit simpin' after the pussy of the American dream and get outta here.' And we did. Lived in some hole in a wall somewhere where the alley cats all looked coked up. But I still remembered what the Devil told me. 'Son, you ain't done.' You bet your ass I wasn't. Told Mike what we oughta do. 'Look at this motherfuckin' world, Mike. Feast your eyes on the have and the have-nots. The game is fuckin' rigged. We were born at the bottom of the fuckin' food chain, and those fat fuckin' cats are gonna keep eating more and more people like you and me until the whole goddamn solar system is revolving around their asses. And what are we gonna do? We're gonna keep bending over and taking it up the ass like we're oblivious to what's going on out there? Pretty damn stupid. Pretty fuckin' weak.' Truth is, those motherfuckers write the rules. Know what that means we gotta do? We gotta play our own game."

He dug around in his pocket until he pulled out a pack of cigarettes. "They say it's a dog-eat-dog world, but I don't believe that's true. I think that's some bullshit they tell you 'cause they wanna make it look like the game's equally matched. My ass." Coils of white smoke twisted across the windshield and burned nicotine into my nostrils. He rolled down his window. "Everybody knows the wolves are eating the chihuahuas. Takes a chihuahua to bite back." He snapped his lighter shut.

I nodded. "I get that—"

"So we start recruiting more people. It's how it goes. Enough people have enough of somebody's shit, they look for a solution. And Nerd, he's probably about the best goddamn thing that ever happened to D3vil's Krew. I get a phone call from him before I ever meet him, and I say, 'Who's this?' Says his name is Arin, and he can build a bomb. I'm skeptical because I don't even know how this son of a bitch found me. But he wasn't lying. He can make bombs; he can make bullets—that son of a bitch has the kind of skills that take you from a scavenging street rat to a planning street rat." He laughed. "We get Jackie and Axe, Pip, who's just a kid, but he's got balls. People die. People go away, but we spread. I got my crew, and I got a million other Krew members saying fuck you to anyone who tells 'em they ain't shit."

"Did you ever have a dream?"

"What?"

"Like, a dream?" I shrugged. "I used to wanna be a writer. Guess I still do—"

"Yeah. Thought I'd be a lyricist when I was a kid."

"A lyricist? You like writing music?"

"Used to. You can't make money doing shit like that in this world. Not unless you're, like, Kanye West or some hot shot."

"That what's on your chest? Your arm?"

He looked down at his tatts. "Yeah. I wrote 'em a long time ago."

"They're pretty good."

"Thanks."

"Do you still write?"

He paused. "Sometimes."

I nodded. "Sometimes I still write."

I thought he'd be bored of me or wouldn't be interested in what I had to say, but then he asked, "What do you write? What's your genre?"

I parted my lips, but my answer got stuck in my throat.

He raised his voice. "What do you write?"

"Whatever comes to mind. Sometimes, I write about my family. Sometimes, I write about me. Maybe an old guy out on the steps. I guess I write about people. Yeah. That's what I write about. People."

"You ever publish anything?"

"No."

"Why not?"

"I don't know. Maybe I will one day."

He took a drag and tapped the ash out the window. "Cool."

"I agree with you, though. Can't make money off that kind of shit—"

"I think we need more of that." He flicked his cigarette out the window and crossed his legs over the dash. "We need more artists..."

I forgot Mike was back there until he said, "Amen to that."

I cracked a smile.

Richie looked to the back of the van and chuckled. "We need more artists, more writers, more musicians. Artists say the kind of things nobody knows how to verbalize." He sighed. "Hell, that's why I do it."

I nodded. "Maybe that's why I do too." That might've been more for me than anyone else.

"Crazy shit happens, it gets recorded and lives forever. And crazy shit happens in this business—I never told you about the time some jackass ran me over with a truck. Huge brawl. This motherfucker thought he'd kill me, but I got back up."

"Jesus. Then what?"

"I beat his ass, that's what."

I chuckled.

"Two fractured ribs, a broken collar bone...still beat his ass to dirt."

I never thought Richie could get me to smile. "You're lying."

"Swear to God."

Mike laughed.

Richie turned around. "You remember that? Don't you, Mike?"

"Crazy shit." Mike laughed.

"See? Mike remembers. I went to jail, and that dude got to walk," Richie said. "That's how bad I beat his ass."

"And you're still telling the story."

"I don't die easily."

"I got a question. I read something back at the church. Some sort of history book, I guess, for D3vil's Krew."

"Yeah-yeah. I know what you're talkin' about."

"Said something about a church pastor that went bankrupt. I'd heard that story before."

"Yeah."

"I didn't know D3vil's Krew had anything to do with it."

"Shit. Long story. Basically, you had some rich whack job pastor that wanted to boost his success, start a megachurch, sell some shit, you get it. But instead of getting a loan, and I got an idea why, he decided he was going to go through us to get the money. 'You sell a bunch of drugs, we split the price.' I said, 'Where am I gonna get the money to get that many drugs?' He said he'll take care of that, but in the end, we both prosper.

"You're probably thinkin' what I'm thinkin'. Why doesn't the dude get the Italian Mafia or Yakuza or some fancy shit like that to work with him? I'll tell you why. 'Cause they ain't damn near stupid enough to fall for that kind of shit. Go out, get some trash street gang run by some twenty-something who's not seeing nothin' but dollar signs in front of his eyes. If I'd known then what I know now...

"Anyway, this guy becomes a multimillionaire televangelist overnight. They don't even know the only reason for his success is that he made a deal with the Devil."

"He didn't hold his end of the deal? Did he?"

He shook his head. "I told him he was done."

"I read what happened."

"The Lord giveth, the Lord taketh away."

He stopped talking and I stopped talking while the van bumped along the road. That intermission that happens between conversations that leaves you thinking about what you said. Don't know if there's a reason for it. Maybe it's just a natural part of human interaction.

"If there's anything to learn from that story," Richie said, "it's don't let anybody fuck you over. I don't care if they got five dollars or five billion."

I glanced at Richie's cigarette. "Mind sharing one of them?"

"I thought you were done smokin'."

"I thought so, too."

He tossed the pack in my lap.

I picked it up, popped it open with my thumb, grabbed one with my lips.

"Keep writing, Bird." He handed me the lighter. "Maybe it'll move somethin'."

# 17

Pops used to say money is sweeter when you can taste the fruits of your labor.

I never asked for anything for free. Not as an adult. But with my new lifestyle, what was labor? How did we put it into terms?

About a week after "tour," Richie had me come by the church and meet him at the conference table. Just me and him. He had the briefcase full of money on the table. A roll of cash lying in front of him.

"Here." He slid it to me. "Five percent."

I took the band off it, counted it, and lifted my head to see his face, but he wasn't looking at me.

I wrapped the money back in the band. Pushed out my chair.

He closed the briefcase.

I got out of my seat, almost slid the money in my pocket but stopped. "Sorry."

"What?"

"I thought there'd be more."

"Five percent. Like we said."

"I know, but—"

"What?"

I rubbed the back of my neck.

"You ain't satisfied?"

"It's not like I bailed halfway."

"All you did was drive the van. You get your share for what you contributed. Five percent."

"I got you guys out of trouble."

"Yeah. Part of the job."

"I went through a lot."

"We all did."

"Come on, Richie. It ain't fair."

His face hardened. "You accusing me of shorting you? I don't cheat my guys out of what's owed to 'em. That ain't-my-code. All you did was drive the fucking van. When you get out and make some real shit happen, then we can negotiate. 'Til then, five percent. Don't argue with me, or you can walk out of here with nothin'. Dismissed."

What makes someone a bad person?

Is it the things they do? The way they think? Or the stuff they say? If I can sit down and have a conversation with a murderer, and that murderer feels the same way as me about everything in life, whose sin's the biggest? Is it theirs because they're a murderer, or am I just as bad for thinking like one? Would I kill? Could I kill? How human will I be if I do? Maybe I already killed. And then you got to ask yourself, what the hell is a sin? I've committed a million of them since the day I was born, and the only person who's ever shown compassion for me when I couldn't forgive myself was the Devil. It's about then you start to realize you're the villain.

Hiding a van behind a bunch of trees while the cops flew by wasn't enough to impress Richie. I'd have to step up the game.

I did some things I never thought I'd do in my entire fucking life. I got a gun. I loaded it. I put a black mask on my head. I went out. By myself. Me and my bike. Dead of night. Waited. For folks who weren't paying attention. Folks who were alone. I discriminated. I didn't break into any cheap-looking homes or mom and pop shops. I didn't steal purses from single moms. I didn't mug any dudes in tattered pants and holey shoes. Something in me wouldn't let me do that.

But when a Mercedes Benz pulled up to an ATM, I got out my Glock and held it to a guy's head, and I did it without letting him know my heart was pounding, and my nerves were bouncing, my breathing was short, and my face was sweating.

"The money. Give it to me. Now."

He didn't hesitate. After he hopped back in his car and drove off, I said sorry. I don't know to who, but maybe somebody was listening.

I broke into stores, not unlike the way I saw the Krew do on "tour," checked for cameras, kept my head down, broke the glass with my gun, and if an alarm went off, I raced out of there like fire was on my ass. If not, I went in there, got what I could and scrammed.

I held a pawnshop worker at gunpoint and got him to give me all the money in the cash register.

Put on a pair of sunglasses, pulled the hood down over my head so you couldn't see the top of my face, slid into a cab, and kept the gun towards his waist. Told him to give me his wallet. I didn't take any credit cards or debits, nothing like that. There were a couple of hundred-dollar bills in there. I only took one and a twenty. Cab driving probably sucks.

After some time, you stop thinking about it. Or you try not to. Just part of the job. Then you start counting your money.

I shot someone.

He wasn't coming after me. He didn't attack me. He didn't ask for it. I pussied out like a bitch.

He was working the convenience store late at night. The only one in there. Barred windows and security cams. I wasn't the first person to rob this place. He was minding his own business. Late night, probably an eight-hour shift. Maybe twelve. Having to put up with angry customers. Having to put up with bad kids. Having to put up with thieves like me. Just part of the job.

I took a deep breath before I went in there. Parked my bike in the shadows. Put my mask on, pulled my hood over my head, kept my hand on the gun tucked away in my jacket.

I marched in there half confident, half coward. Pulled the gun out and pointed it at his face.

He threw his arms in the air.

"Empty the cash register. Hurry!"

He shook and stared at me a long time, in my eyes, a gaze. I couldn't tell if it was fear or if he was trying to talk to me without any words, but he did what I said. He opened the cash register. Never stopped glancing up and meeting my eyes.

I thought I could channel Richie. "Hurry the fuck up!" But it didn't have the solidity and brashness of Richie's voice. It had the anxiety and unsureness of mine. "I said hurry up."

He took out the money. Put it out on the counter, twenties, fifties, hundreds. When I reached to grab it, he made a quick move. Reached down under the counter.

I didn't think. I shot him. In the arm. He fell back, and everything inside me—around me, beneath me, above me—stopped. The earth stopped spinning. The cars stopped driving. The world went silent. My ears stopped working. My muscles, my limbs, my lungs, my heart. I was paralyzed. Numb.

I shot somebody.

He lay on the ground, clenching his arm. I grabbed the money, stuffed it in my bag. I started running but turned around. Looked at the door, looked back at him. "Sorry...I'm sorry." I ran out the door.

I heard about it on the news.

*"Police are searching for an assailant who robbed a convenience store last night..."*

He suffered an injury to the arm, but he lived. And his wife and his kids were happy to see him.

I had a bag of dirty money. I brought it to the church the next day, found Richie sitting at the conference table, and dropped it in front of him. He looked at the bag and looked at me like he didn't know who, what, or when.

I unzipped it and pushed it to him.

## 18

Pops used to say that drugs were a gateway to Hell.

Windows and balconies were decorated with turkey signs and red and yellow leaves on the day that Richie had me meet him at the conference table.

"I was gonna have Axe and Mike go with you, but I needed them somewhere else. I think you can handle this on your own."

I nodded, but I didn't feel as confident as I hoped.

He pushed a black bag across the table. "Show them the money. Let 'em count it. Make sure you bring back all the drugs. If something ain't right, give me a call. We'll handle the rest."

When I got my first job as a delivery driver, I feared I'd get lost on my route. Seems overwhelming the first time you do it. You got a GPS. You got things you need to deliver. Stops you need to make, and you got to do it in a certain amount of time. Fuck up too much, and it's your job. Job? It's your livelihood.

I was driving with a fake license plate. Or a stolen one. The D3vil's Krew never kept the same license plate. I never came up with an excuse for the cops if I ever got pulled over.

The Krew checked the brake lights every day, the headlights, the blinkers. They checked the tires, the wing mirrors. Made sure there was no good reason for a cop to pull over the van. So everything else was left up to me.

Once I got pounds of cocaine stuffed into the back of the van, what was I supposed to do if a cop pulled me over? Better drive with caution. The last thing I needed was a wreck.

I almost couldn't find the crumbling remains of what used to be a warehouse. Now, it was just four walls of decay with boarded-up windows. It stood in the middle of a slum where the roads are so narrow you can hardly fit the van. I couldn't even put it into the GPS. GPS couldn't read it. There's another building a few blocks down from it, Richie'd told me. Plug that in, and you should be able to find it from there. Big ol' warehouse, green metal roof, everything's boarded up. Ya can't miss it. Pull up to the back garage door. They know you're coming.

I pulled up to the back garage door, a big rusted metal wall with graffiti all over it. Didn't know if I should call anyone. Didn't know if I should wait. The last thing I wanted was a bunch of dudes coming out with rifles, thinking I was a cop or somebody looking to rob their drugs.

I got a phone call, though, and I answered it.

"Richie sent you?"

I looked around. "Uh, yeah."

Guess Richie gave them my number. Maybe every criminal in New York had my number now.

"Stay where you are. We're gonna open the door."

The garage door rolled up. A guy in a black hoody waved me in from the middle of the doorway. He backed up as I slowly drove inside. He put his hand up, and I stopped.

I didn't open the door right away. I didn't know how many guys there were. Maybe ten. Maybe fifteen. But they all had guns, either in a holster on their waists or a rifle on their backs.

The guy who waved me in tapped on my window.

I rolled it down.

"You got the money?"

I swallowed. "Yeah. It's right here."

"Step out."

They carried out two suitcases and put them down in front of me. "Open 'em up," he said. "Let him see it."

They unzipped all three bags. I didn't even know what to look for, but he looked at me like he was searching for confirmation.

"Yeah." I nodded. "That's good."

They zipped the suitcases.

All I saw was guns. Not enough places for me to hide. Too much wall for anyone to hear me scream. If I fucked this up, I was done.

"The money."

I nodded. "Yeah." I went to the van, grabbed the bag off the passenger's seat. I don't know how much money was in there or how much was owed. I did what Richie told me, unzipped it, held it out in front of them.

The guy dug through it, took out a wad, flipped through it.

My heart almost cracked my ribs.

"Alright." He jerked his head. "Load the van."

I handed him the bag.

He smiled, something I didn't think he could do. "Pleasure doing business with you."

I called Pip one weekend to see if he wanted to hang out. He wouldn't have to pay for my beer and pizza like he used to.

He told me he was going to pick up his son that day and asked if I wanted to come along. If I wanted to meet him.

I wasn't much for kids, but as much as Pip talked about that little guy, I kind of did want to see what he was all about.

I walked to Pip's place, and he drove me down an avenue where the town-homes stood three feet away from each other, and the garage doors were tucked up underneath the porches. As suburban as the urbs can get. The street was clean. No graffiti or overflowing trashcans. No discarded pallets or broken glass. No rats or roaches or dirty-looking cats with bloated bellies.

He pulled up to a half-brick-half-wooden house with iron porch rails. "You wanna get out?"

"Yeah," I said. "Why not?"

I got out after him and followed him up the steps to a screen door that had a wreath with pink, white, and yellow flower petals and a wooden plaque that said *Family*. He rang the doorbell.

A woman, barefoot and wearing a floral dress, opened the door. The first thing my eyes fell on was the bump in her belly. A black woman, curvy, big in the chest and hips. Had her hair up in a short fro with a pink bow that wrapped around it.

She smiled when she saw Pip, opened her arms. "Hey, Elijah." She pulled him into a hug and looked at me over his shoulder. Her brows furrowed. She sized me up, and her tone changed. "Who's this?" Like she had a sixth sense about what my relation to him was.

Pip turned to me. "This is Nolan. He's a friend of mine. Nolan," he turned back to her, "this is Tasha. Caelin's mom."

She stepped back and crossed her arms.

"I helped him out in an alley one night when someone tried to mug him. He's a good dude."

"Daddyyyyyyyyy...!" Caelin ran to the door and threw his arms around Pip's legs.

Pip threw him up in the air and caught him in his arms. Caelin kicked his legs and laughed. Tasha's face softened and turned into a smile when she heard her son giggle.

She chuckled. "Where are you going?"

"We're just gonna take him for some ice cream and out to the park afterward."

"Yaaaay," Caelin squeaked. "Ice cweam."

Pip patted him on the back. "Yeah. Doesn't that sound like fun?"

Tasha tilted her head. "Have him back by seven."

"Sure thing."

It got quiet. Pip turned his gaze to the bump in Tasha's belly. "How long?"

"About three more months. I wish she'd hurry up, though," she laughed, "cause this back's been killing me."

"Have you decided what you're going to name her yet?"

She rubbed her belly. "Angelica. I just hope she's as angelic as her name." She nudged his shoulder.

Pip chuckled, then everything got quiet again. "I hope she has your dimples."

Tasha put both hands at the top of her bump. The ring on her left finger glittered like the glint in her eye when she looked away from Pip.

"Ready for the wedding?"

"Yeah. My mom and I went and picked out a dress the other day." She held her hand out in front of her and gazed at her ring. "Mrs. Marcus Anderson. Can you believe that? Already?"

Pip craned his neck. "You've got yourselves a nice place."

"Way better than that shit you and me lived at when we had Caelin."

"Hell, yeah."

They both laughed.

"What the hell was that?" she said. "One hundred square feet? Why was that even legal?"

Pip shrugged. "I dunno."

They both stopped laughing at the same time, sighed in a way that seemed awkward and yet sentimental.

She sighed. "We're talking about me quitting my management job and either working part-time or staying home with the kids full-time. I'm not too sure about it yet, but he's selling real estate, and it's doing good, so I think we'll be alright."

"Hey, congratulations. On everything. On the baby, the wedding..."

She nodded. "Thank you...thank you..."

"I wish you the best."

She leaned against the doorway. "You too." The look in her eyes said she meant it in a different way. "I'm glad you came by. I..."

Caelin'd been staring at me the whole time. Had that look on his face kids get when they want to ask you something but don't know what. "Are you my daddy's fren?"

I never really knew how to talk to kids. I scratched the back of my head. "Yeah. We're friends."

"Will you keep him from being sad? Sometimes my daddy gets really sad, and I hug him, and then he's not sad anymore. But I can't always be there to hug him because Daddy doesn't live with me and Mommy and Marcus, so will you hug him for me so he doesn't get sad?"

Pip petted Caelin's hair. "What are you telling him?"

"Remember," Tasha said, "seven o'clock."

"Seven o'clock." Pip turned to me. "Come on."

I followed him to the car. He put Caelin in the back seat and buckled his seatbelt. Got in after me and started the car.

"Ice cweam!" Caelin clapped his hands.

"Yeah." Pip pulled out onto the road. "Ice cream."

"Elijah," I said.

"Yeah. Hardly hear that anymore."

"Better than The Mad Twink."

"Daddy, what's a twink?"

Pip and I paused before we laughed.

I hadn't done anything wholesome since before I could remember. I'd forgotten what it was like. The last few months, the only thing I could taste was blood and drugs, so a banana split had a zing to it I couldn't explain. Watching Caelin drip chocolate ice cream on his shirt and get more ice cream there than in his mouth, I had to ask myself, was I that before? Did my pops ever take a napkin and tuck it into my shirt, rub the stains off as much as he could the way Pip did for his son? Was I that? And then you look at this kid and you realize there's nothing going on in his life but that ice cream. Cartoons and toys and his pops, who's his whole world, who sells drugs out on the corner and commits armed robbery. But he's his whole world, along with his ma and soon his baby sister. That's it. That's all that matters. And when you see the lights in his eyes, you got to wonder if those lights twinkled and glittered in yours, blinding you to everything outside. You got to wonder, where did they go?

I didn't even like kids, but I was laughing. I was feeling fuzzy. Feeling something in me that almost made me forget I watched a man get shot to death not that long ago. Like I didn't get rid of his body. Almost made me forget the nightmares I had about that. Like I didn't see that man standing next to me during a sleep paralysis episode the other night.

It'd been a long time since I did anything wholesome. I forgot what wholesome was. Maybe I needed it. This little kid sitting across from me, he don't know shit about the world and what's going on in it, and I'm praying to a God that probably doesn't exist that nobody or nothing robs that kid of the vibrance in his laugh or the color in his cheeks or the bright lights making his eyes look like they've got the sun shining out of them. What I'd give to be that again.

We walked to a playground after ice cream. Pip pushed Caelin on a swing for a little while, but I guess Pip got tired. All that ring-around-the-rosy and spinning him on the merry-go-round, I guess, but Caelin still had energy, which reminded me why I never wanted kids.

"Stay where I can see you." Pip collapsed next to me on the bench.

Caelin spun around in circles with his arms out like a helicopter before he ran off to the slide.

Pip sat quietly. He could gaze at his son and all the life would be in his eyes, but they faded to gray the longer he sat as the wind whisked beneath the cracks of our coats and made him shiver.

"How ya doin'?"

"Huh?" He blinked several times. I think he forgot where he was. He nodded. "Good."

"He's a good kid. He's gonna be alright."

"I know."

I tucked my hands into my pockets, watched red and yellow leaves tumble across the pebbles and concrete.

"He's gonna find out one day, though. Even if nobody tells him." He nodded, staring out in front of him either at his son or nothing at all. "When I was his age, my dad, who I guess was actually my step-grandfather. Complicated shit, but he was the biological father of my aunt, who was raised as my little sister. He was my father. Or I saw him as my father. He went to work. He brought home most of the money. He was married to Mom. He taught me to ride my bike. A father—" he swallowed, took a deep breath and balled his lips "—He got put away when I was six. Drugs. I didn't even know that's how he made his money." He shook his head. "He abandoned my family." He looked at me. "He abandoned me."

"You don't gotta continue this lifestyle."

He shook his head. "I'm too far gone." He chuckled. "I was gone when I started. I always credit the Krew for helping me survive, but that's not true. The only thing keeping my ass alive is Caelin. I know that. But if I didn't have the Krew, what would it be? Maybe drugs? Maybe alcohol? I watched my dad come home drunk one day and beat my mom bloody. He wasn't a bad person, yet it happened. I'm not gonna be that to my son." He turned his gaze back to Caelin. "He doesn't know I'm a monster yet."

"We're all a bunch of monsters in this fucked up world. What makes you special?"

"I got a track record."

I sat back and dropped my shoulders. "Someone else is going to raise your kid."

"I'm just happy he can have a healthy, normal life. That's all that matters." He dropped back against the seat and stared up at the sky. "I know the day is going to come when my son is gonna wonder why I'm in prison." He parted his lips but didn't say anything.

The wind blew a whistle that sounded like a broken flute.

"When that day comes, he'll have a family and a home and a father there to support him."

He looked out at the playground. Furrowed his brows. "Cay?" He looked left and right. "Caelin?" He jumped up, raised his voice. "Caelin?"

"He couldn't have gone too far."

Pip hurried onto the playground. "Caelin!"

I got up, looked under the slide and up at the top of the jungle gym. I turned around, and there was a guy holding Caelin up under the monkey bars.

Pip raced past me and grabbed his son. "I told you to stay where I can see you." He clenched his fists and got in the guy's face. "The fuck were you doing?"

The guy threw his arms up. "I was just helping him on the monkey bars."

I ran over and grabbed Pip from behind.

"Sorry," the guy said, "It looked like he needed help."

Pip looked at Caelin, back at the guy.

The guy trembled, hands in the air.

Pip dropped his shoulders and shook his head, embarrassed. He rubbed his temples, took Caelin's hand. "Don't run off like that again."

"Sowry, Daddy. I wanted to pway on the monkey bars."

Pip sighed. "I know. You're not in trouble. I just—" His face turned red. He looked towards the ground like he tried to hide his shame. "It's late. Your mom wants you home by seven."

"Pwease, Daddy. Can we stay a little longer?"

"Nuh-uh. Your mom's gonna have my ass if I don't get you home on time," he picked him up, "and you don't want her to have my ass, do ya?"

Caelin laughed. "Dat's a bad word."

Pip smiled like he'd made an active effort to forget what just happened. "Come on."

He didn't say much on the way back to his ex-girlfriend's. Mumbled some things under his breath that I don't think he noticed I saw.

"That's what happens," he said. "You're always on edge."

He pulled up to the house.

Tasha sat on the porch, and a tall black man in a polo shirt and a pair of thick-framed glasses, dreadlocks pulled back in a bun, handed her a steaming cup. Maybe coffee, maybe hot chocolate.

He sat beside her and placed his hand on top of hers on the armrest. She put her hand on top of her belly and dragged her fingers from the top of her bump to the bottom of its curve.

Caelin jumped out of the car, and Pip got out after him.

Tasha's fiancé waved. "How you doin', man?"

Pip smiled and waved back. He didn't have any contempt in his eyes. No anger, like I guess I thought he would. Just sadness. Maybe envy. Maybe regret.

He kneeled. "Be good for your mother. Alright?"

"Okay, Daddy."

He pulled Caelin into a tight embrace. "I love you."

When Pip stood, he stood slow, watched his son run up the porch steps and the kid's mom telling him to go clean up for dinner. She waved at Pip. He smiled, waved back, and didn't turn to the car until Caelin was in the house. Even then, he waited, the contemplative gaze I'd grown used to holding him still.

He let out a deep breath, got in the car.

I stared at him, his downcast eyes, the slight upward curve of his lips that contradicted them.

He put the key in the ignition. The engine rumbled before it started.

"What?"

I shook my head. "Nothing."

He drove onto the road. "I never had a father who told me he loved me."

I looked out the window and watched the house disappear behind us. Now that I thought about it, my pops never did, either.

# 19

A rowhouse in Queens, red brick, concrete stoops, and rusty steel rails. Turkey vinyl stickers on the windows just above the air vents and AC units. Yellow roots climbing through the pavement cracks and trees whose leaves had dried and shriveled, crumbled up and drifted to the ground standing half naked like the molting fledglings that don't hang out that time of year.

I'd gotten used to carrying a gun with me. So much so that I started grabbing it the way I grabbed my wallet before leaving the house. It became a habit. But I made sure I didn't bring nothing but a notebook.

I climbed the stoop and knocked on the door. I didn't think I'd actually do this, but at one point in my life, I was supposed to be a writer, and I found that I wasn't writing the way I used to. Sad, with all the inspiration floating around out there. But money. And stress. Time. You find things start to change as you do, growing and learning.

I rang the doorbell.

She had sweatpants on. A cropped shirt, showing the little bit of fat on her belly that sat on top of the hem of her pants. A scar that ran just below her belly button.

"Nolan?" She said. "Elijah told me you'd be coming." She had age lines from her nose to her mouth, but they were faded, like they knew they were too early to be on a face that young. She had eyes like Pip's and a smile like Pip's. Pip, if he were a woman.

She stepped back and opened the door all the way.

"Thanks." I nodded and walked in.

It smelled like coffee and sage.

"Tamera. Right?"

She nodded. "Yeah. You can sit in the dining room. Did you want a coffee? Tea?"

"That's alright. Thanks." I walked into the dining room and sat at a round, wooden table with a floral tablecloth and two seats. The only thing that separated the kitchen and dining room from the living room was a half-wall. Everything was floral. Floral couch, floral curtains, a floral wreath by the kitchen doorway. Cheap carpet with nicks in it, cracks in the walls, stains on the wood of the kitchen floor. Stacked bowls and glasses by the sink, a collage of photos on the fridge. One of her and Pip together. That one was framed on the wall. Plaques on the walls, posters, people standing in front of the sunlight at the edge of a cliff or atop of a hill with their fists in the air, *Growth, Strength, Courage Doesn't Always Roar.*

She brewed herself a coffee and took a seat across from me. "Got any plans for Thanksgiving?"

"Not sure." I opened my notebook on the table, pulled my pen out of the spine. "If you're not comfortable with this we don't have to do it. I just wanna hear your story."

"I'm good."

"Thanks for this. When Pip told me about your story, I couldn't stop thinking about it. I think a lot of people will feel the same way."

"Are you going to publish it?"

I parted my lips but paused, shrugged. "To be honest, I'm not all that sure what I wanna do just yet. I wanna be true to your story. For sure. But I don't know how I wanna approach it."

"You're not the first person to interview me. I've been in a documentary."

"Yeah?"

"Uh-huh. Pregnant Kids. You can find it online."

I closed my notebook, crossed my arms, and leaned against the table. "First, I feel like I gotta tell you I'm sorry. Growing up must've been rough."

She shook her head. "The past is the past. I wouldn't take back anything. I've got Elijah, even if it put me in the hospital for all the back problems."

"What happened to his father? Do you know?"

She shook her head. "Last I heard from him, he and his family moved to New Jersey. I think."

"You don't plan on having any more kids?"

She shook her head. "To be honest, the thought of pregnancy again is sort of a nightmare."

"Because of the back pain? And surgeries?"

"I was ten."

I nodded. "I gotcha."

"We didn't have enough money to pay for all the surgery, and it just put us in even more debt."

"I'm sorry."

"But maybe...I dunno. Can I say something?"

"Go for it."

"I was not his mother. Because of circumstances. But I wish I could've been—not with my situation—but if I'd been an adult and married and had financial stability." She took a sip of coffee and set the cup back down with a thud. "I know what he does. He's been at it even when I was popping pills. And," she shrugged, "I don't think he knows anything else." She sighed. "I've got a nephew who's my grandson who came into his life as unexpected as *he* came into *mine*. I think I told you wrong. I said I wouldn't take anything back. I would. If I could go back, I'd have given Elijah up to a family with a nice house and two loving parents that could keep him on track."

She lifted her cup with both hands, turned her head towards the window. I couldn't tell if she was even talking to me anymore. "He got all caught up in drugs and money—and that Richie."

"Yeah—"

"I hate that fucking man."

Coffee steam rippled across the red in her hardened eyes.

She reached across the table and put her hand on mine. "I'm sorry." She smiled. "This was supposed to be about my pregnancy."

"You're good." I took out my notebook. "Tell me about your life growing up. After giving birth."

"It was hard. Not much space, lots of siblings. No money. Making mistakes. Lots of mistakes. I hated my grandmother for years after what she did to me, but then when I think about it, and I put myself in her shoes, I ask myself, would I have done the same?"

"Did you ever have a dream?"

She smiled. "No one's ever asked me that before. I guess you've got one." She glanced at my notebook.

"Used to."

"I think...my dream..." she rubbed her lips together. "I would give everyone in my life a home. My siblings, my mother, my nephew, his mother, even my grandmother. A real home, wherever they wanna live. Whatever size or shape, however many rooms. They could call it their own. Have protection from the world, a sense of normalcy. Have something to put their name on. Maybe some satisfaction. If everybody was satisfied," she wagged her finger, "I think some lives might've been saved." She fell back against the seat. "Don't know what it would take, but I think I'm still dreaming."


The D3vil's Krew got together for dinner on Thanksgiving. I didn't even know they celebrated Thanksgiving.

I thought about hanging with them, and I probably should've. Maybe that was where I belonged, but I got an invite from my sister. After it's been a minute since you've seen the fam, you get curious. Even when you grow up feeling like the black sheep of the family, left out in the rain because you ain't as good as they wanted you to be, didn't turn out the way you're supposed to, you got to wonder what they're going to say, how they're going to look at you, the kind of questions they'll ask. And they're family. Even if sometimes they don't act like it, they're still family, and it's almost an obligation.

My sister held dinner at her house in Staten Island. Every time I got a look at the white planks, cobble steps, balconies and bay windows, I couldn't believe we were related.

I brought a pie I didn't even bake. Axe put it together for me, and I didn't tell nobody that the whole night, only that a friend baked it.

When I rang the doorbell, I felt a nervous cramp in my chest I hadn't felt since asking out my crush to the middle school dance, only I didn't have to fear my boner was showing. But even that might've been less embarrassing than being around a bunch of rich people, knowing you're the younger brother whose only skill in life was crime. And driving vans.

"Glad you could make it." Katelyn reached out and hugged me.

"Hey, sis." I stepped inside. I didn't even know what kind of tile I was standing on, but it was white and glossy and more than anything I could afford. I handed her the pie.

"Looks good. Did you bake it?"

"Nuh-uh. Got it from a friend."

I followed her to a dining room that was separate from the breakfast room and kitchen, which I never had growing up or any place I ever lived in. A glass table with golden legs that crisscrossed underneath it like some kind of abstract sculpture and round lavender chairs. That modern look. I didn't want to see Pops, but there he was, standing around with a wine glass in his hand like he came from some sort of prestigious background. Like he was used to this kind of thing. Like he was born into it. No, Pops. You grew up poor like I did. You're working class. Been working class since you were old enough to lift a hammer. What little scraps you got were thrown to you after you busted your ass for more than sixty hours a week. And Ma, in an evening gown I know she bought from a discount store, linking arms with Pops, talking to some other people I may or may not have ever met. I asked myself why I came.

If the Krew were here, what would they do? Maybe they'd steal a vase or something. Set some shit off over the last slice of pie. Get themselves kicked out.

Pops saw me and threw open his arms, wrapped me in a hug and patted my back. "If it isn't my good-for-nothin' son." He said it playfully. I know he didn't really mean it, but he meant it. "Where you been all these years? Why don't you ever call?"

"I've been busy."

"Your sister tells me you found a new job."

"Uh...yeah. I've been working for a drug company. I do all the delivery. Y' know? Delivering drugs to people's houses."

"How's that working for ya?"

"It's taking care of the bread."

"That's what it's about. See? All that worry you had. Turns out, you didn't need my money after all." He shook my shoulder. "Let's just hope you keep this one."

"I'm in good standing."

I hadn't seen my brother-in-law in years. He reminded me I was under-dressed, walking up to me in a white cotton shirt and plaid blazer, leather loafers. I guess they all did. I didn't get the message I wasn't supposed to wear a dingy leather jacket and jeans, biker boots that looked like they'd taken a couple of trips through the jungle. But the accumulation of everybody's cologne rolled into a cloud pretty much smothered whatever funky smell I was carrying after riding a motorcycle.

"Nolan." His smile was whiter than the hanky he kept in his front pocket.

I waved. "What's up, Steve."

"How long's it been?"

"Beats me."

"We're real sorry about the money."

"Nah." I shook my head. "Don't worry about it."

Katelyn came up behind him and linked arms with him. Yesterday, she linked arms with a clumpy pillow and slept on a holey, spring mattress. He wouldn't even know what that was like. What did those two even talk about? How'd they even meet?

Or maybe she just followed the rules. Did everything right. Go to college, Pops used to tell her. You're a pretty girl. You're young, you're vibrant, you can get any kind of man you want. Find one that makes a lot of money. Know what a woman's nature is? To take care of a house, to take care of a husband, to take care of a child. Don't listen to all this new age bullshit, Katelyn, I'm your pops. I've lived in this world, and I know what's best for you. Get you a well-adjusted man, sweetheart. One that goes to church, keeps his hair trimmed, his beard groomed, his pants pressed. You take care of him, he'll take care of you. Because that's what a man is about.

Maybe I should've followed the rules. Maybe I'd have been picking up six-figure checks instead of drugs every night.

Katelyn called me as much as I called her. But I remember when she wanted to be a photographer.

Steve tapped the side of his glass with a fork. "We're about to start dinner, but before that, why don't we go around the room and say what we're thankful for."

"Family," Pops said. "We're all here. We're all alive, my beautiful wife, my daughter. *Both* my sons. Even if one only calls when he needs money." Everyone chuckled and looked at me. Pops raised his glass. "There's nothing more important than family."

They all clapped, but I hesitated before I did. If I told myself that last line was directed at me, I'd have felt like an accusative dick, but sometimes Pops did shit like that. Or maybe I was a dick.

As we went around the room, everyone shared their thoughts on gratitude. Career successes, new cars, vacation trips, all kinds of stuff. Stuff that I said I'm not going to be a little shit about. If I had money and opportunities, I'd brag too. I'd be telling everybody, hey, I got this new car. A new Lambo, a new Bugatti. I got a penthouse that overlooks Manhattan. I just took a trip to Hawaii where I had cute girls in hula skirts fan me while I drank a piña colada out of a coconut.

But it all seemed so shallow. So out of touch. Family milestones and political successes. Or maybe I was jealous because I had nothing to say.

"How about you, Nolan?" Steve asked.

All eyes were on me.

I cleared my throat. I'm the only one here looking dirty and about to drink a wine that didn't come from a box for the first time in four, five, six years. "I'm...uh...I'm thankful we could all be here."

They started clapping, but Pops cut in. "That's all?"

"Yeah. It's kind of like you said, Pops. We're here with family. I get to meet some new people. That's something to be thankful for."

"Surely you're thankful for more than that. What's been going on in your life? You got a new job, didn't ya?"

The memory of that guy getting shot to death flashed across my eyes. I blinked as if some crazy shit like that was just going to rinse out like a piece of debris. "Ye...yeah."

"And you're making money?"

I nodded. "I am."

"So there ya go. You keep up, you'll meet the right woman, and you'll be able to support a family of your own someday."

"It ain't that simple, Pops."

"Sure it is. It took you a long time coming, but I think you're starting to mature."

"No. I mean, life ain't that simple. And it ain't about maturity."

"You don't know what life's about. And you don't know what you want."

"That ain't the point."

"What *is* the point?"

I didn't say anything.

"You got a point, make it."

I sighed.

"Now, don't you think when you stop fighting it and hold down a job for once, you'll be able to find some value in life?"

I ain't say a thing.

"Right?"

If I opened my mouth, the situation would escalate.

"Right?"

I nodded.

I didn't even realize how quiet the room had gotten until Pops took a drink of wine.

Steve laughed nervously, "Know what? We should probably sit down and eat. Don't want the turkey to get cold."

Katelyn and some of the other women brought the food to the table. I thought about eating in the kitchen, and maybe I should have, but I didn't want to look like a wuss, hiding from my father, rage-quitting like a twelve-year-old who lost the boss battle in a video game. Not that an eventual rage-quitting wasn't inevitable.

Told myself I just wouldn't talk to him. Wouldn't look at him. When I was a little kid, I used to look up to that man. Maybe because I didn't know nothing. Before you hit maturity, you got no opinions of your own. Your parents are the people who feed you, play with you, tuck you into bed. You don't ask no questions when they're yelling at the TV on election day.

I hadn't had alcohol that wasn't beer, boxed, or hard liquor in so long, I forgot it could taste good. Sparkling white Moscato. The price was probably close to three digits or beyond. I knew I wouldn't drink nothing like that for at least another year. Unless I came by Christmas, but that sounded like a dead deal.

The food was cooked perfectly, the yams, the turkey, the stuffing. Tasted like restaurant food. Real restaurants. The kind I couldn't afford.

Everything was going great until Pops said, "Hear you moved up at your job, Steve. Seven figures?"

Steve dabbed his mouth with a napkin. "Yeah. Marketing director. Which is great, considering..." he turned to Katelyn "...should we tell them yet?"

She whispered. "We *were* gonna tell them earlier."

Steve took her hand on the table. "We're pregnant. Guess we should've mentioned that when we shared what we're thankful for, but we weren't sure we wanted to tell you yet."

"Congratulations," Ma said. She stood and clapped, and everybody joined in.

"It took a while and a few tries, but here we are."

"Check that out," Pops said. "I'm gonna be a grandfather. Nolan, why are you just sitting there? You got a new niece or nephew on the way."

I clapped, but it came with no emotion.

Pops raised his glass. "A promotion, a new kid. Now that's what I call taking care of responsibility." He chuckled. "If I could only get another kid of mine to—"

"Stop it, Pops."

"You know I'm just teasing you, Nolan. I believe in you. That's why. It's not that I think you're a failure; I just know you can do better. Kind of like when you used to bring home Ds and Fs on your report cards. It wasn't that I didn't believe in ya, I just knew you were better than that—"

"Stop it!"

The eyes of everybody in that room were on me. People who owned homes. People with beach houses. People with seven-figure jobs. People I didn't fit in with. People who Pops didn't fit with. People my sister had to marry into. People who'd have never sat down to dinner with a working-class, yuppie wannabe like my father if Steve hadn't put a fancy-looking ring on his pretty daughter's finger.

"It's like I said." Pops waved his fork at me. "You're a bit late coming, but I think you're starting to mature."

"Pops, I been working since I was eighteen years old. Fuck it..."

They gasped.

"...Before that. 'Cause even when I was hustling Adderall to my classmates, I was doing it 'til the bones in my knuckles showed..."

"You sold your Adderall...?"

"...And what'd I get? A roach-infested apartment? Five goddamn years at a business that threw me out the door because they were worried about their money but couldn't give a shit about mine." I shoved my chair back and jumped out of my seat. "And that's just it, ain't it? That's all that it is in the end. Money. That's what his promotion's about, that's what you've spent years destroying your body over, and that's what I've been out here sacrificing my sanity over night after night."

"One day, when you man up and stop waiting for handouts, you'll get it."

"Fucking handouts," I laughed. "Are you really that daft?"

"Listen to yourself. That's your problem. Quit running around here chasing after dreams—"

"I ain't chased a dream since I was sixteen, Pops. I'm a grown-ass man—"

"Then act like one."

"You spent more than twenty years banging hammers in the rain and snow for a goddamn penny. Every day. Every minute of your time. Did it ever dawn on you that's the only life you'll ever live?"

"It put food in your mouth, didn't it? Put a roof over your head?"

"That ain't what I'm sayin', Pops."

"Let me tell ya somethin'." He pointed a stiff finger at me. "I worked 'til my hands bled so that you and your sister and your mom could have everything you got. Know why? It ain't 'cause I care about you. I do, but that ain't why. It's because that's what a man does. You grow up, you become an adult, and you earn."

I balled my fists, stepped back, exhaled. "Thanks for dinner, sis," I nodded at Katelyn, cut my eyes back at Pops. "I ain't hungry anymore." I turned and marched to the door.

"That's how you're gonna win your battles, huh?" Pops called. "Like a little girl. Keep walkin'. Come back when you're a real man."

I went outside and called Richie.

"We already ate," he said. "But you can stop by if you want."

By the time I got to the church, the streetlights lit up the sidewalks. I used to be nervous when I went outside at that time of night. Now, I was thinking someone should be nervous about me.

I got in there, and it smelled like turkey and weed. Just what I'd expect. Empty containers and uncovered half-eaten food shared the bar counter with beer bottles and liquor canteens. The music from the stereo changed from rap to rock. Jackie and Axe were playing beer pong on a foldable table they dragged in front of the bar counter. Mike and Richie were shooting pool. Arin was smoking a joint at the bar, playing a game on his laptop. Pip was sitting next to him on his phone.

Despite the clutter, the cracks in the walls, the frigidity of the room except where the heat from the wood burner and tabletop heaters hit, funky smell and everybody looking like they just rolled out of bed, something about that image was kind of comforting. Like you can take off your mask, stretch your legs. Maybe not despite it; maybe because of it.

Boxed Moscato on the bar counter. I laughed.

Mike looked up from the pool table. "What's funny?"

I shook my head. "Nothing."

I ate a cold slice of turkey meat, a dip of overcooked stuffing, and a slice of pecan pie I know Axe didn't bake. But I know he baked the cake because that was about the only thing that tasted good. Then I had to think about these four idiots prepping food last minute, yelling at each other about whose gonna cook what. Did Pip bring anything? Probably not. Why'd they even cook anything? But I guess it's the same reason they had a hand-painted turkey holding an AR-15 at the front entrance I had a suspicion Mike drew. Or the same reason they hung up orange string lights in the kitchen. A pumpkin on the turntable. I guess folks just like to celebrate.

I stayed on the couch after I grabbed my plate. Watched Jackie and Axe play beer pong, listened to Richie tell Mike to pay up when he beat him in pool. I liked listening to those two hang together. There's always laughter and reminiscing, I guess because they've known each other so long. But it didn't protect me from my own thoughts. Even when I bit into Axe's cake, took a drink of beer, took a hit from Arin's joint, I could feel the frustration pressing against my skull. I'm lying in front of a rustic wood burner with a beer. The heat's cozy and the flames are popping in a way that would make anybody feel like a kid the night before Christmas, but I ain't feeling nothing but the need to punch a wall. Because my pops was on my mind. And I walked out of there and let him get the last word. And then I had to ask myself if he was right. I didn't know what right or wrong was anymore.

I talked to Pip. He sat beside me on the couch. At first, I thought I'd avoid the topic. Started talking about movies, music, trivial shit, but at some point, it came out. He told me that, as a father, all he wanted was what was best for his kid, but he didn't always know what that was.

You can never get a straight answer from Pip.

Every time I looked at the time, I said I was leaving in about five minutes, but eventually I dozed off, and by the time I woke up and realized I was still there, it was four in the morning. All the lights were out; everybody had gone home or to bed. Even though I'd fallen asleep and woken up in a cold sweat in a cold room, thinking about my father with just a little bit of fire still flickering in the wood burner, I still didn't get off my ass. Threw a block of wood in the wood burner and wasn't sure I was doing it right, but I'd seen Arin do it before I dozed off. Just hoped I didn't burn the church down. Richie said he don't die easily. His charred ass would've probably kicked my ass down the street.

Moonlight seeped through the cracks of the window boards. There was a sky outside I couldn't see, but that sky went on forever.

I didn't realize I dozed off again until I woke up to the smell of coffee.

Arin walked out of the kitchen with a mug. "Didn't know you were still here. I could've gotten you a blanket." He sat in the chair beside the couch.

I rubbed my eyes. "Am I an idiot?"

He took a sip of coffee. "You want me to answer that honestly?"

"I saw my pops at dinner yesterday at my sister's house. First time in years. He looked..." I scratched the back of my head. "...tired. Doesn't move as well as he used to. He doesn't admit it. He can try, smile and all that, but he's been working construction for over twenty years and all that time in the heat's aged his skin. Makes him look ten years older than what he is."

"Could just be the result of getting old." Arin shrugged. "Some folks age faster."

I sighed. "Could be."

"Everything alright?" He smiled uncomfortably. "You're lookin' a little restless."

"I am." I sat up. "What does it mean when you let someone belittle and berate you, yet you still wanna make 'em proud? You just want a pat on the back? Or a hug? A genuine fucking hug? Does that make me an idiot?"

He chuckled. "I think it makes you human."

"You said that like it's funny. That how ridiculous I look?"

"No. I mean...shit." He stopped smiling. "We're all a little bit ridiculous. Part of being alive." He took a sip of coffee. "When I was growing up, my dad had expectations out the ass. I took a lick if I fell below an A plus. Top that with after-school activities and AP classes, chess team—did I ever get a hug? Ha! I got a belt to the ass."

"I forgot you grew up with money."

"Doesn't make a difference. I went all the way to Princeton just to make that dude proud. Honor roll student. Still never heard he was proud of me. You'd think, after all that, I'd stop caring. I didn't. Bad as he treated me, as impossible as his standards were to live up to, you think I would, but I never stopped caring. I just stopped trying."

"Why do you think that is? I mean, your pops had money; mine was broke as an old man's dick. Yet they both got that thing in common. What do you think that's all about?"

He shrugged. "Could be a generational thing. Could be regret. Beats me. I never thought my dad hated me."

"I don't think my pops hates me either."

"But that's just it, isn't it? Maybe they're just trying to figure out how to love."

"I yelled at him yesterday. We got into a huge fight. I walked out, and I can't tell if I'm being gaslit or if I deserve to feel like shit."

"I don't remember the last time I saw my family. They don't even know whether or not I'm still alive. Do I feel like shit about it? Yeah. Half the time I do."

"I don't think I'm ready to estrange myself from my family just yet. I think I'm wantin' something else."

"You shouldn't. You'll look back on it later in life."

"What was the last thing you said to your pops?"

"I don't even remember. Was I on the phone? Might've been in person. Maybe...good luck. 'Cause you're gonna need it." He took a long drink of coffee and set the cup on the end table. "And so am I."

# 20

One day, Richie put me in a curly black wig, a pair of glasses, and a mustache that looked like Freddy Mercury's.

The wife posted their weeklong vacation on social media. Cancun. Photos of Gucci sandals and Louis Vuitton sunglasses. Margaritas by the beach from last year's trip. Spending Christmas in Paradise! Can't wait!

Arin was multitasking when he scrolled through that shit on the desktop computer. Pouring back a beer with one hand, handling a computer mouse with the other. "See? This is the problem with marrying a trophy wife. She might have meat in the back but none in the skull. If I were to get married, I want a hot piece of ass and a hot piece of mind." He laughed.

He sent out a phishing email under the guise of the folks who ran their security system. Told them the company needed to do a checkup on their system. They'll be sending someone out to your house on Friday. It were me, I wouldn't be so dumb to fall for that one, or at least I like to think I wouldn't, but the Krew went all out. Changed the license plate. Even stuck a ladder on top of the van.

Arin looked more ridiculous than I did. Had a long blond wig on with a backwards hat, a pair of thick framed glasses. He even dyed his goatee.

"I'm Toby Renalds. How ya doin'? We're from HX security, here to check up on your security system." Don't know if Arin ever took any acting classes, but he was selling it. Had a clipboard in his hand, a pen behind his ear.

The blonde lady at the door reminded me of those chicks you see on reality TV shows about housewives who carry little purses with dogs in them, or maybe she'd be a host on some daytime knock-off of *The View*. Smiling even when she's not smiling, eyebrows like she's surprised 24/7, lips swollen and poked out like she'd gotten into some jacked-up science experiment that went wrong and crossed her DNA with a duck's. Leopard print jumpsuit and heeled slippers with fluffy feathers on the toe.

She giggled. "Thanks for calling ahead of time. I almost forgot."

Biggest house I'd ever been in. A modern home. Three stories. Didn't even look real. Looked like something on the cover of *Home Décor*. Or some celebrity home on *MTV Cribs*. South-facing windows, ceilings as tall as two stories. Checkered floors at the entrance and white marble in the living room, black and white Persian rug, white leather sofas, a marble coffee table that looked like a black and white block of abstract art—goddamn! We went in looking to hack the security system, wound up down in the wine cellar, where we ran into a vault.

Arin licked his lips and said, "Holy shit. Look what we got here," took a picture, ran upstairs, and nodded at the woman before we got the hell out of there.

The whole crew showed up a week later in black hoodies. The street looked like a postcard picture, bourgeois winter wonderland. Snowmen and snow forts. They don't shovel the snow off the sidewalks like that where I come from. Snow like that means saving extra money for when the heat bill goes up. Or a freezing unit. Always have a backup battery heater just in case.

We waited in the van just far enough away to see the house through a pair of binoculars. All the lights were out. Didn't look like anyone was home.

Arin typed on his laptop. "System's shut down. Cameras are off. We're in the clear."

Slush crunched beneath the tires as I slowly pulled up in front of the driveway. Arin clicked his mouse, and the gate opened.

I drove up the driveway past a marble fountain whose icicles made it look like a giant antique chandelier with strings of diamonds dangling and glistening from its edges. I stopped the van in front of the door. We looked around before we jumped out. Arin knocked, put his ear against the door. He tried the knob. It cracked open. He looked back at us, nodded.

Soon as we stepped in, the ceiling lights came on one by one down the entrance. When we got to the living room, Richie hit the light. The room was the size of two of my units. That TV wouldn't even fit in my unit. How much were those wooden walls? How about that painting? Almost made your chest hurt.

Richie craned his neck back, walked around in a circle. "Nice."

"The wife posted the whole vacation plan online," Arin said. "Whole family's gone for the week."

"That's why you keep your business to yourselves, kids. Nobody gives a flying fuck about what you're up to except criminals and creepos—" Richie laughed, jumped and spun in the air. "I LOVE THIS SHIT!"

Maybe I loved it too. Which didn't make no sense because a part of me was feeling guilty, but a part of me wanted to take off my shoes and feel that Persian rug beneath my feet. Aside from Arin, who I guess had seen too many abstract paintings and marble floors to be impressed, those broke fucks were running around the house like a bunch of hamsters dropped in a new cage. Richie pointed to this object and that object—that painting's gotta be worth a limb. Make sure you grab the big-ass vase. That stereo's gonna look good in my bedroom.

The dining room had a chandelier with long white light bulbs that came down in a spiral above the table and mesmerized me when I looked up at it. It almost made me forget where I was, like it was a wormhole that would take me from Dirt Poor World to one where all the houses can afford trippy chandeliers. The kitchen had an aquarium built into the wall. The breakfast table was in the room right, next to the parlor, which had two white leather lounge chairs across from a black sofa made of a material that probably cost more than my soul. It had one of those built-in glass fireplaces with multicolored flames. A marble coffee table with a gold frame.

Mike plopped down on the sofa and rummaged through the books on the table. "Check it out. A cigar case." That cigar case was encrusted in gold and diamonds. And the black cigar he popped in his mouth had a golden strap on it.

"You don't even know how to smoke that, you stupid son of a bitch," Richie said.

Mike flipped him off.

Richie laughed. "If I didn't love you, motherfucker, I'd break your goddamn finger."

Mike took out his lighter.

"You're supposed to cut off the end, dipshit." Richie grabbed the cutter off the table. "Here. Tell me what it tastes like."

I walked to the back of the room and gazed at the photos on the wall. Headshots. Guys in suits from different times. One as far back as the 1920s, one from the 60s, the 90s, 2000s, today. Everybody's last name was Pinkerman.

Jeffrey Pinkerman. Founder of Gold Real Estate. 1923.

I stared at those photos until I didn't realize I was even staring anymore. Even if I tried to put my feet on that rug, my coat on that coat hanger, my ass on that couch, the reality was, I couldn't imagine what that was like. When I breathed, I didn't smell mildew and old cigarettes. I smelled a dustless room and the smoke of a hundred-dollar cigar. I saw the eyes of people gazing at me from gold-framed portraits. Smiles on their faces. Satisfaction in their eyes. I couldn't tell if it was jealousy brewing or anger or self-pity. Whatever it was, I didn't like it, but the photos were bittersweet. I could stare at them and live vicariously or stare at them and feel like shit about myself.

Richie startled me. "Ain't it a damn shame? Some of us come from wealthy pussies with a free handout, and some of us come from the dirty pussies of street prostitutes. Life's a gamble." He swatted me on the chest. "Let's go crack that vault."

He left, but I was still looking, thinking about that sky Pip showed me. He liked to think there was a better version of him out there somewhere. Maybe there was another me out there, too. Which one had my face on a wall like that?

I got down to the cellar after Richie and Arin were already there. There were bottles of wine probably over a hundred years old, every brand, every variety, red and white, laid in rows side by side like a library of wines. Wooden shelves and stone walls. Leather chairs and a glass table in between them. A polished bar counter and a red billiards table. The vault door had a touchscreen system.

"Swear to God, there'd better be something in this bitch," Richie said.

"Gotta be something." Arin pulled his laptop out of his bag. "If you had a safe room, wouldn't you keep your valuables there?"

"Shit if I know. I don't ever think about having a security system. That's what God made guns for. This gonna take long?"

"I don't know yet." Arin sat on the floor and put his computer in front of him. "They got a settings?"

"Jesus. You don't know how to get into this thing?"

"Every system's different, alright. I never worked with one like this."

Richie tapped the screen. "What are you looking for? Options or some shit?"

"Look for a serial number."

Watching them crack into a vault wasn't the suspenseful excitement of a crime thriller like I thought it would be. It was the tedious blah of watching class project partners argue about an idea. I grabbed myself a bottle of wine and went upstairs.

I don't know where Mike went, but I could still smell his cigar. Axe had the phonograph going in the living room, found himself some Bach, Beethoven—I don't know the difference, but he sat on the chair with his eyes closed, the nightstand lamp on, moved his hand up and down like he was some old music scholar. Maybe he was. Axe never talked much.

The house had an elevator I only checked out because it existed. I stopped on the second floor. Got to say, I couldn't resist opening every room door. You got to wonder what's inside a house like that. Place had a game room with a bar counter. A whole room with black lights sectioned off just for PC gaming. I never got into gaming, but if I knew somebody with that kind of setup, I might have.

I rode the elevator to the top floor. Light seeped beneath the door of one of the bedrooms. I opened it, poked my head inside. Looked like a master bedroom. They had a staircase inside, and I thought, who the hell has a staircase in their bedroom? Rich folks.

I heard rummaging. I went up, found Jackie digging through a vanity drawer.

"Can you believe this shit?" She said. "This chick's got an entire floor just for her closet."

She wasn't lying. The number of shoes against the wall looked like a display at a department store. Dresses and fur coats, hats, dress coats, blouses, and stuff I didn't know what it was. Had a counter in the middle of the floor with a glass window at the top that displayed sunglasses and jewelry. White tile and a black fur rug.

"This stuff's gotta be worth thousands." She dropped a diamond-crusted necklace into the bag. "Who the hell needs this much shit? Look at this." She held up two diamond bracelets, three gold earrings, and a pearl necklace. "This could buy me a whole apartment." I couldn't tell if she was angry or amused. "Me and Lacy are hustling every day 'til our fingers bleed just to get a damn roof over our heads, but if someone dropped just one of these necklaces in our laps, haha." She gazed at the jewelry in her hand. Got quiet. Her eyes lingered, unblinking like she was staring through the gold and diamonds at something out of reach. "I wonder how much this chick's gonna miss any of this. Or if she'll just buy a new one without really thinking about it. Here." She tossed me a gold necklace with a diamond heart. "Christmas is coming up. Give your mother something nice."

I held it in my hand.

"I'd have given something like that to Lacey if she was still in my life. She'd have hated it, but still."

I slid the necklace into my pocket.

Still had that bottle of wine in my hand. I headed back to the elevator, stopped on the first floor.

I grabbed a wine glass out of the kitchen. Axe still sat in the living room listening to classical music. Had his eyes closed, still doing that thing with his hands, and I wondered if he was even with us anymore. I walked past him to the door, stepped outside on the patio.

My breath looked like I'd taken a long drag. You could see the entire city from up there. The buildings. The lights. Looked like a photograph.

The infinity pool had three fountains that weren't frozen. Mist rose off the water. I'm guessing they had one of those heated pools. I took a seat in a conversation pit that had a table with a firepit. I wasn't sure how to light that thing, but I fooled around with it until I figured it out.

I took a lighter out of my pocket and lit the lid until it popped off the bottle, poured myself a glass. I swirled the wine around the glass because I'd seen rich people do that, and if I stared at the pool and the open city, the fire in the firepit, if I felt the leather beneath my ass enough, I might feel like I was one of them.

I was almost scared to drink it. Wine like that ain't cheap. I sipped it, and it was bitter, but I guess that's how rich folks' wine tastes.

What if I'd have grown up in a place like that with Pops and Ma, Katelyn? What would've been different? I wouldn't have been a good for nothing. I wonder how Pops would've been, though. I wonder if he'd have been happy instead of pretending to be. Katelyn was living this kind of life now. She did everything right.

I gazed up at that sky Pip was always staring at. I guess somewhere up there, I did grow up in a three-story house with an infinity pool and a game room. Me and Pops actually got along.

Pops gets home early because he's got enough inherited riches to have a work-life balance. Plus, he can take as many vacations as he wants. He's not sweaty or tired. He's got a lot of energy. I'm nine years old, and he helps me with my homework. He doesn't yell at me; he's got patience because he's not stressed out from being overworked. Ma comes in from the kitchen. She's got that necklace around her neck that Jackie gave me, only it wasn't stolen. Pops bought it for her. Nine-year-old me is looking through the window. It's almost summer, a few more days before school's out. Katelyn's out back swimming in the infinity pool. She's going to go to a good college one day because she's smart, and we've got the money to send her someplace super expensive. There's never a day where Pops has to put in overtime. There's never a night where we eat boxed freezer food because we can't afford too many groceries. I never run the shower water only to feel cold water hit my ass. Pops doesn't worry about bills. He never worries he won't get enough hours to keep his family secure. He never locks himself in the bathroom with a canteen of whiskey, crying because deep down he feels like a failure, not wanting his family to know that he has those moments. Even though I always knew. He has that perfect nuclear family. The one he always believed in.

The door opened. I turned around. Pip grabbed a wine glass from under the outdoor kitchen counter, walked across the granite, and took a seat by me. If I'd seen those glasses, I wouldn't have wasted time going to the kitchen.

He grabbed the bottle off the table and poured himself a drink.

"Better enjoy it," I said. "We're rich for one night."

"If I could get my son all this, I'd never have to worry about a thing again." He took a drink, stared out at the pool or the city lights that glistened across his irises and splashed different hues of white on his cheeks. He shook his head. "He wouldn't need it." He shook his head again. "He wouldn't need any of this."

"Remember what you said at the bar that time? About why you don't believe in God?" I nodded. "I think I get it now."

He sat back and let out a heavy breath. "You asked me before what my dream was. I don't remember what I said, but if you asked me now, I'd say for everyone to be happy."

I chuckled. "That's what you said last time."

"Did I? Guess I oughta elaborate then. I want everyone to be happy. Me, you, Richie, the rest of the Krew. My family, your family, the folks who live at this house. I want everyone happy. And I want everyone happy without this shit." He flicked the edge of the glass.

"You think that could ever happen? Sounds like a utopia."

"It is a utopia, but no. I don't think it could ever happen."

"But if it could, what do you think needs to happen?"

"Pfft. People have been trying to figure that out for centuries."

"And?"

He shrugged. "What are *you* gonna do about it?"

I parted my lips, shook my head.

"If the answer was easy, we'd have found it a long time ago."

"Maybe it's up there." I pointed at the sky.

He snorted a laugh. "What? You think there's a God you can pray to?"

"No." I shook my head. "But there's a big ass universe. We keep starin' at it, maybe we'll find an answer."

"I've been staring at that sky all my life. The only thing it's told me is that any answers we find, we're gonna find down here on earth."

There was no money in the vault.

# 21

Cracker Joe moved to New York, but he didn't join house crew.

He'd stop by sometimes to hang out. Said he wanted to buy a few guns from us. He said that when I met him at the party. We got good guns. Richie showed him what we had. Cracker Joe took two. Said he'd be back for more. I asked him why he didn't join up with house crew. He was already a Krew member. He just shrugged. Can't be a lone wolf and be part of the Krew, but house crew wasn't the only Krew in New York. I never knew how all that shit worked, but I liked Cracker Joe. He was the kind of dude you could shoot the shit with and not have to be too serious.

I got an invite to a Christmas party Ma and Pops were throwing. I was surprised they sent me one.

I didn't go. I thought about it, but it would have just been another incident like Thanksgiving.

I held on to that necklace Jackie gave me at the mansion. Ma was going to ask, how'd you afford something like this? And I was going to say it was on sale.

Maybe it had already been a Christmas gift. A child to a mom. A husband to a wife. Maybe it wasn't fair, but that lady had dozens of diamonds, plenty of silver and gold jewelry. This was going to be Ma's first one. Even the Devil's got to show his ma some love sometime.

I sent it to her in a Christmas package I wrapped myself along with a card. *Merry Christmas. Love you, Ma.* And then somewhere towards the bottom, I wrote, *Sorry.*

I'm not sure if that was for her or Pops or what specifically I was even apologizing for. But I felt like I needed to say it.

I sent my sister and her husband a card. *Congrats on the new baby!* I didn't send Pops anything. But that's alright. He didn't send me nothing either.

Pip gave his kid a stuffed bear and Transformer. Said he saw him on Christmas and spent time at the house with Caelin's ma and soon-to-be steppops. Then I wondered if the rest of the crew had families at all. Not Arin anymore. Maybe Axe. Nobody knew where Axe went when he wasn't hanging around the church. Maybe a girlfriend. Maybe a kid. Maybe a wife he wasn't telling nobody about. Maybe the crew just got each other. Sometimes that's the only kind of family you need, I guess.

They celebrated Christmas like they celebrated Thanksgiving. Beers instead of eggnog. Weed instead of mistletoe. They put up a Christmas tree and decorated it with anarchy signs, skulls, and strung-together bullet shells. Put a dirty boot at the top instead of a star. It wasn't even a Christmas tree, it was a twig tree they dug up from God knows where.

They had a white elephant that seemed out of place for them, and I ended up with an empty beer can. For whatever reason, that empty beer can became a decoration on a bookshelf I only ever filled with CD collections and a bunch of hats.

I happened to run into Cracker Joe at the coffee shop one morning. He asked me why I brought my laptop with me. I told him I'm a writer. It's what I do. Or what I *did.* But I'm getting back into it.

"What made you move to New York?"

It took him a while to answer. He had his elbow on the table, his chin in the palm of his hand, almost like a dreamer. He shrugged. "Looking for something new."

I opened my computer. "Tired of the old?"

"You can say that."

I nodded, but I wasn't paying attention.

"Sometimes, when things aren't working out, you have to take a leap. Maybe a dangerous one if need be." He pushed his glasses up on his face. "Maybe something stupid."

He didn't make eye contact with me.

"What are you talking about?"

"Drama." He ran his fingers through his hair. "Of the kind you don't wanna get tangled up in."

"You're probably right. I got enough shit to deal with right now." I opened my doc. "Who've you been hanging with? Where you stayin' at?"

"Some folks. I'm in the area." He put his hands in his coat pockets and dropped back against his seat. "How long have you been with your crew?"

"Been some months now."

He nodded, but he wasn't looking at me. Looked zoned out, staring out the window like he was talking to himself. "You know what they do if you leave 'em, right? They cut that tattoo off your back. Leaves a scar there forever." He turned his face to me, smiled. "But you got nothing to worry about. I think they like you."

"I think they like you too."

"I know." He nodded. "I've been their friend a long time. What made you join?"

"Money."

"That's everybody's story."

"Desperate times. Matter of fact, the night I got my tattoo, I—" I was talking faster than I was thinking. "You ever do something stupid? Something you can't go back on? Know what I mean?"

He nodded, but he wasn't looking at me again.

"I made a split decision before because I was desperate at the time, and it still stalks me everywhere I go. I know it'll catch up to me. At some point. And I can't tell nobody. I can't apologize. What's done is done."

Now, he gave me eye contact. And he didn't break it. He looked in my face like he was staring at the mirror. "What'd you do?"

I shook my head. "Told you. I can't tell nobody." I broke away from his eyes. "It was a long time ago. Can't take it back now. All I can do is hope I don't get caught."

"Did you steal from your crew?"

I froze. Couldn't tell if he was reading my mind or what. I shook my head.

"Good." He stood. "Because that would be a mistake. But I get where you're coming from."

I stopped him before he could walk off. "What are you doing out here, Joe? Really? You moved all the way out here to New York. Whatever happened with *your* crew in Jersey? Ours is the only one in the Bronx. I know you're not out here by yourself."

"I told you, I'm looking for something new."

He zipped up his coat and walked out the door. I got up and watched him make his way down the sidewalk.

He didn't get into a cab or stop at the bus stop. An SUV pulled over and picked him up. I didn't know who-all Cracker Joe knew or where he hung out, so I didn't ask any questions.

## 22

I strapped a gun to my waist.

Richie sent Jackie and Pip with me. Two bags of coke. Get the money, head home.

I pulled up to the warehouse. The garage door was already open. One of their guys stepped out and gestured for me to park the van. I parked it just outside the door. Jackie and Pip got out before me. I followed them into the warehouse.

No matter how many places like that I saw, they never stopped being shady. Hard-faced guys standing around in black hoods would always put me on edge, even when I became one of them. Dripping spray paint and rusty abandoned buildings, crumbling steps, dirt-covered floors.

Something about these dudes was an extra kind of shady. Don't know if it was the way they were standing around kind of confident, kind of proud. Had that look in their eye, an expression that wasn't quite poker face but wasn't telling nothing either. Hands in their pockets, arms crossed, and there were more of them than us. Three of us, five of them. Not counting the three or four standing in the part of the building the light hardly hit.

I don't think I was the only one feeling it.

"Why's pretty boy here got his hand on his gun?" one of their guys said.

"Pip." Jackie jerked her head.

Pip took his hand off his gun.

"You got the goods?" the guy said.

"Yeah," Jackie said. "You got the money?"

"Yeah." He nodded and one of the guys from the back brought up a bag and handed it to him. He gave it to Jackie.

I'm thinking, good. I'm thinking, now we just gotta give them the drugs and get the hell out of here. Drug runs suck. I'd do anything but a drug run. Heists suck too, but I don't got to do anything at a heist but drive the van. Try not to get caught, try not to get shot. Drug runs make you get involved with other lowlife scumbags like yourself, and you're all thinking the same shit because you don't trust each other. That was the business. It sucked.

I was starting to step back, turn around, but Jackie furrowed her brows. She raked her fingers through the bag. "This ain't the money."

"What do you mean that ain't the money?" The guy said. "You're lookin' at it."

"Nah." She shook her head. "It's counterfeit." She shoved the bag into his chest. "It's fuckin' counterfeit."

"This ain't counterfeit."

"You think I ain't been around the block?"

"Bitch—"

She slugged him in the face, and he stumbled. Grabbed his gun.

Pip whipped his out, shot, but the guy dove to the side.

Everybody's shooting. Bullets are flying around like death gnats. Me and Jackie hurriedly duck behind a concrete staircase. Pip jumps behind a brick column. He's shooting, Jackie's shooting, and I'm screaming shit in my head, but I got my gun. I'm holding it. I got my finger around the trigger, but my back's against the wall. I'm swallowing hard.

It's going through my head. How the fuck did this happen? Where did it go wrong? I played the whole drive out there, getting out of the van, the counterfeit incident like a movie reel. And then I thought about how I didn't want to see anybody die again. Still hadn't recovered from that first time.

I peeked around the corner. Somebody poked out from hiding, took a shot at me, but got popped in the shoulder. I don't know if it was Jackie's bullet or Pip's.

The garage door was a good three or four meters from the staircase. If we were going to get to the van, we'd have to hold them back.

Jackie looked at me, eyes moving over me to see if I've been hit. "What's wrong?"

Everything, I'm thinking. Everything's wrong. I'm getting shot at. I'm making a drug deal. I somehow went from a blue-collar package delivery driver to a criminal felon in less than a year. It's all wrong. It's all fucked up.

I peeked out again. First thing I saw was a gun aimed at my head. I gasped. Locked my finger around my gun's trigger but flashed back to when I shot the guy at the convenience store.

Jackie shot my opponent before he could shoot me. "Get to the van."

I don't know if he was dead or injured, but one second later, I would've been fucked.

"Don't think about it, Bird." She heaved. "Just pull the trigger."

The van was closer to me than her. Pip was still behind a column in the middle of the room. Even if I did get the balls to run out, how the hell was he supposed to catch up with us? I'm thinking maybe we should just wait until they run out of bullets, but that never happens in movies, and it probably wouldn't happen here, either.

Jackie jerked her head and waved for Pip to come on.

Bullets fired. Jackie peeked, fired back.

Pip ducked, hurried across the floor, but a guy behind another column aimed at him. Jackie was distracted. I don't think Pip saw him.

An image of Pip holding his kid flashed across my mind. He'd just celebrated Caelin's birthday. The gunshot went off before I realized it was mine.

I learned that day that the human head jerks forward instead of back when a bullet hits it. I still don't know why.

That guy was dead.

I killed him.

"Get to the van!" Jackie's scream mixed with the blare of gunshots and the ringing in my head. "Get to the van!"

I couldn't feel my face. My breathing stopped. It seemed like the whole mechanism of time crashed and left me standing in a paused reality. I could hardly stand on my feet, but Jackie swatted me. I woke up, ducked down, and did what she said.

The three of us hurried to the van, threw open the doors, jumped inside. The key was already in the ignition. My hand shook so hard I could barely turn it. I put the van in drive, slammed on the gas. The van skirred, flew off the curb, raced down the road, but I wasn't present. My body was, but I wasn't. Everything was red.

"Bird!" Jackie shook me. "Are you okay?" She said it like she'd already just asked me, and I feel like I heard her ask right after she asked Pip the same thing, but every sound hit my ears like it came through a closed window.

"Huh?" I blinked and shook my head. "Ye-yeah. I'm alright."

"Richie's gonna be pissed..." Her words disappeared again.

The gunshot popped in my head.

I killed him.

He was involved in some business he wasn't supposed to be involved in, but so was I. He was armed and shooting, but so was I. Might be he ended up in the same circumstances I ended up in. No job. No money. Stuck between a rock and a hard place, making bad decision after bad decision. Damn. I didn't mean it. He was about to shoot Pip. But what if he had a kid like Pip? What if he had a whole family? Maybe that's why he was there.

I killed him.

I could look down the road all I wanted, but I wasn't seeing shit. Just black. When I rolled forward, the headlight would break through the dark, and the streetlights would coat it gold, but up ahead was just more black and cold and snow and a distance I couldn't measure. Driving down a road, trying to focus but not focused at all. Driving a route but not knowing where I'm going. Feeling the steel bars of a prison cell press against my face and the hard rock of death against my back, but still moving. Still trying to breathe.

I killed someone.

He was a person like anyone else. A criminal like me. Maybe a father like Pip. He was somebody's son. Somebody's friend.

Pops used to say, you got to do what you got to do, and sometimes it's not the thing you wanna do.

When I was a kid, I thought the only thing that would ever dirty my hands was ink. The scribblings of a breakthrough author who grew up poor but made his dream a reality. Now, they were wet with somebody's blood.

Who was going to write about that?

# Two Years Later

# 23

Pops used to say the water's only shallow when you first step in it.

I'd shaved half my head and got a bird tattooed on the shaved side. People asked me what kind of bird it was. Is it a dove? A raven? I told them it depended on how I was feeling that day.

The water's only shallow when you first step in it, and it's cold and uncomfortable, and at first you want to jump out of it, but if you sit in it long enough, you start to get used to it. You start to get comfortable. You're swimming around, and before you know it, you're out in the deep. Tell you what. You don't want to get out of the water at this point. It's too cold out there.

Two years ago, I said I would be a temporary criminal. Get in there, do a couple of petty crimes until I could make rent, get a job, then ditch that joint, maybe change my name, maybe hide out until they forgot me, and get my life back together.

So what the hell was I doing in a high-speed chase?

If I thought back, I could remember. Richie told me we were running a heist. Told me they needed to get in there, get out before the cops showed up. It wasn't even in NYC. It was somewhere out in New Jersey. A pawnshop. Evening. Mid spring. I didn't want to. I wanted to take that day to meditate and figure out my life, but Richie told me if I bailed on him, he would eat me, and I believed him because he was Richie.

So, I've got three cops on my ass. I don't know where I'm going. I don't know what to do. There're two semi-trucks up the road in the right lane and the one I'm in, and I have to do something rash.

It's not the first heist where the cops showed up. It's just the first one where I didn't have a plan to evade them before the pursuit got too intense. I don't know if somebody inside snuck away and called 911. I don't know if a security alarm went off. I don't know shit. But the cops pulled up when my crew were sprinting out the door. Arin threw the door open before they left the building, and I raced towards the highway before they shut it all the way.

I took the left shoulder, raced around the semi.

I'm in an episode of *Fast & Furious.*

I sped up at the bridge, cut through two cars. The cops were back on my ass. Richie clung to the door. "See if you can lose 'em."

I cut across the road, flew for the toll last minute. One cop cut a turn too soon, slammed his brakes, and smashed into the side of the bridge. But the other two were still in pursuit.

There was no way in hell I could outrun these bastards no matter how good a driver I was. We were either going to run out of gas or crash. I had to think of a plan. But it might not be one anyone liked.

I checked my surroundings. An exit. A gas station. A town off the highway. Lots of buildings. I needed to lose them. How do you lose them? You got to distract them. How do you distract them?

I careened off the exit, pulled into the gas station.

Richie pulled out his gun and looked out the window. "What the hell are you—"

"Wait."

I checked my surroundings. A road to the left of me, a road behind me, a building to my right. I had a chain-link fence in front of me. Two apartment complexes, with a parking lot that separated them, a straight shot towards an alley. I didn't know where that led, but I could either let the cops take me in or find out.

"What the fuck are we doing, Bird—"

"Stay put." I won't pretend like my heart wasn't racing. I took a deep breath. Four cop cars pulled behind us, beside us. They got out, guns ready. If I fucked this up, we were dead.

"Step out of the vehicle! Hands above your head!"

I waited until they all got out. Put the van in drive.

"Bird—"

"Get down."

"What the fuck are you do—"

"Get down!"

I slammed the gas. The gunshots went off. One of the back windows shattered. The van broke through the chain link fence, flew off the curb. I cut through the parking lot, turned into the alley, sped through the trash, discarded pallets, and muck until I came out the other end.

I don't know if the cops knew where I'd gone, but red and blue lights flashed through the rearview mirror on the other end of the alley.

I made a right, made a left, dodged a bus, took a wrong turn. I peeked through the rearview.

One of the cops flew around the corner but was struck by a bus. The bus blocked the street corner. Two cops slammed to a stop; one smashed into the bus.

I made a left and wove through cars until I saw what looked like a sanctuary.

The yellow bar was down, but it was an auto meter. No security guards. I busted through it. Prayed to the Devil there weren't any cars on my way up. The parking spots were mostly empty.

I drove until I reached the top floor. Parked in the corner. Flickering LED lights made me think I was waiting in limbo. They were the only lights. The headlights, but I cut those as soon as we pulled into the parking lot. A shadowed closed-off area of walls and concrete pillars. The kind of surreal prison you're running in forever in your nightmares. I didn't hear any sirens or see any flashing lights. But I was feeling wearier than I should've. My head pounded. My hands fell off the wheel because they were too weak to hold onto it anymore.

I looked in the back to make sure everybody was alright. I didn't see any blood.

"I think we lost 'em," Richie said. "Holy shit." He laughed. "Bird does it again."

They laughed. They talked about getting the window replaced, the license plate changed, how we were going to get back home.

I dropped my head on the steering wheel, arms limp.

"Bird."

If Richie hadn't said anything, I might not have felt it. That was definitely blood running down my back. Pain in my shoulder.

"Shit. He's been shot."

That's when their voices started to blur, and I was seeing double.

"Where's the bullet wound?" Arin's voice.

"The back of his shoulder." Richie's voice.

"Get him out the car." Jackie's voice.

The door opened behind me. I saw Pip's face through my window. He opened the door, Axe pulled me out and lay me on the concrete.

They're all standing around me, looking at my back. Arin gets out a knife and cuts my shirt off.

"How bad is it?" Richie's voice.

Arin, "We're gonna have to get it out,"

Jackie, "We can't do that right here."

Richie, "Ain't like we can call an ambulance."

They're pacing back and forth. They're talking over each other. Arin's got my shirt pressed against my wound.

Pip, "*Somebody's* gotta do *something*."

Mike, "There's alcohol in the back. We can stitch him up with..."

Their voices muffle.

Arin, "That might not work if..."

My hearing's in and out.

"For fuck's sake..." Richie's voice.

Everything doubles until it's all a blur. I can't hear them anymore. It all goes black.


I woke up on the couch.

As my vision cleared, blurred blacks and browns became the familiar rusted iron and cooking logs in the wood burner. I didn't know what time it was. I didn't see any sunlight seeping through the window boards. I had a bandage around the back of my shoulder.

"You awake?" Pip's voice came from behind the couch.

I moaned and rolled over. "What the hell happened?"

"You took a bullet to the shoulder. Lost a lot of blood, but we got it out just in time."

I rubbed the side of my head. "How'd you do that?"

"Consider it a miracle."

Arin sat at the bar counter, raised his beer in the air. "He's alive." He took a drink.

They were all back there. Arin, Axe, and Jackie at the bar. Pip standing behind the couch. Mike came around and nudged my shoulder. Guess it didn't dawn on him it hurt like shit. "Glad to see you're awake."

Richie, sitting at the dining table, his phone screen smearing neon across his face—he'd had it harder than me. Growing up with a mother who may or may not have loved him. Growing up with no money. Selling drugs at twelve, shooting guns at fourteen. Don't know who or what he was by the time he was legally old enough to throw back a whiskey. Him and Mike. Mike had a steppops who didn't love him. A ma who chose somebody else over him. Probably wouldn't be much if not for Richie.

Jackie had it harder than me, too. Living out there on the streets had to be rough. Trying to take care of not just yourself but somebody you care about, then losing that somebody. Not knowing what happened to them. Not knowing if they're alive, and maybe that's the whole reason she's alive.

Pip had it harder than me. Waking up and realizing his sister's his ma. He's the product of some fucked-up shit nobody wants to talk about. Too many kids, too little money. A pop that went to jail before he was old enough to grasp the concept.

Axe. I didn't know nothing about Axe. He didn't talk enough.

Arin. I could say fuck Arin because he never knew what it was like to go hungry, but lying there on that couch looking at all those broken have-nots, drinking beer and smoking cigarettes like booze and tobacco was the snake in their lives that promised an Eden nothing else would offer—shit, I felt like shit about myself. Makes you think those days you got picked on because you wore the same old cheap clothes every day weren't that bad. Kind of makes you grateful for your own poor upbringing, even if you didn't have a dime to your name. Go back and tell your child self, cheer up, kid, maybe your parents can't afford to buy new shoes, maybe the other kids are bullying you because your parents can't afford the clothes and toys and gadgets theirs can, but at least you ain't that. I don't know if that said anything about them or about me. But I got to thinking about how Pops took that tiny amount of money and tried to give us a normal life complete with vacations and after-school activities, and I didn't know how to feel about that. Confused, angry, maybe even a little bit grateful at the same time. If I was willing to admit it.

"I'm gonna head home," Pip said. "You need anything, give me a call." He patted my shoulder but not the side that hurt.

I nodded. "Thanks."

He walked to the door.

"I'm gonna get out of here too," Axe said. "Say, take care of yourself, Bird." He followed Pip out the door.

Arin and Jackie went upstairs. Richie disappeared into his room before I even realized he was gone. So that left me and Mike.

He picked up the beer bottles off the counter, emptied the ashtray. He even got a broom out of the closet, swept the floor, which answered a question I wondered for two years: who the hell cleans up around here?

"You plan on hanging out here all night?" he asked.

"Don't know if I'm well enough to walk to the bus stop."

"I could give you a lift."

"I probably should've said this when everybody else was here, but thank you. I mean it."

He leaned over in front of me, and his hair hung over the side of his cheeks like bronze curtains. He tucked one side behind his ear, smiled that smile I came to know better than I ever imagined. When I first met this guy, he had a gun pointed at me and told me to scram. Now, he was smiling at me. Looking in my eyes like he was an older brother. "We're not just gonna let you die."

Mike had gotten more tattoos since then. He had a new one on his neck. I don't know who did it or what it meant, but it was a fist. Maybe it stood for fighting. Maybe unity. Maybe only Mike knew. I didn't want to ask because I wanted to interpret it myself.

"Thanks." I sat up but moaned once I realized how painful it was to do so.

He dropped the broom against the wall and sat in that old, tattered, plaid chair.

"How am I still alive?"

"It didn't hit nothing serious. And the bullet wasn't that deep. You got lucky."

I rubbed my bandage. "I guess I did."

"When I got shot, they were gonna leave my ass for dead. Richie said fuck that. I had a bullet 'bout where yours was, only mine was in there deeper."

"When was this?"

"Pre-Krew days. Might've been, shit, twenty years ago. Me and Richie hadn't even dropped out of school yet. He got the bullet out by himself, didn't know what the fuck he was doing, and I was conscious the whole time."

"Bet that hurt."

"You bet your ass it did. And that sucker wasn't coming out. Can you believe it? That crazy son of bitch bit down on it and pulled that shit out with his teeth." He laughed.

"Seriously?"

"Yeah. Spat it out to the side. Had blood all over his mouth. Bro looked like a goddamn vampire. I said, if I don't bleed to death, I'm dying of infection."

I joined him when he laughed this time. "You guys go way back, huh?"

"Way back. We went to junior high together. Got into shit together."

"And then you started The D3vil's Krew."

"He did. I joined."

"But it was just you two?"

"Yeah."

"And you're still here today."

"That's called loyalty."

"Do you ever have doubts about it? Even after all these years?"

"All the time. But it's ride or die. Like that bullet we got outta you. What if Richie had left *me* to die?"

I paused.

He smiled. "When was the last time you smoked a joint?"

"I dunno. Couple of months ago."

"You're 'bout past due. Don't ya think?" He got up, grabbed his stash box off the counter, pulled a joint from a plastic bag, lit it. He took a hit, held that shit in until he coughed. Came back around and passed it to me. "It'll make you feel better."

"Thanks."

He sat on the armrest of the couch. "It was something different early on."

"What?"

"The Krew. Pfft. Don't get me wrong, we were always a bunch of scallywags hustling dope and breaking into cars, but I feel like when we started this thing, we aimed for a revolution. Something. Instead, we just get shot in the streets or shoot somebody else for no reason but money."

"Reality gets in the way."

"That what it is? D3vil's Krew was supposed to leave its name. The ideas me and Richie had back in the day are dead. So, what is all this?" He shifted around, stared at my face like he was trying to communicate something that maybe I'd have understood if I were there with him and Richie when it all began. "Pass the joint."

I reached up and passed it to him.

He took a hit, held it, let the smoke roll out through his nose. "When me and Richie ran away way back when, know what he said to me? He said, 'The Devil ain't done with me yet, Mike. Maybe God gave up on me, but I'm still alive.' We were in some abandoned building. You could see all the city's scum and dirt through the cracks in the walls. That's where we were bunking for the night. All the homeless motherfuckers. Drunk motherfuckers. Smelled like shit, and he said, 'I'm alive for a reason, Mike. So are you. So we gotta make something happen.' Man, we didn't make shit happen. Kept doing the same bullshit we've been doing for the last some odd years, and you know what? I think he was wrong. We're not alive for a reason. We're just alive. I still believe in The D3vil's Krew's motto." He shrugged. "But the Krew's just like us. Alive. But for what? It all goes in vain."

I ran into Tasha at the grocery store.

She had a two-year-old girl in the front of the grocery cart. A wedding ring on her finger. A bump in her belly.

"Hi, Mister Nolan." Caelin had gotten bigger since the first I met him, his father's features more noticeable in his face.

"Caelin." Tasha turned. When she saw me, she paused. She grabbed Caelin's hand. "Come on."

"Hey, how've you been?" I waved, but before she saw it, she'd taken Caelin and walked out of the aisle.

I stopped beside her at the endcap, rubbed the back of my neck. "What brought you all the way out here?"

She picked up a cereal box, turned it over, and didn't so much as glance at me. "The local store didn't have what I'm looking for."

"So, you're having another baby?"

"Yep."

"Guess your hands are gonna be full."

She put the box down and pushed her cart to the next endcap. She had her back to me. Picked a jar of peanut butter off the shelf.

"Do you know if it's gonna be a girl or boy yet?"

"Girl." She dropped the jar in the cart, turned into the aisle.

It wasn't like I wasn't getting the memo, but sometimes you feel like you got to say something.

I sighed. "I'm sorry."

She still had her back to me. "What are you apologizing for?"

"I dunno. Whatever you're mad at me for."

"I don't even know you. Why the hell would I be mad?"

"Then I'm sorry for whatever's got you hating me."

She finally turned around, but she crossed her arms when she looked at me.

"I know you hate me, but I'm not responsible for what Pip does."

"It ain't you I hate." She looked me up and down. "Don't give yourself that credit. It's all of it I hate. The whole damn thing."

"You're not even with him anymore."

"He's the father of my son, Nolan. That's your name, right? But I hear they're calling you Bird now."

I looked away from her face and pressed my lips together.

"You think just because I'm not married to him means I don't sit up at night worried about him?" She looked me up and down again. "But guys like you treat this whole thing like it's some kind of joke." She walked off.

I followed her down the aisle. "A joke? After the shit we'd seen? Wake up, lady. Look at the world around you. Nobody's jumping into this life because it's all shits and fucking giggles. The big guys wrote the rules a long time ago. I'm just trying to play it my own way."

"Who are you now? Richie?"

"Truth is truth. It's all one big game written in their favor. Maybe you got lucky enough where you can sit comfortably in the matrix, but the rest of us are playing it the best way we know how, and if that ain't by their rules, then that ain't by their rules."

She stopped. Only time I'd ever seen a look like that on somebody's face was when they were about to cut me. She pointed an acrylic fingernail at me like she'd jab me in the chest. "I don't need some Buffalo white boy telling me how the system is broke. You think I ain't lived out there in those streets? I grew up in the ugliest parts of the Bronx, motherfucker. I worked a job when I was sixteen to help the single mother raising me and my four younger siblings keep the lights on. I busted my ass more than your sorry ass has excuses." She flared her nostrils. Took a deep breath and exhaled. "And then what? I get knocked up before my seventeenth birthday and end up getting my ass grabbed, busting tables every day just to make ends meet, living in a shithole in the middle of the slums. You think I ain't never been desperate?"

"So what? You settle down with a guy that makes six figures, and you forget."

"I haven't forgotten shit. I see what goes on out there, and I've seen what people do trying to survive. I was almost married to that, but I made a decision not to be a part of it."

"You got lucky."

"What I got is sense."

I relaxed my shoulders, sighed. Rubbed the back of my neck.

Her eyes softened, and her look of contempt dropped into a look of pity.

"I know how I got myself into this," I said. "I just can't seem to find my way out."

She rubbed her temples. "Look. I get it. I've had my run-ins with the law. It's rough out there, and it don't seem like anybody cares." She looked me in the eye with a long, uneasy pause. "But if you keep up, you're either going to end up in prison or dead."

# 24

Kids are like Silly Putty.

Sometimes you look at a kid, and you think I'll never be that again.

I'm never going to be six years old again. I'm never going to have the blissful naivety that was both protection and danger. Running around with other kids, never thinking about what a day is. A day is just a moment in time. There's no tomorrow or next year. There're toys and cartoons, games, fingerpaints. Adults are lumbering giants who complain about jobs and the president, the economy. What's an economy? You're six years old; you're building castles. You're shooting your sister with a water gun. You're not worried about the stock market or what's going on in the news, bills, how much money you have to save if you're going to take a vacation, buy yourself something nice. The world is just moving, and you're in that moment, breathing, experiencing, laughing about nothing and everything, but you don't even know it. You're a kid forever until you're not anymore, and you don't think about how it will all be over and done. It'll never happen again. One day, you wake up, and it's too late. You're not a kid anymore.

Sometimes you wish that in those naïve years, you could pinpoint what made you into the person you are today. Take a time machine and remove all the things that sent you down the wrong road. But you can't do that.

I guess the only thing a breath can do is pray that life has graceful hands when molding a child.

I watched Pip with his son one day at his apartment. Called Pip up earlier that day, asked if he wanted to hang out. He said he was spending time with Caelin that afternoon, but I was welcome to stop by. I usually let Pip have his quality time with his son, but I was bored.

Caelin had his backpack with him. It's weird—kids always grow faster than you think they will. Always changing. Took me 349 years to go from four to seven years old. Took that kid one minute.

They're silly putty.

"Did you wanna play with my toys, Dad?"

"That sounds like fun." Pip smiled. "What did you bring?"

He crossed his legs on the floor. After seeing this guy shoot rounds of bullets into people and knock other guys out with a punch, I can't explain the feeling of seeing his eyes light up when he crossed his legs beside his first-grader.

Caelin poured all the toys out of his bag. Action figures and bouncy balls, broken crayons. He picked up a plastic gun that made kapow sounds when he pulled the trigger.

"Where'd you get that?"

"Marcus bought it for me."

Pip gripped the gun's barrel. "Why don't we play with something else?"


The more I saw Cracker Joe, the more his smile couldn't play pretend anymore.

His eyes darted across the room, looking at everything but me, anytime I saw him. For two years.

We made it a thing to meet at a burger joint a few blocks from where I stayed. Or it became a thing on its own. Used to do it once a month or so, then, naturally, it became an every other weekend thing. Funny how that happens.

The ceiling fan turned, even though the diner was already cold. Dingy curtains and dusty blinds. Bacon grease. Makes your stomach hungry and sick at the same time.

The waitress came by and wiped down our table. Pulled silverware from a white, cotton apron and dropped two greasy menus in front of us.

"A beer," I said.

The TV hung behind the bar counter. Gang violence. Three people shot. Two suspects. Cracker Joe turned his eyes away from it when it cut to a commercial. "I can watch how the world's going to hell and read a burger menu on the same wall." He shook his head and laughed. "Boy, are we fucked."

The waitress came back with my beer and a water for Cracker Joe. "Ready to order?"

"Give us a minute," Joe said.

She nodded and walked away.

Joe opened his menu. He ordered the same thing every time, so I knew he wasn't looking at it.

I opened my menu. I always ordered the same thing, too.

"A whole lot of meats." He turned the menu over.

"You don't like meat all of a sudden?"

He wasn't looking at me, and I wasn't looking at him.

"No. I do." He pushed his glasses up on his face. "There's just a lot of it. Know what's interesting? We're the only animals to domesticate other animals. It's how we can have all this meat, farms and pets, all that, but you gotta think about it—you a dog fan? You like dogs?"

"I never had one, but yeah. I guess I like 'em alright."

"Yeah? Think about it. There had to be a time when someone came across a pack of wolves, and they said, 'You know what? I'm going to work with that group of vicious carnivores." He chuckled.

I did, too. "Maybe they were desperate."

"Had to be. Think about what it took to make that happen. There had to be some level of trust between both species."

"Yeah."

"It's not just a symbiotic relationship. I mean...they say dogs are man's best friends."

"At the end of the day, they're animals, though. And so are we. They're gonna do what they need to survive, and we're gonna do the same."

"Right."

"I'm sure you probably had a wolf that acted out, though. Maybe stole some food for himself."

"Had to be." He flipped his menu back over. "That's nature."

I took a swig of beer. "That's survival."

"Not always. Sometimes, I think animals do things for selfish reasons."

"You think that?"

"Yeah. I mean...there's always two sides to a story. I'm sure nature has a justification."

"Nature?"

"Yeah." He looked up and paused. Nodded. "Nature." He flipped his menu back over. "What if ten thousand years ago, a wolf stole food from the tribe that tamed him and brought it to another tribe?"

"Be better than if he ate it for himself."

He looked at me. I looked at him.

I took a swig. "Why'd you do it?"

He shrugged, shook his head. "Why'd *you* do what *you* did?"

# 25

Pops used to say, show me your friends, and I'll show you who you are.

Imagine driving a group of dangerous people back from some business out of state. Imagine showing up at the base and finding the door open. Imagine the looks on everyone's faces when you all pull out your guns and silently step into the building. Imagine checking every room, floor, and hallway, finding no one there. But what do you find upstairs?

They left the door open. Dust particles floated around in the midday sunlight exposing empty metal shelves. They cracked the gun safe. Every gun gone. The money bag too.

Richie didn't say anything at first. He stared at it. Had his back to the rest of us, arms at his side with his gun hanging in his hand.

I was scared to look at his face.

His voice was so low you could hardly hear it. "Did they take anything else?"

Mike shook his head. "Doesn't look like it."

Richie raised his shoulders when he inhaled like he nearly lost control of whatever was clawing up his throat.

"Push comes to shove," Arin said, "we might have to get money out of the other safe."

I stopped breathing for a second.

"We won't be getting shit out of the safe," Richie said. "We're getting our money back."

Jackie looked out the window. "Who do you think could've done it?"

"I don't know." Richie slammed the safe shut. The echo rattled the windows. He turned on his heel and marched to the steps. "But when we find the motherfucker, he's dead."

I didn't sleep that night at all. I stared into a black room. When I'd first joined D3vil's Krew, I stole money from their safe. That secret crime rose up my chest every now and then, and I swallowed it back down like puke.

I'd tried time and time again to get the safe to open, but it wouldn't budge, so returning the money was a lost cause. It was either a matter of time, or luck would have to show up at my door, shake my hand, tell me it was giving away free miracles, and get me out of whatever shit I'd gotten myself into.

Richie put Arin on the task of finding the gun thief, and Arin poured back a beer with nonchalant ease because he knew what I knew. He knew what I'd known for a long time. I didn't know what would happen, but I knew something was about to pop off, and then you got to ask yourself, what happens next? You got to ask yourself if the only reason you never spoke up about it was because you knew you were no better. Nobody was any better. Everybody in the Krew was a fucking thief. That's how we played the game.

I asked Cracker Joe, the last time I saw him, whether or not he ever had a dream. He said no.

He never believed in dreams.

Almost two weeks after the guns were stolen, I got an invite to the church. When Arin does a job, Arin does a job fast, but Arin didn't do that job fast. Nonchalant, apathetic Arin wasn't going to say why. But I think I know why.

They'd invited every Krew member in the area—other cities and boroughs in New York and bordering states. Had a whole basement full of people. Anybody with their shirt off had the same tattoo. Music. Drinking. Drugs. Cage fights. It was a Krew party if I ever saw a Krew party.

Then the music turned off. Richie walked into the pen. He raised one hand in the air, and everybody from the pen's fence to the back of the basement stopped dancing, stopped drinking, stopped chattering, stopped laughing. This man was the motherboard that shut everything down.

I don't know how they got Cracker Joe out there. I don't know if they kidnapped him in the middle of the night. I don't know if they threatened his family. I don't know if he was foolish enough to think it was just some ordinary party, but he had to know that they knew or were going to find out.

They didn't drag him into the pen. He stood, no tape or chains, untied, in the corner with a cigarette, a pensive look that didn't tell me anything. But it had me thinking some sort of bargain had been made between him and the Krew, one nobody made my business. That's probably why he showed up. I didn't even know he was there until Richie said his name.

Cracker Joe tossed his cigarette to the side, stomped it out, and joined Richie.

"You see this man?" Richie held his arms out to the crowd. "Get a good look at him. Calls himself a member of The D3vil's Krew. One of the crews out in Jersey." He paced back and forth behind Cracker Joe, who stood unwavering in a swarm of sparkling dust particles. "But you know what happened when me and my boys came back home not long ago." Richie nudged him on the shoulder. "Tell 'em, Joe."

Joe snorted and spat to the side.

"That's alright. You've got the right to remain silent, but I think these good people got a right to know what you been up to. Wouldn't you all agree?"

The crowd woo-hooed and applauded.

"Cracker Joe, here, stole our guns and our money..."

They booed, pointed their thumbs down, threw trash at the pen.

"...and now, he's going to tell us what he did with it."

"I sold them," Cracker Joe said.

"To who?"

"I can't give that up."

"You a Krew member, or you belong to someone else?"

"I don't know."

Richie punched him in the face, and Cracker Joe almost stumbled over. He spat a wad of blood.

"What about the money?"

"We split it. They got most of it."

He punched him again. The crowd cheered.

"We're gonna figure it out with or without you," Richie said. "You might as well make this easier on yourself."

Joe flared his nostrils and swallowed. "The Rhats."

"Why'd you do it?"

"Money."

"That it?"

"No. I wanted to join their crew."

"Why? The D3vil's ain't good enough for ya?"

The crowd booed.

"Damn," Richie said. "Took you that quick to rat, maybe you *are* a Rhat." He turned to the crowd and raised his hand.

Everyone got quiet.

"We had some pretty good fights tonight. Yeah?"

They cheered.

"Got some good K.O's, won some bets. Tonight," Richie said, "I wanna challenge Joe to a brawl."

The crowd went crazy, clapping, whistling, shouting, spinning their shirts around in the air.

"What do ya say, Joey, my boy." Richie grabbed Cracker Joe by his hair and pulled his face close to his own. "It ain't negotiable."

He socked the glasses off his face. Cracker Joe stumbled back. His glasses slid across the floor and smashed against the side of the fence.

The crowd went insane.

Richie punched him and punched him again.

Cracker Joe got a punch in. Dodged one of Richie's, punched him again, in the mouth, but Richie spat out a wad of blood and came back full force.

Cracker Joe couldn't even get his arms up. Blood ran down his nose, poured out of his mouth.

Richie punched him and punched him again.

Cracker Joe spat his teeth to the side. Both eyes swelled shut. Nothing was left on the top row of his mouth but bloody gums.

Richie didn't stop. He grabbed Cracker Joe by his shoulders, kneed him in his stomach, and did it again. Again, after that. He grabbed his head and kneed him twice in the face. He punched him in the nose, and Cracker Joe fell back flat.

Richie wasn't done.

He got on top of him. Punched him in the face. Left fist. Right fist. Left fist. Right fist. A puddle of blood spread across the floor.

Cracker Joe's arms and legs lay splayed out beside him, his head dropped to the side, eyes shut and swallowed by his own swollen brow, cheeks darkened like rotting fruits, nose smashed and crooked. Black and blue, red. I'm not sure there was a face left. There was no need to check for a breath, a pulse.

He was dead.

Richie got up, chest heaving, body soaked in sweat. He wiped the blood off his cheek with his arm.

The crowd was silent.

"You see this?" Richie made eye contact with everyone. "This is what happens to a fucking traitor!" He pointed a stiff, bloody finger at Cracker Joe. "You stab D3vil's Krew in the back, this is the result."

Richie clutched his fists before a wide-eyed crowd, blood rolling down the side of his face, shoulders moving up and down, sweat rolling down his neck.

They cheered.

I picked up Cracker Joe's glasses. Wiped off the blood with the hem of my shirt.

The left lens was cracked. The nose bridge was bent.

The bloodstain still lay on the floor.

The fence door creaked when I opened it. I walked out of the pen, climbed the steps. I went up to the second floor and stopped at the top of the stairs.

Arin sat at the computer like I'd thought.

"Cracker Joe told me about how you guys would place money bets on chess matches back in the day." I smiled a small, solemn smile. "Nerdiest gambling I ever heard of."

He wasn't looking at me. He had his eyes on the computer, fingers moving across the keyboard at speeds I had never seen from anyone else. "Yeah." His cigarette bobbed up and down between his teeth. Always smoking something. Always drinking. Always had something in his hands, combatting the tics that made him have to keep moving. "We were best buds back in college."

I walked up to the Arin, one hand in my pocket, the other wrapped around Cracker Joe's glasses.

"How'd you sleep?"

He kept his back to me. "Pretty good," he chuckled. "Considering the stress lately."

I stared at the glasses and let out a heavy breath. I lifted my gaze to Arin. "Do you care?"

"I care this computer's slowing down on me."

"Arin."

"There we go. Just needed to let it load a sec."

"Last night. All of it. I haven't been able to get it out of my head."

He shook his head, responded with a playful tone. "No one told you ya had to come."

"You don't feel guilty?"

He took the cigarette out of his mouth and tapped the ash in the tray beside him.

"Do you feel anything at all—"

"Yeah." His tone hardened. "I feel."

"Then why'd you do it?"

"It's my job."

The clacking keys echoed against the walls.

"He was an old friend," I said.

"Yeah. It sucks."

"But it's your job."

"He betrayed the Krew."

"So he deserved to die?"

"That wasn't my call."

"But you knew what would happen."

"Yeah." He nodded. "I did."

"When you figured out who was responsible, did it ever eat at you?"

He didn't say anything.

"Were there any questions you had to ask yourself?"

He didn't say anything.

"And then when you told Richie, did it get down in your chest?"

Clack, clack, clacking.

"Did it hurt?"

Clack, clack, clack.

"But you already knew, didn't you? You knew long before anyone asked you to investigate. You just didn't tell. Something in you wouldn't let you do it. So now I gotta ask you something. What finally made you ignore that voice?"

Clack, clack, clack.

"How can you do that? Just sit there typing whatever bullshit you're doing on that computer? Like it doesn't matter. You sold him out!"

He whipped his chair around. "Nobody wanted to kill him. Not me. Not you. I can promise you, not even Richie. Nobody wanted any of this. But it happened. So we dealt with it."

"He was a friend. Not just a friend, a member of the Krew—"

He slammed his hand on the desk. "You've been in this gig for nearly three fucking years, and you still haven't found out yet that's the kind of shit you signed up for?" His chest heaved.

I don't know why, but mine did too.

We stared at each other. He wasn't going to admit to the tears forming in his eyes.

"You sold him out," I said.

"I did my job."

"You killed him."

"I didn't kill anyone. Richie did the killing. I did what was assigned to me."

"But you let it happen. You're partially responsible."

"Alright." He nodded. "That's the case, then why don't you call the cops? Tell them we murdered somebody, burned his body, threw his ashes over the bridge. But you're not, are you? Doesn't that make you just as responsible?"

I swallowed.

He dropped his head. Rubbed his brow. Rubbed his eyes. He slowly raised his head, turned his gaze from mine. His words came out slow and gravelly. "What was I supposed to do? Lie?" He turned back around to his computer.

"I was talking to Mike. The D3vil's Krew used to be about something, y' know? Used to stand for something."

"Go home, Nolan."

"Now all it is is just fighting and killing and stealing."

He raised his voice. "Go home, Nolan."

I balled my lips. Took a deep breath. I walked up to his desk, dropped Cracker Joe's glasses beside him.

He looked down at them and up at me.

I went home.

# 26

I did a dumb thing, but I guess we all did something stupid that day.

We got extra rifles from Krew members outside the Bronx. Pistols tucked away in drawers and under the floorboards. Arin made bullets.

Richie didn't ask for backup but told the crew down in Brooklyn to be ready if we called. But that wouldn't be necessary.

Richie had me pull up to some old rowhouse that looked like it was put together with popsicle sticks.

Axe kicked the door open, and we hurried with assault pistols into what looked like a frat boy's dorm room. The counters looked like a junkie's workspace. Beer cans and ashtrays. The whole place had the skunky stench of weed. Three dudes chilling out on holey couches and a lounge chair smoking a bong, one guy with a joint. We surrounded them, and their hands went up slowly.

"Where's my shit?" Richie shouted.

One guy glanced at the other guys. "What shit?"

"Don't play fucking dumb."

"We don't know what you're talkin' about."

"The guns. The money."

"We don't know."

"Who does?"

"We don't fuckin' know."

"I better start hearing some answers, or bullets are gonna start flyin'."

"Does this look like the kinda place that's stashing guns and a load of cash?"

"Your crew. Where are they keeping my shit?"

"I don't know what you're talkin' about."

Richie shot him in the foot.

"Fuck!" He clenched his foot and fell off the couch.

Richie aimed at a different guy. "The goddamn guns!"

"Okay! Shit! Fuck! Okay!" His shoulders heaved. "We got a tip from one of your guys. We broke in when you were gone and took the guns and the money."

"I know that much. Where's it at?"

"It ain't here—"

"Where the fuck is it?"

That guy looked at his buddy. His buddy looked at him, and the one with a bullet hole in his foot rolled on the floor, foot clutched, blood seeping through his fingers, teeth clenched, face red and soaked in sweat.

"If I gotta ask again, so help me God...so help me fucking God..." Richie walked up to the guy on the chair and pointed his gun at the middle of his forehead.

"The warehouse," the other guy said. "The fucking warehouse. But we're not involved in none of that shit, man. We told 'em it was stupid—"

"What goddamn warehouse?"

"The one on South Lane. By that old factory. I don't know if that's where they're keeping your shit, man. Honest to God. But that's where they hang out. You can probably find 'em there."

Richie turned around to that guy, walked up to him.

The man raised his hands higher.

Richie took the joint from between his fingers, took a long drag, and passed it back to him. "I swear to God if I don't find what I'm looking for, I'm coming back." He jerked his head towards the guy rolling on the floor. "And you'll have more than your fuckin' toes to worry about."

When we got back to the car, Richie slammed his fist against the glove compartment. "The fuckin' Rhats!" He did it again, over and over, made the whole van rattle. "The fuckin' Rhats! How did I not see this? Should've taken those motherfuckers out a long time ago." He rolled the window down and fired five shots into those guys' windows. I can't tell you if any of the bullets hit anyone, or if the violence was enough to calm Richie. "Drive."

I put the van in reverse.

The warehouse sat on a street corner between broken and God don't give a shit. Shattered glass and spray paint.

We got out with our pistols ready, peeked through hanging wood planks and shattered windows. Didn't look like anybody was in there.

We went around to the back. The door was unlocked, which made everyone hesitant. We got behind the wall. Jackie suggested we find another way in. The back door unlocked like that could mean they were waiting on the other side, but we didn't see nobody through the window. Richie pushed the door open, got back behind the wall. He peeked. We all did but didn't see anyone.

He waved for us to follow him inside. I felt like a cop on a drug bust, which is pretty ass-backward, I guess.

Wasn't much light, but what there was shined through the window and left sparkling dust particles looking like cigarette embers. They had to know we were coming. Maybe they didn't know when, but they had to know it would happen. So, they had to be ready. But this warehouse was huge. Not nearly as renovated as the church. Made your nose itch to hang around here. Smelled like mildew. Had a dusty couch on the side of the wall, a mattress in the middle of the floor, a wooden table. Probably had a light switch too, a generator outside. You knew somebody was living here or hanging out here or something. We looked behind the couch, behind the walls, the columns, didn't find a single person.

We looked through every room, kicked open every door. Nobody.

We looked upstairs, inside the cabinets, the closets. Nobody.

Didn't find the guns either. Nor the money.

"Should we wait for 'em?" Mike asked.

"No," Richie said. "We'll come back, ride out here every night. Keep an eye on 'em. They'll be back eventually."

We headed out to the alley.

"I got a hunch," Mike said.

"What do you mean?"

"You think those guys back there were telling the truth?"

"I don't know what to belie—"

A gunshot shattered the back window just behind Richie's head.

"Get down!" Mike shouted, and he and Richie hurried behind a rusty garbage bin. Me, Jackie, and Axe jumped behind the stoop, Pip behind an old truck on the other side of the alley.

Five guys hung out the windows of a raggedy SUV, popping bullets into the rusted fire escapes and decaying brick. We fired back.

They got back into the vehicle, slammed the gas, but before they could get too far, Pip aimed for the tire and sent the car spinning onto the sidewalk on the other side of the street.

We ran out of the alley and ducked behind a basement entrance to a boarded-up building that might've been a speakeasy once.

The wheels turned, but the SUV wasn't moving. The back wheel was caught in a pothole. The blown-out tire spun until it ripped off, and the naked rim sprayed sparks everywhere. The whole street smelled like burning metal and gasoline.

We fired at the vehicle. They fired back.

The SUV yanked, the wheels turned, and the vehicle jumped out of the pothole and sped down the street. The bare rim scraped against the bumpy pavement, screeching like a saw against lead.

We ran out to the sidewalk and shot at the SUV. The back passenger window rolled down. One of their guys got up on the windowsill and fired a shot.

Mike shoved Richie out of the way, and the bullet hit him in the back. He turned and fired one last shot before he hit the ground.

The bullet scraped against the SUV, startled the shooter, and he fell out the window, tumbled down to the road. The SUV slammed to a stop and reversed, but we blew out the back windows, and it sped off without him.

Richie got on his knees and turned Mike over, shook him. "Mike." He shook him again. "Mike."

Mike wasn't moving. His eyes stared forward, arms splayed out beside him. Blood trickled down the sides of his mouth, sheeted his bottom lip.

"Mike." Richie shook him again.

Mike wasn't moving.

Richie patted him on the cheek. "Come on, Mike. Come on." He looked up at Arin. The only time I'd ever seen helplessness in Richie's eyes. "What can we do?"

Arin let out a heavy breath. He shook his head.

Richie patted Mike on the cheek, slapped him. "Come on. Come on." His voice, usually a gravel road, was a threadbare whisper, frayed at the edges.

Mike wasn't moving.

Richie got up, stumbled back. "Fuck!" His voice screeched like he couldn't get air in his lungs. "Fuck!"

He turned around and sprinted after the shooter.

The guy stumbled off the ground, limped for his gun. Richie shot. The shooter threw his hands in the air as the bullet bounced off the concrete.

Me and the rest of the crew ran to Richie.

"Don't kill him," he said.

The shooter took off with a limp. Didn't make it halfway down the street before we jumped him, got a hold of his arms.

Richie punched him in the face, busted his nose into blood. He balled his fists, gritted his teeth, shoulders heaving. He punched him again. Hacked up a loogy, spat on his cheek. "Tape him up. Throw him in the back."

We dragged him to the van. Richie stopped beside Mike's body. He kneeled, put his fingers on Mike's eyelids, and shut them.

I turned and looked down at Richie, at Mike lying like his wings were broken beside him.

Richie held Mike's head. "I ain't leavin' him here."

I thought I'd say something, but nothing came out. I nodded.

"We'll get a big wooden board, mix his ashes into paint. Paint him with a joint hanging off his lip." He placed his hand on Mike's, gripped it tight. "He'd have liked that."

# 27

I wrote a story about a robot.

A lot of different hands had programmed it. Programmed and deprogrammed until it didn't know what its purpose was anymore. Or if it ever really had one. It wandered around with no emotions, doing what its programmers programmed it to do. It hadn't the capacity to ask itself what it wanted.

It was built to preserve its battery, but batteries were fragile. So that's all the robot sought to achieve, preserving its battery, and though its steel got colder and its wires got tougher, the battery was still fragile. The robot determined the best way to preserve it was to not let anyone know its fragility.

By the time the robot became advanced enough to ask itself what it wanted, it forgot it even had a battery. It wanted to be state-of-the-art. It wanted to be equipped. It wanted to be strong. But what it didn't know was that it wanted to be human.

I watched two Krew members die in less than two weeks. One of them was killed at the hands of another Krew member. The other, those same hands held his head and closed his eyes after he died.

Richie hung a picture of Mike on the wall with the other fallen Krew members. A photo where he had a paintbrush between his teeth and a smile on his face broader than the caboose of a graffiti artist's canvas. Home before he went home.

Michael Rae Stevenson

1989-2026

*"May this motherfucker rest in all the big titties, dank kush, and
cash the high towers of Hell have to offer!"*

Sometimes, Richie would stop, drop his elbows on the bar counter, and stare
at it until the whites of his eyes started to change colors.

And if you asked him about it, he'd say it is what it is. People die. Part of the
business. What's important is we get our money and guns back.

Richie kept Mike's killer behind the steel bars beneath the basement stairs. I
always wondered why they had those bars. I guess I knew now.

He had us cuff his hands and tape up his legs. Said he wasn't letting him go
until he got his money back.

After three days, the guy had a swollen black eye, blood dried under his
nose, swollen cheeks, and two missing front teeth. After a week, he lay in a fetal
position.

Richie sent me down to the basement to give him his food and water. Left-
overs on a plate, a bowl he could bend down and slurp from. I slid it beneath
the bars. Didn't like looking at him but couldn't help but stare.

Sweat and dirt made him look like an abstract oil painting. He breathed like
he was down to one lung, and even that sounded clogged and damaged. Bruises
up and down his arms, his legs.

I sat beside the bars, bent my knees in front of me, crossed my arms on top. "Just tell 'em what they wanna hear. Might get you out of here—"

"Fuck you."

I reached under the bar and pushed his plate closer to where he could reach it. "They're not gonna let you go."

"My guys are coming. They're gonna fuck your guys up real bad. Wait and see."

I nodded, shrugged. "Maybe." I took my arms off my knees. "You killed my friend. Y' know? He was a good guy. He did some shit. Some really bad shit, but...he wasn't a bad person."

"I don't give a fuck."

I nodded. "He liked art. Wanted to be an artist. Loved giving people tattoos. I think if he were presented a different path in life, he'd have taken it, but somehow, he ended up where he did. And now he's dead. I hate what you did to him, but I don't blame you." I shook my head. "I've killed people's friends too."

He looked at me a long time.

"What's your name?"

"I ain't telling you that."

"Fair. My name's Nolan. Sometimes they call me Bird because of how I fly down the road, y' know?" I chuckled. "I was a package delivery driver before I joined the crew. What were you before you got in with the Rhats?"

He hesitated. Furrowed his brows. Didn't look like he would say anything, but he slowly parted his lips. "Car mechanic."

"Yeah?"

"Lost the job. Couldn't find a new one. Got kicked out of my apartment, ended up on the streets. Started selling rock, next thing you know..."

"It happens that way."

"Yeah." He nodded. "It does."

"You got a family?"

"No. Used to want one. I guess not anymore. Not after what my life became."

"I get it."

"I ask myself all the time, what is this all even about?" He sighed. "I'm sorry I killed your friend."

"Don't worry about it. I told you. I got blood on my hands, too."

Richie came downstairs. I got off the floor and stepped back.

Richie looked at me with his brows knitted. "What is this? A playdate?" He knocked on the bars. "Lunch over."

Dude hadn't even touched his plate yet.

Richie unlocked the door, went in, and kicked the prisoner in the stomach. The guy clenched his gut and gagged.

Richie pulled a gun from the back of his pants, kicked the guy onto his stomach and stepped on his back. He kneeled, dug his knee into his spine and the gun barrel into his back at the same spot Mike received his bullet. He leaned down to his ear. "You don't know how fucking bad I wanna pull this trigger right now."

Sweat beaded the prisoner's forehead.

"But I need my shit." Richie raised up. "I'm gonna ask one last time. The money. The guns. Where are they hiding 'em?"

The prisoner took three heavy breaths. "Up your ass."

Richie pistol-whipped him.

"I gotta ask you again, I'm gonna start cutting shit off and shipping it to your friends."

"Go fuck yourself."

He struck him again. Got off his back. The longer Richie looked at him, the more he ground his teeth. He shot two bullets beside the guy's head. "Fuck!"

"You might as well just kill me," the prisoner laughed. "I ain't saying sh—"

Richie kicked him in the stomach. He stepped back, paced in a circle, kicked him again. Again. Again.

The prisoner rolled over on his knees and gagged a string of blood. He fell on his side. "My guys are gonna come for you."

"Good. We'll be waiting."

Richie left the cage and locked the door.

"He gets you to the money, he gets out of here, right?" I asked.

Richie stopped walking but kept silent.

"Right?"

"Make sure he eats. I don't need him dead."

Axe baked a cake.

He topped it with red cream that contrasted with the white icing underneath. He frosted it with sprinkles and crystal sanding sugar that blended into the icing until all the white was hidden by a mix of different colors, and the red cream streamed from the top of the cake and rinsed the sprinkles and sugar into a hardened puddle at the edge of the plate.

He cut me a slice. Tasted good, but it had a thick outer layer, and you couldn't taste the icing until you got through that layer.

"When did you start baking?" I put a plate of crumbs, red cream, and sprinkles on the bar counter.

"You like it?"

I smiled. "Have I ever not liked your cakes?"

He walked into the kitchen. "I've been baking since I was a kid."

"What got you into it?"

He got quiet. "Did you want another slice?"

"I'm good." I shifted around on the bar stool, rested my elbows on the counter and gazed at the faces on the memorial wall. Only one of them I recognized.

"I don't know you that well, Axe."

"Beer?"

I didn't even see him beside me. He handed me a bottle. I didn't really like cake and alcohol together, but I took it anyway.

I popped the cap off. "That's a big wall." I took a drink. "A lot of people died. I don't think I ever really paid attention to it until Mike's face ended up on it. That could be any of us. Easily."

Axe leaned against the counter and looked at what I was looking at. He cast his eyes down, clasped his hands on the counter. Squeezed until the veins and tendons poked through his skin.

"It's been over two years, and I still don't really know you. Don't take this the wrong way, but if your face is on that wall, I don't know how that might make me feel. All I'd be able to say is, he made good cakes." I set the bottle down. "I look at that wall, and it runs across my mind—everyone. What will I feel when it's Jackie? What will I feel when it's Arin? Pip? What would anybody feel if it were me up there? Would they care?"

"I'd care."

I chuckled a little. "You would?"

"Yeah." He nodded. "I would."

"That's good to know."

He sat down next to me. "I started baking when I was ten. The other kids used to make fun of me for it. Said boys don't bake, but it was something my grandma taught me. She believed life shouldn't just be surviving. Life should be living. It's better to live one short life full of pleasure than one long life just existing." He shifted all the way around on the bar stool, away from the pictures on the wall. He took a long drink of beer, held the bottle in his lap. He stared out at nothing, with a look I was used to seeing on Pip's face. "She was the only person who took care of me. My mom got put away for drug abuse. Last time my dad saw me, I don't even remember." He nodded like he was admitting to something. "Grandma died when I was fourteen." He took a drink.

"Sorry to hear that."

"They put me in foster care, but I didn't like it, so I ran away. Squatted in different places. Lived with different people. Took me a while to admit that I was homeless." He took another drink. "Richie was in jail when I joined the Krew. It was actually Mike who was calling shots at the time. I met him through a guy who hooked me up with a dealer when I needed to make ends meet."

"Can I ask you something? How did your grandma die?"

"She got sick. She was a young grandma. Too young for Medicare. Couldn't afford healthcare, and what she got from her job was a joke."

"What did she get sick with?"

He pulled one side of his mouth into a bittersweet smile. "Diabetes."

I gazed at the crumbs and sanding sugar in the middle of the plate.

"No matter how bad things get, I can always bake something. It's the only thing I got left of her."

I sat still. "You didn't join D3vil's Krew just because of the money? Did you?"

He took a drink. "In some ways, I don't even remember joining."

"I get that."

"I don't wanna die." He slowly turned his head, looked me in the eye. "I don't wanna die, but...I..." he froze, his mouth left open mid-speech. "I don't know how to live. It's this life. I don't know how to live without this life, but if it don't kill me..." A tear crawled to the corner of his eye.

"We all have to die." I held my bottle to my lips but didn't take a drink. "But when you do, it don't got to be in this life."

"She was seven years old." He turned his gaze towards his lap, gripped his bottle with two shaking hands. "She was spending the night at her dad's. She had her stuffed bear in her arms when they found her on the couch. The bullet went clean through her head, so I always hoped she didn't feel anything. The news said there'd been a shoot-out. A stray bullet went through the window, and..." tears rolled out of both his eyes, ran down his cheeks like streams of melted ice.

I rubbed his back.

"It was my bullet. I shot that little girl. Over some fucking drugs." He swallowed. "And what did I get? A rent payment in. A couple thousand dollars. That man watched his daughter die over a couple thousand dollars. That child's life was wasted over a couple thousand dollars. But I..." Tears splatted the palms of his hands. "Here I am." He looked at me. "I can't stop."

I rubbed his back.

He let the tears run down his eyes until they left nothing but wet residue on his cheeks.

"Grandma loved to live." He shook his head. "She wouldn't be proud of me."

I found myself on the church's third floor. The library I don't know if anyone even remembered.

I wasn't looking for anything in particular. I don't even know what brought me up there. But I found something. An old composition notebook. Had Richie's name on it. Lyrics and poems.

*I polished my gun tonight.*
*The angels said a prayer, and the crows took flight.*
*I hope that God can hear me cry,*
*And knows that snakes don't always lie.*
*He knows the truth is in the fruit,*
*So why'd He bar us from its root?*
*I can't beg for mercy and vengeance all the same,*
*But there's got to be more than sin to a name.*
*I polished my gun tonight.*
*The angels said a prayer, and the crows took flight.*
*I think that God forgot my eyes,*
*But the Devil's not in disguise*
*He's just ignored,*
*Bought and whored.*
*He don't want money, he don't want love*
*Just the soul of a fallen dove.*
*And if I bring him my feathers, he'll bring me my cash,*
*Store it with the rest of his stash*
*Made of the other broken wings and fallen dreams*
*That God didn't bother to redeem.*
*I polished my gun tonight.*
*The angels said a prayer and the crows took flight.*
*I'll look death in the eye, and it'll look at me.*
*Get down on one knee.*

I'll tell it no, throw away its ring.

Remind that son of a bitch it was just a fling.

The raven's rapping on my window, my door,

But I can't ignore it anymore.

I'm no human, I'm what's left of a seed

After the vermin and maggots came to feed.

Whatever used to live in my chest,

Has gnawed its way through my breast,

And now nothing pulsates, nothing breathes.

Just waiting for the raven to leave a message about me.

Until that day, I won't be free

The angels are praying for me,

But they're all praying in vain.

Given the lives I've slain.

So, help me God.

*-Richie Bryant*

He had a whole book full of them.

## 28

Cradles
  Blankets
  Arms and breasts
  The air is clear, the water's right,
  Come deal with the Devil tonight.
  Laughter
  Games
  Spray paint and beats
  The air is clear, the water's right
  Come deal with the Devil tonight.
  Camels
  Needles
  Pixies and dust
  The air is clear, the water's right.
  Come deal with the Devil tonight.
  Bibles
  Crosses
  Bullets and toys

*The air is clear, the water's right.*
*Come deal with the Devil tonight.*

*-Richie Bryant*

I asked the prisoner if he ever had a dream. He told me dreams were for people too afraid to wake up.

Richie had me drive the Krew late one night.

We carried guns.

I stopped on a street with one light. Houses that looked like Lego set pieces, tall but crunched together like whoever squeezed them choked them so hard it made the brick crumble. Barred windows and doors. Wooden rooftops. Telephone poles with tangled wires hanging and drooping like a bum's greasy hair. Beer bottles on the lawn. Cigarette butts in the cracks and potholes of the pavement.

"Why don't we just break in?" I pulled my ski mask over my face. "Seize 'em? Bring 'em back? We can throw 'em in the cell with the other guy."

"You don't call the shots," Richie said. "Besides. We need to send a message that D3vil's Krew don't fuck around."

"It's a rowhouse."

Richie cocked his rifle. "Aim for the windows."

I looked in the back, and by the looks on everyone's faces, they weren't feeling good about it either.

"I just think there's a better—"

"Aim for the fucking windows! You blow a stray bullet through somebody's grandma, that's on you."

Arin slid the back door open. I took in a deep breath, held that shit in like I was holding back a puke that would go away if I denied it. Rolled down the window.

Richie handed me my rifle. Everybody in the back aimed theirs out the door. I got up on the windowsill. Richie took the first shot, and before anyone could exhale, the house got eaten bite after bite by a swarm of bullets. The windows shattered. The doors splintered. Concrete blocks exploded. The drainpipe dropped off the brick. The wood boards busted. Looked like it caught a flesh-eating disease. Like some type of jiggers infected and consumed it in seconds. Made my skin crawl.

"Alright! Alright!" Richie shouted. "Get back in. Let's move."

They shut the door. I threw my gun inside and slammed on the gas. Looked through the rearview mirror. Nobody was following me, but I had a weight that sat on my chest no matter how I tried to shake it off. You'd think a man would get used to it. He just gets better at pretending it's not there.

I woke up the next day with a stiff neck and a crick in my back. It's what happens when you don't get any sleep.

Grabbed my phone off the nightstand. The first thing that popped up in the news was a story about a drive-by shooting. Three people killed. No named suspects. Victims thought to be involved in a street gang called the Rhats.

It didn't end there. It would've been nice if it ended there, but it didn't. Three days later, the Rhats thought they'd retaliate. Or maybe they thought they'd take us out and pick up their guy. A fool's move if you ask me. Not just because they already tried to pull a similar trick in the alley the first time we went after them, but they ought to know that we took notes. Richie caught word from Krew members in Brooklyn that they were headed our way. I can't say how those Krew members found out about it, but I'm guessing somebody threatened somebody.

They showed up in two SUVs, but our guys showed up in three. We had Krew members hiding on the other side of the street, behind our SUVs, behind abandoned buildings, a basement entrance, trash bins—every corner. House crew stayed in the building, tucked up under the windows on the third floor. We aimed our guns out the window.

Soon as the Rhats rolled up on us, a bullet burst through the first SUV's windshield and shattered glass across the hood. Chaos rained down like a blizzard from Hell. Return fire cracked graffiti-stained brick, blew out a streetlight, planted bullets into the pavement. Booming staccato rattled the walls, turned the street into a thunderstorm of vengeance. The reek of gun smoke choked the air. A bitter taste numbed my tongue. Bullet shells were cockroach corpses scattered across the road; where one landed, another followed.

There were more of us than them, and they were surrounded. They had no protection. Maybe bulletproof vests, but the bullet-riddled doors of the SUVs ought to tell you the vehicles were no shields. They retreated.

*"A Texas construction worker died in the hospital yesterday afternoon after being denied a water break..."*

"What do you think of that?"

I met with Pip at the bar. Same bar we always went to.

"Think of what?"

I reached into a basket of fried pickles. "That."

*"The family of the victim are looking to press charges; however..."*

"What are we doing?" I said. "They're not gonna give us the money back."

"We'll get it back one way or another—"

"It doesn't matter."

He stared at me.

"That's not where my mind's been."

He looked behind him at the TV on the wall.

"It's not what's been on your mind either. Shouldn't be."

He took a bite of fried pickle.

"We get the money back, and then what? Somebody else steals our shit. They strike back because we struck back." I leaned forward and lowered my voice. "People get killed." I took a swig of beer. "And it's just gonna keep happening over and over and over again."

He wiped his mouth with a napkin. "That's the life we live."

"I talked to Mike before he died. He told me what the Krew used to be about. Or *tried* to be about."

"I know." He took a swig. "But that ain't who we are."

"And why not?"

He set his drink down.

"I feel like everywhere I go, I'm hearing that right there." I pointed at the TV. "If it ain't passing out dead, it's somebody's starving in the streets. Evictions. Somebody's grandma died because she was too young for Medicare, but her low-wage job couldn't even take care of her healthcare."

"There's nothing we can do about it."

"You sure about that?"

He looked at me. I looked at him.

"Why are we here?"

He parted his lips but didn't say anything.

"What the fuck did Mike die for?" I dropped my head back against the seat. "What the fuck are any of us dying for?"

"What do you suggest we do?"

"Let's get together with everybody at the church. If Richie's not going to make use of D3vil's Krew, I will."

I visited the church the next day. Sent a text message to everybody but Richie. Wasn't about to risk him ruling against my idea and having the whole thing called off. I told everybody to meet me on the third floor.

There wasn't a whole lot of room up there. The whole floor was basically just an attic, but Jackie and Arin found a seat at the chess table. Pip plopped down on some old dusty lounge chair. Axe leaned against that. I stood next to Richie's manifesto.

"I turned on the news yesterday," I said. "I think D3vil's Krew's been beating around the bush far too long."

"Why'd you bring us up here?" Jackie asked.

"It's time to act."

She furrowed her brow. "Okay?"

"I mean it. D3vil's Krew is a powerful force. We proved that with the Grace Redemption Church back in 2014; we can prove that with the world. We're still here today for a fucking reason."

"Okay, but why'd you call us up here?"

"Yeah," Arin said, "And where's Richie?"

"Richie doesn't care about nothing but that business with The Rhats right now. I can't risk him fucking this up." I put my hand on the manifesto. "But we can get back to this right here."

They looked at each other.

"I say we get out there, and we raise hell. We break shit. We scream shit. We turn something over. Maybe we can get others to join us. If we put as much energy into this as we do heists and drugs, we can make something happen."

They took another look at each other.

I waited for a response.

Jackie sat back in her seat, crossed her arms. "What's in it for us?"

I shook my head. "Really?"

"Yeah. What am I gettin'?"

"The nation's on fucking fire, Jackie—"

"The nation's *been* on fire. You think some little street rats are gonna put it out?"

I clenched my fists. "You had a girlfriend, didn't you? Lacey? Loved her more than anybody in your entire life, but you haven't seen her since the two of you went to jail trying to survive in some shithole you were thrust into. You think she's living the American dream right now?"

She turned her eyes away from me.

"There's a broader picture we're looking at." I gestured to everybody. "You want a better world for your kid? You want everybody to have healthcare? Tired of eating shit? The first thing we have to do is make it known we're not gonna bend over and take it anymore. I'm not saying it's gonna happen overnight. I'm saying we have to push back."

Jackie leaned forward. "What's-in it-for-us?"

I stepped back and dropped my hands in my pockets.

Their faces had no more interest than a dog who knows he ain't getting a treat when you tell him to roll over.

I sighed. "First thing we gotta do is cause a disruption. Break some shit, loot some shit. Whatever you steal, you get to keep. Sell it. Do whatever you want."

She dropped back against the seat. "Alright. I'm in."

Everybody agreed to it. Maybe for the money. But I like to think D3vil's Krew just didn't like to admit what they were really feeling.

# 29

Richie used to say sometimes you need a little bit of chaos to get things shaking.

Jackie and Arin brought the van out to me. I don't know what they told Richie, if they told him anything at all, but Richie was so caught up in the mayhem and drama with the Rhats, I don't think he paid attention to anything anymore.

Pip and Axe were already at my place. We left with guns and liquor bottles. Ski masks and hoodies. Spray paint.

Waited until the store closed, the manager locked the doors, the security gates came down. We hit one target that night. It wasn't a random decision. The company was known for supporting legislation against workers' access to healthcare and lost wages.

We kicked down the security door. The alarm screamed. We shot up the dresses, designer hats, Gucci purses, and sunglasses, leopard print jackets, Prada bags, and satin robes. Watched them pop and tear and break until they shredded into debris. We shattered the jewelry display glass and grabbed every necklace, diamond ring, and bracelet inside, pearls, silver, and gold. Crammed fur coats and gator-skin boots into bags. Grabbed lipstick tubes and scribbled all over the mirrors. *Enough! Enough!* Smashed the perfume bottles and dropped a lighter in it. Watched the flames unfold like popping red feathers. We lit liquor bottles and smashed them against the shelves. Raced out the door.

I took my spray paint can out the side of my belt, shook it. *Enough!* I didn't
know what else to say, and I didn't have a lot of time, so I quickly sprayed an
anarchy symbol next to it. Sirens wailed around the corner, so I left it at that.
Jumped into the van and sped off with the rest of my crew.

People had already gathered. People with their phones out. People with their
hands clasped. By the time the firetrucks passed us, my chest tickled. I wanted
to cough. I wanted to laugh. I did something bad. I did something good. I did
something evil. I did something noble. I did something crazy.


*"An act of vandalism left NYPD puzzled last night..."*

It hadn't even been one day yet.

*#Enough!*

*#Enough!*

*#Enough!*

Everywhere. YouTube videos and TikTok. Facebook posts and Twitter.
Videos of the firemen hosing down the building. Photos of the spray paint I
tagged on the brick. *Enough!* People supporting it. People condemning it.

Nothing but a bunch of criminals destroying property.

Solidarity!

Someone ought to line up whoever did it. March 'em to the gallows.

Solidarity!

They're anarchists trying to destroy this country. Crazy fucking socialists.
Commies. Left-wing wacko commies!

Eat the rich! Solidarity! Enough!

I didn't think we would get that far, but we got that far in that little time, and
I sat up that morning and poured myself a coffee, watched all of it unfold with
a smile and a tinge of fear.

*"There are currently no named suspects, and police are investigating whether
this was an act of terrorism..."*

They knew what it was.

The D3vil's Krew still hadn't gotten back the money or the guns. But what we did get was an email. Richie said that the Rhats agreed to back down. All they wanted was their guy back. They'd trade us the money and guns for him. Richie said he'd agree. Said he'd meet them under a highway bridge somewhere outside the city and make the exchange. No weapons.

I didn't have a good feeling about it.

We showed up when the last sunrays turned the sky red, and the crows dotted the clouds.

We put a sack over the prisoner's head, taped his hands behind his back. Had him in the passenger seat with the window rolled down so they could see him.

"I don't think this is a good idea," I said.

"It ain't about what you think." Richie opened the door. "It's about getting my money back." He got out, and Pip and Jackie followed him, stood behind him on the cracked pavement.

The Rhats stepped out of the SUV. There were six of them. Three of them carried black duffel bags.

"That the guns?" Richie asked.

The guy in front said yeah.

"What about the money?"

A seventh guy got out of the back seat with a black briefcase.

"That all of it?"

He handed the briefcase to Richie. Richie opened it, squatted down, and leafed through the money. "Looks good." He jerked his head.

Axe got out and dragged the prisoner out of the passenger seat. He fell onto his knees, and Axe pulled him off the ground.

"Give 'em the guns," the guy in front said.

They handed the first bag to Richie, the second to Pip, and the third to Jackie. The three of them looked inside.

Richie zipped up the bag. "Everything where it's supposed to be?"

"Yeah," Pip said.

Jackie said, "It's all here."

Richie nodded.

Axe marched the prisoner forward.

I squeezed my eyes shut, took a deep breath, and let it out slowly. Rubbed my face.

Axe shoved the prisoner to the ground. The guy in front lifted him by his shoulder and pulled the bag off his head. His eyes widened. He almost fell over. By the time he looked up at Richie, Richie had a Glock pointed at him. Planted a bullet between his eyes. The man didn't even have time to process the fact that the prisoner wasn't their guy. It wasn't a prisoner at all. It was Arin.

Richie, Pip, Jackie, and Axe immediately opened fire. The seven Rhats tried to turn around, run back to the SUV, but they were face down in a pool of blood before they even reached the door.

Richie got in the passenger seat.

"That wasn't fair," I said.

"What ain't fair is somebody breaking into my space and taking my shit. Think there's gonna be no consequence?"

"You made a deal, and you broke it."

"Tough titties." He shut the door. "Mess with my money, you fucked up."

I said under my breath, "That ain't what D3vil's Krew is supposed to be about."

"Huh?"

I shook my head. "Nothing."

"You got something to say, spit it."

I sighed.

"Get your act together, Bird. I don't need anybody going pansy on me. Got it?"

I held my breath.

He slapped me in the back of my head. "I asked you something!"

"Yeah." I nodded. "I got it."

He shuffled around in his pocket until he found a pack of cigarettes. Popped one in his mouth, took out his lighter. "Broke the deal—ha!" He said to himself, "Wait'll you see what I break next."

I sat against the seat and stared at him while he let the flame nibble the end of his cigarette and stared towards a fading horizon. "You got your money back, Richie. What more do you need?"

Not even a week passed before we drove to the Rhat's base. We didn't go looking for anyone. We left with liquor bottles and lighters, assault rifles. We shot up the warehouse from the van, shredded the wooden boards, busted the windows. We got out, lit the bottles, tossed them through the windows. Watched the flames eat the building from the inside out until the entire warehouse was swallowed whole.

When the rest of us ran back to the van, Richie stayed, a shadow in front of the giant bonfire made from his bloodthirst. He stepped backward before he turned around and joined the rest of us in the van. The fire flickered in his eyes like cigarette cinders. He grinned, but his glare spoke louder.

He wasn't done.

He had us burn down another base. Drive around town and look for anyone who had the Rhat's mark tattooed on their back. Then we'd follow them. Maybe back to their place, maybe someplace else, but I'd let him out of the van, and he'd get out with a hood over his head and a gun in his hand.

He wasn't done.

He got Krew members from other boroughs and states involved. In all, there were more of us than them. If they had a few soldiers, we had a whole army. I asked Richie if he was going to let it go. He said no one fucks with The D3vil's Krew.

I think they learned their lesson.

No one fucks with The D3vil's Krew.

But that wasn't the only thing on my mind. *#Enough!* had become its own movement. And I wasn't done.

I and everyone who wasn't Richie brought our guns again, liquor bottles and spray paint. We broke into a clothing store, shot up the clothes on the rack, scribbled lipstick on the mirrors. But we weren't alone this time.

Once the spray paint hit the brick and the burning merchandise glowed through the windows, other people joined in. Regular people. People off the streets. Broke through the glass, kicked down the doors. They looted and smashed and cheered and raised their fists and their middle fingers. They screamed. A car crashed through the window of a neighboring building, and people poured inside, people from the back seat, people from the streets. I don't know where they all came from. When we showed up, we entered through the back alley, where there were no pedestrians, but when we came out, there was a crowd that multiplied like cells.

Then the red and blue lights flashed. The black and white cars skirred onto the sidewalks. The ambulances showed up, the firetrucks. Cops got out with batons, pepper spray, guns and Tasers. A war was on. I stopped and gazed at it. Dumbfounded. Proud. Terrified.

This happened because of me.

There was a part of me that wanted to join in, but a part of me that knew I needed to get the hell out of there while the going was good. Once the tear gas exploded, I ran back to the van, made sure my crew were all there, and hit the road.

The next day, the news went on about how a riot broke out. Five people injured, several arrested. Video after video. Article after article. Talking heads and online debates. Got so bad, even politicians were mentioning my antics.

I didn't know whether to laugh or cry.


Richie didn't know I was there.

He had his elbows on the bar counter, his eyes on Mike's memorial picture.

I was coming out of the bathroom, but I stopped when I heard him talking. Peeked through the door crack.

"Boy, we sure had a good run, didn't we?" He spoke like he was having a conversation. Like Mike was going to come out of there, laugh, and say, sure did, then light a joint or a cigarette, throw back a shot of whiskey, pretend he wasn't dead.

"I tell ya what," Richie said, "a lot of shit's been going down since you been gone, and I gotta admit, sometimes, I don't know what to do. Just what I know *how* to do." He hung his head. "Maybe that's why I need you back. Keep me levelheaded. Something like that."

Mike's smile was unmoving.

"I got the money. Guns, too. All of it."

The floor wasn't swept. The counter wasn't shined. The graffiti was dry and chipped. There was an empty shot glass on the bar counter next to Richie.

He smashed it against Mike's photo. "Why'd you have to go and fucking die? Why didn't you just let me get hit? THAT BULLET WASN'T FOR YOU!" He shoved over a bar stool, dropped his elbow on the counter, pressed his fingertips against his eyelids.

His face turned red. Veins poked through the side of his head. He shook.

He took his elbow off the bar counter and moved his hand around the back of the bar stool like he didn't know what to do with it. His fingers quivered. He licked the tear that ran from his cheek to his mouth.

The door screeched.

He looked my way, and when he saw me, he quickly turned away from me and dropped his head. His voice came out low. "You goin' home?"

"Not yet. I need to ask Arin something."

"Should probably hurry up and do that then."

He leaned against the counter, his shoulders up, his head down, face hidden behind his hair.

I nodded. "Alright."

He wiped his eye.

Just something I noticed.

# 30

"What do you plan on doing with him?"

Richie poured down the rest of his beer and slammed his glass on the bar counter. "Don't know yet."

I rummaged through my pocket for a pack of cigarettes. "You've had him here a long time."

"I know."

"Guy's half dead." I popped a cigarette in my mouth, lit it.

Richie cut his eyes at me. "Don't try and make this your business."

"It kind of already is, though. Isn't it?" I shrugged. "I'm involved in this too."

"Gimme one of those."

I tossed him the pack, slid him the lighter.

He put one in his mouth, tilted his head as he lit it. He turned around on the barstool, leaned back against the counter with his elbows on top. "Hashtag Enough. I feel like I'm hearing that everywhere."

"Sounds like it's a good thing." I nodded. "Folks don't wanna eat shit anymore."

"Hmm..." he blew out a cloud of smoke. "I hear that."

"Maybe some change will happen."

"Reminds me of my idealist days during Occupy Wall Street." He shook his head. "Kids."

He took the cigarette out of his mouth. I took a drag, blew out smoke that looked like ghost hair.

"I hear they're burning down buildings," he said. "Tagging anarchy symbols on the walls. Sounds a little half-assed."

"How?"

"Because if you're gonna fuck shit up, then fuck shit up."

"How would you do it?"

"If I were to do it, I'd be ready to die. But let's get real. There's no sense in sacrificing life for liberty."

"Why not? You risk your life every day dealing drugs and shooting guns. Why not put it someplace that matters?"

"That ain't the same thing."

"Sure it is. You're just blind to it—"

"That ain't the same thing." He shifted in his seat, tapped his cigarette off in the ashtray. "Do you even know what anarchy is?"

I inhaled a long drag of burning nicotine.

"Any idea what that shit's about? And when you get it, then what?"

Curls of smoke drifted from my mouth.

"You fix things, right? It's just like magic." He snapped his fingers.

"That ain't the kind of anarchy I'm talkin' about."

"Tell us the one we can wish upon a star about, and it's gonna wave its wand and fix our problems overnight like the motherfuckin' blue fairy."

"Nothing gets fixed at all if we don't act."

He stubbed his cigarette out in the ashtray. "I don't want you taking my guys with you anymore."

"We're making ourselves heard."

"You think you're gonna be a little freedom fighter, burn down a couple of buildings, start a couple of riots, and that's gonna give 'em a run for their money? Tell ya something, we play our game and stay in our place. Maybe it'll kill us, but at least it won't be in vain."

"Everybody's dying in vain. You think Mike's death was for a noble cause—"

"Hey—" He jumped off the stool. "Mike died for this." He held out his arms. "He died for you. He died for me. And everybody in this goddamn crew."

"And what did he get?"

He flared his nostrils. "I been around the block, buddy. Been there. Done that. Tell ya somethin' I learned. They don't back down. They come full force."

"Don't let anybody fuck you over. That's what *you* told *me.*"

He rubbed his temples and shook his head.

"Don't bend over and take it. *You* wrote those words."

"Jesus Christ. You wanna take somebody with you for your personal vendetta? Find somebody else. Those are my men, this is my crew, and I call the shots."

"Vendetta?" I laughed. I got out of my seat, threw my cigarette on the concrete.

"Where the hell you are going?"

I marched to the basement.

He followed me.

I threw open the door, turned on the light, and stomped down the steps. "What do you call this?" I stepped backward to the prisoner's cell. "You annihilated everyone in his whole crew. You got your shit back. What's the sense in keeping him anymore except for him to suffer?"

"Jesus Chri—"

"You can't keep a man suffering!"

The prisoner lay in fetal position in the corner of the cell, half dead, half alive. Malnourished. Dark rings around his eyes. Sallow, sweat-soaked skin.

Richie licked his lips. "That's what happens when you touch my money."

"Not everything's about money, Richie."

"What? It ain't money keeping a roof over your head? Cramming food down your gullet every goddamn day? Wasn't it for money that you joined this gig? My mother was a prostitute." He slapped his chest. "My whole existence is about money."

He glared at me and bared his teeth, but I knew the truth, and it was shimmering in the corner of his eye. He just wouldn't admit it.

I shook my head. "None of this has been about money. Or the guns. Not even from the start. You know well as me what it's really about."

He inhaled like he was going to say something, but nothing came out.

I pulled a gun from the back of my pants.

"What the fuck are you—"

I shot the prisoner in the head.

"You piece of shit." Richie charged at me.

I turned the gun on him.

He stopped. Clenched his teeth. "Get that gun out of my face." His shoulders heaved. "Or so help me God..."

Silence swallowed up everything but the sound of breathing. I stared him in the eyes. He stared directly back into mine. I clenched my fist, balled my lips.

He didn't look scared. Didn't look intimidated. Not even nervous. Just...ready.

I lowered the gun. "Sorry."

He walked up to me, snatched it from my hand, and released the magazine. Slugged me in the face.

I stumbled back.

"I'm gonna let you off with a warning this time." He put his hand around the back of my neck and pulled my face to his. "You're in my territory, and I call the shots."

Ma called me one day. Told me to come out to the house.

I hadn't visited my parents' house in Buffalo in years.

I might get the occasional call. Might call them. Ma, anyway. I might see them at a get-together for the holidays at somebody else's house or a restaurant or something, but I forgot what it felt like to stand in that old wooden house. With the creaky floors and the low ceiling. The peeling wallpaper that looked like it was pasted on with glue sticks.

I was reluctant. I asked why she wanted me there. It wasn't like they invited me over any other time. She didn't give me much of an answer. Just, you need to see your father.

About what?

There shouldn't be a what, she said. Said he was my father. We may have our differences, but at the end of the day, we're still blood, and if I kept running away from him, I would regret it.

And as much as I wanted to fight her on that, she wasn't wrong.

So, I went out there, my bike and me. Made a stop at a motel in Pennsylvania, then finished the rest of the drive the following day.

When I stood in front of the house, those things I thought I'd forgotten were there like they never left my memory in the first place. The American flag hanging over the porch rail. The white bench on the porch and its peeling paint. The chipped planks on the window shutters. The rust on the drainpipe.

I didn't go in with a sense of ease. I spent two to three years walking into warehouses occupied by armed criminals and creeping down back alleys to make trades with violent drug dealers, yet I never felt as uncomfortable walking into a place as I did walking into Ma and Pop's house. In some ways, I'd have rather met with the drug dealers.

I climbed the steps, knocked on the door, and that old wood smell hit me like it never left me.

Ma opened up. She hugged me and let me inside. Pops sat on the couch in front of a commercial about how buying an SUV will save your kid from cancer. Katelyn sat on the couch, too, with my almost two-year-old nephew I hardly knew. Katelyn got up and hugged me, and even though he probably didn't know my face, the almost two-year-old wrapped his arms around my knees.

"Steve not coming?" I asked.

"He had to work," Katelyn said.

"You came all the way out here, too? What's the occasion?"

Ma came in from the kitchen with a pan of cookies. "It's been a long time since we got together as a family. I thought it would be good for us." She set the pan on the coffee table.

That old coffee table. I hadn't seen it in years. Ma probably just polished its wood. It still had that nick I put in it when I was ten. Hit it with a baseball I wasn't supposed to be playing with in the house. Thought I could cover it up with a blanket. Then Ma asked what that blanket was doing there. I said I thought it needed a tablecloth. Pops got on me good for that one.

Pops looked thinner than the last time I'd seen him. Paler. Bags under the eyes. Was Pops getting old? Had I been away from my own father so long, I didn't even see him age? But his changes happened quicker than I would've expected. And they didn't look all that natural.

Pops looked at me with his brows furrowed. He didn't get up, but he held out his arms. "Come 'ere, son. Let me get a look at you."

I walked over and gave him a hug. It was kind of awkward. No hug from my father ever felt sincere.

I stepped back.

He tilted his head. "Put on a little muscle, didn't you?" He smiled. "Been working out?"

I nodded.

"What's that on your head? Another tattoo? What kind of bird is it?"

"It's nothing."

He sighed. Nodded. Not the reaction I expected. He didn't scoff at my hair. Didn't yell at me for getting another tattoo.

"Grab a cookie," Ma said. "Hurry up before they get cold."

My nephew already had his hands in the tray, crumbs on his hands and lips. Ma giggled. "Or before the baby eats them all."

I looked at my father. He didn't look like he wanted to look back at me, but he did. And he did it like he didn't recognize me.

I grabbed a cookie off the tray, bit into it. I'd forgotten how good Ma's baking was. I hadn't eaten nobody's baking but Axe's in a while, and while his baking may have been delicious, it didn't remind me of my old bed. It's kind of amazing, the things that don't mean nothing to you until they're gone. Then you got to ask yourself—is that some sort of trickery of the brain? I hated that house when I lived there. Now, it felt like my flesh and blood.

"How's the job been?" Pops reached forward and grabbed a cookie.

"Good."

"You still doin' the same thing?"

"Yeah."

"How'd you get those scars?"

I shrugged.

"You've got 'em on your face."

Ma came around and lifted my chin with her fingers. "You do."

"Life's rough, Pops." I threw the rest of my cookie in my mouth. "Kind of like you always told me."

*"Hashtag Enough has sparked a wave of vandalism across the country, leaving many business owners in fear for their property and safety..."*

"Bunch of criminals." Pops waved the remote at the TV. "That's all they are."

I sat on the couch's armrest. "I think there's more to it."

"Nuh-uh." Pops shook his head. "They're destroying property. And get off the couch like that. Have some manners."

I got up. Slid my hands into my pockets.

"People work hard to build their businesses, and for what? So some entitled brats can go and wreck it?"

"It's not that black and white."

"Don't tell me you agree with that behavior."

"I wouldn't touch any mom-and-pop shops, but I think big chain stores will be alright."

"Do you or do you not agree with it?"

"Yeah." I nodded. "I do."

Pops stared at me, and I turned my head to avoid looking at him. The room fell silent except the TV. Katelyn picked up her kid and carried him to the kitchen.

Ma looked at me, turned her head to Pops, back at me, and back at Pops again. "Let's change the conversation."

"You got a beer?" I asked. "I need a drink."

Pop's expression tightened. "You know better than to have that kind of drink in front of your mother."

"A drink's a drink, Pops. You don't care if she sees me with wine. What makes a beer any different?"

"It's disrespectful—"

"It sounds like order for the sake of order."

He glared at me.

"Tradition for tradition's sake. And some traditions just need to be broken."

Ma blinked her eyes rapidly and turned to Pops. "I can get him a beer. It's fine." She walked to the kitchen.

"What's gotten into you, son? Something about you is different. I don't know if it's your attitude or that tattoo on your head, but I ain't likin' it."

"It ain't like me and you ever got together and sang kumbaya before, Pops."

"I know. But something ain't right."

Ma came back with a can of beer, handed it to me.

Pops crossed his arms, leaned forward. "Who've you been hanging out with?"

I popped open my can. "Y' know, for a long time, I didn't have any friends at all. Couldn't find the time because of work." I took a swig. "I haven't really been hanging with anyone. 'Cept coworkers."

"Is that who's got you siding with criminals?"

I said under my breath, "They're not criminals."

"They are." Pops looked back at me with wide eyes and a red face. "What good comes from destruction? Huh? They think they're helping someone? They're making people lose their jobs."

"Yeah...I know. And we thought about that, and it sucks, but there's a bigger picture. You gotta make sacrifices for the overall goal."

"We?" He raised one eyebrow and cocked his head. "Have you been out there too?"

I rubbed the back of my neck, paced.

Pops clenched his fists and waved them like he was banging on an invisible table. "Have you?"

I stopped, craned my neck.

"Answer me."

I slammed my beer on the table and threw my arms out. "Jesus, Pops. Jesus. Is this why you had me come out here? So you can scold me for another thing? Hadn't gotten your fix yet? I get it. You hate me."

Pop's posture stiffened. His eyes dulled.

"You always hated me. I don't do anything right. I'm your dumb kid. I'm not as good as your son-in-law. Your real son. I'm the one you regret. Just say it to my face."

"I don't hate you. I'm just afraid for you—"

"Yeah? Save your pity. I made it this far without your help, I don't need it now."

"Why are you so damn stubborn—"

"I dunno, Pops. The apple don't fall too far from the tree—"

"I don't even know you anymore—"

"You never knew me. You never took the time. The only thing you knew was who you wanted me to be, but I'm not that, Pops. I'll never be that."

"I failed with you—"

"Then why the fuck did you bring me out—"

"Your father has cancer!" Ma marched between me and Pops. She looked at him. She looked at me. "He's got lung cancer. That's why I asked you to come out here."

The silence was ugly.

I scratched the side of my head, looked at Pops. "When were you gonna tell me this?"

Pops dropped back against the seat and let out a heavy breath. "I didn't know how to tell ya, son. Every time we get together, it's this. The same back and forth. I don't want that."

I wouldn't let myself admit it, but I felt a burn in the back of my eyes. I clasped my fingers on top of my head and looked down at the floor. Opened my mouth, shook my head. "Is it...Is it...?"

"We don't know." Ma's voice was low.

I paced, rubbed my face with both hands, ran my fingers through my hair. "Remember how the doctor used to tell you..." I swallowed, licked my lips, swallowed again. "Remember how the doctor used to tell you, you gotta quit working those hours?" My voice shook. "Remember?" I stopped pacing, waved my finger at Pops. "Remember how they told you, you gotta quit breathing in all those fumes, all that sawdust?"

"The hours were mandatory."

"That it? That supposed to make it okay?"

"I..." Pops slowly shook his head. "Nolan...."

"They told you what it was doing to your body."

I thought he would yell at me, but he didn't. The redness faded from his face, his eyes softened, and all he did was nod.

"How about your healthcare? That gonna cover it?"

"Let's not turn this get-together into this."

"It already is this. It's been this."

"I did what I had to do to take care of my family."

"You think they ever cared about your family?"

"I'm just glad I was given a job—"

"You're dying, Pops!" My breath caught in my throat. "You're fucking dying. What does a job matter if you're dead? Are you ever gonna wake up?" I stormed to the door.

"Where are you going? You're not gonna drive all the way back when ya just got here, are you?"

"I don't..." I shook my head. If I didn't get out of there, I might let go some tears. "I don't know."

I stepped outside, dropped my hands on the porch rail, and stared down at a tiny garden of shrubs I'd known all my life. I squeezed my eyes, stopped the tears from coming, swallowed down what was hurting me.

My hand shook so badly I could hardly reach into my pocket. I managed to get out the pack of cigarettes and my lighter, but I could hardly light it. Couldn't tell what was more frantic, my mind or my hands or my lips. Couldn't tell what to do next. Felt stupid yet righteous at the same time. The worst goddamn feeling. I couldn't look at Pop's face, but I couldn't leave him. And I didn't even want to think about the future. What might happen if I left now and didn't see or call Pops again?

I leaned against the porch, and I smoked that cigarette until it was nothing but an orange speck, and then I took out another and smoked it.

Wasn't nothing but me out there. Just my stupid thoughts and a setting sun.

## 31

*"Working over 55 hours a week causes almost 7% of annual deaths..."*

I cut off the TV.

Had my computer in my lap, sat on the very edge of a couch cushion that hadn't been dropped on the floor to make way for a mattress since I left to go back to Buffalo. Hadn't even thought about pulling out the mattress, making my bed. Or eating. Or showering. Or brushing my teeth.

My knee bounced.

Shit's been in my head living as rent free as the crust punks the landlord just ran out of the lobby. But even a shithole like my apartment was a nicer place for squatters than the rundown filth that was my head.

I took a sip of coffee, tapped the ash off the end of a wrinkled cigarette crumbling between my fingers. I pulled it to my lips, and the ash peppered my keyboard. I blew it off. Ran my fingers across the keys with my right hand.

**Gregory Daniels**


**Gregory Daniels, CEO of Steel & Strong Construction Co.**

## Gregory Daniels Salary: 3.5 M

Three-point five mil. Three million five hundred thousand dollars. Three-point five. A year.

Pop's worked for Steel & Strong for as long as I'd been born. When I was four, I didn't know what a job was. When I hit puberty, I wondered why we didn't have much money. When I became an adult, and was old enough to hunch over a computer and smoke a cigarette, obsessing over a rich guy I'd never met, I asked the kind of questions a blissful brain shouldn't ask.

I don't know if I'd spent too much time with Arin or if the criminal mind I'd developed over the past couple years had grown to possess me, but I dug around Gregory Daniels' information until I knew more about him than his own ma. Then I came across something. Don't know how, don't know what I clicked last or the time before that or the time before that, but I was down at the bottom of the rabbit hole. What I came across lit the kind of black lightbulb above my head that you don't get until the need for vengeance rolls through your nervous system with an intensity you didn't know you could feel.

A banquet. Had a location. Had a time.

I had a crew. And a plan. A picture of the building. A shot of its entrance. Its exit. Its guard shack.

I dropped back, didn't even realize I'd smoked the last bit of my cigarette. Smiled.

I didn't text Pip until two days later when I had a solid plan. Two straight days of thinking this thing over—my brain was overheated. But I texted Pip, then Jackie, Arin, Axe, added them to a group chat. Met up with them in the back of the church one night. Told them a little bit of what was up, what I was planning, and that there'd be a bunch of silver spooners there. They could take whatever they wanted. I encouraged it. Just save something for me. I wanted to sell it, turn it into cash, and hand it out to the poor struggling and barely-getting-by saps out there.

As for my role at the banquet, I had something bigger in mind.

"What's that?" Pip opened the van door. He had this apprehensive look on his face I didn't like. He'd had it since we'd met tonight. "You keep saying you got something big planned, and you want us to go with you, but you won't tell us what."

I tucked my gun in the holster beneath my jacket and a can of spray paint in my belt. "Let's go."

I didn't drive up to the guard shack until everybody pulled their masks over their faces, their hoods over their heads. I showed up late on purpose.

The guard opened the window, but when he did, he was met by my Glock. "Hands up!"

He threw his hands in the air.

"Don't move."

My guys had already gotten out of the van and run around the shack. They kicked down the door.

The guard flinched.

"I said don't move."

"I'm sorry." He trembled and took heavy breaths. "I...I'm sorry."

Jackie grabbed him from behind and wrapped tape around his mouth. They taped his hands together, his feet, opened the door, and Axe tossed him in the closet.

"Is it good?" I asked.

Jackie gave me a thumbs up.

Pip grabbed the guard's phone.

Arin looked at his computer monitor. "There're two guards by the entrance."

"Alright." My palms should've been sweating. My bones should've been shaking. Maybe I'd grown used to this.

Everybody got back in the van. I drove to the entrance slowly, casually, but I didn't see anyone in the parking lot. Just Lamborghinis, Bugattis, Bentleys, Rolls-Royces—the kind of cars that could buy me a mansion if I put them all together. The building was made of glass, shaped like a piece of modern art, angles and designs that made a guy wonder if its insanity was all a comedic reflection of his own inner world.

They shoved open the glass doors, assault rifles pointed like they were going into combat. I don't even think the guards knew we were there before Jackie shouted, "Hands up!" She had her gun at one guard's head. Axe had his pointed at the other. "Drop the guns! Kick 'em to me. Walkie-talkies, too. Slowly."

Somebody screamed. I walked through fancy white tablecloths and bowled candles, the fragrance of cologne and perfume, silk gowns, cashmere suits, and high-class people running in circles and jumping beneath the tables like the rich folk roach bomb just exploded.

I pointed my gun. "Hands up! Everybody!" I had Pip and Arin behind me.

Jackie walked the guards to the floor with everyone else, kicked over any tables. "Off the floor! Now! Hands where I can see 'em!"

She was better at that than me. I let her handle it.

While she confiscated the pearls from everyone's necks, the earrings and gloves, bracelets, and watches, my eyes fell on my target. Don't know if it was a Godsend or a Devil's send, but he was already on the stage. Eyes wide. Mouth agape. Hands in the air. Trembling. Four-piece suit, diamond-crusted watch, a pepper-colored toupee that probably cost more than Pops' whole house. Gregory Daniels.

I climbed the stage.

He stepped back. Looked behind himself. Took another step. Stumbled.

"Don't move." I pointed my gun at him.

"What do you wan—"

"Shut up." I grabbed the can of paint with my other hand and sprayed *Enough* in red. "Right there." I gestured with my head. "That's where they're gonna find you."

"Maybe we can work something out."

It started as a chuckle, then it turned into full laughter. I didn't know why. I didn't know the emotion, but it came out, and it hurt and felt good at the same time. "Work something out?" I rubbed my temples. "Work something out. This is what it takes, huh? A gun at somebody's head. So, all this time, we've been doing it wrong." I laughed. "People like you don't give a fuck about anybody's kid or anybody's mom or anybody's dad or—let's get real—any-FUCKING-body until the gun's at your head." I took a deep breath. "Because you don't care about anybody's life but your own."

He gulped. "That's not true—"

"My pop's dying right now. He worked for your company. Worked his fingers to the bone just to take care of his family." My eyes stung. "Sixty plus hours a week and still living paycheck to paycheck—the least he could get is some decent healthcare. Do you care about him?"

"I...I'm sorry."

"Sure you are." I paced back and forth, rubbed the side of my head, and rubbed my hands on my face. "Here's what's gonna happen. I'm taking that suit, I'm taking that watch, and I'm taking those shoes, and I'm using it to take care of my pop's medical payments that you and your company didn't bother helping with. In fact, a little birdy told me that you donated to some legislation that made it hard for workers like my father to get access to medical care. Glad you care."

"It's not what it sounds—"

"Shut up." I walked up to him slowly. "And then when they find your body, right here on the stage where you and your pompous fucking friends patted each other on the back for the crimes you committed, they're gonna know what you did." I shook the spray can. "They're all gonna know. And they're gonna talk. And maybe all the greedy bastards like you will realize nobody's putting up with this bullshit anymore."

I moved my finger to the trigger and held my breath.

"You don't have to do this—"

"Shut up!"

"Please. I'm sorry about your father—"

"Shut up!"

"This won't solve anything. Just...it isn't worth it...put the gun down."

"I'm not gonna tell you again to shut the fuck—"

The last time I heard a crash that loud everything was on fire.

## 32

When I was fifteen, I snuck out to a party.

I'd gotten grounded the week before because I skipped math class to go smoke in the back of the school with some friends. Pops told me I wasn't allowed to leave the house for three weeks. Not for anything but school and church. But I'd gotten an invitation from a girl who hung out with the popular, rich kids. Folks who knew folks who knew folks. Everybody was going to be there. The hottest chicks in the school. Gonna be one of the best parties of the year.

So, me and a group of my friends got together and made plans to sneak me out. I told them to meet me at eleven o'clock. Pops worked extra hours. He could barely stay awake during the day, let alone at night, and Ma always went to bed around ten. Tap on the window.

They showed up at eleven like we'd planned and tapped on the window. I did the ol' pillow under the blanket trick. Y' know, just in case. We rode to the party in a beat-up, 1998 Mustang. The driver wasn't supposed to be driving because he didn't even have a real license, just a permit.

We got to the party at 11:30. I danced my ass off, drank, smoked, made out with a girl whose name I never learned.

Everything from that night is like the last memories of a dream just before they start to fade. Everything but one thing, and I can still hear it in my head clear as day.

"Whose dad is that?" Immediately after whichever kid said that, I knew whose dad it was.

Pops, in pajama pants, a wife beater with a hole, night slippers, showed up and didn't say anything. Don't know how he found me. Don't know how he knew where to look, but those kids made way for him when he grabbed my arm and dragged me out of that house.

They didn't let me live that one down until graduation.

A black SUV shot through the window like a bullet on steroids. Glass slid across the marble and showered the tabletops. Gasps mingled with screams. I stumbled, but I still had my gun on Gregory Daniels.

The SUV skirred and slammed to a stop. The driver's door flung open. He had a ski mask on, a hood over his head, but I recognized that voice and that walk soon as he jumped out of the van.

"Did my idiot lackeys crash your party? I'm so sorry." He pointed his pistol at me.

Six other guys with assault rifles got out of the SUV. I guessed other Krew members from other boroughs.

Broken glass crunched beneath Richie's boots as he made his way down the table aisle and towards the stage. He waved his fingers at me like he was asking me to come over. "Drop the gun."

"No. Not 'til I get justice."

"Drop the fucking gun, Bird."

"No—"

He shot me in the hand. I dropped my gun.

Gregory fell on his hands and knees, crawled towards my pistol.

Richie pointed his gun at him. "Touch it, and I swear to God I'll spill your brains all over this boujee fucking floor."

Gregory stopped and threw his hands up.

Richie jerked his head towards the window. "Come on. Let's go."

I shook my head, squeezed my blood-soaked fingers. "No."

"I said get in the fuckin' van."

"I'm not going." I reached for my pistol.

Richie aimed his gun at my head. "Don't you touch that fuckin' gun."

I stopped. "Just let me do this. I need to do this—"

"You're all emotion, and you ain't thinkin'." He picked up my gun. "Go to the fucking van before I lose my shit and blow away everybody in this goddamn building." He turned around and waved both guns. "All of you. Get in the fucking van. We'll talk about this on our way back."

I looked at trembling Gregory Daniels. I looked at the patrons of the party. They looked at me and Richie. Like a nightmare. Like a sitcom.

All of my efforts were in vain.

"Go to the fucking van!"

I followed Richie out of the building.




Pip sewed up my hand and wrapped it in bandages. And when he did, he didn't say much. Just, "Don't apologize."

Richie didn't say anything to me on the way back. He didn't say anything to me when we got in the church.

He stared at me—a cold, hard glare, like he waited for me to speak first. And everybody was there, everybody was watching, standing around the living room, except Mike hanging on the wall with a smile on his face like he was the only one of us who had any peace of mind.

"How'd you know where we were?" I asked.

"Don't worry about that." Richie walked up to me, rubbing his brow. He crossed his arms. "The fuck were you thinkin'?" He said it in a low, crinkly tone, like his voice had dealt with enough stress and was ready to throw in the towel.

"I think you know—"

He put up his hand. "Shut up." He looked at Arin and Axe on the left of him, Jackie and Pip on the right. "First, you take my guys out..." he poked himself in the chest. "My guys. And you did it after I warned you not to—"

"I think they can think for themselves—"

He put his hand up. Took two deep breaths. "And then what did you go out there to do? Let me ask you something. What'd you think was gonna happen if you'd taken that guy out? You think they would've let that go? That guy has a billion-dollar net worth. He ain't like the disposable scavengers crawling up and down the slums like you and me. You off one like him, guess what happens to you."

"I leave a message."

"You leave a bump in the dirt, and nobody remembers your name."

"The old you wouldn't have said that."

"You don't know shit about the old me."

I smiled sarcastically. "I talked to Mike before he died. He told me what D3vil's Krew used to be about. It was supposed to leave a name."

He stared at me like he was searching for something to say but gave up halfway.

"Or have you forgotten?" I half-smiled. "I thought you weren't done yet."

His face reddened.

"You told me you woke up in a hospital bed when you were seventeen years old, and you realized you had a job to do."

A vein twitched on the side of his head.

"You couldn't die yet because you weren't done—"

"Jesus Christ!" He threw his arms out. "I quit. I give up. I gave up a long time ago, alright? The big dogs eat the little dogs. That's the game—"

"Change the game."

"You can't change the fucking game!" He shook like he was having a spasm. His breathing was loud. His face was hard red. He blew out a long, steady breath. "Holy shit..." he rubbed his brow, paced in a circle. "Holy fucking shit. I thought like you too." He stopped. "I thought I could spray a couple buildings, break a couple things, and somebody would say, 'Hey, those kids are fuckin' shit up. Somebody oughta listen to 'em.' But it don't work that way. I been out there before. I seen it all. Listened to the chants, seen the protests, been in 'em, the peaceful ones, the riots—SHIT DON'T CHANGE!" His shoulders moved up and down. His face was covered in sweat. His nostrils flared, breathing like he couldn't get enough air in his lungs.

I swallowed. "Nothing changes until somebody says it does."

"You think that somebody's gonna be you?"

I shook my head. "Not just me."

I looked at Pip. I looked at Jackie. Axe and Arin.

They looked at me.

Richie glanced to his left and glanced to his right. His voice was low. "Think."

They stepped. Slowly. One by one and lined up. Side by side.

Behind Richie.

I nodded. "Yeah? You're gonna give up too? What about Grace Redemption Church? What about that manifesto hanging upstairs? Huh? There's a whole movement because of us."

"At the end of the day," Richie walked closer to me, "the best thing we got is each other and what we know how to do. You can go back out there and buy, buy, buy, let 'em put a boot on your throat, and as soon as you step over the line, they'll take everything from you. Or you can get behind me."

I shook my head. "You're just a bunch of thugs."

"That's the game." His eyes narrowed as if recalling a bitter memory. "You gotta be like 'em, and you gotta think like 'em. You can't do that, you're gonna get eaten by 'em." He slapped his chest. "I learned that at an early age. Then I thought I could take 'em on. Boy, was I wrong. They're bigger than you, they're more powerful than you, and they got the world on their side. All we got is guns."

"I got a thirst for justice."

"That's naïve."

"Don't act like you're better when you kept someone in a cage over your dead fucking friend—"

He punched me in the face. I stumbled back. He punched me again. Went for another blow. I dodged it and slugged him in the face. It hurt like shit. My wound pulsated. I decked him again. He decked me back. Next thing I knew, we were rolling on the ground, swinging punches like mad monkeys.

Everybody watched from behind, standing in a blobby line. Nobody jumped in.

Richie got on top of me and got his fingers around my throat. He squeezed until not a sliver of air could pass. My face numbed. My eyes felt like they were bulging out of my head.

Richie's tangled, sweaty hair hung down and tickled the sides of my cheeks. His face was red, and all I could see were black pupils glaring through near colorless eyes.

"I'm going to give you one more chance." He breathed. "Get behind me. Or walk." He tightened his grip. "But if you walk through that door, that tattoo's coming off your back."

I couldn't even gulp.

He let go of my throat.

I gasped and gripped my neck.

He got off me, walked backward, and stood before his crew.

I got off the floor. Looked at the guys, looked at the door. Looked at the guys, looked at the door. I squeezed my eyes shut, took a step.

Got behind Richie.

# 33

*"No severe injuries have been reported. Investigators believe the suspects were members of the Enough movement. Gregory Daniels tells reporters he feared for his life, but..."*

My phone vibrated. I grabbed it from the armrest. Pops.

I didn't even know he had a Skype.

I dropped back against the couch. Stared at the screen. Let it ring.

If I didn't answer it, I might've regretted it later. I sighed.

"Hey, Pops. Why'd you wanna video chat? Thought you didn't believe in all that stuff."

Pops looked tired. Like he'd lived and worked three or four lives, and his body just realized it was time to age. "Because I wanna see you." He nodded. "I wanna see my son."

A chill went through my veins.

"My grandparents immigrated to this country on the promise of opportunity. They were poor. All they had was what they could carry on their backs, but they said this is the land of the free, and they were gonna make it. And uh..." his eyes reflected a mix of joy and melancholy, "they passed that on to my pops, and my pops passed it on to me...something to believe in." He looked away from the camera, and his eyes turned red. No tears dropped out, but I was taken aback. "When you were born, and your mother handed you to me for the first time, I said, 'I'm going to give him everything my hands have the capacity to give. No matter what that takes.' I made it my life's purpose to protect you and your ma and your sister, to provide for you and lay down my life for you if I had to."

"It's not that I don't appreciate you, Pops, I just—"

"Hold on. I'm not done."

I swallowed.

"With everything that I did, the hours that I worked, the money that I made to support the family—but I guess that's where I messed up. I put so much time and energy into being a man that I forgot to be your father." He patted his chest. "I am your father. And I guess..." he turned his eyes like he had lost track of what to say "...I guess somewhere down the line, I forgot what that really means." He dropped his shoulders. "I don't know if I'll be here in three years. I don't know if I'll be here tomorrow. But what I do know is I don't want to be on my deathbed having let my son down." He nodded. "I don't want you to hate me."

I combed my bangs to the back of my head. "I could never hate you."

"I'm sorry that I waited 'til a time like now to finally tell you this. I should've said this a long time ago, but maybe it takes seeing my own mortality to fracture some of that pride." He sat still. "I'm sorry I wasn't a father to you."

I rubbed the back of my neck.

"There's a lot that we're not going to agree on, and that's alright." He shrugged. "I love you." He looked me in the eye. "Because you're my son, and I'm proud of that. No matter what path you choose to take in life."

I smiled, felt a tear burn the back of my eye, and that choking feeling you get when you don't know what to say.

"These upcoming days, months, years, however long I have here on this earth. That's what I wanna do. I wanna be your father. Your pops. Maybe we can go out, go for a beer, go fishing..." he chuckled. "I dunno. What do you like to do?"

I chuckled, shrugged.

"Guess we'll figure that out later."

I nodded. "That sounds like a good idea."

"Yeah? But no politics." He laughed. "You still writing?"

"Yeah."

"Good. Maybe that's what we can talk about. We can talk about that next story. I believe you're gonna make something out of it one day." He stared at my face with a sentimental smile. "Anyway, I gotta get going. Let's talk about getting together another time."

"Alright, and Pops..."

He almost ended the call but stopped.

"Thank you." I took a moment to let the words sink in. "For everything you did for me." And to conjure my own. "I love you too."

# 34

Richie had me come by the church. Said it was important.

It wasn't a drug run or a heist. No break-in or convoluted scheme. It wasn't even about #Enough. He had everybody there. Axe and Arin at the bar, Jackie behind it, leaning up against the counter with her head hanging down. Pip in the living room chair. I came in last.

Richie had a gun in his hand. He paced the floor in front of the bar counter.

When I walked in, he looked at me and waved his hand. "Come in. Join everybody else." He said it in a casual tone, but there was something more to it. Something he was trying to hold back.

"What's going on?" I asked.

"Come here."

I joined the room, but I didn't sit down. Everybody was quiet. Faces uneasy.

Richie kept pacing. Every time he turned around, it made my hands sweat a little. He was restless. He was moving all weird, cracking his neck, clenching and unclenching his fist. And he had that gun in his hand.

"It's been a rough year." He paced faster, harder. Looked at Mike's photo, looked at the ground, hung his head and ran his fingers through his hair. "I think I've been fair to everybody in this crew. We're a body, a system. You play your role, you get your pay. I don't fuck around with that." He finally stopped marching and turned around to the bar. "I put my faith in you people."

Jackie lifted her head. "What's this about, Rich—"

"I didn't say you can speak."

He started pacing again.

"If somebody has anything to say, I suggest he say it," he cocked his gun, "cuz I'm gonna find out no matter what."

I almost looked towards the door, but I didn't want to make myself obvious. There wasn't anywhere I could go anyway. Didn't want to turn my eyes towards the ground. Didn't want to sweat. Guess all I could do was hope he couldn't see the blood draining from my face.

"Ride or die, right? I look out for him; he looks out for me—we're a brotherhood, right?" He raised his voice. "So why the fuck is somebody stealing from me?"

Jackie's forehead wrinkled. "Nobody's stealing—"

Richie pointed his gun at her. "Don't say another word."

She hung her head.

"We got our money back. That's good. But we had a scare, so I opened the money safe. Everything looked right, but something was off."

Arin parted his lips. "Maybe there was some sort of misunder—"

Richie pointed the gun at him. Arin lowered his head.

Axe had his fingers clasped on his lap, his knee bouncing.

Richie rolled his shoulders. "I said, 'Must just all be in my head,' but nah. I had a hunch. So, I counted that shit. Came out short. Didn't say nothin' about it because I wanted to believe in my crew, but I had a hunch, so I counted it again. Then I counted it again...then I counted it again..." He blew out a breath. "Blood's about to fucking spill tonight."

Jackie slowly raised her hand but kept her eyes towards the counter.

"What?"

"Maybe it was The Rhats. I mean, they stole the guns and the money. And who knew how to crack a safe like Joe?"

"I wanted to believe that so bad, so fucking bad. But when those assholes stole our shit, they were sure to leave everything open and everything dry. They showed no shame. Whoever did this took the time to screw the screw back on the vent, which means our culprit," he sneered, "tried to hide it." He waved the gun around. "I love my crew, so this is going to hurt so fucking bad, but we can't have a traitor in our midst. It taints the whole group. Fess up."

Nobody spoke. Sweat ran down all our faces. Everybody was pale, wasn't breathing right, but I was the only one who had reason to hide.

"No contenders? That's alright. Somebody did this before the Rhats. I counted the money a few weeks back. It came out short. Before then, I ain't touched it in almost three years. Can anyone tell me? What big change happened almost three years ago?"

He grabbed me by my shirt, slammed me against the bar counter, shoved the gun barrel into my mouth. "Give me one fucking reason why I shouldn't blow your head off right now."

Everybody jumped out of their seats.

"Come on, Richie," Jackie cried. "You don't even know for a fact it was him."

"Anyone could've taken it within that time," Arin said.

Richie chuckled. "Oh-ho. I've had my eye on this motherfucker since he walked through that door." He crammed the gun down my throat.

I gagged. The cold gun barrel burned a bitter, tangy taste on my tongue and shot a sharp shock through my gums.

"He takes my fucking guys out behind my back. Disobeys my orders—Why should I trust this son of a bitch—"

"I did it."

Richie whipped his head around.

Pip stood, breathing hard, both fists clenched. "I did it. I took the money."

Richie pulled the gun out of my mouth and turned around.

"My son was starting school. I used it to help him pay for clothes and supplies."

Richie marched up to Pip. Pip didn't move. Richie raised the gun. Pip's breathing was shaky, but he stood with his chin up. He squeezed his eyes shut. Swallowed.

Richie had the muzzle an inch from Pip's head. First time I'd ever seen his hand quiver while holding a gun. He licked his lips, flared his nostrils, squeezed his eyes tight when he blinked.

"R-Richie—" I stuttered. "Richie. He didn—"

He struck the side of Pip's face with the gun. Hard enough to make him stumble but not enough to make him fall.

Pip gripped his face.

Richie tucked the gun into his pants and headed to his room. "Get your shit together."

When I was a kid, I watched a documentary on chimpanzees.

The male chimp challenged a higher-up chimp to a brawl in a fight for dominance. They do that. And if that doesn't work, they'll build a coalition.

Sometimes, when you're lying around by yourself, you get to thinking about shit. Especially when you don't got the TV on, and you're sprawled out on the couch, got your third beer in your hand, and you're able to be honest with yourself.

It's funny how people follow the leader and follow the leader and follow the leader and don't really question it. You just kind of do it, y' know? Don't think about it. Maybe that's a safety mechanism. At the end of the day, folks just want to survive. And if you're doing a lot of fighting or too much thinking, it gets in the way. You can't just go with the flow. Maybe our ancestors realized that a long time ago.

But it's funny how, at some point, we'll have it up to here. At some point, you realize if you keep putting up with abuse, that's all you're going to get.

People will follow a leader just so long as that leader proves he's the toughest bastard out there. The biggest. The most dangerous. Until another tough bastard comes along and he says, hey, fuck you. Takes the crown. Most folks don't have the balls to do that. Maybe that's why the guy who does have the balls to do it becomes the next leader. Maybe it's got less to do with him whooping the other guy's ass and more to do with the fact he showed he's got balls of steel.

Maybe there're guys who got balls of steel who don't know they got balls of steel because they don't ever try. They're not the leadership type. But if they were ready, willing, and able, they'd take the throne.

You can't do anything alone in this world. You always got to have somebody else. If being in D3vil's Krew has taught me anything, it's that. That old song about needing somebody to lean on—they ain't shitting.

Sometimes, I think, when people cross the line, it's time to take charge. Life's too short to let people walk all over you. Especially when you know what needs to be done. Not just for you.

If you keep looking at your guns, you're going to eventually ask yourself, is this being used in vain? Does it have to be? And if I'm going to pull the trigger, it needs to be pulled for the right reason.

There's such a thing as a food chain. Some animals are always at the top of that thing. But how did they get up there? They were apex. How were they apex? Evolution. How did they evolve? They adapted. They got stronger. Before there were lions, there were rodents burrowing in the earth. You think no blood was shed in that frame of time? No end of a reign?

I let a man stuff a gun down my throat after choking me and keeping a guy in a cage to suffer.

I don't know much about leadership or power or chimpanzees, but there was once a king who lorded over an entire kingdom. He was strong, he was powerful, and he didn't take shit. He'd been king for as long as anybody could remember. The land was prosperous, the army undefeatable, but the king had become consumed by his own power.

The people didn't question it. The people didn't challenge it. And everybody in the city tolerated whatever shit the king had to throw at them because no one was willing to take on the almighty.

But there came a time and there came a boy who'd been nothing but a server to the king all his life. He didn't question it. He didn't challenge it until one day, he'd had enough. He went to the other peasants, and he said, if I were king, it would all be different.

They didn't listen to him, and he continued serving.

But another day came when the boy had enough, and he went to the other peasants and he said, if I were king, things would be fair.

They didn't listen to him, and he continued serving.

But another day came where the boy had enough, and he went to the other peasants, and he said, I am now king.

Confused, the peasants asked the boy what the hell happened to the last king?

The boy showed them the blood on his sword and, with a triumphant smile, said, oh how the mighty hath fallen.


I stopped by Pip's apartment. I didn't bother calling beforehand.

The bruise Richie gave him made his face look like a discarded apple. You could tell he tried to cover it with his hair, but it didn't do much good.

"I'm sorry."

He sat down on the couch. "I told you not to apologize."

"Guess I owe you my life. You didn't have to stick up for me."

"Why'd you take the money?"

"Rent. I didn't think it would go this way."

He gazed at a TV that wasn't on.

I dropped my hands into my pockets, leaned against the armrest. "How you feelin' about Richie right now?"

Pip didn't respond.

"There's something that needs to be done, and I think you know what that is."

"Why are you asking me?"

"Look what he did to your face."

Pip shook his hair over his cheek.

"Look what he did to the Rhats. Look what he had us do. We don't get it together, eventually, it's gonna be him or us."

"If you plan to pull this thing off, you'd better do it discreetly. The rest of the Krew find out what you did, it's gonna be your head."

"That's why I need your help." I turned around and faced him. "Two heads are better than one. You and me work together, we can cover it up, make it look like some sort of accident."

"You're adamant about this? Aren't you?"

"Yeah." I nodded. "I am."

He stared at my face like he was waiting for a crack in my expression, and when he didn't get it, he looked away.

"Richie's after nothing but money. And power. He's no better than the folks he used to fight against. He will mow each of us down if it means he gets to the finish line."

Pip sat still.

"And he's in our way." I walked around the couch and stood in front of him.

He still refused eye contact with me.

"There are bigger things that we gotta do. If we can talk to the rest of the Krew and get everyone on board, we can make change. But we gotta get rid of Richie first."

He turned his eyes to me.

"That night, when we did that drive-by shooting on the Rhats not too long ago. At the rowhouses. Did that feel right? None of us wanted to do that. None of us wanted to cheat the Rhats the way we did." I leaned down. "None of us wanted to see Cracker Joe die. That was all Richie." I put my hand on his shoulder. "He held a gun to your head, Pip."

Pip clenched and unclenched his fists.

I stood up straight. "If we work together, no one would even have to—"

"Richie saved my life." He got up, finally made eye contact with me. His expression was fierce. Cold.

I stepped back.

"He saved my life." He blinked his eyes and shook his head like he was trying to gather his thoughts. "I hear what you're trying to say. I don't deny that things are fucked up. Richie's fucked up. But look at you."

I took another step back, raised my chin, flared my nostrils.

"You thought that was a good idea? At the banquet?" He shook his head. "What did you expect to fix with that?"

"We needed to leave a message—"

"Your dad is sick. Possibly dying. And you feel like Gregory Daniels is responsible." He furrowed his brows, nodded in a short, quick motion. "I get it. I'd have been mad, too. Hell, I might've had some of the same ideas, but that wouldn't make them right."

"You told Richie. Didn't you?"

He dropped his hands on his hips, let out a heavy breath, nodded.

"Why the hell would you do that?"

"Because I knew you'd do something stupid."

I gave him a sharp look.

"Killing Gregory Daniels wouldn't have made you a hero. It would've just made you a killer."

I chuckled sarcastically. "I'm already a killer."

"So what?" He shrugged. "You looking to add more tally marks to that kill count? What'll that do for ya?"

# 35

If I made a list of my favorite bosses, Richie wouldn't be at the top.

Maybe that's because he knew he was an asshole.

I didn't tell anyone I was coming. I let myself in.

Didn't wait until nightfall. It was afternoon.

After I did it, I was going to flee the state. Do away with my name. Don't know what I planned to tell my family. Guess I figured I'd worry about that after the deed was done.

I sat up thinking about it all night. Thought about what Pip said, too. If I'd have dreamed, it'd have been the same shit over and over again like a blood-covered merry-go-round.

I had to stare at my face in the mirror. Had to stare at it for a long time. You don't notice the scars on your face or the creases in your skin until you realize you don't fully recognize the person looking back at you in the mirror. Change can be good. Change can be bad. But it's always necessary.

Sometimes, when I think about that morning, I try to remember everything on my mind in those twenty-four hours leading up to it. But I never can. Maybe that's because there was so much going on in there, it all equated to nothing. Running around like ants from a runover mound. The mayhem and fire, the crashing that goes on in a skull can leave the whole body numb. But that won't stop the hands from doing what the mind feels it has got to do.

And then the prefrontal cortex or the amygdala or whoever is blabbering on back there will try to tell you to stop. You push back against it.

Put a cork in it!

Once a mind is made up, I guess a mind is made up.

I had my gun in my pants. I walked in and checked Richie's room. He wasn't in there. I checked upstairs. Arin on the computer, Jackie taking a nap in her bed. Arin said hi to me. What's up? Asked me if I was looking for something.

I didn't respond.

I had a hunch about where Richie might be. It wasn't wrong.

I opened the basement door slowly and made sure it didn't screech. I tiptoed down the steps, hung onto the handrail and looked around the room. He was standing behind the staircase with his hands in his pockets, staring at the metal bars that confined a living person not long ago. He didn't turn around. Didn't glance at me.

I slid my gun out of my pants, crept down the stairs, aimed the gun at the back of Richie's head. I took a deep breath. I didn't want to do it with my eyes closed. Not because I wanted to revel in spilled blood. Not because I was afraid. Because I needed to see it and make sure. There was always something about Richie that seemed immortal to me.

I cocked the gun.

"If you're going to send me back to Hell, you'd better have two extra bullets for the other people in this church." He didn't turn around. "And I hope you got a good escape plan. D3vil's Krew's not gonna let you get away that easily."

"Turn around."

He hesitated but did what I said. Had his head tilted to the side with an attitude I was used to seeing on his face. "I can't say I blame you, though. A lot of people want me dead. I won't act like I haven't thought about it myself."

I lowered the gun but raised it back up.

"Hopefully, D3vil's Krew will get back on track," he said. "Been a bumpy road. I know everybody's ass is hurting."

He stared at me.

I stared at him.

The silence was nauseating.

He pulled a pack of cigarettes from his pocket, popped one in his mouth. Pulled out his lighter.

My hand trembled. I put two hands on the gun.

He lit his cigarette, took a long drag with his eyes closed, blew out a cloud of smoke. "I was never able to get that ring thing goin' on. Know what I mean? With the smoke?"

I sighed and relaxed my shoulders. Lowered the gun.

Richie blew out another cloud of smoke.

I put the gun back in my pants.

Richie walked over to the throne I remembered from my initiation but forgot was even there. He didn't sit on it. He sat on the floor in front of it. He leaned his head back, with his cigarette between his lips.

I walked over and sat beside him.

"Look at us." He took the cigarette out of his mouth. "Two dumb fucks sitting on the floor together. We got the same beliefs. The same desires. But one of us wants to kill the other, and the other...he's batshit enough to watch him do it." He chuckled and shook his head.

I smiled, too, once I thought about what he said.

"The fuck are we? Huh?"

I shook my head. "I dunno."

"You wanna smoke?" He reached into his pocket. "Have a smoke. Here." He handed me the cigarette pack, the lighter.

There was one cigarette left in there. I pulled it out with my lips.

"Yeah, this world fucks everybody up the ass. It's got two crazy anarchist fucks like you and me at each other's throats. How in the world does that happen?"

"Like you said. The world." I took the cigarette out of my mouth. "It fucks everybody up the ass."

We both laughed.

He got quiet. I got quiet. Sitting next to each other, the picture was almost too perfect, like we were going to break into some sort of dramatic music number where the piano starts playing and he sings the second verse of some sappy ballad I started out of nowhere. That wouldn't even make sense.

"In my perfect world," he said, "Mike wouldn't be dead. He'd be an artist. He'd be making tattoos for big-name celebs. Have one of those shallow fuckin' reality TV shows, and everybody'd know his work." He hung his head, licked his lips. "I'd be writing music. Not even just for the money. I'd be writing the kinda shit that speaks to people. Helping 'em make sense of this crazy fuckin' world." He took a long drag. "D3vil's Krew wouldn't even exist." He shook his head. "It wouldn't need to."

He tapped the ash off his cigarette. "When I was—I dunno—'bout six, maybe seven, I heard gunshots outside my window. First time I ever heard that shit in my entire fuckin' life. I didn't even know what it was." He took another drag. "And my ma grabbed me and threw me on the floor and jumped down there with me. I still remember the look on her face. She was scared shitless. I don't know if I ever seen her scared like that. Ma was a tough broad, but that scared the fuck out of her. She said, 'When you hear that. You get on the floor. You don't look out the window. You don't wait. You get down.'" He rubbed his temples. "I try not to let myself think about it, but I know that somewhere, at some point, some other kid's ma told 'em that same thing. But that time, the gunshots were mine."

I tapped the ash off my cigarette once I realized it was halfway burned.

"So what do we do? What are we? What the fuck is D3vil's Krew? A bunch of fucking lost souls or what?"

I reached into my pocket, took out my wallet, pulled out all the cash. I held it out to him, and he looked at me wide-eyed.

"That ain't all of it," I said. "I'll have the rest back to you tomorrow. I promise."

He didn't say anything, just took the money.

I got off the floor, stomped out my cigarette. Got my keys out of my pocket and unhooked the key to the church, handed it to him. "Good luck. Go easy on the crew for me." I headed for the steps. "And for the record, I don't think you should give up on that dream you have. I think," I shrugged, "you oughta try and do something with it."

I climbed the stairs and grabbed the doorknob.

Before I walked through, he said one more thing to me. "Keep writing, Bird."

*I'm the boy you killed,*
   *The one you raped, beat, and lied to,*
   *Staring at God or the NYPD.*
   *Politicians, schools, society—*
   *Whoever molded me.*
   *You say I'm a monster; I'll be your monster.*
   *I'll devour you whole and shit out your bones.*
   *I'll absorb your power, destruction, everything you own,*
   *And I'll take it all for me,*
   *Set it all on fire and set the rest of the world free*
   *Because there's nothing worse than a bird who can't fly*
   *Can't sing.*
   *So, I'm giving the world back its wings.*

*-Richie Bryant*

# 36

# TEN MONTHS LATER

Pops used to say people come into your life for a reason and for a season.

Sometimes, it's easier to see into the future than to look into the past.

I published a book. Self-published under the pseudonym Bird. Wrote it right after the day I left the Krew. Sort of. Some chapters I wrote after a mission, a moment, a thought. Compiled it into a novel.

It didn't become a bestseller. I think maybe ten people read it. But they said it resonated with them. That was good enough for me.

I got a job. Found myself in an office answering phone calls, sipping coffee. Coffee tastes better with a cigarette.

I only got the job because my sister knew somebody who knew somebody, and she told them about me and how I had office experience because I liked to write or something like that. It worked out. Paid better than most office jobs. So, it took care of my rent. And it didn't require guns.

Working again was like being the only beer on a table full of sodas. At some point, I thought I'd get used to it, but I never did. Just felt like sitting. Waiting. Like something exciting was supposed to happen, but it never did. Had a couple of acquaintances in the office. They invited me places, to lunch, to birthday parties. I'd go. But.

I think when you've spent years living on the edge of a cliff, it's hard to bring yourself back to the center. You get a taste of a new life. Something exciting. Dangerous. Not that it's good for you. Still.

And then you find yourself missing people. The people that were supposed to be your enemies were your best friends. On the news, you hear about break-ins and drug shit going on. You wonder if it's your guys. Maybe it is, and then you want to run back out there, give it one more go just for old times. You can't. You shouldn't. It's bad. There's a Mr. Hyde living inside. Problem is, you already still can't sleep because you're feeling like one day the cops are going to show up at your door. Might not be today. Might not be tomorrow. But it'll happen.

I guess me and Pops could never be best friends, but in my time bonding with him, I saw a human there. Somebody I never really saw growing up. Somebody vulnerable. And in some ways I could hardly tell that he was my father, but there was a man that I looked up to and honored as a child, and when he came out in that human being, I realized that I missed him. I didn't even know I was missing him. But I was glad when I found out. You realize you got more in common with your pops than you expected. We weren't going to vote for the same president, but we could make fun of the same movies, and that was enough.

I wish I could say it all ended there, but that would be a lie. I started the shower water one day after work. The news was rattling on outside the bathroom door, *"The Enough movement still continues as riots have moved to downtown Los Angeles..."*

Took off my shirt. Looked in the mirror.

I turned around.

I used to ask myself why Richie never made me remove it, but after ten months, I gave up guessing. I guess you could say he forgot, but probably not.

I tried to avoid looking at it when I got by a mirror, but I couldn't. It was there, twisting and turning, drawing the face of the devil like cursive letters. It somehow managed to be both beautiful and ugly at the same time. A scar and a work of art. History and a revelation. Mike's hand put it on me.

I worked in Manhattan. Took the subway. Had gotten off at the station, about to head home when I ran into a body I forgot carried so much muscle.

Still the biggest dude I'd ever seen. Wearing a t-shirt that was about to rip. Jeans that made you think he skipped leg day. A shaved head with *D3K* tattooed on the side.

"You're in a suit." First thing he said to me after ten months of not seeing him and over two years together of doing the kind shit that most people don't imagine doing because it brutalizes the conscience.

"Yeah." I nodded. "I'm wearing a suit."

"So you got a good job?"

"Pays the rent. You still baking?"

"Sometimes."

I chuckled. "I'd kill to have one of your cakes right now. Office work wears you down."

He nodded, but it came with no expression.

"Maybe..." I rubbed the back of my neck. "Y' know, we can...get together. Be like old times."

He nodded slowly. "That would probably be fun."

"Yeah." I cleared my throat. "I think it would."

I couldn't tell if he was looking at me or past me.

"And maybe you could bake something...maybe call up Pip. See if he wants to hang..."

His face was a misplaced mask.

Mine probably was, too.

"Say...Axe...?" I scratched my head. "What are you doing out here?"

The train rolled by, the ground rumbled, my feet vibrated.

Axe stood with his hands in his pockets. "What's it like out there? In the world?"

I chuckled and tried to lighten the mood. "Boring."

He didn't laugh.

"Everything alright?"

"At some point," he furrowed his brow and looked left to right like he forgot what to say, "I think everybody's sins catch up to them."

I nodded. "Maybe."

"I think everything I did in my life, I did in the name of fear. Fear of getting in trouble. Or death. But what do you do when the only thing you fear becomes life itself?"

I didn't know how to answer that.

"At some point, you have to face retribution."

"What are you saying, Axe?"

"You can try to make amends. But it doesn't fix anything. At some point, you can't heal all the scars. And then you realize you're the one making them. You can't heal them, but you can stop new ones."

"Huh?"

He pulled his hands out of his pockets, looked at his palms, turned them over and looked at the back. "The only time these hands have been put to good use is when they're feeding someone cake." He looked up from his hands and at me. "I don't wanna scar anyone else. But some things are easier said than done."

"Where have you been the past ten months? You still with the Krew?"

"I don't know if I'm broken." He stepped back close to the edge of the tracks.

"Axe...hey. Why don't you come back with me to my place? We can talk over a beer."

"We never really got to know each other. And that sucks. Because I always saw you as a friend. Everybody. You've all been like brothers to me, so I don't want you to think I don't care about you guys. I do. Probably more than anybody. But at some point, you gotta stop running. And not just from the cops." Axe looked to the side. The ground rumbled. The train rolled out of the tunnel. "I'm sorry."

He jumped onto the tracks. The train rushed by.


I hadn't talked to Pip since I'd last seen the Krew. It was kind of awkward.

He didn't know I had a job or that I'd begun hanging out with my pops. And I hadn't the nerve to call him up and ask him about his son.

I don't know if they knew what happened to Axe. I guess that's why I called. They'd find out anyway.

I tried to get off the phone with him. Leave it at that, but it wasn't going to be that easy. I knew that. Maybe that's why I never called. Right when I told him goodbye, talk to you later (though I didn't plan to), I put the phone back against my ear. Hoped he hadn't hung up yet.

"Hey...you still there? How's the Krew doing? They alright?" And the next thing I knew, I'd invited myself to the church.

When I stood in front of the church, my heart raced. My chest tightened. I wasn't ready to see everybody again. It's funny how months can feel like years, depending on the memories you have with a place. Or with the people. And when those memories can't be defined as good or bad, it adds an extra layer.

I walked through the chain-link fence, knocked on the door. Richie answered. He stood still for a long time. He didn't scowl at me or shout or cuss me out. He hugged me, warm and tight. I didn't know that was a thing he was even capable of.

"We know about Axe," he said. He jerked his head back, and I followed him inside.

Everyone was there. Cigarettes, beer, but no cake. Jackie and Arin at the bar counter. Pip on the plaid chair. Mike smiling from the wall. House crew was down to four people.

"How's life been treating you?" I sat on the couch.

They shrugged. "Good." "Getting by." "Same shit it's always been."

And then we talked. About life. About the past. The future. And everything in between. I didn't even realize the time had passed. The sun went from painting the sky solid blue to stroking it purple and red. For a second, I thought I was a Krew member again, and we were going to go on a drug run tomorrow.

"Gettin' pretty late. I gotta work tomorrow." I stood. "Guess I'll head out. Take care of yourselves." I didn't leave without stopping, turning around, gazing at the pensive look on Pip's face. "How's your son been?"

He lifted his head and blinked several times like he'd been gone and snapped back to the present. "He's good." He smiled slightly. "Thanks for asking."

I nodded. Turned around.

Sometimes I ask myself, if I'd gone straight home instead of calling Pip and visiting the church, I wonder how things would be now.

I didn't make it out the door. Almost like the cosmos got in bed with time, and everything that I'd done, the blood that I'd shed, the people I'd hurt, the sins I committed, caught up to me as soon as I put my hand on the doorknob.

"Police! Open up!"

There was never any proof of who it was, or when they'd told them, or how long they took to find us, or how they knew who, what, when the things that we'd done. I could probably make a guess. But somebody left it in a snail mail.

An anonymous tip.

The cops broke the door in. Shields and helmets. Guns.

Pop! Pop! Pop! The stereo exploded, beer bottles shattered, the couch tore to shreds. We jumped down, faces to the floor, hands on our heads, except Richie.

Richie ran to his room.

I don't know what the tipper told them, but we weren't armed. Not until Richie peeked out from behind the wall and sprayed the cops with an automatic. They ducked, put up their shields.

Richie waved to us. "Get to the van."

We got off the floor, ran to the back of the building. Pop! Pop! Pop! The trash barrel blew to bits, Mike's photo dropped off the wall, Arin was shot in the back.

I caught him before he could collapse. Richie tossed me the keys. We ran to the garage and jumped in the van.

I looked in the back. "Is he alright?"

Jackie held Arin. "Let's go."

I looked out the windshield. "What about Richie?"

I started the van. Waited.

"We have to go, Bird."

Waited.

I licked my lips, slammed on the gas, busted down the garage door.

Richie came running.

"There he is."

But he wasn't alone. He turned around, fired two shots. I didn't drive until he jumped in the van. I put the van in drive before he shut the door. Slammed on the gas, sped around the building onto the road.

He whipped his head around. "How's Arin?"

Jackie looked at the blood soaking her hand. "We need to get him to the hospital."

Richie slammed his fist against the door. "Shit."

The cops were behind us.

"We can't get someplace safe? Get it out ourselves?"

"It's too deep."

"We can't go to a hospital right now."

"We have to, or he'll die."

Pip took off his shirt and pressed it against Arin's back. Arin was unconscious.

I weaved through traffic, jumped the curb, rode along the sidewalk, and skirred back on the road, just missing a pedestrian. I made a left, a right. Sped down an alley. I didn't have a plan this time.

"So what are we doing?" I looked through the rearview. "Are we gonna find a hospital?"

"We can't risk that."

I hit the highway, saw two semis up ahead. I slowed just enough for the cops to get right up on me, before I cut the steering wheel, hit the shoulder, and two cop cars ran straight into the truck trailers.

"Where are we going?" I panicked. "What are we doing?"

"I don't fucking know." Richie rolled the window down. He stuck his head out, pointed his gun. Fired. He hit the tires of one of the cops. It spun and slammed against the rail.

"We gotta get Arin to a hospital."

"Shit." Richie fired and shattered the windshield of another cop, but it didn't slow the car down. "These motherfuckers don't quit."

I cut around another semi and saw an exit up ahead, but I wasn't off the bridge yet. Then I thought about every action film I'd ever seen in my whole life. The kind of shit that happens in movies don't happen in real life. If I tried what they tried, we'd probably die. But we were probably going to die anyway.

I followed construction signs, busted through a chain link fence with a caution sign. I didn't have anything planned. Seat of the pants.

A cement truck took out two cop cars. A crane took out another. I didn't hit the road again until I looked through the rearview and didn't see any more cops behind me, then I sped to the nearest parking garage and slammed the brakes.

I threw off my seatbelt. "We're gonna have to change vehicles." I looked in the backseat. "How's Arin?"

Jackie's face was distraught. "He's lost a lot of blood."

I shoved open the door. Went around to the driver's seat of the car parked next to ours. It was unlocked. I flung open the door, got down below the seat, hotwired it.

Jackie and Pip got out of the van, both carrying Arin. "We gotta get him to a hospital, Richie," Jackie said.

"Then what?" Richie pulled his hair, paced. "You don't think they're gonna see us? Turn us in to the cops?"

"If we don't, he'll die."

Richie stared at Arin, nostrils flared.

Arin lay limp, head slumped over, one arm around Pip's shoulder, one arm around Jackie's.

Richie stopped and stared at Arin, and no matter how he may have tried to hide the look of worry on his face, his eyes dampened. "Fine. We'll drop him off in front of the hospital, but we can't stay. We do that, we're all dead."

We rode back out onto the highway, now in a gray Honda. The windows were tinted like we needed. Cops were everywhere. Coming up behind us. Passing us in the other lane.

I tried to drive the speed limit as much as I could with shaking hands and sweat pouring out of my palms like a rinsed rag.

I pulled up in front of the hospital.

"Alright." Richie looked to the back. "Lay him out on the bench. Knock on the door but hurry up. Don't let 'em get a look at your face—what?"

Jackie didn't say anything.

"What's wrong?"

Jackie's lip quivered. Richie looked at Pip. Pip shook his head.

Jackie raised the palm of her hand and let Richie get a look at the blood. "He's already dead."

Richie's eyes widened. He froze. "You're kidding, right?"

Jackie shook her head.

Richie craned his head back, stared at the ceiling like he was having a conversation with God. He squeezed his eyes shut. "Okay." He nodded. Maybe trying to get his composure, maybe trying to catch up to reality. "We can't stay here."

"Where can we go—"

"I'm trying to think!" Richie breathed two heavy breaths. "We got cash. We'll find a motel. We'll leave Arin here and...I don't know—Jesus! I don't fucking know!" He dropped his elbow on the center console, pressed his fingers against his eyelids. "Maybe...maybe somebody will notify his family—Jesus. I don't know if Arin's still got family. Only people he ever talked to was us."

We left Arin on the sidewalk, rode around until we found a motel that accepted cash. I don't know if they had our pictures floating around out there, but nobody made contact with the staff when we walked in. Kept it short. We need a room. Three people. Dropped off three hundred dollar bills.

This motel wasn't the dingiest place in the world, but it looked like hell. Peeling linoleum, flickering hallway lights, a shower that looked like someone scrubbed it with dog shit. But nobody was planning on making this a vacation.

We turned on the TV.

*"A high-speed police chase took place today after..."*

Richie lay on the bed with his hands crossed over his stomach, staring up at the ceiling like he was dead. Had a cigarette between his lips, moving it up and down like he was trying to write out his name.

Pip sat at the edge of the bed. Jackie leaned against the wall with her arms crossed. I stood in front of the TV with my hands in my pockets, staring at the screen, the blue glare reminding me of that scene from *Poltergeist* where the dead came back and tried dragging everyone back to Hell with them.

Yesterday, I sat at an office desk and drank coffee.

Axe was dead. Arin was dead. And both of them died right in front of me. None of that hit me until I was staring at a bright TV that burned my eyes. Movement. Picture. Commercials. But nothing in the world was moving. It was one paused video I kept trying to press the rewind on.

Arin was right there in the church with us. We reminisced. We laughed. He was right there. I was going to come back and see everybody again tomorrow. That same night he wasn't there anymore.

Neither was Axe.

Reality sank deep enough into my bones to make the marrow boil. My whole body ached. My stomach twisted. But what can you do when everything just keeps moving forward, and it don't give a shit about you?

"We were gonna go to San Francisco." Richie's voice was a fried hum that melded into the A/C's. He took the cigarette out of his mouth, chuckled. The streetlights gleamed through the window, and the shadows of long, hanging blinds left him behind bars. "Me and Mike. Back in the day. Sittin' around. 'Say, Richie, know what would be a good idea? If we went to San Fransisco someday, man. We gotta go sometime, maaaaan. It's calling our name, maaaaaan...San Fransisco.' 'What's out there in San Fransisco?' I said. He said, 'We won't know 'til we go.' San Fransisco, where it's sunny and warm. We can learn to surf. When were you ever gonna surf, Mike? Get outta here with that shit." The smile on his face reminded me of an old dog with an old chew toy. I wasn't even sure who he was talking to anymore, but it didn't look like it was anyone in the room. "Said we were gonna hitch a ride out there, live like vagabonds. Lay out on the beach. Leave all this shit behind. No more fighting. No more stealing. No more drugs. We didn't know what we were talkin' about. Matter of fact, we were high as fuck." He closed his eyes, squeezed them until his lids started to twitch. "We were gonna paint the world to life." He got quiet. "I never been to San Fransisco."

He inhaled a long drag of smoke and let out a ghost that drifted to the window and vanished before it could curl between the cracks of the blinds. "We were supposed to leave for San Fransisco two years before I started D3vil's

Krew." He only moved his arm and kept the rest of his body still when he reached up and dropped his cigarette in the ashtray. He rested his hand back over his stomach, his chest raised and slowly lowered. "We were gonna paint the world to life."

"I saw my son today." Pip raised his head from the slumped-over position he'd been frozen in since we'd got here. "I...uh...gave him a long hug. Told him I loved him. No matter what happens." He dropped his head into his hand, combed his fingers through his hair.

The room was the kind of silence only the twisted could love.

Jackie started laughing. She started off laughing slowly at first. Quietly. But then it grew. Turned into roaring laughter. Uncontrollable.

Richie waited until she finished and cleared her throat. He didn't yell. There wasn't any anger in his voice. No frustration. He didn't even look at her. Turned his eyes towards the window where the streetlights and TV light nested in his pupils like fireflies. He said it in a voice devoid of any emotion. "What's funny, Jackie?"

She paused. "Life."

Richie had the bed. I spent that night on the floor. I didn't get no sleep. I got flashes of Axe and Arin dying again and again in my head. Their eyes. Their bodies. They were alive again. Moving and laughing and baking, typing on the computer. We were having conversations. Mike was there, too. And then they were dead. I kept telling myself to sleep because if I went to sleep, then I could wake up, and if I could wake up, I could prove that it was all a nightmare.

But I didn't wake up from any twisted dream. I was disturbed by a bang on the door.

"Police!"

If we hadn't been overwhelmed, we might not have been so stupid. Maybe we would've thought twice before leaving the van in a garage where we stole a car whose owner could describe it, give the license plate number. So cops could look for it in a motel parking lot.

The cops kicked the door in, poured in like someone just filled the trough. Richie shot the window and shattered the glass. We climbed out onto the fire escape, hid behind the wall.

Pop! Pop! Pop! The fire escape rattled. Police cars surrounded the building. Cops on the ground. Cops in the motel.

The ones below us hid behind their car doors and had guns aimed at us.

I looked back at the door. I looked at the ground. Next thing I knew, Richie had jumped from the rail and dove into the garbage bin. He climbed out, rolled over the edge, raced around the building, dodged every bullet.

I realized I didn't have any other choice.

I jumped too, followed Richie, felt a bullet whip right past me, and ignored the reality that one inch closer, one second earlier, my life would've been gone. Richie ran through the hedges of the building next door, jumped a fence, and when I caught up to him, he'd run to the back of an open truck trailer lying rusty in an alley.

I climbed back there with him.

"It's too early in the morning for this shit." He tried to catch his breath.

Pip caught up to us, but he had Jackie leaning on his shoulder. He helped her inside before he finally climbed inside himself.

Cop cars sped past us, but they weren't done with us yet. Just giving us a head start.

It was dark back there, and I could hardly see, but what little sunlight broke past the rusted door showed blood spilling out of Jackie's mouth. She choked, gargled. Her body convulsed. She had bullet holes in her stomach, in her side, in her chest.

Richie sat against the wall with his knees up, his arms in his lap. He dropped his head.

I looked back at Jackie, at Pip. "What can we do?"

Pip's mouth was open. He started to shake his head but stopped like he didn't know if there was another response to give.

I took off my jacket, pressed it against Jackie's wounds, best I could. "We're gonna figure something out, alright. Hold on. We're gonna...we're..."

She stopped moving.

I shook her. "Jackie." I shook her harder. "Jackie."

I wasn't looking, but Richie's voice moaned behind me, "The cops are gonna circle around soon."

I gazed at Jackie's face. All I could see was that girl who taught me to be resilient. I closed her eyes.

We checked the area before we got out. Had no idea where to go. I looked to Richie because that's what I always did. That's what everyone always did. But Richie didn't say nothing. He walked and we followed.

Pip didn't say nothing, either. He walked with his hands in his pockets. Everybody's head was down, but his was down in a different way. Not just trying to hide from the cops but hide from everything. Maybe even himself.

"Maybe," I said, "if we can find a place to lie low, we can get Brooklyn Krew to come and get us. Ride us to another state."

Neither one of them said anything.

"Or maybe we can go to them."

Glass crunched beneath our shoes. Cigarette butts looked like shat-out noodles in the cracks beneath the curb. The garbage bin had trash bags halfway to the second floor, and the dried spray paint of #Enough soaked into decaying, crumbling skin of old brick.

We didn't have a car. Cab driver might turn us in. Only damn thing we could do was walk.

"Okay." Richie nodded.

I had to stop for a second to digest the fact that he said anything at all after a long time of walking aimlessly down a cracked road.

He exhaled a heavy breath. "Let's get out of this alley."

Richie called Brooklyn Krew, told them where to meet us, but they couldn't meet us there. Cops were scoping.

Worst time of the day. Broad sunlight where birds should be singing, and kids would be heading off to school. Nobody should be trying to get away with nothing during an hour like that, but we made it a good ways down the street without getting caught. Didn't stand too close to each other. If the cops saw three dudes, shaped like us, standing side by side, that would've been it. Every time a cop cruiser rode by we went the other way. NYPD was on our asses like tattoos on a drunken night.

"We're about a mile from the subway station," Richie said. "If we can make it another block, then we can cut the alley and—"

A cop car rolled up beside us. We looked away, lowered our heads. Turned the corner.

He followed us.

"Shit," Richie whispered.

We walked faster.

He turned on his lights.

We ran.

He sped after us.

We cut into an alley. The cop jumped out of the car and chased after us on foot.

We'd just made it to the other end of the alley when another car pulled up on the street in front of us. The other cop still chased us on foot. He pulled out his gun.

We took a right out of the alley. Three more cop cars pulled up on the road.

We jumped behind a van.

"Shit!" Richie shouted. "Shit! Shit! Shit!"

Cop cars lined the streets. Blue and red lights bounced off the windows and brick, flickering like fucked-up Christmas lights. Pedestrians had their phones out.

"Only a mile, right?" I tried to catch my breath. "Right?"

Richie nodded. "Yeah."

"Then we can make it. They're probably already waiting. Or maybe we can get there. Find a basement or something to hide in."

Pip peeked out. "How are we supposed to get from here to there? There're cops everywhere."

Richie dropped his head back against the van. "We might have to make a run for it."

There were cars parked on the side of the streets. Cops trying to get a hold of pedestrians.

"If we head east," I said, "we might be able to get out of here."

"They're gonna catch us," Pip said.

"We'll have to figure it out as we go."

I looked at Richie's face. There wasn't anybody in there. He was stiff. His eyes weren't blinking.

"Richie," I said.

He flared his nostrils and breathed real heavily.

"Richie."

He pulled his gun out of his pants. Gripped it tight.

"Richie!"

He took a deep breath. "D3vil's Krew's gonna live forever."

He ran from behind the van and fired.

They fired back.

I didn't even look. I could hear it. Pop! Pop! Pop!

Me and Pip crawled quickly from behind the van and hightailed it around the corner. Found a guy getting into his car. I threw him out of the way and jumped in the driver's seat. Pip jumped in the passenger, and we sped to the subway station. Weaved through the traffic, cut between cars.

I would love to say that was it. Would love to say I drove down the steps of the subway station, slammed the brakes just before hitting the tracks, hopped on the train, and got the hell out of there to meet up with Brooklyn Krew, but God knows I couldn't have been that lucky.

There were cop cars all around the station. Parked on the side of the road, across the street. Every corner.

I slammed the steering wheel. "Fuck!"

I glanced at Pip. He stared out the window. The only way I could describe the look on his face is a kid daydreaming. Longing to go home.

I didn't know where to turn from there. I just kept driving. There were cops all over the road, but I kept driving. I knew they were behind me. Looking for me. Probably knew what car I was driving. Probably knew the license plate, but

I kept driving. Until I reached Bronx-Whitestone Bridge and realized we were running out of gas.

I pulled over at the end of the bridge. We got out. I didn't know where I was going. I needed a place to hide, think.

We ran beneath the bridge, across the stones, to the bank.

There weren't any red and blue lights. No sirens.

"Damn!" I said. "Damn! Okay...let me just gather my thoughts."

I looked left. I looked right. City. Pedestrians.

Pip had his hands in his pockets. He stared out at the water.

"Pip." I paced. "Think. Maybe we can call somebody." I shuffled around in my pocket. "Get Brooklyn Krew to meet us somewhere else." The battery was dead on my phone.

"You're fuckin' kidding me." I hit the button. The only thing that came on was a no-battery screen. "You're fuckin' kidding me!" I smashed my phone on a rock. "Let me see your phone."

Pip walked out from under the bridge and sat down on the rocks. He shuffled around his pocket until he pulled out a pack of cigarettes, put one between his lips.

"Pip. Your phone."

He lit the cigarette, craned his neck, gazed at the sky. "It's better to stare at, at night, but it's nice to see the sun for a change." He reached into his pocket. Didn't take his eyes away from the blue and gold above his head but handed me his phone.

I took it but kept my eyes on Pip.

He wasn't like me. His shoulders were relaxed.

I shook my head, turned on his phone. "Shit!" I said under my breath. "Pip."

He wasn't paying attention.

"What's the password?"

He took a drag, let the breeze blow the hair off his shoulders before he parted his lips. "My son's name."

My hand shook. I started typing.

"It's like a painting," Pip sighed, "huh?"

I didn't mean it when I did, but I looked up at the sky. It was almost a kneejerk sort of thing, or maybe there was someone inside of me that wanted something else. Somebody that wasn't panicking but wanted to know what it was like to just be alive. Maybe he'd been in there for a while.

If I didn't know any better, I'd think it was the first time I ever saw a cloud. Or the sun. Or the outstretched wings of birds. Or the quiet water ripples. Or the city beneath the horizon.

For the first time in a long time, the earth rested.

I spelled Caelin's name wrong. Then, when I started to ask Pip how it was spelled, I didn't. Or my lips wouldn't part. Or the guy inside who wanted to see the sun held my tongue. When I thought I was going to ask how to spell the password, I took a seat instead.

"Y' know?" I let myself smile. Just a little. "This would be really beautiful if our asses weren't in trouble right now."

"I think it's more beautiful this way."

Red and blue lights were closing in.

I got up. "Come on, Pip. We gotta go."

He put his hands behind his head, dropped back against the rocks, and crossed his legs.

"What are you doing? They're here."

His eyes were the twinkle of sunlight on the river's ripples.

Red and blue lights surrounded us.

"We gotta go." I started to run, but he grabbed my hand.

I looked at him. I looked around me. The cars were getting closer, the sirens louder.

He tugged on my arm.

I looked at him. I looked around myself again. I looked back at him and the drops of sunlight on his cheeks.

I relaxed my shoulders. Hesitated.

I sat beside him, stretched out my legs, crossed my arms behind my head, and dropped back against the rocks.

Stared up at the sky.

Pops used to say people come into your life for a reason and for a season. I guess that season was finally over.

# ABOUT THE AUTHOR

Iggy Black has been an author and artist since 2005, enjoying aggressive music and absurdist comedy because nothing else is fun anymore. The author derives inspiration from both Mark Twain and Dee Dee Ramone. Stories range from the inner journeys of bottle throwing street dwellers to pot smoking mushrooms discussing the fundamentals of the human condition. Live fast, have a beer, and go out and do something fun tonight because life is too short.